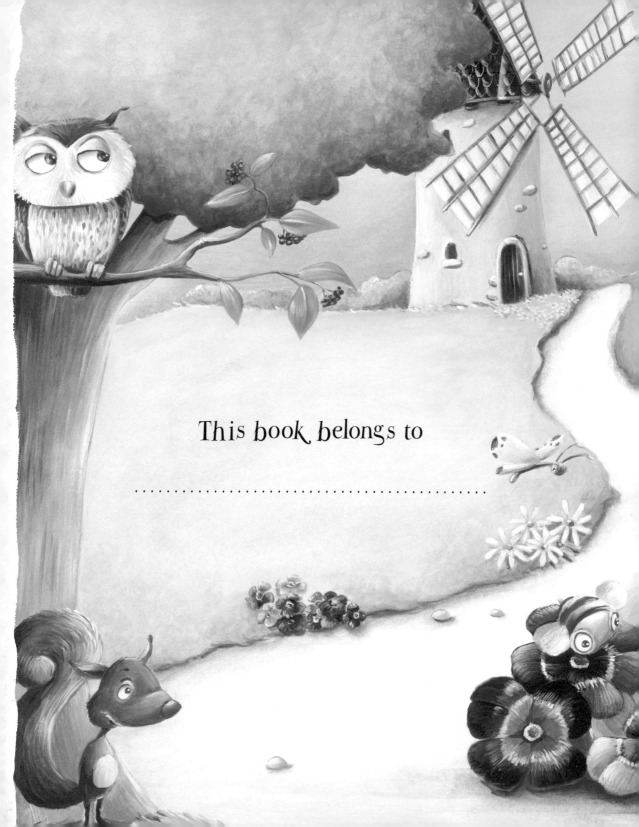

This book belongs to

....

100 Classic Stories

Compiled by Vic Parker

Miles
KeLLy

First published in 2007 by Miles Kelly Publishing Ltd,
Harding's Barn, Bardfield End Green, Thaxted, Essex, CM6 3PX, UK

This edition printed in 2014

12 14 15 13 11

Publishing Director Belinda Gallagher
Creative Director Jo Cowan
Senior Designer Simon Lee
Cover Designer Rob Hale
Editor Rosie Neave
Production Manager Elizabeth Collins
Archive Manager Jennifer Cozens
Reprographics Stephan Davis, Anthony Cambray,
Jennifer Cozens, Thom Allaway
Assets Lorraine King

ISBN 978-1-78209-519-4

Printed in China

British Library Cataloguing-in-Publication Data
A catalogue record for this book is available from the British Library

ACKNOWLEDGEMENTS
The publishers would like to thank Bruno Robert (Plum Pudding)
for supplying the cover artwork.

All other artwork from the Miles Kelly Artwork Bank

Made with paper from a sustainable forest

www.mileskelly.net
info@mileskelly.net

For 4–6 year olds

Fairytale Magic

The Magic Porridge Pot   19

The Twelve Dancing Princesses   26

The Frog Prince   31

Cinderella   36

Snow White and Rose Red   42

Rumpelstiltskin   48

The Elves and the Shoemaker   55

The Princess and the Pea   61

The Three Wishes   65

Animals Big and Small

The Lion and the Mouse 69

Why the Manx Cat has no Tail 72

Chicken Licken 76

The Three Little Pigs 78

Why the Robin has a Red Breast 84

Androcles and the Lion 88

The Ugly Duckling 91

The Three Billy Goats Gruff 96

The Greedy Dog 100

The Cat and the Mouse 103

The Moon and Stars
and Rainbows

The Star Maiden and the Flax Flowers   108

How Jumbo Went to the Moon   113

The Lad Who Went to the North Wind   117

Kaatje's Treasure   121

Snow Daughter and Fire Son   125

The Moon Caught in the Marsh   129

The North Wind and the Sun   133

East of the Sun and West of the Moon   135

Boys and Girls

The Sorcerer's Apprentice   142

Goldilocks and the Three Bears   146

Peter and the Wolf   150

Dick Whittington and his Cat   154

The Precious Stove   159

Little Red Riding Hood   165

The Gingerbread Boy   169

Jack and the Beanstalk   172

Liam and the Fairy Cattle   178

Wizards and Witches, Giants and Genies

Hansel and Gretel   183

Amal and the Genie   189

Snow White and the Seven Dwarfs   194

The Giant Who Counted Carrots   202

The Mermaid of Zennor   207

The Seven Ravens   211

The Twelve Windows   218

Sleeping Beauty   225

Rapunzel   231

Teeny-tiny   237

For 7–9 year olds

Spells and Enchantment

The Pot of Gold	245
The Wild Swans	248
The Pied Piper of Hamelin	255
Belle and the Beast	259
Pandora's Box	266
Tomlin	270
Hop-toads and Pearls	274
The Firebird	278
The Red Shoes	285
The Magic Tinderbox	289

Favourites

Seven at One Blow	296
Ali Baba and the Forty Thieves	300
The Little Matchgirl	307
St Christopher	310
Thumbelina	313
Babushka	318
Rip Van Winkle	323
A Tall Story	328
The Adventures of Sinbad the Sailor	330
The Old Woman and her Pig	334
The Brave Tin Soldier	337

Feathers, Fur and Fangs

Puss in Boots   341

The Wonderful Tar Baby   346

The Dragons of Peking   349

The Hare and the Tortoise   354

The Elephant's Child   357

The Moon in the Pond   360

The Last of the Dragons   365

Giants, Witches and Enchantments

Baba Yaga, The Bony-legged Witch   375

The Selfish Giant   380

Aladdin and the Lamp   384

In the Castle of Giant Cruelty   392

Freya and the Brising Necklace   396

David and the Giant   401

The Fisherman and the Bottle   405

The Giant's Wife   409

The Thunder God Gets Married   414

Royal Adventures

The Emperor's New Clothes   418

The Little Mermaid   424

The Golden Touch   431

The Nutcracker Prince   434

The Sword in the Stone   439

Ricky with the Tuft   443

The Happy Prince   449

Myths and Legends

The Beginning of Life   455

The Creation of the Navajo People   461

Ra's Secret Name   467

The Murder of Osiris   473

The Trojan Horse   479

Kotan Utannai   483

The Hound of Culan   489

Yama-Kumar and the Healing Gift   495

Daedalus and Icarus   501

The Detah of Baldur   505

Index of Stories   510

CLASSIC STORIES

FOR 4–6 YEAR OLDS

This beautifully illustrated collection features tales of magical creatures, mischevious animals and daring adventures. Within these pages, children will be introduced to many famous characters, including Little Red Riding Hood, the Gingerbread Boy and Rumpelstiltskin. Each of the stories in this section has been especially selected for 4–6 year olds, and the pages have been designed with younger readers in mind, helping to bring a world of wonder and magic to life.

FAIRYTALE MAGIC 19

ANIMALS
69 BIG AND SMALL

THE MOON AND STARS
AND RAINBOWS 108

BOYS AND GIRLS
142

183
WIZARDS AND WITCHES,
GIANTS AND GENIES

Fairytale Magic

The Magic Porridge Pot

a Swedish folk tale

This is the story of an old porridge pot. One day, just before Christmas, a poor old farmer and his wife decided that they needed to sell their last cow as they had no money left, and no food in the cupboard. As the farmer walked sadly to market with the cow, he met a very strange little man on the road. He had a long white beard right down to his toes, which were bare, and he wore a huge black hat, under which the farmer could only just see the bright gleam of his eyes. Over his arm he carried a battered old porridge pot.

"That's a nice looking cow," said the strange little man. "Is she for sale?"

"Yes," said the farmer.

"I shall buy your cow," declared the strange little man, putting the porridge pot down with a thump. "I shall give you this porridge pot in exchange for your cow!"

Well, the farmer looked at the battered old porridge pot, and he looked at his fine cow. And he was just about to say, "Certainly not!" when a voice whispered, "Take me! Take me!"

The farmer shook himself. Dear me, it was bad enough to be poor without beginning to hear strange voices. He opened his mouth again to say, "Certainly not!" when he heard the voice again. "Take me! Take me!"

Well, he saw at once that it must be a magic pot, and
he knew you didn't hang about with magic pots, so he said
very quickly to the strange little man, "Certainly!" and
handed over the cow. He bent down to pick up the pot, and
when he looked up, the strange little man had vanished into
thin air.

The farmer knew he was going to have a difficult time
explaining to his wife just how he had come to part with
their precious cow for a battered old porridge pot.

She was very angry indeed and had started to say a lot
of very cross things when a voice came from the pot,

"Take me inside and clean me and polish me, and you
shall see what you shall see!"

Well, the farmer's wife was astonished but she did as she
was bid. She washed the pot inside and out, and then she
polished it until it shone as bright as a new pin. No sooner
had she finished than the pot hopped off the table, and
straight out of the door. The farmer and his wife sat down
by the fire, not saying a word to each other. They had no
money, no cow, no food and now it seemed they didn't even
have their magic pot.

Down the road from the poor farmer, there lived a rich
man. He was a selfish man who spent all his time eating
huge meals and counting his money. He had lots of
servants, including a cook who was in the kitchen making a
Christmas pudding. The pudding was stuffed with plums,
currants, sultanas, almonds and goodness knows what else. It

was so big that the cook realised she didn't have a pot to boil it in. It was at this point that the porridge pot trotted in the door.

"Goodness me!" she exclaimed. "The fairies must have sent this pot just in time to take my pudding," and she dropped the pudding in the pot. No sooner had the pudding fallen to the bottom with a very satisfying thud, than the pot skipped out of the door again. The cook gave a great shriek, but by the time the butler and the footman and the parlour maid and the boy who turned the spit had all dashed into the kitchen, the pot was quite out of sight.

The porridge pot in the meantime trotted down the road to the poor farmer's house. He and his wife were delighted to see the pot again, and even more pleased when they discovered the wonderful pudding. The wife boiled it up and it lasted them for three days. So they had a good Christmas after all, while the old porridge pot sat quietly by the fire.

Spring came, and still the porridge pot sat quietly by the fire. Then one day the pot suddenly trotted over to the farmer's wife and said,

"Clean me, and polish me, and you shall see what you shall see."

So the farmer's wife polished the pot till it shone as bright as a new pin.

No sooner had she finished than the pot hopped off the table, and straight out of the door.

You will remember that the rich man was very fond of counting his money. There he sat in the great hall, with piles of golden guineas and silver sixpences on the table, and great bulging bags of coins on the floor at his feet. He was wondering where he could hide the money when in trotted the pot. Now the cook had been far too frightened of the rich man's temper to tell him about the pot stealing the Christmas pudding, so when he saw the pot he was delighted.

"Goodness me!" he exclaimed, "The fairies must have sent this pot just in time to take my money," and he dropped several bags of money in the pot. No sooner had the bags fallen to the bottom with a very satisfying clink, than the pot skipped out of the door again. The rich man shouted and hollered, but by the time the coachman and the head groom and the stable lad had run into the great hall, the pot was quite out of sight.

It trotted down the road to the poor farmer's house. He and his wife were delighted to see the pot again, and even more pleased when they discovered the bags of gold and silver. There was enough money to last them for the rest of their days, even after they had bought a new cow.

As for the battered old porridge pot, it sat quietly by the fire for many a long year. Then, one day, it suddenly trotted straight out of the door. It went off up the road until it was out of sight, and the farmer and his wife never saw it again.

The Twelve Dancing Princesses

a retelling from the original story by the Brothers Grimm

The king was very puzzled. He had twelve daughters, each one as beautiful as the moon and the stars, and he loved them above all the riches in his kingdom. But every morning the princesses would appear yawning and bleary-eyed, and with their shoes worn quite through. Every evening the king would kiss them good night and lock the door behind him. So how did they get out? And where did they go? The princesses certainly were not letting on.

Buying new shoes every day was costing him a fortune so the king determined to solve the mystery. The court messenger was sent to all four corners of the kingdom to issue the king's proclamation that he would give the hand of one of his daughters in marriage to any man who could discover the secret. But should he fail after three nights he would be banished forever.

Needless to say there were plenty of young men willing to risk banishment to win such a prize. But they soon found the princesses were too clever by half. Before they retired for the night, the princesses sang and played their musical instruments and fed them sweetmeats and rich honeyed mead. Before they realised it morning had come and there were the sleepy princesses and twelve pairs of worn-out shoes.

The king was beside himself. Only the court shoemaker went about with a smile on his face.

Now into the kingdom at this time there wandered a penniless soldier. He read the proclamation and had just decided to try his luck when an old woman came slowly down the dusty road. The young man offered her some of his bread and cheese, and as they sat peaceably together the old woman asked where he was bound. When he had explained she said, "Well, I may be able to help you. You must not drink the mead those cunning princesses offer you, for it is drugged. Pretend to be asleep, and you shall see what you shall see. This may help you," and the old woman handed him a silvery cloak. "Whenever you wear this you will be invisible. Use it well!" and the old woman disappeared.

"Well, perhaps I will succeed now I have magic on my side," murmured the young man as he set off for the palace. By now the king was tearing his hair out. The court shoemaker had taken on extra cobblers to help keep up with the demand for new shoes every day. The princesses were falling asleep into their bowls of porridge at breakfast every morning.

The young man bowed deeply to the king and smiled at all the princesses. He ate a hearty supper but when the eldest princess gave him a goblet of mead he only pretended to drink it. Then he yawned loudly and let his head droop as if he had fallen asleep.

The butler and the first footman dumped the young

man onto the bed placed
across the door of the
princesses' bedchamber. He
cautiously opened one eye
and gazed around the
room. The princesses were
putting on gorgeous velvet
and brocade dresses
and rings and
necklaces. They
giggled and
whispered as they
brushed their hair,
powdered their faces
and then pulled on
the brand new
jewelled slippers

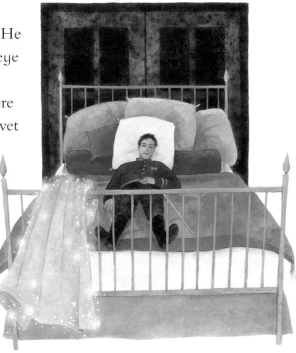

that the shoemaker had only delivered a few hours earlier.
The eldest princess clapped her hands three times. A trap
door opened up in the floor and they all swiftly descended
down a steeply curving staircase. Just as soon as the last
princess had disappeared the young man flung the magic
cloak round his shoulders and rushed after them.

He found himself in a wondrous garden where the trees
were covered in rich jewels, sparkling in candlelight.
Musicians played whirling tunes and he saw all the
princesses dancing with the most handsome princes. The

young man was spellbound, but he managed to keep his wits about him. He reached up and broke off a branch from one of the jewelled trees and hid it under his cloak. Then he ran back and lay down on his bed as though he had never stirred. So it happened on the second and the third nights.

It was with a weary voice that the king asked the young man at breakfast on the fourth day if he had found out where the princesses went at night. The king sat up very quickly when the young man told his tale and produced the branches from the trees. The king was delighted and the young man chose the youngest sister for his bride. And they all lived happily ever after. Except, of course, the court shoemaker, who always made the young man's shoes just a little too tight so they pinched.

The Frog Prince

a retelling from the original story by the Brothers Grimm

Once upon a time, there lived a very spoilt princess who never seemed content. The more she had, the more she wanted. And she just would not do what she was told.

One day she took her golden ball out into the woods, although she had been told by her chief nanny that she must embroider some new handkerchiefs. She threw the golden ball high up into the sky once, twice, but the third time it slipped from her hands and, with a great splash, it fell down, down into a deep well. The princess stamped her foot and yelled, but this did not help. So she kicked the side of the well, and was just getting ready for another big yell, when a very large frog plopped out of the well.

"Ugh!" said the princess. "A horrible slimy frog, go

away at once," but the frog didn't move. Instead, it spoke.

"What are you making such a fuss about?"

A talking frog! For a moment the princess was speechless, but then she looked down her nose and said,

"If you must know, my most precious golden ball has fallen down this well, and I want it back."

With a sudden leap, the frog disappeared down the well. In the wink of an eye, it was back with the golden ball. The princess went to snatch it up, but the frog put a wet foot rather firmly on it and said,

"Hasn't anyone taught you any manners? 'Please' and 'thank you' would not go amiss, and anyway I have a special request to make."

The princess looked at the frog in utter astonishment. No one ever dared talk to her like that, and certainly not a frog. She glared at the frog and said crossly,

"May I have my ball back, please, and what is your special request?"

The frog did not move its foot, but bent closer to the princess.

"I want to come and live with you in the palace and

eat off your plate and sleep on your pillow, please."

The princess looked horrified, but she was sure a promise to a frog wouldn't count so she shrugged her shoulders and said, "Course you can," and grabbed her golden ball from under the frog's foot and ran back to the palace very quickly.

That night at supper the royal family heard a strange voice calling,

"Princess, where are you?" and in hopped the frog.

"Oh bother!" said the princess. The queen fainted. The king frowned.

"Do you know this frog, princess?" he asked.

"Oh bother!" said the princess again, but she had to tell her father what had happened. When he heard the story, he insisted the princess keep her promise.

The frog ate very little, the princess even less. And when it was time to go to bed, the king just looked very sternly at the princess who was trying to sneak off on her own. She bent down and picked the frog up by one leg, and when she reached her great four-poster bed, she plonked the frog down in the farthest corner. She did not sleep a wink all night.

The next evening, the frog was back. Supper was a quiet affair. The queen stayed in her room, the king read the newspaper, and the princess tried not to look at the frog. Bedtime came, and once again the frog and the princess slept at opposite ends of the bed.

The third evening, the princess was terribly hungry so she just pretended the frog was not there and ate everything

that was placed in front of her. When it came to bedtime, she was so exhausted that she fell into a deep sleep as soon as her head touched the pillow.

The next morning when she woke up, she felt much better for her good sleep until she remembered the frog. But it was nowhere to be seen. At the foot of the bed, however, there stood a very handsome young man in a green velvet suit.

"Hello, princess. Do you know that you snore?" he said.

The princess's mouth fell open ready to yell, but the handsome young man continued, "I don't suppose you

recognise me, thank goodness, but I was the frog who
rescued your golden ball. I was bewitched by a fairy who
said I was rude and spoilt," and here the young man looked
sideways at the princess whose mouth was still hanging
open, "and the spell could only be broken by someone
equally rude and spoilt having to be nice to me."

The princess closed her mouth. The king was most
impressed with the young man's good manners, and the
queen liked the look of his fine green velvet suit. Everyone
liked the fact that the princess had become a very much
nicer person. Before long it seemed sensible for the princess
and the handsome young man to get married. They had
lots of children who were not at all spoilt and everyone
lived happily ever after. The golden ball and the green
velvet suit were put away in a very dark cupboard.

Cinderella

a retelling from the original tale by Charles Perrault

O nce upon a time, when there were still fairy godmothers, there was a girl called Cinderella. She lived with her father and his new wife, and her two new step-sisters. The step-mother did not like Cinderella very much, mostly because she was so much nicer than her own two daughters. Cinderella was also much prettier. Oh, but the step-sisters were ugly!

Cinderella had to do all the work in the house as the ugly sisters were also very lazy. They spent all the father's money on new clothes and endless pairs of shoes, and then went off to parties leaving poor Cinderella with piles of stockings to mend.

One day a very grand invitation arrived. The prince was looking for a wife, and had decided to give a ball in three days time for all the young ladies in the land. The ugly sisters could talk about nothing else. They bought lots

of new dresses and many pairs
of matching shoes, and
then spent every hour
trying them all on. They
made Cinderella curl their
hair and iron their ribbons
and powder their noses.
Cinderella was so
exhausted running
around after them
that she had no time
to look into her own
wardrobe to choose
what she should wear.

In a waft of perfume,
the ugly sisters swept out
of the door into the carriage
without as much as a thank you to
Cinderella. She closed the door sadly, and went to sit by the
fire in the kitchen.

"I do wish I could have gone to the ball, too," she
sighed.

There was a sudden swirl of silver stars, and there in
front of Cinderella stood an old lady with a twinkle in her
eye, and a wand in her hand.

"You shall go to the ball, my dear Cinderella. I am
your fairy godmother," she said, smiling at Cinderella.

"Now, we must be quick, there is much to do! Please bring me a large pumpkin from the vegetable patch. Oh, and six mice from the barn, and you will find four lizards by the water butt."

Cinderella did as she was bid. With a wave of the wand, the pumpkin was turned into a glittering golden coach and the mice into six pure white horses. The lizards became elegant footmen, dressed in green velvet.

"Now you, my dear," said the fairy godmother, turning to Cinderella. A wave of the wand, and Cinderella's old apron disappeared and there she stood in a white dress, glittering with golden stars. Her hair was piled on top of her head and it too was sprinkled with stars. On her feet were tiny glass slippers with diamonds sparkling in the heels.

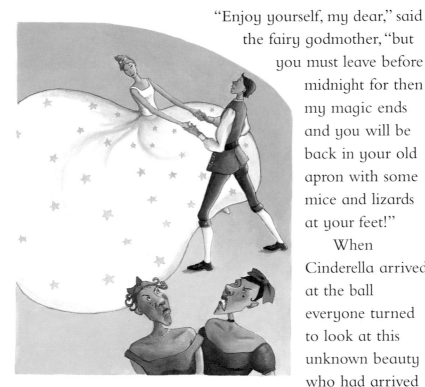

"Enjoy yourself, my dear," said the fairy godmother, "but you must leave before midnight for then my magic ends and you will be back in your old apron with some mice and lizards at your feet!"

When Cinderella arrived at the ball everyone turned to look at this unknown beauty who had arrived so unexpectedly. The prince hurried over to ask her to dance and then would not dance with anyone else all evening. The ugly sisters were beside themselves with rage, which of course made them look even uglier.

Cinderella was enjoying herself so much that she forgot the fairy godmother's warning, so she had a terrible fright when the clock began to strike midnight. She turned from the prince with a cry and ran down the stairs of the palace into her carriage, and disappeared as suddenly as she had arrived. One of the tiny glass slippers with diamonds sparkling in the heels had slipped from her foot as she ran. The prince picked it up and turning to the crowded ballroom declared, "I shall marry the girl whose foot fits this slipper!"

Cinderella, meanwhile, had just managed to reach her garden gate when all her finery disappeared, and by the time the ugly sisters arrived home, both in a towering rage, she was sitting quietly by the fire.

The next morning, the prince went from house to house looking for the mystery girl whose foot would fit the tiny glass slipper. But no one had feet that small. He reached Cinderella's house where first one ugly sister and then the next tried to squash their huge feet into the slipper.

"Please let me try," said a quiet voice from the corner, and Cinderella stepped forward. The sisters just laughed in scorn but they soon stopped when they saw that the tiny slipper fitted Cinderella perfectly. There was a sudden swirl of silver stars, and there in front of Cinderella stood her fairy godmother with a twinkle in her eye, and a wand in her hand. In an instant, Cinderella was clothed in a gorgeous dress of cornflower blue silk decorated with pearls. On her feet she wore tiny white boots with blue tassels.

The prince whisked Cinderella off to the palace to meet the king and queen, and the wedding took place the very next day. Cinderella forgave the two ugly sisters, she was that sort of girl. But the prince insisted the sisters spent one day a week working in the palace kitchens just to remind them how horrid they had been to Cinderella.

Snow White and Rose Red

a retelling from the original story by the Brothers Grimm

Once upon a time there was a widow who had two daughters, Snow White and Rose Red. Snow White was quiet and gentle, Rose Red was wild as the hills, but they loved each other, and their mother, so the little house in the woods was a happy one.

One winter's evening as they all sat round the fire there was a knock at the door. Rose Red opened it and gave a scream. There stood a great big brown bear! But in a deep rumbly voice the bear said,

"Please do not be afraid. All I ask is that you let me sleep by your fire tonight. It is so cold outside."

"Of course you may shelter with us," said the mother. And she called the girls to set the soup on the stove and to put another log on the fire.

"Would you brush the snow from my fur, please?" asked the bear. Rose Red fetched the big broom and carefully brushed the bear's great shaggy coat. Snow White gave him a great bowl of hot soup and the bear gulped it down in one. Then he stretched out in front of the fire and was soon fast asleep.

In the morning Snow White let him out of the cottage and he padded off into the forest through the deep snow. But in the evening, he returned and once again Snow White and Rose Red and their mother looked after him. After that the bear came every night all through the winter, and they all grew very fond of him. But when spring came, the bear told them he would not be returning any more.

"I have to guard my treasure. Once the snows have

melted all kinds of wicked people try to steal it," he said
and giving them all a hug he set off through the forest.
Just as he passed through the garden gate, his fur caught on
a nail. For a fleeting moment Snow White thought she saw
a glint of gold, but the bear hurried off and was soon out
of sight.

A few days later, Rose Red and Snow White were out
gathering berries to make jam when they came alongside a
fallen tree. Then they saw a very cross dwarf, tugging at his
beard which was trapped by the great tree trunk.

"Well, don't stand there like a pair of silly geese! Come and help me!" he shrieked.

Well, no matter how hard they tugged Rose Red and Snow White were not strong enough to lift the tree, so Rose Red took her scissors out and snipped off the end of the dwarf's beard. He was absolutely furious, and snatched up a big bag of gold from the tree roots and disappeared without a word of thanks.

Some days later the girls' mother said she really fancied a piece of fish for supper, so they went down to the river to see what they could catch. But instead of a fish, there on the bank they found their friend the cross dwarf again. This time his beard was all caught up in his fishing line.

"Don't just stand there gawping," he yelled, "help me get free!"

Snow White tried to untangle it but it was impossible so she too snipped a piece off his beard. He was quite white with rage, but just grasped a casket of jewels that lay at the water's edge and turned away without a word of thanks.

It was the Spring Fair a few days later. The girls decided to go and buy some new ribbons for their hats, and their mother wanted needles for her embroidery, so they set off early in the morning. They had not gone far when they heard a terrible shrieking and crying. They ran towards the sound, and there once more was the cross dwarf, this time struggling in the huge talons of an eagle. They tugged and tugged and the eagle had to let go.

"You have torn my coat," muttered the ungrateful dwarf and picked up a basket of pearls and hobbled off as fast as possible. The girls just laughed and continued on their way to the fair.

They had a wonderful time, and it was quite late when they walked slowly home. The sun was just sinking behind a big rock when, to their astonishment, they came across the dwarf again. There spread out on the ground in front of him was a great pile of gold and precious jewels and pearls.

Suddenly the dwarf saw Snow White and Rose Red.

"Go away! Go away! You horrid girls are always in my way," he shouted. But just then there was a huge growl and the great brown bear stood by their side. With one huge paw he swiped the dwarf up, up into the sky and no one ever saw where he fell to

earth again. The bear turned towards
Snow White and Rose Red and as they
looked, his great shaggy coat fell away.
There stood a handsome young man, dressed
in a golden suit of the richest velvet.

"Do not be afraid, Snow White and Rose
Red," he said smiling. "Now you can see who I really
am. That wicked dwarf put a spell on me so he could steal
all my treasure, but you have broken the spell by
your kindness."

They all went home, laden with the treasure. They
talked long into the night, and it was all still true the next
morning! Snow White
married the handsome
young man who, by
great good fortune,
had a younger
brother who
married Rose
Red, so they all
lived happily
ever after.

But if you
ever find a dwarf
with half his beard
missing, I would be very
careful if I were you.

Rumpelstiltskin

a retelling from the original tale by the Brothers Grimm

nce upon a time there was a miller. He was a foolish man who was always boasting. Then he went too far.

The king was riding past the mill with his huntsmen one day. The miller's daughter was sitting in the doorway, spinning. The king could not help noticing that she was a very pretty girl so he began talking to her. Her father came bustling up and began to tell the king what a splendid daughter she was.

"Why, your Majesty, she can even spin straw into gold!" boasted the ridiculous miller.

Needless to say, the poor girl could do nothing of the sort but the king thought this was an excellent way to refill the palace treasure house which was rather empty, so he took her back to the palace. He put her in a room with a great pile of straw and told her he wanted to see it all spun into gold the next morning, or else it would be the worse for her.

As soon as the door was locked she began to cry. The task was impossible. Then she heard a thin little voice.

"Do stop crying! You will make the straw all wet, and then we will have no chance of turning it into gold!"

There in front of her stood a strange little man. He had a tiny round body with long skinny legs and huge feet. His clothes looked as if they had seen better days, and on his head he wore a tall battered-looking hat.

"If you give me your necklace, I will do what the king has asked of you," he snapped.

The miller's daughter

unclasped her necklace and handed it to the little man. He hid it deep in one of his pockets, and sat down by the spinning wheel. The spinning wheel turned in a blur. The pile of straw grew smaller, and the mound of shining gold grew higher. As the first light of day shone in through the window it was all done. The strange little man disappeared as suddenly as he had appeared.

The king was delighted with the great pile of gold, and asked the miller's daughter to marry him. She was too shy to reply so the king just took her silence as her agreement and married her anyway that afternoon.

For a while all was well. But then the treasure house grew empty again so once more the poor girl, now the queen, was locked in a room with a pile of straw and a spinning wheel.

As the queen wept, once more the strange little man appeared. The queen asked him to help her again, and offered him all the rich jewels she was wearing. But the strange little man was not interested in jewels this time.

"You must promise to give me your first born child," he whispered.

The queen was desperate. But she promised and the little man sat down at the spinning wheel. A great pile of gold appeared by the side of the spinning wheel, and by dawn the straw had all gone. The king was delighted and for a while all was well. Then the queen gave birth to a beautiful baby, and she remembered with dread her promise to the strange little man. Seven days after the baby was born, he appeared by the side of the cradle. The queen wept and wept.

"There you go again," said the little man crossly, "always crying!"

"I will do anything but let you have my baby," cried the queen.

"Very well then, anything to make you stop crying," said the little man, who by now was dripping wet from all the queen's tears. "If you can guess my name in three days, I will let you keep your baby," he said and disappeared as suddenly as he had appeared.

The next morning the little man appeared by the side of the cradle. The queen had sent messengers out far and wide to see if anyone knew the strange little man's name.

"Is it Lacelegs?" she asked.

"No!"

"Is it Wimbleshanks?"

"No!"

"Is it Bandyknees?"

"No!"

Then the little man disappeared as suddenly as he had appeared.

The queen sent out even more messengers to the lands far beyond the borders of the kingdom. The second morning the strange little man appeared by the side of the cradle.

"Is it Bluenose?" the queen asked.

"No!"

"Is it Longtooth?"

"No!"

"Is it Skinnyribs?"

"No!"

And the little man disappeared with a nasty laugh.

The queen waited up all night as her messengers came in one by one, and just as she was giving up all hope of saving her precious baby, in came the very last one. He was utterly exhausted but he brought the queen the best of news. In a deep, deep, dark forest he had found a strange little man dancing round a fire, singing this song.

Today I brew, today I bake,
Tomorrow I will the baby take.
The queen will lose the game,
Rumpelstiltskin is my name!

The strange little man appeared by the cradle. The queen pretended she still did not know his name.

"Is it Gingerteeth?" she asked.

"No!" said the little man, and he picked the baby up.

"Is it Silverhair?" asked the queen.

"No!" said the little man, and he started to walk towards the door, with a wicked smile.

"Is it Rumpelstiltskin?" asked the queen, and she ran up to the strange little man.

"Some witch told you that!" shrieked the little man, and he stamped his foot so hard that he fell through the floor and was never seen again. The queen told the king the whole story and he was so pleased his baby and his queen were safe that he forgot to be cross with the miller who had told such a terrible fib in the first place!

The Elves and the Shoemaker

a retelling from the original story by the Brothers Grimm

There was a time when everyone believed in elves. The shoemaker and his wife in this story certainly did!

The shoemaker worked very hard indeed from morn to night. The shoes he made were of the finest leather, and he was good with his hands, but business was slow. One night he found he only had enough leather left for one more pair of shoes. With a heavy heart, he cut the leather carefully and left the pieces ready on his work bench to sew the next morning. He blew out the candle, and crossed the yard from his little shop into the house.

"Wife, I do not know what we shall do. I have just cut out the very last piece of leather in the shop," he said sadly.

"Don't be too gloomy, husband," said his wife with a tired smile. "Perhaps you will be able to sell this last pair of shoes for a fine price. Wait and see what tomorrow brings!"

The next day the shoemaker was up early as usual. When he pulled back the shutters in the shop, you can imagine his surprise when he saw not pieces of leather ready to sew on the bench, but a fine pair of ladies' shoes with delicate pointed toes. The stitching was so fine you would think it had been done by mice. He put the shoes in the window of the shop, and before long a rich merchant came in and bought the shoes for his new wife, paying the poor shoemaker double the usual price. The shoemaker was delighted at this turn in his fortunes, and bought enough leather to make two new pairs of shoes.

Once again, he cut the leather carefully, and left the pieces ready on his work bench to sew the next morning.

The next day the shoemaker was up even earlier than usual. His wife came with him as he went into the shop, and pulled back the shutters.

"Oh husband," she gasped, for there on the bench stood two pairs of the finest shoes she had ever seen. There was a green pair with red heels, and a pair so shiny and black the shoemaker could see his face in them. He put the shoes in the window, and very quickly in came a poet who bought the green pair with red heels, and not far behind him there was a parson who bought the shiny black pair. And both paid him a great deal of money for the splendid shoes with stitching so fine you would think it had been done by mice.

This continued for many days. The shoemaker would buy new leather and leave the pieces cut ready on his bench at night, and when he came back in the morning there would be the most exquisite shoes. The shoemaker's reputation spread, and his shop was soon full of customers, anxious to buy his special shoes. Before long the shoemaker and his wife were no longer poor, but they still lived simply as they had little wish for the luxuries of life. It was enough to be happy and healthy. One day, the wife said, "Husband, I think we must see who it is who has given us this great good fortune so we may thank them."

The shoemaker agreed, so that night after laying out
the cut leather pieces and blowing out the candle, he and
his wife hid behind the door of the shop. As the town hall
clock struck midnight, they heard a scampering of tiny feet
and little voices, laughing. Two tiny elves slid out from
behind the skirting board and climbed up onto the bench
where they were soon hard at work, stitching away with
tiny stitches that were so fine they might have been done
by mice. The elves sang as they stitched, sitting cross-legged
on the bench. But 'oh!' they looked poor. Their trousers
were ragged, their shirts were threadbare and their poor feet
looked frozen as they had neither socks nor shoes. In a
twinkling of an eye all the leather was used up, and there
on the bench stood many pairs of shoes. The elves slipped
away, laughing as they went.

The shoemaker and his wife looked at each other, and then and there both decided to reward the little craftsmen. The next day, the shoemaker took some scraps of green and yellow leather and, with the tiniest stitches possible, he made two little pairs of boots, yellow with green heels. The wife took her sewing basket and some scraps of cloth and, with the tiniest stitches possible, made two little pairs of red velvet trousers and two smart green jackets with shiny silver buttons. Then she knitted two little pairs of yellow socks, with the tiniest stitches possible.

That night, the shoemaker did not cut out any leather. Instead he laid out the clothes and the boots with the socks, and once again he and his wife hid behind the door of the shop.

As the town hall clock struck midnight, they heard a scampering of tiny feet and little voices, laughing. The two tiny elves slid out from behind the skirting board and climbed up onto the bench. When they saw the gifts, they clapped their hands in delight and, laughing merrily, flung off their old rags and tried on their new clothes and the boots. They looked splendid. Still laughing and smiling, they slipped away behind the skirting board, and the shoemaker and his wife never saw them ever again.

But once a year when the shoemaker opened the shop in the morning, on his bench he would find a special pair of shoes with stitching so fine you would think it had been done by mice.

The Princess and the Pea

a retelling from the original story by Hans Christian Andersen

The prince was very fed up. Everyone in the court, from his father, the king, down to the smallest page, seemed to think it was time he was married. Now the prince would have been very happy to get married, but he did insist that his bride be a princess, a real true and proper princess. He had travelled the land and met plenty of nice girls who said they were princesses, but none, it seemed to him, were really true and proper princesses. Either their manners were not quite exquisite enough, or their feet were much too big. So he sat in the palace, reading dusty old history books and getting very glum.

One night, there was the most terrible storm. Rain was lashing down, and thunder and lightning rolled and flashed round the palace. The wind kept blowing out the candles, and everyone huddled closer to the fire. Suddenly there was a great peal from the huge front door bell.

And there, absolutely dripping wet, stood a princess. Well, she said she was a princess, but never did anyone look less like a princess. Her hair was plastered to her head, her dress was wringing wet and her silk shoes were covered in mud. She was quite alone, without even the smallest maid, and just where had she come from? But she kept insisting she was a princess.

We will see about that, thought the queen. While the dripping girl sat sipping a mug of warm milk and honey, the queen went to supervise the making of the bed in the second-best spare bedroom. She didn't think it necessary to put their late night visitor in the best spare bedroom, after all she might only be a common-or-garden duchess. The queen told the maids to take all the bedclothes and the mattress off the bed. Then she placed one single pea right on the middle of the bedstead. Next the maids piled twenty mattresses on top of the pea, and then twenty feather quilts on top of the mattresses. And thus the girl was left for the night.

In the morning, the queen swept into the bedroom in her dressing gown and asked the girl how she had slept.

"I didn't sleep a wink all night." said the girl. "There was a great, hard lump in the middle of the bed. It was quite dreadful. I am sure I am black and blue all over!"

Now everyone knew she really must be a princess, for only a real princess could be as soft-skinned as that. The prince was delighted, and insisted they got married at once, and they lived very happily ever after. They always slept in very soft beds, and the pea was placed in the museum, where it probably still is today.

The Three Wishes

an English folk tale

There was once a poor fisherman who lived by the edge of the sea in a tumbledown old cottage. He lived with his wife, who was always grumbling no matter how hard the fisherman worked.

One evening he threw the nets out for one last try before it grew dark. He had caught nothing all day. As he began pulling the nets in the fisherman's hopes rose: the nets were heavy. But when he hauled them over the side of the boat there was only one tiny fish lying at the bottom. Then the fish spoke. The fisherman rubbed his eyes in astonishment.

"Please throw me back into the sea," said the fish. "I am so small I would not make much of a meal for you."

But the fisherman was tired and hungry.

"Even though you are small I cannot throw you back. My wife would not be pleased if I came home empty handed." he said with a deep sigh.

"I will grant you the first three wishes made in your cottage if you let me go," said the fish, "but I should warn you that wishes do not always give you what you really want."

Well, the fisherman did not hear the fish's warning. All he heard was the bit about three wishes, and he thought that finally his grumbling wife could have whatever she wanted. So he carefully untangled the tiny fish from the nets and placed it back in the sea. With a flick of its tail the fish disappeared deep, deep under water.

The fisherman ran all the way home and in great excitement told her all about the tiny fish. But instead of being pleased, she just shouted at him as usual.

"Trust you to believe such a thing! Whoever heard of a talking fish? You must be daft husband," and she slammed down a plate of dry bread and a rind of cheese in front of the poor fisherman.

"I wish this was a plate of fine sausages, I am so hungry," said the fisherman wistfully.

No sooner were the words out of his mouth than there was a wonderful smell and there in front of him was a plate of sizzling sausages! He was delighted and reached for his knife when his wife yelled at him,

"Why couldn't you have wished for something better? We could have had chests of gold and fine clothes to wear!" And this from the woman who had refused to believe his story only a few moments before. "You stupid fool! I wish the sausages were at the end of your nose!"

There was a ghastly silence as the wife looked at her poor husband. Hanging from the end of his nose was a great string of sausages. The fisherman remembered what the fish had said – the first three wishes made in the cottage.

The fisherman and his wife pulled and pulled at the sausages, but it was no good. They were stuck fast. There was nothing for it, they would have to use the last wish.

"I wish the sausages would disappear," said the fisherman sadly, and they did in a flash. So there they sat, the poor fisherman and his grumbling wife. No delicious supper of sizzling sausages and, much worse, no magic wishes. The fisherman never caught the tiny fish again, and as far as I know, his wife never stopped grumbling. Wishes do not always give you what you really want.

Animals Big and Small

The Lion and the Mouse

a retelling from Aesop's Fables

The lion was very hungry. As he padded through the tall grass, something rustled by his feet. He reached out a great paw, and there was a squeak. He had caught a tiny mouse by the tail.

"Oh please let me go, dear lion," cried the tiny mouse. "I should be no more than a single mouthful for you. And I promise I will be able to help you some day."

The lion roared with laughter. The thought of a tiny mouse being able to help such a huge creature as himself amused him so much that he did let the mouse go.

"He would not have made much of a meal anyway," smiled the lion.

The mouse scuttled away, calling out to the lion,

"I shall not forget my promise!"

Many days and nights later the lion was padding through the tall grass again when he suddenly fell into a deep pit. A net was flung over him, and he lay there helpless, caught by some hunters. He twisted and turned but he could not free himself. The hunters just laughed at his struggles and went off to fetch a cart to carry the great lion back to their village.

As he lay there, the lion heard a tiny voice in his ear.
"I promised you I would be able to help you one day."

It was the tiny mouse! And straight away he began to gnaw through the rope that held the lion fast. He gnawed and chewed, and chewed and gnawed, and eventually he chewed and gnawed right through the rope and the lion was free. With a great bound, he leapt out of the pit and then reached back, very gently, to lift the tiny mouse out too.

"I shall never forget you, mouse. Thank you for remembering your promise and saving me," purred the great lion.

So the tiny mouse was able to help the great lion. One good turn deserves another, you see?

Why the Manx Cat
has no Tail

a myth from the Isle of Man

The rain was falling in torrents, and there were great storm clouds building up. The rivers were overflowing and the fields looked like lakes. Noah decided that the time had come to fill his ark as planned with two of every animal that lived. He called his sons Shem and Ham and Japeth and they began rounding up the animals and leading them gently onto the ark.

First came the big beasts, the giraffes and lions and elephants. Then came the cows and the sheep and the pigs. Then came the foxes and the rabbits, but not together of course. Then came the birds and the grasshoppers and the ants, who were rather nervous of the elephants' feet. Finally came the dogs, but only one cat, a big ginger tom cat. The she-cat, who was a stripy tabby, had decided that she would like to go mousing one last time, as she realised she would not be able to eat a fellow passenger when they were all cooped up in the ark.

Mrs Noah called and called her, but still she did not come. Cats are always contrary and she was no exception. Noah looked at the rising water and told Mrs Noah that he would have to pull up the gangplank as the ark would soon be afloat. All the other animals were settling in to their various stalls, and what a noise there was! Roaring and mooing, trumpeting and baaing, snorting and squawking. Toes and flippers and trotters and paws got stood on, fur and feathers were ruffled and horns and long tails got stuck, but eventually everyone was in place.

Noah began to pull the great door of the ark to, and just as he was about to shut it fast, up pranced the she-cat, soaking wet but licking her lips. She managed to slip through the gap in the nick of time but her great plume of a tail was caught in the door as it slammed shut. She turned round and her entire tail was cut off! The cat was very cross, but Noah told her it was entirely her own fault and she would have to wait until they found land again before she could have her tail mended.

Forty days and forty nights later, the flood was over and Noah opened the great door of the ark once more. First out was the she-cat, and she ran and ran until she found the Isle of Man, and there she stopped, too ashamed for anyone else to see her. Ever since then the cats from the Isle of Man have had no tails. Nowadays they are rather proud to be different.

Chicken Licken

an English folk tale

One fine day Chicken Licken went for a walk in the woods. Now Chicken Licken was not very bright, and he was also rather inclined to act first and think after. So when an acorn fell on his head, he decided immediately that the sky must be falling in. He set off as fast as he could to tell the king. On the way he met Henny Penny and Cocky Locky.

"I am off to tell the king that the sky is falling in," he clucked importantly.

"We will come too," said Henny Penny and Cocky Locky.

So Chicken Licken, Henny Penny and Cocky Locky set off to find the King. On the way they met Ducky Lucky and Drakey Lakey.

"We are off to tell the king that the sky is falling in," clucked Chicken Licken importantly.

76

"We will come too," said Ducky Lucky and Drakey Lakey.

So Chicken Licken, Henny Penny, Cocky Locky, Ducky Lucky and Drakey Lakey all set off to find the king. On the way they met Goosey Loosey and Turkey Lurkey.

"We are off to tell the king that the sky is falling in," clucked Chicken Licken importantly.

"We will come too," said Goosey Loosey and Turkey Lurkey.

So Chicken Licken, Henny Penny, Cocky Locky, Ducky Lucky, Drakey Lakey, Goosey Loosey and Turkey Lurkey all set off to find the king. On the way they met Foxy Loxy.

"We are off to tell the king that the sky is falling in," clucked Chicken Licken importantly.

"What a good thing I met you all," said Foxy Loxy with a cunning smile. "I know the way, follow me."

So Chicken Licken, Henny Penny, Cocky Locky, Ducky Lucky, Drakey Lakey, Goosey Loosey and Turkey Lurkey all set off behind Foxy Loxy. He led them all straight to his den where he ate every single one of them for his dinner! So the king never heard that the sky was falling in. (It didn't, of course).

The Three Little Pigs

an English folk tale

There once was a mother pig who had three little pigs. They were very poor indeed, and the day came when the mother pig could no longer look after the family. She sent the three little pigs out into the wide world to seek their fortunes.

The first little pig met a man carrying a big bundle of straw.

"Oh, please may I have that bundle of straw to build myself a house?" asked the first little pig. The man was tired of carrying the bundle of straw so he gladly gave it to the first little pig.

The first little pig built a very fine house out of the bundle of straw, and he lived there very happily. Then along came a big bad wolf.

"Little pig, little pig, let me come in!" shouted the wolf.

"No, no, not by the hair on my chinny chin chin. I'll not let you in," squeaked the first little pig.

"Then I'll huff and I'll puff, and I'll blow your house down," yelled the wolf. And he did. He huffed and he puffed and he blew the straw house down. The first little pig ran away as fast as his trotters would carry him.

Now the second little pig met a man carrying a bundle of sticks.

"Oh, please may I have that bundle of sticks to build myself a house?" asked the second little pig. The man was tired of carrying the bundle of sticks so he gladly gave it to the second little pig.

The second little pig built a very fine house out of the
bundle of sticks, and he lived there very happily. Then along
came the big bad wolf.

"Little pig, little pig, let me come in!" shouted the wolf.

"No, no, not by the hair on my chinny chin chin. I'll
not let you in," squeaked the second little pig.

"Then I'll huff and I'll puff, and I'll blow your house
down," yelled the wolf. And he did. He huffed and he puffed
and he blew the stick house down. The second little pig ran
away as fast as his trotters would carry him.

Now the third little pig met a man carrying a big load
of bricks.

"Oh, please may I have that load of bricks to build myself a house?" asked the third little pig. The man was very tired indeed from carrying the big load of bricks so he gladly gave it to the third little pig.

The third little pig built a very fine house out of the big load of bricks, and he lived there very happily. Then along came the big bad wolf.

"Little pig, little pig, let me come in!" shouted the wolf.

"No, no, not by the hair on my chinny chin chin. I'll not let you in," squeaked the third little pig.

"Then I'll huff and I'll puff, and I'll blow your house down," yelled the wolf. And he tried. He huffed and he puffed but he could not blow the brick house down.

"Little pig, little pig, I am coming down your chimney to get you," bellowed the wolf.

"Please yourself," called the third little pig who was busy with some preparations of his own.

"Little pig, little pig, I have my front paws down your chimney," threatened the wolf.

"Please yourself," called the third little pig who was still busy with some preparations of his own.

"Little pig, little pig,
I have my great bushy tail down your chimney," called
the wolf.

"Please yourself," called the third little pig who was now sitting in his rocking chair by the fireside.

"Little pig, little pig, here I come!" And with a great rush and a huge SPLOSH! the big bad wolf fell right into the big pot of boiling water that the clever little pig had placed on the fire, right under the chimney. The wolf scrabbled and splashed and scrambled out of the big pot and ran as fast as ever he could right out of the front door. And he was never seen again. The third little pig managed to find his two brothers, and they went and fetched their mother. And they are all still living happily together in the little brick house.

Why the Robin has a Red Breast

an Inuit legend

In the land where it is always winter all the time, there once lived a man and his son. It was so cold that they lived in a house made of snow, and their clothes were all made of fur.

But even with the warm furs it was cold in the snow house. The man and his son needed a fire as well. They needed it to heat the snow house. They needed it to have hot food to eat. So they could never let their fire go out as without it they would surely die.

Whenever the father went out hunting, he would leave his son with a great pile of wood. The fire burned brightly by the entrance to the snow house. The first thing the boy had learned was never ever to let the fire go out.

Now one of the creatures the man was always hunting was the great white bear. The great white bear hated the man and used all his cunning to hide from the hunter. The bear saw that the fire was precious to the man and his son. He thought that if only he could stamp out the fire with his huge white paws, the man and his son would fall into such a deep cold sleep that they would never wake again. So the great white bear watched and waited for his chance.

One day the father fell ill. All day he tossed and turned on his bed. He was not able to go out hunting. The great white bear watched as the son fed the fire with sticks as his father had taught him. The next day, the father was no better. The son looked after him as well as he could but by now he was growing hungry. At night he could hear the great white bear prowling round the snow house, and he was afraid. The third day the father hardly moved at all, and the boy had to fight to keep his eyes open. He put some more sticks onto the fire, but eventually he could keep his eyes open no longer. He fell into a deep, deep sleep.

The great white bear pounced. He stomped and stamped and put the fire out with his huge white paws. Then he padded away, leaving the boy and his father to their fate. It grew bitterly cold in the snow house. Frost and snow gathered round the furs on the bed, and round the boy's furry hood. Still he slept on and on. Both father and son grew stiff with cold.

The boy had one special friend. It was a tiny little
brown bird called a robin. The boy used to feed the robin
and let it shelter in the snow house when the blizzards blew.
The little bird came hopping up to the snow house and he
saw right away that all was not well. He twittered round
the boy's head, calling to warn him that the fire had gone
out. But still the boy slept on, exhausted by all his efforts to
look after his father. The robin scratched among the ashes
where the great white bear had stomped, desperately
looking for just one tiny ember that was still alight. He
found one tiny spark, and he began fanning it with his little
wings. He flapped his wings for all he was worth and
slowly, slowly the flame caught. It spread to another piece
of stick, and still the robin flapped and flapped his wings.

The heat was growing now, and the robin's feathers were scorching. More and more sticks caught alight, and the brave little robin felt his chest feathers burn red with heat.

The boy woke with a start and leapt to his feet. He saw the fire was nearly out, and he rushed to pile on more sticks. He did not see his tiny friend flutter off into the darkness outside. It grew warmer in the snow house, and to his great joy the boy saw his father was stirring on the bed. His eyes were clear and the sickness had passed. In the distance, the great white bear stumped off a long way from the snow house. He could see he was not going to get the better of the hunter and his son.

The next time the robin came to the snow house for food, the boy was puzzled to see the little brown bird now had a bright red breast. But he was never to know why.

Androcles and the Lion

a retelling from the Fables of Phaedrus

Many thousands of years ago there lived a poor slave called Androcles. Life was very miserable for slaves. They barely had enough to eat, and if they didn't work hard enough they were sent to Rome to be thrown to the lions.

One day, Androcles had a chance to escape. He didn't hesitate. He ran and ran, and ran again until he was utterly exhausted, so he crawled into a forest to hide

until he regained his strength. He was just settling down to
try to sleep when a great lion hobbled out from behind a
tree. At first, Androcles was absolutely petrified. He was just
thinking how very unfair life was that he should manage to
escape, only to be eaten by a lion, when he realised the lion
was not about to jump on him, but was holding out his paw
helplessly. Androcles stepped cautiously towards the lion. The
paw was all swollen and bleeding, and when Androcles
looked closely he could see why. There was a huge thorn
stuck in between the claws, which must have been causing
the lion considerable pain.

    Androcles pulled the thorn out,
and cleaned the wound before
wrapping it in leaves to keep
it dry. The great lion licked
Androcles with his very
rough tongue and then
lay down beside
him and went to
sleep. He kept
Androcles warm
all night. In the
morning the lion slipped
away very early and Androcles continued on his way.

    Years passed. But one day Androcles' luck ran out and
he was captured by his master's men and sent into the arena
to fight. The trap door was opened and a huge lion came

bounding up to Androcles. He closed his eyes, waiting for certain death. But then he felt a rough tongue licking his face. It was his lion! The crowds cheered with delight at this unexpected turn of events, and the emperor made Androcles tell the story of how he had taken the thorn out of the lion's paw. The emperor decided to free Androcles, and said that the lion could go with him. Androcles kept the lion's coat well brushed and his paws free of thorns, while the lion kept Androcles warm in bed at night, and so they both lived to a very ripe old age together.

The Ugly Duckling

a retelling from the original story by Hans Christian Andersen

The mother duck was waiting for her eggs to hatch. Slowly the first shell cracked and first a tiny bill and then a little yellow wing appeared. Then with a great rush, a bedraggled yellow duckling fell out. He stretched his wings and began to clean his feathers. Soon he stood proudly beside his mother, watching as his sisters and brothers all pushed their way out of their shells.

There was only one shell left. It was the largest, and the mother duck wondered why it was taking so much longer than the others. She wanted to take her babies down to the river for their first swimming lesson. There was a sudden loud crack, and there lay quite the biggest and ugliest duckling she had ever seen. He wasn't even yellow. His feathers were dull brown and grey.

"Oh dear," said the mother duck.

She led the family down to the river, the ugly duckling trailing along behind the others. They all splashed into the water, and were soon swimming gracefully, all except the ugly duckling who looked large and ungainly even on the water.

"Oh dear," said the mother duck.

The whole family set off for the farmyard where they were greeted with hoots and moos and barks and snorts from all the other animals.

"Whatever is that?" said the rooster, pointing rudely at the ugly duckling. All the other ducklings huddled round their mother and tried to pretend the ugly duckling was not with them.

"Oh dear," said the mother duck.

The ugly duckling felt very sad and lonely. No one seemed to like him, so he ran away from the farmyard and

hid in some dark reeds by the
river. Some hunters came
by with their loud noisy
guns and big fierce dogs.
The ugly duckling
paddled deeper
into the reeds,
trembling with
fear. Only later
in the day, as it
was growing
dark, did the
ugly duckling
dare move from
his hiding place.

All summer he
wandered over fields and
down rivers. Everywhere he went people
laughed and jeered at him, and all the other ducks he met
just hissed at him or tried to bite his tail. As well as being
ugly, the duckling was very lonely and unhappy. Soon
winter came and the rivers began to freeze over. One day
the duckling found himself trapped in the ice. He tucked his
head under his wing, and decided that his short life must
have come to an end.

He was still there early the next morning when a
farmer came by on his way to feed the cows in the fields.

The farmer broke the ice with his shoe, and wrapped the ugly duckling in his jacket then carried him home to his children. They put the poor frozen ugly duckling in a box by the fire, and as he thawed out they fed him and stroked his feathers. And there the ugly duckling stayed through the winter, growing bigger all the time.

Now the farmer's wife had never had much time for the ugly duckling. He was always getting under her feet in the kitchen, and he was so clumsy that he kept knocking things over. He spilt the milk in the bucket from the cow. He put his great feet in the freshly churned butter. He was just a nuisance, and one day the farmer's wife had enough. So, in a rage, she chased him out of her kitchen, out of the farmyard and through the gate down the lane.

It was a perfect spring day. The apple trees were covered in blossom, the grass was green and the air was filled with the sound of birdsong. The ugly duckling wandered down to the river, and there he saw three magnificent pure white swans. They were beautiful and so graceful as they glided over towards the bank where he stood. He waited for them to hiss at him and beat the water with their great wings to frighten him away, but they didn't do any such thing. Instead they called him to come and join them. At first he thought it was a joke, but they asked him again.

He bent down to get into the water, and there looking back at him was his own reflection. But where was the ugly duckling? All he could see was another great and magnificent swan. He was a swan! Not an ugly duckling but a swan. He lifted his great long elegant neck, and called in sheer delight, "I am a swan! I am a SWAN!" and he sailed gracefully over the water to join his real family.

The Three Billy Goats Gruff

a folk tale from Europe

In a mountain valley beside a rushing river, there lived three billy goats. One was very small, one was middle-sized and one was huge, and they were called the Three Billy Goats Gruff. Every day they would eat the lush green grass beside the river, and they were very content.

One day, however, the Three Billy Goats Gruff decided they would like to cross the river and see if the grass was any greener on the other side. The grass was actually no greener, nor was it any tastier, but they all felt they would like a change. First they had to find a way to cross the rushing river. They trotted a good way upstream before they found a little wooden bridge. After a good supper of lush green grass, they decided to wait until the next morning before crossing the little wooden bridge, so they settled down for the night.

Now, what the Three Billy Goats Gruff did not know
was that under the little wooden bridge there lived a very
mean and grumpy troll. He could smell the Three Billy
Goats Gruff, and he thought they smelled very good to eat.
So the next morning when the Three Billy Goats Gruff had
had a good breakfast of lush green grass, the troll was
hiding under the little wooden bridge, waiting for his
chance to have a good breakfast too.

"That little wooden bridge does not look too strong,"
said the very small Billy Goat Gruff. "I will go across first to
see if it is safe," and he trotted across the little wooden
bridge. But when he was only halfway across, the mean
and grumpy troll leapt out of his hiding place.

"Who is that trit-trotting across my bridge?" he roared.
"I am going to eat you up!"

But the very small Billy Goat Gruff wasn't ready to be

eaten up just yet, so he bravely said to the mean and grumpy troll, "You don't want to eat a skinny, bony thing like me. Just wait till my brother comes across, he is much bigger," and with a skip and a hop, the very small Billy Goat Gruff ran across the bridge to the lush green grass on the other side.

The middle-sized Billy Goat Gruff started to cross the little wooden bridge, but when he was only halfway across, the mean and grumpy troll roared at him.

"Who is that trit-trotting across my bridge?" he roared. "I am going to eat you up!"

But the middle-sized Billy Goat Gruff wasn't ready to be eaten up just yet either, so he bravely said to the mean and grumpy troll,

"You don't want to eat a skinny, bony thing like me. Just wait till my brother comes across, he is even

bigger," and with a skip and a hop, the middle-sized Billy Goat Gruff ran across the bridge to the lush green grass on the other side.

Now the huge Billy Goat Gruff had been watching all

the time. He smiled to himself and stepped out onto the little wooden bridge. By this time the mean and grumpy troll was getting very hungry indeed, and he was even meaner and grumpier when he was hungry. He didn't even bother to hide, but stood in the middle of the bridge looking at the huge Billy Goat Gruff who came trotting up to him.

"Who is that trit-trotting across my bridge?" he roared. "I am going to eat you up!"

"Oh no, you won't!" said the huge Billy Goat Gruff, and he lowered his head and with his huge horns he biffed the mean and grumpy troll into the rushing river. The water carried him far away down the river, and he was never seen again. The Three Billy Goats Gruff lived happily for many more years eating the lush green grass, and they were able to cross the rushing river just whenever they wanted!

The Greedy Dog

an English tale

There was once a very greedy dog who just ate and ate. Whenever he saw anything that looked good enough to eat, he would just open his mouth and gobble it all up. The postman wouldn't come near the house anymore, ever since the greedy dog mistook his ankle for an early breakfast. He would stand at the gate and throw the letters in the general direction of the letterbox. The paperboy just refused to go anywhere near. Visitors knew they had to come with a juicy bone or they wouldn't get as far as the front door.

One day the greedy dog was out wandering round the shops. He loved doing this as there were always lots of really good smells for him to investigate, and sometimes old ladies, who didn't know any better, would give him sticky buns to eat.

As he walked past the butcher's shop, the greedy dog started to lick his lips. There in the window was a great big steak. It looked juicy and very good to eat. The greedy dog decided that the steak would make a very nice meal. So he watched and waited outside the shop. Soon one of his favourite old ladies walked down the street and into the butcher's shop. The greedy dog sidled in alongside the unsuspecting old lady. She wanted sausages and mince and goodness knows what else, so while the butcher was looking after her, the greedy dog pounced. He grabbed the steak and galloped out of the shop before anyone really had time to realise what was happening.

Then there was a great hue and cry. The butcher ran out of his shop with a bellow of rage, the little old lady fainted, and everyone in the street joined in the chase. But the greedy dog knew all the back streets, and he was soon far away and longing to eat his steak. He ran through the back streets until he came to the canal. He was just about to cross the bridge when he caught sight of another dog, right in front of him, and this dog also had a great juicy steak in his mouth! Well now, you and I know that what he was looking at was his own reflection, but the greedy dog did not know that. All he saw was a second steak that he might have so, with a great fierce bark, he leapt at the other dog.

But instead of gaining another meal, the greedy dog found himself very wet indeed, and he had lost his own steak! It would be good if I could tell you that from that day onwards the greedy dog was better behaved. But I am afraid his manners did not improve, and he is still looking for the other dog. . .

The Cat and the Mouse

a retelling from the original story by the Brothers Grimm

N ow this is the tale of a wily cat and a foolish mouse. The mouse lived in a bare mouse hole under the pulpit in the church. The cat lived on an old cushion in the vestry. They had met on several occasions, the mouse usually whisking herself away very fast to the safety of her hole. She did not like the look of the cat's claws.

But one day, the cat called on the mouse at home.

"Miss mouse," a purry voice said, "why don't you and I set up home together? We could live in the bell tower and look after each other. We could share our food, too."

The mouse thought

about this carefully. She had never been fond of cats ever since her great grandfather had been supper for the farm tom cat one cold frosty night. But she could see that there would be benefits. The cat had a nice smile on his face. So she agreed.

They put their savings together and bought a pot full of fat for the winter. The cat said he would hide it away safely under the altar where no one ever went, and so it was done. They both promised not to touch it until the weather became really bad.

The mouse went about her business, quite happy in her new home, although she found the stairs a wearisome business. But the cat could not stop thinking about the pot of fat. So he thought up a plan.

"Miss mouse, my cousin has just had a kitten," he said looking at the mouse with his green eyes. "And she would like me to be godcat. I should like to go to the christening, would you mind?"

"Not at all, Mister cat," said the mouse. "I have plenty to do today."

But the wicked Cat went straight to the pot of fat and ate the top off. Then he went to sleep for the rest of the day. When it was evening, he stretched and strolled back up to the bell tower.

"Did you have a nice time?" asked the mouse

"Oh yes, very nice," said the not very nice cat.

"And what is the kitten called?"

"Topoff," replied the cat.

"Topoff?" asked the mouse. "That is a very strange name. Still I suppose cats have different family names," and she went on with her work.

All went quietly for a few days but then the cat had great longings for the pot of fat again so he went to the mouse.

"I find I have another new godkitten. Would you mind if I went to the christening?" said the cat, his green eyes half closed.

"Another godkitten?" said the mouse. "My, my you do have a big family."

And the beastly cat slunk off and ate up half the pot of fat. When he sauntered back up the stairs that night the mouse was waiting.

"Well, how did it all go?" she said. "What is this kitten to be called?"

"Halfempty," replied the cat.

"Halfempty?" said the mouse. "I have never heard such a thing before."

But the cat was asleep, a secret smile twitching his
whiskers.

Well, as you can imagine, it was not long before that
greedy cat wanted some fat again.

"Miss mouse, just imagine! I have yet another
godkitten. I should really go to this christening too," said
the cat.

Miss mouse thought it all very strange but she was a
kindly creature so she waved the cat off to yet another
christening. The cat, of course, just scuttled downstairs, slid
under the altar and licked the pot of fat quite clean. He
came back very late that night.

"Now what strange name did your family give this new
kitten?" asked the mouse crossly. She had a headache from
all the noise in the tower when the bells rang.

"Allgone," said the cat.

"Topoff, Halfempty and now Allgone!" the Mouse said

in disbelief. "Well, I am very glad I am not a member of your family. I couldn't be doing with such weird names," and she went to sleep with her paws over her ears.

There were no more christenings for a while. The weather became colder and colder, and the mouse began to think of the little pot of fat hidden under the altar.

"Mister cat," she said one frosty morning, "I think it is time we collected our pot of fat. I am looking forward to a lick."

We will see about that thought the cat, but he padded downstairs behind the mouse. She reached under the altar and brought out the pot, but of course when she looked in it was all empty.

"What a foolish mouse I have been!" she cried. "Now I see what a wicked cat you have been. Topoff, Halfempty and Allgone indeed!"

"Such is the way of cats," said the greedy cat, and he put out a paw to grab mouse. But she was too quick for him, and dived back into her dear little mouse hole under the pulpit.

Never again did she trust cats, ever, ever.

The Moon and Stars and Rainbows

The Star Maiden and the Flax Flowers

an Austrian fairytale

Peter the goatherd lived high up a mountainside with his mother in a little wooden house. A fast flowing river dashed down the valley, lush green meadows on either side. These meadows were full of flowers, bluebells, daisies and buttercups. In the summer, Peter took the goats even higher up into the mountains to the small patches of green grass that grew among the rocks. The goats wore bells round their necks, and all day long these bells would jingle as the goats leapt from rock to rock. In the evening, Peter would play his pipes and the goats would all gather round him for the journey back to the house and the barn where Peter's mother would milk them.

One evening as they all trotted back down into the

barn, Peter's mother called out to him.

"Where is the white nanny goat and her two kids?"

Peter looked round. They were not there.

"I saw them as we came down the valley, I will go and look for them," he said as he turned and blew his pipes again, calling over the meadow. But they did not appear. Peter set off up the mountain track again. He knew he had to find the goats before it grew too dark: climbing over the rocks would be a dangerous task with only the stars to guide his steps. He did not dare leave looking until the morning as he was afraid a wolf might snatch them away.

He climbed higher and higher, playing his pipes all the while, but he could not find a trace of the nanny goat and her kids. All night he searched without any luck. But in the summer the nights are not long, and just as he thought he could go no further, the rising sun tipped the mountain tops with pink. He sat down exhausted and closed his eyes for a moment. He heard the first calls of the birds as the light gradually crept over the grey rocks. And as he listened, he heard a soft voice calling his name.

"Peter, Peter," and with the

voice he heard a gentle bleating. He leapt to his feet and looked all round. He could see no sign of the goats. The voice came again.

"Peter, Peter," and as he looked up at the rocks above him, he saw a beautiful girl, dressed in a long blue cloak. Her eyes were blue too, as blue as the morning sky. She stood in front of a cave Peter could not remember seeing before. From underneath her cloak peeped the white nanny goat and her two kids.

"Call them, Peter," she said and he put the pipe to his lips and blew a joyous tune. The nanny goat and her two kids bounded down to stand by his side. Peter stroked their rough heads and looked up to the girl. She was so beautiful, he felt quite tongue-tied. She smiled at him and laughed gently.

"You are a good goatherd, Peter. I have watched over you and your herd for many a long day. When I found your nanny and her two kids last evening I brought them up here to keep them safe from the wild beasts through the night."

Peter was still silent. He was so overcome he couldn't even find the words to say thank you to the beautiful girl with the blue eyes. She beckoned him towards the cave.

"I should like to give you a gift to remember me by, Peter. Would you like to choose? Look inside the cave," she said as she stood aside. Peter gasped. Inside the cave there were great mounds of precious stones, diamonds, rubies and emeralds. Peter finally found his tongue.

"Who are you?" he whispered.

"I am Hertha, the Star Maiden," the girl replied. "I look

after all the little ones, the kids, the lambs, the little rabbits and the birds in the air, the new leaves and flowers, even the babies in the cradles. Now Peter, all these precious stones come from deep inside the earth, so what will you have?"

"My mother and I have all we need. We have food and clothes and our little wooden house. We have our goats and their kids. We have no need of precious stones," Peter said proudly.

The girl seemed very pleased with this reply.

"Good, Peter! I am pleased to see you are content but I would still like to give you something."

Peter smiled shyly at her.

"I should like some of those beautiful blue flowers growing by the entrance to the cave."

Peter had never seen the flowers before, they had slender stems and sky blue flowers, just the colour of the girl's eyes. She clapped her hands in delight.

"That is my very own flower, Peter. It is called flax. I shall give you some seeds to sow as well and my flowers will bring much good to you and your people." And she gave Peter a handful of tiny golden seeds. As he looked at them lying in his hand, the girl's cloak billowed around her and she was gone. So was the cave with all the precious stones, but there at his feet was a bunch of the pale blue flowers. Peter and the goats went happily downhill back to the little wooden house where his mother was waiting anxiously for him.

Peter planted the golden seeds, and the next year the flax bloomed like a blue cloud in the valley. Then early one mid-summer morning, Hertha suddenly appeared and showed them how to dry and then comb the flax to make it into linen. And so the little blue flowers were indeed a gift that brought much good to everyone.

How Jumbo went to the Moon

an English tale first told by Joyce M Westrup 1936

Jumbo was a dog, a small woolly dog with a great plume of a tail. He belonged to two brothers who had decided after travelling the world that they wanted to settle down. So they looked for a place to build a house. They searched and searched and searched, and eventually they found just the right spot. They had discovered a little clearing in a great green forest, with a stream running by.

"This is the spot!" said the brothers to Jumbo and they all began work straight away on their new house. Jumbo didn't do very much other than run around barking, but he thought he was helping. The brothers cleared a big square in the grass, and then the eldest brother took his great axe and began chopping down a tall tree for the roof.

A huge great voice said, "Who said you could chop

down my trees?" and a
big ugly face looked
down at the brothers
and Jumbo from
above the tree. It was
a giant, and he looked
very cross.

"We wanted to
build our new house
here," said the younger
brother bravely.

"Well, you can't!"
said the giant and he
stomped off back into the forest.

Now the brothers were very fed up at this turn of
events. They had spent such a long time looking for a good
place for their new house. They sat and thought about what
to do for ages. Jumbo helped them think by going to sleep.
Then the elder brother said, "I have a splendid idea. Let's
dig a very deep, deep pit and then cover it with branches so
that when the giant comes along again he will fall into the
pit and then we can build our house on top of him!"

So they set to work, and Jumbo helped with the digging
because he was good at that. Soon their giant trap was
ready, and the elder brother took up his great axe again.
He had only chopped his third chop when the giant came
stomping down the path shouting at the top of his huge

voice, "I thought I told you not to… HELP!" he yelled as
he fell down the deep, deep pit. Well, it was a very deep,
deep pit and the giant just could not get out. The two
brothers cut down lots more trees and soon they had built a
very nice house indeed, right over the deep, deep pit. They
made a trap door in the kitchen floor so they could send
down meals to the giant. The brothers were quite kind-
hearted in this way, and it was the giant's forest after all.

Now the giant was quite well brought up, but the one
thing he was very bad about was
eating his crusts. He just dropped
these onto the floor of the pit,
and before long he was knee
deep in crusts.
Then he had a
splendid idea.

He piled all the
crusts up into one
great heap, and
when he climbed up
this heap he found
he could reach the
trap door. He
pushed the trap
door open very
carefully and
scrambled out.

He found it was night-time and everybody, including Jumbo, was fast asleep. The giant bent down and scooped up the entire house in his great arms and he hurled it up, high, high into the sky. The two brothers landed on a star each, but Jumbo fell on the moon. They are all quite happy up there, and if you look very carefully sometimes you can see Jumbo, waving his great plume of a tail. I don't know what happened to the giant but I am sure it was a long time before anyone dared try to build a house in his forest again!

The Lad who went to the North Wind

a retelling from Popular Tales from the Norse by George Webbe Dasent

There was once a lad called Snorri who lived with his mother in the far north. They were very poor, and there was never very much food on the table. One day Snorri decided to visit the North Wind to see if he could do some work for him. But he was no good at huffing and puffing, and he couldn't blow big waves at sea, so the North Wind gave him a magic tablecloth.

"All you have to do is lay the cloth on the table and say, 'Cloth serve me, please!' and you will have food enough," said the North Wind.

Snorri thanked him very much and set off home. But it was soon dark so he stopped at an inn for the night. He spread the cloth out on a table and said, "Cloth serve me, please!" and there in a trice was enough food to feed everyone at the inn. All the other travellers were very grateful to Snorri, but the landlord saw a chance to make life easy for himself. When the lad was asleep, he stole the cloth and put an ordinary one in its place. Of course Snorri knew nothing of all this until he arrived home and tried to show his mother the North Wind's gift. Snorri decided to go back to the North Wind.

"That cloth you gave me didn't last very long," Snorri complained. "One meal and that was that."

Now the North Wind guessed what had happened so he gave Snorri another gift. This was a goose that would lay golden coins.

"All you have to say is, 'Goose fill my money bag, please!' and you will have plenty," said the North Wind.

Snorri thanked the North Wind and once again set off home, stopping at the same inn as before. He went into the stables to talk to the goose, but the landlord followed him and saw all that happened. Late at night, the landlord's wife put an ordinary goose in the place of the magic one. Of course Snorri knew nothing of all this until he arrived home. Snorri decided once again to go back to the North Wind.

"That goose you gave me didn't last very long," Snorri complained to the North Wind. "One bag of money and that was that."

The North Wind guessed what had happened so he gave Snorri a final gift. This was a stick that would beat whoever it was told to.

"All you have to say is, 'Beat, stick, beat, please!' and it will go on until you tell it to stop," said the North Wind.

So Snorri thanked the North Wind and set off home, visiting the same inn again. Snorri was not a foolish lad and he too had guessed that the landlord was the thief. So when he arrived at the inn, he made a great show of the stick and then lay down, pretending to sleep. The landlord found another stick and was just about to change it for the North Wind's gift when Snorri sat up and shouted at the top of his voice, "Beat, stick, beat, please!" and the stick began to beat the landlord. Well, didn't he shout and didn't he roar! He ran round and round the room.

"Stop! Stop!" the landlord cried, but Snorri only laughed.

"Where is my tablecloth and my goose?" he shouted above the landlord's roars of pain. "If you give me my property back I will see if I can persuade the stick to stop."

"Please get your stick to stop beating my husband," the landlord's wife cried. "Here is your tablecloth and your goose," and she thrust them into Snorri's hands.

Only then did Snorri say, "Stop, stick, stop, please!"

The landlord disappeared very quickly, and so Snorri took up the stick and the tablecloth and he tucked the goose under his arm. He lived with his mother very comfortably ever after.

Kaatje's Treasure

a myth from Holland

Hans was a cheesemaker and he lived with his wife Kaatje. They had a small farm near the crossroads by the Old Inn outside the Dutch town of Haarlem. Every week Hans would go to market in Amsterdam with his great big round cheeses, and he would come back with some coins jingling in his pocket, and a few bulbs for his wife to plant in her little garden. Kaatje was a dreamer but Hans loved her very much.

One day as Hans was pressing the cheeses in the dairy, he noticed Kaatje was not singing as usual.

"What is wrong, my dear?" he asked. "You are not as happy as usual."

"Oh, husband, I have had a very strange dream three nights running now. It was so real!" she whispered.

"You and your dreams," laughed Hans. "Tell me what happened then."

So Kaatje told him that she had dreamt she must go to Amsterdam and then walk round the Corn Exchange three times. From then on she would be rich beyond her wildest dreams. Hans thought it was another of her daft wishes, but she was very serious so eventually he agreed to walk round the Corn Exchange three times when he next went to market with his cheeses. And so Kaatje would have to wait until market day. She simply couldn't wait that long so she crept out of the house very early the next morning while Hans was still asleep, and set off on the road to Amsterdam.

She walked and walked, and then some more and eventually she arrived in Amsterdam. She was very excited as she set off round the Corn Exchange. Once. Twice. And a final third time. Absolutely nothing happened. Kaatje sat down with a thump. Her feet were very sore. Her head ached. And she felt very silly. Whatever would Hans say when he heard where she had been. Her eyes filled with tears.

"Can I help you?" a kindly voice said. "You seem to be lost, I have watched you walk three times round the Corn Exchange."

Kaatje looked up and there was a man,

a farmer by the look of him, and he had such a kindly face that before too long Kaatje was telling him her silly dream. Well, he just laughed and laughed.

"I had a dream like that once, but I knew it was only a dream," the farmer said. "I dreamt I had to go to the dairy of a small farm near the crossroads by the Old Inn outside the Dutch town of Haarlem, and under the flagstones I would find a great chest of gold. Quite ridiculous! I think you should go home to your good husband and forget your dreams," and he walked away down the street.

Kaatje could not really believe what she had heard but tired as she was, she went home again as fast as ever she could.

Hans was cross with her at first for going on such a fool's errand, but when she demanded he dig up the dairy floor he just laughed at her. So she picked up the spade and began digging by herself.

The pile of earth grew higher and higher, and Hans despaired for his clean dairy. But then the spade struck something metal. Hans and Kaatje peered down into the hole.

An old rusting chest lay on its side, and spilling out was a great pile of coins! Well, then they both dug away with both hands and soon there was a great pile of gold coins on the dairy floor, enough to keep them in great comfort for the rest of their days. They were content with their way of life so they stayed at the farm near the crossroads by the Old Inn outside the Dutch town of Haarlem, and Hans went every week to market with his cheeses. But Kaatje never remembered a single one of her dreams ever again.

Snow-Daughter and Fire-Son

a German legend

There was once a husband and wife who had longed for many years to have a child. But as no child arrived they grew sad. One winter day they were outside clearing the snow away from their path. It had been bitterly cold, and there were huge icicles hanging off the roof. They sparkled in the sunlight. The wife turned to her husband and murmured,

"I wish I had as many children as there are icicles hanging from the roof."

When they turned to go back inside, the wife looked up again at the roof and sighed. As she did so, a tiny icicle fell from the roof and straight into her mouth.

"Ah, husband!" she laughed, "Perhaps now I will have a snow child!" and they thought no more of it.

But in the spring the following year, the wife did have a baby. It was a tiny girl whose skin was white as snow, and her eyes were like blue chips of ice. As the little girl grew, it was clear she never felt the cold. She would always run around with bare feet, and in the winter she would laugh and roll in the snow as soon as it fell. She hated the warmth, and would hide from the sun in the summer. Indoors, she would sit as far away from the fire as possible. Her mother and father called her Snow-daughter.

One winter's night when a blizzard was blowing, the man and his wife huddled by the fire.

"Ah, husband," said the wife, "perhaps it would have been better if I had produced a fire child," and as she spoke a spark flew from the fire into her lap.

The man laughed.

"You should not say things like that, wife. You never know what might happen."

In the spring the following year the wife produced a fine son with rosy cheeks and flashing black eyes. As the

little boy grew, he was always
complaining of the cold.

In the summer he would
dance in the heat of the sun,
and would stay outside
until the last rays had
dipped over the horizon.
His mother and father called
him Fire-son.

Now, of course, Fire-son and
Snow-daughter could not bear to be close to each other.
Fire-son would complain that Snow-daughter made him
shiver, and Snow-daughter would complain that Fire-son
made her skin burn.

Time passed. Fire-son grew into a fine, darkly
handsome young man, and Snow-daughter grew into a
beautiful shining fair young woman. Their mother and
father died, and Fire-son and Snow-daughter longed to
leave the little cottage and seek their fortunes. But they had
no one other than each other in the whole wide world and
they wished to travel together.

"I just know we should keep together if we are to be
lucky," said Snow-daughter.

"But how can we arrange it?" asked Fire-son. "If I stay
close to you my heart freezes, and if you come close to me
you burn from my heat."

Snow-daughter produced two huge fur cloaks. "If we

wear these we can walk side by side. I shall
not feel your heat, and you will not
feel my cold."

And so they set off. They
travelled for many days,
wandering far and wide, and saw
many strange lands before they
grew weary and decided to stop
a while. Fire-son built himself a
snug wooden hut where he
always had a great fire burning,
and Snow-daughter lived outside
in the open air. When they met
for supper, they would always put
on the fur coats and sit outside.

One day they were sitting outside the hut together in
their coats when the king and all his courtiers came by. He
was captivated by Snow-daughter's beauty, and bade her
tell him who she was and who the fiercely handsome young
man in the fur coat was. And so they told the king the
whole story. He wasted no time in asking Snow-daughter to
marry him.

The king built a huge ice house underground for
Snow-daughter, and he built a house inside a great oven for
Fire-son. So they all lived happily ever after and, thankfully,
when Snow-daughter gave birth to twins they seemed quite
able both to sit by the fire and to dance in the snow!

The Moon Caught in the Marsh

a folk tale from East Anglia

The Moon looked down on the marsh. It was oozy and murky, and people were afraid to cross the marsh at night unless the Moon was shining. It was said that on dark nights the marsh goblins would lead travellers astray and drag them down into the clinging black mud.

Now the Moon did not believe these tales but she decided to see for herself. She wrapped herself in a great dark cloak and slipped down to the marsh. All you could see was her tiny silver feet below the cloak.

But the goblins could see in the dark. As soon as they saw the Moon's silver feet they all crept up close to her and tried to pull at the great cloak with their horrid cold hands. The Moon realised exactly what the travellers had to put up with. And then she heard a cry coming from quite close by. It was a poor man who had come to fetch the doctor for his wife who was going to have a baby. In the deep dark he had tripped over a tree root and hurt his foot.

The beastly goblins ran away from the Moon the moment they heard the man cry out and they began pushing and pulling him here, there and everywhere. The man yelled out in fear, and the Moon was so upset that she flung aside her cloak and shone out in all her bright glory. The goblins scattered, their eyes hurting from the brilliance of the Moon.

The man escaped from the marsh and ran all the way to the doctor, in the clear moonlight. And later that night, his wife safely produced a beautiful little girl with shining white hair. Everyone always said she looked like a moonbeam.

But the Moon was still in the marsh, and she found her tiny silver feet were stuck in the mud. She turned this way and that, but she could not get out. And then she stumbled and fell with a splash into the dark black mud. Instantly her glorious light went out. With wicked cries of delight the

goblins all came
running back, and
rolled a great flat
stone over the
spot where the
Moon lay
trapped. Not
a single
beam of her
light was to
be seen.

Days went
by, and then weeks.
The villagers waited anxiously
for the new Moon but there was no sign of it. When a
month had gone by, several of the villagers gathered
together to decide what to do. The man who had been
rescued the night his daughter was born suggested that
perhaps the Moon might be found near where he had been
caught by the goblins. They set off towards the spot, bravely
determined to find out what had happened to the Moon.
They all carried flaring torches and sang bold songs to
cheer themselves.

When they reached the spot the first thing they saw
was the great flat stone. The next thing they saw was
hundreds and hundreds of nasty spiteful goblins. The goblins
tried to blow out the torches, but the men re-lit them as fast

as ever possible. The men waded out into the marsh and with a huge effort lifted the side of the great stone. Out shone a blinding ray of moonlight. The goblins all disappeared, shrieking in dismay. Slowly, slowly the men lifted the stone and the grateful Moon sailed high into the sky once more. She shone down on the men as they walked home, and she shone the next night, and the next. Best of all, from that day forth there was never a goblin to be seen or heard in that part of the country.

The North Wind and the Sun

a retelling from Aesop's fables

The North Wind and the Sun once had a quarrel about who was the stronger. "I am stronger than you," said the North Wind. "I can blow down trees, and whip up great waves on the sea."

"I am stronger than you," said the Sun. "I can make flowers open, and turn fields of wheat from green to gold."

And so they argued back and forth, day after day. The East Wind and the Moon became very cross with them both and suggested that they have a competition to decide once and for all who was the strongest. A man was walking down the path, and he was wearing a big overcoat.

"Whichever one of you can first get that man to take off his coat is the strongest," said the Moon. And the East Wind said, "And then we will have no more quarrels!"

So the North Wind and the Sun agreed to the competition. The North Wind began. He blew and blew, the

coldest bitter wind he could manage. The great overcoat
flapped round the man's legs as he struggled against the
wind, but he only pulled the coat closer round his neck to
keep out the bitter cold. Then it was the Sun's turn. She rose
high in the sky and shone down on the man in the great
overcoat. Warmer and warmer she shone, until the man
unbuttoned the coat. Still the Sun beamed
down, and finally the man flung off
the coat, sweat pouring down his
face. The Sun had won!

The North Wind blew off
in a great huff, but he did
not dare continue his quarrel
with the Sun. So today when
the fierce North Wind blows
you have to remember that he
is still very cross!

East of the Sun and West of the Moon

a retelling from Popular Tales from the Norse by George Webbe Dasent

Once there was a poor herdsman and his wife who lived in a tumbledown cottage in the north of the country with their family. There were seven sons and six daughters and the youngest daughter was the best of the lot.

One cold winter's night there came a gentle knock at the door. When the herdsman opened it, to his surprise there was a Great Brown Bear outside.

"Herdsman, I would be grateful if you would give me your youngest daughter," said the Brown Bear very politely. "If you do, I shall make you rich beyond belief."

This was a tempting offer, but the herdsman thought he should ask his daughter first. She said, "NO!" very loudly.

But the rest of the family persuaded her that the Brown Bear looked kind enough, and they really could do with the money. So she brushed her hair and put on her cloak, and

off she went with the
Brown Bear.

"Get on my back, and
hold onto my fur tightly," said
the Brown Bear, and she did.
They rode a long way to a
great castle. The Brown Bear
galloped in through the front
door, and there was a table laid
with a delicious-looking meal.
The Brown Bear gave the
daughter a silver bell saying,

"Whatever you want, just ring the bell and it shall be
yours," and he padded away silently.

Well, the youngest daughter ate till she was full and
then all she could wish for was a good sleep. So she rang
the silver bell, and she found herself in a warm room with a
great four poster bed. No sooner had she snuggled down in
the warm soft blankets and blown out the candle than she
felt something lie across her feet. It was the Brown Bear. But
when she woke in the morning he had gone. She rang her
bell for breakfast and then spent a very happy day
wandering round the castle.

And so she settled down to life in the Brown Bear's
castle. But after a while she grew sad. She missed her family.
So the Brown Bear offered to take her home for a visit. But
he warned her, "Whatever you do, you must not spend time
alone with your mother. If you do, there is no telling what

bad luck will follow."

She promised and they both set off. The Brown Bear bounded over the snow, and it seemed no time before she was once again with her family. They now lived in a grand house with many rooms and a servant for everyone. They all thanked her for making their lives so much happier.

Her mother said, "Now, my daughter, you must tell me all about your new life!" and she led her away from the rest of the family. The youngest daughter quite forgot her promise to the Brown Bear and she was soon telling her mother everything. When she came to the bit about the Brown Bear sleeping across her feet every night, her mother let out a great shriek.

"Foolish child! This bear must be a troll in disguise! You must wait until he is asleep, and then take a good look at him. Then you will see what he really is."

So when the Brown Bear had taken her home again, the youngest daughter did as her mother suggested. As she held the candle high above the bed she saw not a sleeping bear, not even a troll, but the most handsome prince ever. But, as she bent closer, some wax fell from the candle onto his shirt and he awoke with a start.

"Alas!" he cried. "What have you done? Had you only

waited, you might have released me from the wicked witch whose spell has turned me into a bear by day. Now I must return to her castle which is East O' the Sun and West O' the Moon, and marry the princess with the three-foot nose."

The prince looked at her once more, his eyes full of tears, and with a rumble of thunder he disappeared. As did the castle and the gardens. The youngest daughter found herself alone in the middle of a forest.

"Well, it is my fault that I have lost the prince so I will just have to try to find him again and rescue him," she said to herself, and she set off to find the castle East O' the Sun and West O' the Moon.

She had walked for seven days and seven nights when she met an old woman sitting by the roadside. The old woman had a golden apple in her lap.

"Do you know where I might find the castle East O' the Sun and West O' the Moon?" the girl asked.

The old woman replied, "No, but my sister might. You can borrow my horse, he will lead you to her. You better take this apple with you, too."

The horse galloped through the night for seven days until they saw an old, old woman sitting by the roadside. The old, old woman had a golden comb.

"Do you know where I might find the castle East O' the Sun and West O' the Moon?" the girl asked.

The old, old woman replied, "No, but my sister might. You can borrow my horse, he will lead you to her. You better take this comb with you, too."

The horse galloped through the night for seven days until they saw an old, old, old woman by the roadside. The old, old, old woman had a golden spinning wheel.

"Do you know where I might find the castle East O' the Sun and West O' the Moon?" the girl asked.

The old, old, old woman replied, "No, but the East Wind will. You can borrow my horse, he will lead you to him. You better take this spinning wheel with you, too."

The horse galloped through the night for seven days until they found the East Wind. He didn't know where the castle was. He suggested the girl try his brother the West Wind and he blew her all the way to the West Wind's house. But he didn't know where the castle was either. So the West

Wind suggested she try his
brother the South Wind, but
when they reached the South
Wind's house he was fast
asleep.

"I think you need to try my
brother the North Wind, but he is
very busy and very fierce," said the
West Wind, and he blew her a long,
long way to the top of a bleak mountain. There they
met the North Wind.

"Do you know where I might find the castle East O'
the Sun and West O' the Moon?" the girl asked.

"Indeed I do," howled the
North Wind. "I will take you
there," and with a mighty gust he
blew the girl and the golden
apple and the golden comb and
the golden spinning wheel until
they reached the castle East O'
the Sun and West O' the Moon.

The girl sat down outside
the castle and began to throw
the golden apple high up into
the air. A window was flung open and there stood the
princess, her three-foot nose resting on the window edge.

"What do you want for your golden apple?" she
shrieked down and her voice was like a saw.

"To spend the evening with the prince," replied the girl.

Well, that was easily arranged, but when she went into his chamber, the youngest daughter found the prince fast asleep. The witch had given him a sleeping draught so the youngest daughter went sadly away.

The next morning the girl sat combing her hair with the golden comb, and it was the same story. The princess with the three-foot nose took the golden comb, but again the prince just slept and slept.

The third morning, the youngest daughter sat outside with the golden spinning wheel, and again the princess stuck her great nose out of the window. But this time, the prince's little page told the prince all about the girl who had tried to wake him the nights before, so when the witch brought him his cocoa he only pretended to drink it.

When the youngest daughter came in, he was awake and waiting for her. As soon as he saw her, the prince was overjoyed and kissed her. Straightaway, there was a terrible shriek from the tower at the top of the castle as the witch disappeared in a flash of green light. The princess found her nose was three-foot longer again, so she ran away to hide and was never seen again.

The prince married the youngest daughter the very next day, and the castle East O' the Sun and West O' the Moon became a happy place. Even the North Wind blew more gently round the battlements.

Boys and Girls

The Sorcerer's Apprentice

a German folk tale

The sorcerer lived in a dusty room at the top of a very tall gloomy tower. His table was covered with bottles and jars full of strange-coloured potions, and bubbling mixtures filled the air with horrible smells. The walls of the tower were lined with huge old books. These were the sorcerer's spell books and he would let no one else look inside them.

The sorcerer had a young apprentice called Harry. He was a good but

142

lazy boy who longed only to be able to do magic himself. The sorcerer had promised to teach him all he knew, but only when he thought Harry was ready.

One day the sorcerer had to visit a friend who was a warlock. The sorcerer had never left Harry alone in the tower before and he did not entirely trust him. Looking very fierce, the sorcerer gave Harry his instructions.

"I have a very important spell to conjure up tonight when I return, so I need the cauldron full of water from the well," he said. "When you have filled the cauldron, you can sweep the floor and then you must light the fire."

Harry was not best pleased. It would take many, many trips to the well to fill the cauldron, and he would have all those steps to climb each time. Perhaps the sorcerer could read his mind, for the last thing he said as he climbed out of the window to fly away on his small green dragon was, "Touch nothing!" and off he flew in a cloud of smoke and flame from the dragon.

Harry watched until the sorcerer was safely far out of sight, and then did precisely what

he had been told not to
do. He took down one
of the old dusty spell
books. For a while
all was quiet in the
tower, and then
Harry found what
he was looking for.
It was a spell to
make a broomstick
obey orders. Harry didn't
hesitate. He forgot the sorcerer's
instructions, he forgot that magic can
be very dangerous. He took the broomstick
in one hand and the spell book in the other,
and read out the spell in a quavery voice for,
truth to tell, he was very nervous. Nothing
happened. Harry tried again, and this time his voice
was stronger.

The broomstick quivered and then stood up. It
grabbed a bucket and jumped off down the stairs. Soon it
was back, the bucket brimful of water which it tipped into
the cauldron. Harry was delighted and smiled as the
broomstick set off down the stairs again. Up and down the
broomstick went and soon the cauldron was full.

"Stop, stop!" shouted Harry, but the broomstick just
carried on, and on. Soon the floor was awash and then the

bottles and jars were floating around the room. Nothing Harry could say would stop the broomstick, and so in desperation, he grabbed the axe that lay by the fireside and chopped the broomstick into pieces. To his horror, all the pieces of wood turned into new broomsticks and they set off downstairs to the well, buckets appearing magically in their hands.

By now the water was nearly up to the ceiling. Wet spell books spun round and round the room, and Harry gave himself up for lost. Suddenly there was a great clatter of wings and a hiss of steam as the green dragon flew into the tower. The sorcerer was back! In a huge voice he commanded the broomsticks to stop. They did. Then he ordered the water back into the well. It all rushed back down the stairs. Then he ordered the dragon to dry everything with its hot breath. Then he turned to look at Harry. And, oh dear! Harry could see that the sorcerer was very, very angry indeed. The sorcerer looked as if he might turn Harry into something terrible, but then he sat down on a soggy cushion with a squelch.

"Right, I think it is time I taught you how to do magic PROPERLY!" And he did.

Goldilocks and the Three Bears

a retelling from the original tale by Andrew Lang

Once upon a time there was a little girl called Goldilocks who lived in the middle of a great forest with her mother and her father. Now ever since she was tiny, her mother had told her she must never, ever wander off into the forest for it was full of wild creatures, especially bears. But as Goldilocks grew older she longed to explore the forest.

One washday, when her mother was busy in the kitchen, hidden in clouds of steam, Goldilocks sneaked off down the path that led deep into the forest.

At first she was happy, looking at the wild flowers and listening to the birds singing, but it did not take long for her to become hopelessly lost.

She wandered for hours and hours and, as it grew darker, she became frightened. She started to cry, but then she saw a light shining through the trees. She rushed forward, sure she had somehow found her way home, only to realise that it was not her own cottage that she was looking at. But she opened the door and looked inside.

On a scrubbed wooden table there were three bowls of steaming hot porridge; a big one, a middle-sized one and a little one. Goldilocks was so tired that she quite forgot all her manners and just sat down at the table. The big bowl was too tall for her to reach. The middle-sized bowl was too hot. But the little one was just right, so she ate all the porridge up.

By the warm fire there were three chairs: a big one, a middle-sized one and a little one. Goldilocks couldn't climb up into the big one. The middle-sized one was too hard. The little was just the right size, but as soon as she sat down, it broke into pieces. Goldilocks scrambled to her feet and then noticed there were steps going upstairs, where she found three beds: a big one, a middle-sized one and a little one. The big bed was too hard. The middle-sized one was too soft. But the little one was just right and she was soon fast asleep.

The cottage belonged to three bears, and it was not long before they came home. They knew at once that someone had been inside.

Father Bear growled,

"Who has been eating my porridge?"

Mother Bear grumbled,

"Who has been eating my porridge?"

And Baby Bear gasped,

"Who has been eating my porridge, AND has eaten it all up?"

The bears looked round the room. They looked at the chairs by the warm fire.

Father Bear growled,

"Who has been sitting in my chair?"

Mother Bear grumbled,

"Who has been sitting in my chair?"

And Baby Bear gasped,

"Who has been sitting in my chair, AND has broken it to bits?"

The bears all clumped upstairs. They looked at the three beds.

Father Bear growled,

"Who has been sleeping in my bed?"

Mother Bear grumbled,

"Who has been sleeping in my bed?"

And Baby Bear gasped,

"Who has been sleeping in my bed, AND is still there?"

Suddenly Goldilocks woke up. All she could see was three very cross-looking bears. She jumped off the bed, ran down the stairs, and out of the door. She ran and ran and ran, and by good fortune found herself outside her own cottage. Her mother and father scolded, but then gave her lots of hugs and kisses, and a big bowl of soup. Goldilocks had certainly learnt her lesson, and she never ever wandered off again.

Peter and the Wolf

original libretto by Sergey Prokofiev

P eter lived with his grandfather at the edge of the forest. Peter used to play with the wild birds and animals in the garden, but his grandfather always warned him not to go into the meadow in case the wolf crept out of the forest.

I am afraid Peter did not always do as he was told, so one day he slipped through the garden gate and into the meadow when he met a duck swimming in the middle of the pond.

"You must watch out for the wolf," said Peter to the duck but she was too busy enjoying herself to listen. Round and round the pond she swam. A little bird flew down and the duck tried to persuade her to come into the pond as well. But as the little bird stood talking to the duck, Peter saw the cat sneak up behind her.

"Look out!" shouted Peter and the bird flew up to safety in the tree.

"Thank you, Peter," she said. The cat was not so pleased. Just then Peter's grandfather came out and saw the open garden gate.

"Peter! How many times do I have to tell you? Come back into the garden at once," he shouted and Peter walked slowly back in.

Meanwhile, at the far side of the meadow, nearest the forest, a grey shape slunk out from under the trees. It was the wolf!

The little bird flew up into the tree, and the cat joined her, although on a lower branch. But the duck was too busy swimming to see what was happening and in a flash the wolf grabbed her and swallowed her whole!

Peter saw it all from the garden.

"I am going to catch that old wolf," he said to himself.

He found a piece of rope and climbed up a tree whose branches overhung the meadow. He made a loop in the rope and hung it out of the tree. Then he called to the little bird, "Can you tempt the wolf this way by flying round his head, please? I am going to catch him!"

The brave little bird darted down very close to the wolf's nose. The wolf snapped his fierce teeth, and only just missed the little bird. Closer and closer they came to the tree where Peter was hiding. The wolf was so busy trying to catch the bird that he did not see the rope. Peter looped it over the wolf's tail, and there he was, dangling from the branch of the tree!

Peter's grandfather came out and he was astonished to see the wolf. Just then some hunters came out of the forest.

"Well done," they cried, "you have caught the wolf. We have been after him for a long time."

And they all went off in a very joyful procession to the zoo. Peter led the wolf at the front, the little bird flew overhead, and the cat padded alongside, taking care not to get too close to the wolf. The hunters came up in the rear with Peter's grandfather. And from deep inside the wolf's tummy, the duck quacked loudly, just to remind everyone that she was there!

Dick Whittington and his Cat

an English myth

Hundreds of years ago there lived a poor orphan boy called Dick Whittington. His only possession was his cat, but everyone in his village looked after him, so he never wanted for a meal or clothes on his back. In return, he worked hard wherever he was needed. Now Dick's greatest dream was to visit the great city of London where, he had heard, the streets were paved with gold.

One day, a waggoner pulled into the village to give his two great shire horses a drink. Dick offered to rub the horses down, and before long he was telling the waggoner all about his dreams of visiting London town.

"Well, you must be in luck today," smiled the waggoner, "for that is where I am bound. Why don't you come with me and I will drop you off back here again when I return tomorrow?"

This was too good
an offer to refuse, so
Dick and his cat waved
goodbye to the villagers
and set off with the
waggoner for London.
When they arrived, Dick
looked round about in
astonishment. Never
before had he seen such
huge buildings, all
crowded so closely
together. And there
were so many people!
Dick set off to explore,
promising the waggoner
he would be back in the evening.

The pavements certainly did not appear to be made of
gold. But he kept on thinking he should just try round the
next corner, and then the next and, before long, Dick
realised that he was hopelessly lost. He stumbled into a
doorway, and worn out with hunger and worry at not
keeping his promise to help the waggoner, he fell fast asleep.

Now as luck would have it, Dick had chosen a very
good doorway to sleep in. The house belonged to a rich
merchant, Mr Fitzwarren, who was very kind and always
willing to help anyone in need. So when he came home

later that evening, Mr Fitzwarren took Dick and his cat indoors and told the cook to give him supper. The cook was very grumpy indeed at having to prepare a meal late at night for Dick who, she thought, looked like a ragamuffin.

The next morning, Dick told Mr Fitzwarren the whole story. Smiling, Mr Fitzwarren told Dick that, as he had found, the streets of London were not paved with gold, and indeed life there was very hard.

"But you look like a strong boy, would you like to work for me, Dick?" he asked. "You will have a roof over your head and a good dinner every day in return for helping in the kitchen and the stables."

Dick was delighted, and he soon settled into the household. He worked hard, and everyone liked him, except the cook. She gave him all the really horrible jobs in the kitchen and would never let him have a moment's rest. But she didn't dare defy her master and so Dick had his good dinner every day.

Now whenever one of Mr Fitzwarren's ships went to sea, it was his custom to ask everyone in the household to give something to the ship's cargo for luck. Poor Dick had only his cat and it was with a very heavy heart that he handed her over.

The ship was at sea for many, many months before they finally came to port in China. The captain and the crew went ashore to show the emperor the cargo they had brought all the way from London. The emperor had known

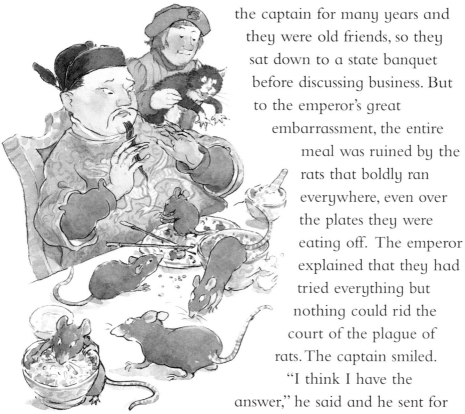

the captain for many years and they were old friends, so they sat down to a state banquet before discussing business. But to the emperor's great embarrassment, the entire meal was ruined by the rats that boldly ran everywhere, even over the plates they were eating off. The emperor explained that they had tried everything but nothing could rid the court of the plague of rats. The captain smiled. "I think I have the answer," he said and he sent for Dick's cat. Within moments of her arrival, there were piles of dead rats at the emperor's feet. He was so impressed that he gave the captain a ship full of gold just for the cat.

Back in London, Dick's life was a misery. The cook was nastier than ever and he didn't even have his beloved cat for company, so one day he ran away, intending to walk home to his village. But he had not gone far before he heard the church bells ringing, and they seemed to say,

"Turn again Dick Wittington,
Thrice Lord Mayor of London."
Dick didn't know what the bells
meant, but he remembered how
kind Mr Fitzwarren had been, so
he turned round again and
went back before the cook
had even noticed that he
was missing. Of course
when the ships came home,
Mr Fitzwarren gave Dick his
fair share and more. This was the
start of Dick's prosperity, and he
even married Mr Fitzwarren's
daughter, Jane. He did become
Lord Mayor of London three
times, but he never forgot
his early days of
poverty and he founded
schools and hospitals for
the poor. He and
Jane had many
children, and
there were
always lots of
cats in their great
house as well!

The Precious Stove

an Austrian folk tale

P eter lived with his mother and father and his brothers and sisters in an old wooden cottage deep in the woods of Austria. They were very poor and the cottage had hardly any furniture, and they might have been very cold in winter were it not for their most treasured possession, a stove. This was no ordinary stove. It was made of white porcelain and it was so tall the gold crown at the top almost scraped the ceiling. Its feet were carved like lion's claws, the talons painted gold. The sides of the stove were painted with flowers and rare birds, in glowing colours, and the door was tiled in blue and gold. It looked very out of place in the poor wooden cottage for it had originally been made for a king's palace. Many years before, Peter's grandfather had rescued it, after a great war, from the ruins of the palace where he used to work. Peter used to draw copies of the flowers and birds on pieces of brown paper with a stub of old pencil.

One evening, as Peter and his sister Gilda lay curled up in the warmth at the foot of the stove, their father came in, shaking the snow from his boots. He looked tired and ill.

"My children, this is the last night you will be able to enjoy our beautiful stove," he said sadly. "Tomorrow it will be taken away as I have had to sell it. We have no money left, and we need food more than we need a grand stove."

The children were horrified, but their father would not change his mind. That night, instead of banking up the stove to keep it burning warmly through the night, he let the fire die down so it was quite cold in the morning. The traders arrived and loaded the stove onto a cart, and off it rumbled down the track towards the town. Peter's mother and father looked at the handful of gold coins the traders had given them and shook their heads. It seemed a poor bargain when all was said and done.

Peter and Gilda whispered together outside behind the wood pile.

"You have to follow the cart, Peter," said Gilda, "so you can see where our stove goes."

So Peter rushed off down the track after the cart, pausing only to stuff a couple of apples into his pocket. The journey into town was slow as the stove was heavy so the cart could not travel very fast, but by evening it had reached the station. Peter crept as close as he dared, and heard the traders arranging for the stove to go to Vienna by train the very next morning. He made up his mind very quickly. Once the traders had gone to an inn for the night, he clambered up and inside the stove. There was plenty of room inside for a small boy, and he knew that air would come in from the grill at the top under the golden crown. He soon fell fast asleep.

When he awoke, the train was moving fast. It sped through snowy forests and past the mighty Danube river. Peter munched his apples and wondered what his parents would be thinking, and just where was he going to end up, and then what could he do, anyway, to keep the stove for his family.

Eventually the train came to a halt and with much banging and clattering all the boxes around the stove were unloaded onto the platform. Then Peter heard a gruff voice.

"Have a care there! That valuable stove is going to the palace, take care it isn't damaged in any way or it will be the worse for you!"

The palace! Peter's knees shook. The palace, why that was where the king lived. Peter sat as quiet as a mouse as he felt the stove lifted up off the train and onto another cart. It clattered through cobbled streets and over a wooden bridge, and then came to a halt. Many voices came through the grill as the stove was moved off the cart.

"My word, the king will be pleased! Look what a fine stove it is," said one voice.

"It must have come from a palace originally, look at the golden crown at the top," said another.

Then there was silence for a while. Peter strained his ears, and his knees shook a little more. Then he heard the swishing of long robes on a polished floor, and a murmur of voices. Then a deep hush.

"Truly, it is a very beautiful stove. I did not expect it to be so fine. Look at the quality of the painting round the sides," said a deep important voice. And then the handle of the door turned and light flooded into the stove. Peter

tumbled out onto the floor as the same deep
voice said, "Good gracious! What
have we here, there is a child
in the stove!"

Peter picked himself up
and looked up into eyes
that were full of laughter.
They belonged to a man
dressed in a bright red
jacket with great gold
tassels and gold buttons.
Many glittering medals
gleamed on his chest. A
great silver sword hung by
his side. It was the king!

Peter was absolutely
terrified, but the king kept on smiling.

"Well, my boy, would you like to tell me how you come
to be inside my new stove?"

A servant rushed forward and grabbed Peter by the
arm, meaning to drag him away, but the king raised his
hand and the man stepped back.

"Let the child speak," said the king.

Well, once Peter found his tongue, he could not stop. He
told the king all about the stove. How it had stood in their
poor cottage for as long as he could remember. How much
the family welcomed its heat in the winter. And he told the

king that his father had been forced to sell the stove for a few gold pieces to buy food.

The king listened in silence while Peter told his story.

"Peter, I am not going to give you back your stove for it belongs here in the palace, but I will give your father several bags of gold, for it is a very valuable stove. And perhaps you would like to stay here and look after it for me?" he asked.

Peter was delighted. And he looked after the stove for the king from that day on. His family never wanted for food again, and every summer they would all come to stay at the palace to see Peter, and the stove of course. When the king discovered how good Peter was at drawing, he sent him to art school and he became a very fine artist. But when he was an old man, all his grandchildren wanted to hear was the story of how he came to Vienna inside a stove!

Little Red Riding Hood

a retelling from the original tale by Charles Perrault

There was once a little girl who lived in the middle of a deep dark forest with her mother and father, who was a woodcutter. The little girl always wore a red cloak with a warm hood and so she was called Little Red Riding Hood.

One day she decided to visit her granny who lived some way from the woodcutter's cottage. She took a basket with a cake her mother had baked and set off. Now the last thing her mother had said to Little Red Riding Hood was, "Don't leave the path, and don't talk to any strangers," but I am afraid Little Red Riding Hood was not really listening. So when

she saw some bluebells growing under a tree she left the
path and began to pick a bunch for her granny. Slowly,
slowly she wandered further away from the path, deeper
into the trees. Suddenly, she was not alone. There in front of
her stood a great big wolf. Now Little Red Riding Hood
had not met a wolf before so she did not realise that wolves
are not the kind of people it is wise to be too friendly with.

"Good day, little girl," said the wolf with a snarly sort
of a smile. "What is your name and where are you going?"

"My name is Little Red Riding Hood. I am going to
visit my granny, and I am taking her a cake to
eat," replied Little Red Riding
Hood.

The wolf was delighted.
Not only a little girl to
eat but a granny
AND a cake as well!

"And where does
your granny live, little
girl?" asked the wolf,
trying very hard to
smile nicely despite
all his fierce teeth.

Little Red
Riding Hood told
the wolf where her
granny lived, and went on

picking bluebells. The wolf slipped away through the trees and soon found the granny's cottage. He tapped on the door and said, in a disguised voice, "Hello, granny. It is Little Red Riding Hood. I have brought you a cake, will you let me in?"

As soon as the door was open, the wolf bounded in, and gobbled the granny all up! He put on her nightcap and shawl and climbed into her bed. Soon he heard Little Red Riding Hood coming and he tried his snarly smile again.

"Hello, granny," said Little Red Riding Hood. "I have brought you a cake and these bluebells," and she came up to the bedside.

"Goodness, granny! What great big eyes you have!" she said.

"All the better to see you with," growled the wolf.

Little Red Riding Hood could not help noticing the wolf's teeth.

"Goodness, granny! What great big teeth you have!"

"All the better to eat you with!" snapped the wolf and gobbled Little Red Riding

Hood up. He gobbled up the cake in the basket as well and then, very full indeed, he fell fast asleep, snoring loudly.

Now by great good luck, Little Red Riding Hood's father was passing by the cottage, and when he heard the terrible snores he put his head round the door to see who was making such a noise. He was horrified to see the wolf so he took his axe and made a great slit down the wolf's tummy. Out jumped Little Red Riding Hood. Out staggered granny. She stitched up the wolf's tummy and told him to mind his manners in future. Then, as there was no cake left for tea, they all went back home, and Little Red Riding Hood's mother made pancakes. I am pleased to say Little Red Riding Hood had learnt her lesson, and she never spoke to wolves again.

The Gingerbread Boy

an English folk tale

One fine sunny day, an old woman was making some ginger biscuits. She had a little dough left over and so she made a gingerbread boy. She gave him two raisins for eyes and three cherries for buttons, and put a smile on his face with a piece of orange peel. And she popped him in the oven. But as she lifted the tray out of the oven when the biscuits were cooked, the gingerbread boy hopped off the tray and ran straight out of the door! The old woman ran after him, and her husband ran after her, but they couldn't catch the gingerbread boy. He called out, "Run, run, as fast as you can! You can't catch me, I'm the gingerbread man!"

The old dog in his kennel ran after the old man and the old woman, but he couldn't catch the gingerbread boy. The ginger cat, who had been asleep in the sun, ran after the dog, but she couldn't catch the gingerbread boy. He called out,

"Run, run, as fast as you can! You can't catch me, I'm the gingerbread man!"

The brown cow in the meadow lumbered after the cat, but she couldn't catch the gingerbread boy. The black horse in the stable galloped after the cow but he couldn't catch the gingerbread boy. He called out,

"Run, run, as fast as you can! You can't catch me, I'm the gingerbread man!"

The fat pink pig in the sty trotted after the horse, but she couldn't catch the gingerbread boy. The rooster flapped and squawked after the pig but he couldn't catch the gingerbread boy. He called out,

"Run, run, as fast as you can! You can't catch me, I'm the gingerbread man!"

He ran and ran, and the old woman and the old man, the dog and the cat, the cow and the horse, the pig and the rooster all ran after him. He kept on running until he came to the river. For the first time since he had hopped out of the oven, the gingerbread boy had to stop running.

"Help, help! How can I cross the river?" he cried.

A sly fox suddenly appeared by his side.

"I could carry you across," said the sly fox.

The gingerbread boy jumped onto the fox's back, and the fox slid into the water.

"My feet are getting wet," complained the gingerbread boy.

"Well, jump onto my head," smiled the fox, showing a lot of very sharp teeth. And he kept on swimming.

"My feet are still getting wet," complained the gingerbread boy again after a while. "Well, jump onto my nose," smiled the fox, showing even more very sharp teeth.

The gingerbread boy jumped onto the fox's nose, and SNAP! the fox gobbled him all up. When the fox climbed out of the river on the other side, all that was left of the naughty gingerbread boy was a few crumbs. So the old woman and the old man, the dog and the cat, the cow and the horse, the pig and the rooster all went home and shared the ginger biscuits. They were delicious.

Jack and the Beanstalk

a retelling from the original tale by Joseph Jacobs

This is the story of how Jack did a silly thing, but all was well in the end.

Jack and his mother were very poor and there came a sad day when there was just no more money left, so Jack's mother told him to take the cow to market and sell her.

As Jack led the cow to market, he met a funny little man with a tall feather in his hat.

"And where might you be going with that fine-looking cow?" the funny little man asked.

Jack explained and the funny little man swept off his hat with the tall feather, and shook out five coloured beans.

"Well, young Jack, I can save you a journey. I will give

you these five magic beans in exchange for your cow."

Now Jack should have realised that this was all rather odd, for how did the funny little man know his name? But once he heard the word "magic" he didn't stop to think. He took the beans at once, gave the funny little man the cow and ran off home to his mother.

"Jack, you are a complete fool! You have exchanged our fine cow for five worthless beans!" She flung the beans out of the window, and sent Jack to bed without any supper.

When he woke in the morning, Jack couldn't understand why it was so dark in the cottage. He rushed outside to find his mother staring in amazement at the most enormous beanstalk that reached right up into the clouds.

"I told you they were magic beans," smiled Jack, and without any hesitation he began to climb the beanstalk. He climbed and climbed until he could no longer see the ground below. When he reached the top there stood a vast castle. Jack knocked at the door, and it was opened by a HUGE woman!

"My husband eats little boys for breakfast so you better run away quickly," she said to Jack. But before Jack could reply, the ground started to shake and tremble.

"Too late!" said the giant's wife. "You must hide," and she bundled Jack into a cupboard. Jack peeped through the keyhole, and saw the most colossal man stump into the kitchen.

"Fee fi fo fum! I smell the blood of an Englishman!" he roared.

"Don't be silly, dear. You can smell the sausages I have just cooked for your breakfast," said the giant's wife, placing a plate piled high with one hundred and sixty-three sausages in front of him. The giant did not seem to have very good table manners, and had soon gobbled the lot. Then he poured a great bag of gold onto the table, and counted all the coins.

With a smile on his big face, he soon fell asleep.

Jack darted out of the cupboard, grabbed the bag of money and hared out of the kitchen. He slithered down the beanstalk as fast as ever he could and there, still standing at the bottom, was his mother. She was astonished when she saw the gold.

Jack's mother bought two new cows and she and Jack were very content now they had plenty to eat every day. But after a while Jack decided he would like to climb the beanstalk again. The giant's wife was not very pleased to see him.

"My husband lost a bag of gold the last time you were here," she muttered looking closely at Jack, but then the ground began to shake and tremble. Jack hid in the cupboard again.

The giant stumped into the kitchen.

"Fee fi fo fum! I smell the blood of an Englishman!" he roared.

"Don't be silly, dear. You can smell

the chickens I have just cooked for your breakfast," said the giant's wife, placing a plate piled high with thirty-eight chickens in front of him. The giant had soon gobbled the lot. Then he lifted a golden hen onto the table, and said, "Lay!" and the hen laid a golden egg. With a smile on his big face he fell asleep, snoring loudly.

Jack darted out of the cupboard, grabbed the golden hen and hared out of the kitchen. He slithered down the beanstalk as fast as ever he could and there, still standing at the bottom, was his mother. She was astonished when she saw the hen.

Jack's mother bought a whole herd of cows and found a farmer to look after them. She bought lots of new clothes for herself and Jack, and they were very content. But after a while Jack decided he would like to climb the beanstalk one last time. The giant's wife was not at all pleased to see him.

"My husband lost a golden hen the last time you were here," and she peered closely at Jack, but then the ground began to shake and tremble. This time Jack hid under the table.

The giant stumped into the kitchen.

"Fee fi fo fum! I smell the blood of an Englishman!" he roared.

"I would look in the cupboard if I were you," said the giant's wife, but of course the cupboard was empty. They were both puzzled. The giant trusted his nose, and his wife didn't know where Jack had gone.

"Eat your breakfast, dear. I have just cooked you ninety-two fried eggs," said the giant's wife, placing a plate in front of him. The giant had soon gobbled the lot. Then he lifted a golden harp onto the table, and said, "Play!" and the harp played so sweetly that the giant was soon fast asleep, snoring loudly.

Jack crept out from under the table and grabbed the golden harp, but as soon as he touched it the harp called out, "Master, master!" and the giant awoke with a great start. He chased after Jack who scrambled down the beanstalk as fast as ever he could with the harp in his arms. As soon as Jack reached the ground he raced to get a big axe and chopped through the beanstalk. Down tumbled the great beanstalk, down tumbled the giant and that was the end of them both!

Jack and his mother lived very happily for the rest of their days. The bag of gold never ran out, the hen laid a golden egg every day, and the harp soon forgot about the giant and played sweetly for Jack and his mother.

Liam and the Fairy Cattle

an Irish legend

L iam and his mother lived by the sea. They had a
small white cottage with a pile of peat for the fire
outside, and a row of potatoes to eat with the fish
that Liam would catch. They had two cows, and Liam's
mother would make butter and cheese from their milk. She
baked bread and gathered sweet heather honey from the
hives at the bottom of the meadow. They did not have much
in life, but they were happy.

But then there came a time when ill luck fell on the
small white cottage. First the two cows died, one after the
other, and there was no cheese to eat. Then the shoals of
fish swam far out to sea and Liam would come home
empty handed. The potatoes rotted in the ground, and Liam
and his mother were hungry all the time.

One day when Liam was wandering along the
shoreline he came across two boys throwing stones at a seal.

He shouted at the boys and
chased them away, but
when he went to see if
the seal needed help
it turned its head
once and looked
deep into his eyes
then slipped away
into the sea. As it
dived into the waves he
saw blood on its head.

Three days later
when Liam and his
mother were sitting by the
fire in the evening there came
a knock at the door. There on the
doorstep stood an old, old man leaning
on a staff. His clothes looked wet through and he
had a large cut on his forehead, but his eyes were gentle.

"I am very weary, might I come in and warm myself at
your fire?" the old man asked.

Liam opened the door wide, and bid the old man come
in. His mother pulled up a stool close to the fire, and
warmed up the last of the soup in the pot while she bathed
the wound on his head. He thanked her kindly, smiling at
Liam, and Liam had the strangest feeling he had looked
into those deep brown eyes before. But he made up the fire

for the night and they all slept peacefully until the day.

The old man looked better for his night's shelter, and as he rose to leave he spoke to Liam's mother.

"I have no money to offer you but I would like to thank you for your shelter and food, and I would like to repay the boy here for his kindness," and he turned and looked at Liam with his gentle brown eyes. "I know you have lost your cows so I will tell you where you can find some special cows who will give you milk such as you have never tasted before. Tonight is a full moon and the sea-folk will bring their cattle up out of the sea to graze on the lush green grass that grows just beyond the shoreline."

Liam's mother laughed.

"I have often heard tales of these marvellous cattle, but in all the years I have lived here I have never seen a fairy cow."

"That is because your eyes have not been opened by a touch with the heather that grows on the grave of Fionn who died all those years ago," said the old man and there in his hand he held out a sprig of heather. "Will you let me touch your eyes, and the boy's too?

Then you shall see what you shall see."

Well, Liam's mother felt she had nothing to fear from this kindly old man and so both she and Liam let him touch their eyes with the sprig of heather.

"Now," he said, "you must gather seven handfuls of earth from the churchyard, and then tonight go to the meadow just beyond the shoreline. There you will see the fairy cattle. Choose the seven you like the best and throw the earth onto each one. They will all run back to the sea, save the seven that you have chosen. Bring those seven back home and look after them in your kindly way and they will be with you always. Now I must return from whence I came. Liam, will you walk with me to the sea?" And the old man looked at Liam with those gentle eyes once again.

So Liam and the strange old man walked to the shoreline. One moment they were together on the sand, the next Liam was alone. But when he looked out to sea, there was a seal, looking at him with gentle brown eyes. Then with a ripple, it was gone under the waves.

That night, Liam and his mother did as the old man had bid.

They gathered the earth from the churchyard and made their way quietly down to the meadow. There indeed was the herd of fairy cattle. They were small, no bigger than a sheepdog, and all colours, brown and black and white and brindled. Liam and his mother choose three black, three white and a brindled one, and Liam crept up behind them and threw the earth onto their backs. The rest of the herd scattered back down to the shore and ran into the waves where they quickly disappeared. But the seven in the meadow stood quietly and showed no fear as Liam and his mother led them home.

From that day on, Liam and his mother had a plentiful supply of rich creamy milk. The little fairy cattle would low gently in the byre and were well content with their life on land. But Liam would never let them out to graze when there was a full moon in case the sea-folk came to claim them back.

Wizards and Witches, Giants and Genies

Hansel and Gretel

a retelling from the original tale by the Brothers Grimm

At the edge of a deep, dark forest there lived a poor woodcutter and his wife, a mean spiteful woman, and their two children Hansel and Gretel. The family was very poor and there was often very little food on the table.

One dreadful day there was no food at all and everyone went to bed hungry. Hansel could not sleep, and so it was that he heard his mother talking to his father. "Husband," she said in her thin spiteful voice, "there are too many mouths to feed. You must leave the children in the forest tomorrow."

"Wife, I cannot abandon our children, there are wolves in the forest!" said the poor woodcutter.

But his wife would give him no peace until he had agreed to her wicked plan. Hansel felt his heart grow icy cold. But he was a clever boy and so he slipped out of the house and filled his pockets with the shiny white stones that lay scattered around the house.

The next morning they all rose early and Hansel and Gretel followed their father deep into the forest. He lit them a fire and told them he was going to gather wood and would be back to collect them. He left them, tears falling down his face.

The day passed slowly. Hansel kept their fire going but when night fell, it grew very cold and they could hear all kinds of rustling under the shadowy trees. Gretel could not understand why their father had not come back to collect them, so Hansel had to tell her that their mother had told the woodcutter to leave them there deliberately.

"But don't worry, Gretel," he said with a smile, "I will lead us back home," and there, clear in the moonlight, he showed her the line of shiny white stones that he had dropped from his pocket one by one that morning as their father had led them into the forest. They were soon home where their father greeted them with great joy. But their mother was not pleased.

Some time passed. They managed to survive with very little to eat but another day came when Hansel heard his mother demanding that the woodcutter leave them in the forest again. This time when Hansel went to collect some more shiny pebbles, he found his mother had locked the door and he couldn't get out.

In the morning, their father gave them each a small piece of bread, and then led them even deeper into the forest than before. All day long, Hansel comforted Gretel and told her that this time he had left a trail of breadcrumbs to lead them safely back home. But when the moon rose and the children set off there was not a breadcrumb to be seen. The birds had eaten every last one. There was nothing to do but go to sleep under one of the great big trees and wait to see what they might do in the morning.

All next day they walked and walked, but they saw nothing but more and more great trees. And the next day was the same. By this time they were not only cold and very hungry but deeply frightened. It looked as if they would never ever be able to find a way out of the forest. But then just as it was getting dark, they came to a little clearing and there stood the most extraordinary house.

The walls were made of gingerbread, the windows of fine spun sugar and the tiles on the roof were brightly striped sweets. Hansel and Gretel could not believe their good luck and they were soon breaking off little bits of the amazing house to eat. But then a little voice came from inside.

"Nibble, nibble, little mouse,
Who is that eating my sweet house?"

Out of the front door came a very old woman. She smiled very sweetly at the children and said, "Dear children, you don't need to eat my house. Come inside and I will give you plenty to eat and you shall sleep in warm cosy beds tonight." Hansel and Gretel needed no second asking. They were soon tucked up, warm and full of hot milk and ginger biscuits and apples. They both fell asleep very quickly. But little did they know they were in worse danger than ever before. The old woman was a wicked witch and she had decided to make Gretel work in the kitchen, and worst of all, she planned to fatten Hansel up so she might eat him!

The very next morning she locked poor Hansel in a big cage and gave Gretel a broom and told her to clean the gingerbread house from top to toe. In the evening, the witch fed Hansel a huge plate of chicken but she only gave poor Gretel a dry hunk of bread. But once she was asleep, Hansel shared his meal with Gretel. And so they lived for many days. The witch could not see very well. So every morning, the witch would make Hansel put his finger through the cage so she could tell how fat he was getting. But clever Hansel poked a chicken bone through the bars so she thought he was still too skinny to eat.

After many days, she grew fed up and decided to eat him anyway, and so she asked Gretel to help her prepare the big oven.

The witch made some bread to go with her supper and when the oven was really hot she put it in to cook. The kitchen was soon filled with the lovely smell of baking bread, and the witch asked Gretel to lift the bread out to cool. But Gretel was clever too. She pretended she couldn't reach the tray, and when the witch bent down inside the oven Gretel gave her a great shove and closed the door with a clang. And that was the end of the witch!

Gretel released Hansel, and together they set off once more to try to find their way home. After all their adventures, fortune finally smiled on them and they soon found the path home where they were reunited with their father who was simply overjoyed to see them again. And what, you might ask, of their mean mother? Well, the poor woodcutter had not had a happy moment since he left the children in the forest. He had become so miserable that she decided there was no living with him. The day before Hansel and Gretel returned, she had upped sticks and left, so that served her right, didn't it?

Amal and the Genie

a Persian fairytale

Many moons ago in ancient Persia there lived a bright young man who knew what was what, and his name was Amal. He was out one day when he had the misfortune to meet a genie. Now sometimes genies can be good news, but this one was in a very bad temper and he was looking for trouble. Amal had to think very quickly. He had no weapons with him, and anyway weapons are no use against genies. All he had in his pocket was an egg and a lump of salt.

The genie came whirling up to Amal, but before he could say anything, Amal yelled at him.

"Genie! You and I should have a competition to see who is the strongest!"

You might think this was very foolish of Amal, but he knew two things about genies. One was that it is always better to take control first, and the second was that genies are not terribly bright. They are fine at conjuring up gorgeous palaces and flying carpets, but they are a bit slow when it comes to basic common sense.

Well, the genie looked at Amal, and then he laughed and laughed. It was not a nice sound, but Amal was not daunted.

"Hah! You don't look very strong," sniggered the genie. "I shall win this contest easily," and he laughed again.

Amal picked up a stone.

"You must squeeze this stone until water comes out of it," he said, handing the genie the stone.

Well, the genie squeezed and squeezed, and huffed and puffed, but, of course, no water came out of the stone. He threw it down in a temper.

"Not possible!" he snapped.

Amal bent down and picked up the stone, and squeezed. And with a scrunching sound, liquid ran down Amal's fingers.

The genie was astonished. And so would you have been

it you had been there. What clever Amal had done was to put the egg in the same hand as the stone, and it was the egg that was broken. But as I said, genies are not terribly bright and this one was no exception. Then Amal said, "Well, I win that one. But now perhaps you could

crumble this stone into powder," and he handed the genie another stone.

Well, the genie squeezed and squeezed, and huffed and puffed, but, of course, the stone did not crumble at all, not even the tiniest bit. The genie threw it down in a temper.

Amal picked it up and squeezed. And as he squeezed, powder fell from his fingers with a grinding sound. The genie was astonished. And so would you have been if you had been there, but you can guess what clever Amal had done. He put the salt in his hand as well as the stone.

The genie was feeling that his reputation was somewhat dented by Amal's performance so he needed to get his own back.

"You are clearly a great and mighty fighter," the genie said to Amal. "I should like to give you a meal to celebrate your achievements. Come and stay the night with me," and he smiled.

But Amal saw the smile, and kept his wits about him. After a dreadful meal (the genie was not a very good cook either) they both lay down to sleep in the genie's cave. Once Amal was sure the genie was asleep, he moved to the other side of the cave, leaving his pillow in the bed to look as if he were still there asleep. Then he watched. As the first light of dawn filtered into the cave, the genie woke up. He picked up a huge club and crept over to where he thought Amal was lying, and he pounded the club down onto the bed, seven times in all. Then he stomped out of the cave to fetch some water for his morning tea.

You can imagine his utter dismay when, on returning, he found Amal singing to himself as he lit the fire.

"Good morning, genie! I thought I would get breakfast ready," said Amal cheerfully. "I hope you slept better than I did," he continued. "Some wretched insect batted me in the face in the night, seven times in all."

Well, at this the genie gave a great shriek and whistled himself as fast as possible into an old oil lamp that lay on the floor of the cave. He wasn't seen again for hundreds and hundreds of years until a young lad called Aladdin happened to find the lamp. But that is another story, isn't it?

Snow White and the Seven Dwarfs

a retelling from the original tale by the Brothers Grimm

T he queen was sitting at the window sewing, and thinking about her baby who would be born soon. As she sewed she pricked her finger, and red blood fell on the snow by the ebony window ledge.

"I wish that my daughter be as white as snow, as black as ebony and as red as blood," she said to herself, and so it happened. Her tiny daughter had snow-white skin, lips as red as blood and hair as black

as ebony, so she was called
Snow White. But the
queen died and the king
married again. His new
wife was very beautiful
but she had a cold
heart, and she did not
love Snow White.

Every morning the
new queen would look
into her magic mirror
and say,

"Mirror, mirror on
the wall

Who is fairest in the land?"
and the mirror would always
reply,

"Thou, oh queen,
Thou art fairest in the land."

So the queen was content. Seven years passed and Snow
White grew into a lovely young girl, with her mother's
gentle nature.

One morning the queen looked into her mirror as
usual, but the mirror's reply filled her with a deep envy.

"Thou, oh queen,
Thou art indeed fair.
But Snow White is the fairest in the land."

She ordered her woodsman to kill Snow White. But he could not bear to do such a wicked deed so he hid Snow White deep in the forest. Poor Snow White wandered about until she was utterly weary.

Suddenly, she caught sight of a light through the trees in the distance. It came from a little house with a lantern glowing in one small window. The door swung open at her touch, so she stepped inside. Everything was as neat as a new pin. A scrubbed wooden table was set, with seven plates and seven cups. Seven little chairs were ranged round the fireplace, and along the back wall there were seven little beds, each with a brightly coloured blanket.

There was a basket of logs beside the fireplace, and Snow White soon had a cheerful fire going. She sat in one of the little chairs and before long was fast asleep.

Now the cottage belonged to seven dwarfs and when they came home that evening, they were very worried to discover Snow White fast asleep. They tiptoed round preparing their supper, but as the wonderful smell of stew filled the room, Snow White awoke with a start. She was very surprised to see seven little faces looking at her, but soon she was telling them how she came to be in the forest. They were very angry when they heard about the wicked queen.

"Might I stay with you?" asked Snow White. "I could look after you, and have supper ready for you every night."

The dwarfs were just delighted with this suggestion, and immediately set about making Snow White her own chair by the fireside and her own bed.

Back in the castle, the queen looked into her mirror in the morning, and asked,

"Mirror, mirror on the wall,
Who is fairest in the land?"
But you can imagine her rage when the mirror replied,
"Thou, oh queen,
Thou art indeed fair.
But Snow White with the seven dwarfs does dwell
And she is fairest in the land."
So the wicked queen disguised herself as an old pedlar,

and searched out the dwarfs' cottage. Snow White did not recognise the queen and invited her in.

"Goodness me, you need new laces for your dress," said the old woman, and she pulled the new laces so tightly that Snow White was unable to breathe.

When the dwarfs came home that evening, they were horrified to discover Snow White lying on the floor as if dead. They lifted her up and, of course, saw the laces. They quickly cut the tight cord and the colour came back to Snow White's cheeks.

"Now you know the queen will stop at nothing," they cried. "You must not let anyone indoors again."

The queen looked in her mirror the next morning, and

went white with rage when it told her Snow White was still the fairest in the land. She disguised herself as a gypsy, selling wooden pegs and combs. Snow White remembered what the dwarfs had said and would not open the door. But the gypsy passed one of the combs through the window, and the minute it touched her hair, Snow White fell down in a faint for the comb was poisoned.

When the dwarfs came home and found Snow White, they immediately suspected the queen. They found the comb and pulled it out, and Snow White sat up, quite recovered. They pleaded with her to be more careful the next morning when they set off for work.

So when a farmer's wife appeared at the door trying to sell apples, Snow White would not even open the window.

"Why, anyone would think I was trying to poison you," said the farmer's wife, who was, of course, the wicked queen in disguise.

"I only want to give you some apples. Look how juicy they are!" and she took a big bite out of one.

So Snow White thought it must be all right and she took the apple. But the queen had poisoned it on one side only, and the minute Snow White took a bite she fell down dead.

This time when the dwarfs came home, there was nothing they could do. Snow White was indeed dead. They could not bear to bury her in the cold earth so they placed her in a glass coffin. They wrote her name on the side in silver and put the coffin in a sheltered part of the forest, and planted wild flowers all round about.

When the queen looked into her mirror the next morning, it gave her the answer she wanted.

"Thou, oh queen,
Thou art fairest in the land."

Years passed. Snow White lay in her coffin, looking as beautiful as ever. The dwarfs watched over her, and one day they found a young prince kneeling by the side of the glass coffin. He had fallen in love with Snow White the moment he had set eyes on her. When the dwarfs saw how deeply the prince felt about their beloved Snow White, they agreed that he take the glass coffin to his palace where he wished to set it in his rose gardens.

As the prince lifted the glass coffin, the piece of poisoned apple flew from her lips, and Snow White opened her eyes. She saw the prince, she saw her faithful dwarfs and she cried, "Where am I? What has happened?"

There was huge excitement as everyone tried to talk at once. The prince wasted no time and asked Snow White to marry him. She agreed as long as the dwarfs could come and live at the palace as well, and they all lived happily ever after.

But what of the queen? She looked in her mirror the morning Snow White and the prince were to be married.

"Mirror, mirror on the wall
Who is fairest in the land?"
The mirror replied,
"Snow White, oh queen,
Snow White who marries
her prince today,
She is fairest in the land."

The queen was so ugly in her rage that the mirror cracked from side to side. And she was never able to look in a mirror ever again as long as she lived.

The Giant who Counted Carrots

a German fairytale

High upon a mountainside there was once a giant who was always very sleepy, and when he went to sleep, he would sleep for hundreds of years at a time. So every time he awoke things had changed a great deal. He spent time as a herdsman, but he did not like being poor. So he went back to sleep. On another visit he spent time as a rich farmer but he found his servants cheated him so he went back to sleep. When he eventually awoke again he wandered down the mountainside to see what he could see.

He came upon a rock pool where a waterfall tumbled down the rocks. A group of laughing girls were sitting dangling their toes in the water. The giant hid and watched. One of the girls was quieter than the others, but to the giant she was the prettiest. Her name was Elizabeth and she was to be married in a few days to the young duke. She and her friends chattered about the forthcoming celebrations as they paddled in the pool, and all the while the giant watched. When they skipped away, his heart grew sad. He realised just how very lonely he was.

He decided to try to win Elizabeth's heart. All through the night he worked. He covered the steep stone under the waterfall with white marble so it sparkled in the clear water. He lined the pool with silver, and filled it with darting golden fish. He covered the banks with rich green grass, planted with sweetly-smelling violets and forget-me-nots and deep blue hyacinths. Then he hid himself again.

When the girls arrived
they were astonished, but
Elizabeth looked
thoughtful. She knew
that some powerful
enchantment had been at
work. She wandered to the
edge and looked deep into
the silver pool, full of the
golden fish. And as she looked
she heard a voice, whispering,
whispering to her to step into the
pool. There was a sudden splash, and
as her friends looked round in alarm,
Elizabeth slipped into the pool. The girls ran
over to the pool and looked into the silver depths. In
vain they tried to find her. When they went home and told
the young duke, he came with all haste to the pool. All the
giant's adornments had vanished. The waterfall fell over
steep and black rocks, the silver lining and the golden fish
had disappeared from the pool, and there was not a single
flower to be seen. Sadly, the duke went back to the palace
and nothing would cheer him.

Meanwhile Elizabeth found herself in the giant's
garden. He begged her to stay with him and be his queen,
but she told him she loved the duke and would not forsake
him. The giant hoped she would forget the duke, but as the

days passed he saw that she grew pale and sad. He
wondered how he could cheer her, and change her mind.
Then he remembered his magic staff. Whatever it touched
would turn into any animal he wished for. He gave the staff
to Elizabeth and for a few hours she was happy as,
first a kitten then a dog then a canary appeared
thanks to the staff. But it was not long before
she grew silent again.

Now the giant grew very good
carrots, and he was very proud of
his carrots. He pulled some for
supper and Elizabeth said she
had never tasted such
delicious carrots in all her
life, which was true.

So the next day, the giant
took Elizabeth out into the fields
round the castle where the carrots
grew. As far as the eye could see
there were carrots, row upon row
of them. Elizabeth asked the giant
how many there were, but he
couldn't tell her that at all. So she
begged him to count at least one
row, and as he began counting she quickly drew the staff
out from under her cloak and touched a black stone that
lay on the ground. It turned into a black horse with great

hooves that pounded the earth as Elizabeth mounted its back and fled down the valley away, away from the giant.

The very next day, Elizabeth married her duke and they lived happily ever after. The lonely giant went slowly back to his garden, and fell into a deep sleep. Many hundreds of years passed and still the giant never awoke. In time grass and plants and trees grew over the slumbering giant, and still he slept on. Over the years the mound that was the sleeping giant became known as Giant Mountain, and so it is still called today. So beware if you see great rows of carrots on a mountain side, you might be very near a sleeping giant!

The Mermaid of Zennor

a Cornish legend

The bell was ringing, calling the villagers of Zennor to Sunday service. It was a simple little granite towered church, built to withstand the wild winds and weather that could roll in from the sea. Matthew Trewella stood in the choir stalls and looked at the new bench he had been carving. It was nearly finished and wanted only one more panel to be carved.

As the voices of the congregation rang out in the hymns, a sweet pure voice was heard. A voice that no one had heard before. When the villagers turned to leave at the end of the service, there at the back of the little church stood the most beautiful woman any of them had ever seen. Her dress was made of soft rustling silk, at one moment green, the next blue, like the sea. Round her neck she wore a gleaming necklace of pearls, and her golden hair fell down her back almost to the floor.

As Matthew walked out, the woman placed her hand on his sleeve.

"Your carving is beautiful, Matthew."

Matthew blushed and turned his rough cap round and round in his great red hands, his deep blue eyes wary.

"Why, thank you ma'am," he managed to stutter before he fled out of the church. Where the beautiful lady went no one quite saw.

The next day Matthew was hard at work, carving the decoration of leaves that went round the edge of the bench when he heard the soft rustle of silk. There stood the woman again.

"What will you put in the last panel, Matthew?" she whispered. And she smiled into his deep blue eyes. Matthew sensed a strong smell of the sea in the tiny church as he bent to get up off his knees but when he looked up again, there was no sign of the woman.

The next Sunday the lady was in church again. She looked deep into Matthew's eyes as she sang the hymns, and when he walked slowly out, as if in a dream, she was waiting for him.

"Will you carve my image in the last panel, Matthew?" she asked and her voice was gentle and sighing like the withdrawing tide on a shingle beach. Matthew's deep blue eyes gazed far over her head, out towards the sea, but he did not reply. Only the schoolmaster and his wife noticed that the seat where the woman had sat was wet, wet with sea water. But they said nothing.

Time passed, and every Sunday the woman came to church. Matthew seemed like a man in a dream, his eyes always looking out to sea. The final panel was still not finished on the bench. November came, and with it the mist curled up from the sea. Night after night a light was to be seen late in the church. The gentle sound of wood chipping drifted out with the mist, but no one ventured into the church.

It was the parson who

discovered the finished bench when he went in to open up the church one morning. The church floor was wet, wet with sea water. The stub of a candle stood among a great pile of wood shavings on the floor. The final panel of the bench was the best Matthew had ever carved. It was a mermaid, long hair falling down her back, the scales of her great fish tail in deep relief. She looked almost alive.

Matthew Trewella had not slept in his bed that night, nor was he ever seen again in Zennor. The mysterious woman never came to church again. The schoolmaster and his wife never talked of the wet seat. Only the fishermen would shake their heads as they sat talking on the winter's evenings. They would talk of the mermaid they had seen off the coast, and of the young man with the deep blue eyes who was always swimming by her side.

The Seven Ravens

a fairytale from Poland

There was once a poor widow who had seven
great sons and a daughter. The daughter, Anne,
was a good girl, but the seven brothers were wild
as the hills. One day the widow was baking a blackberry
pie. As she rolled out the pastry the
whole noisy troop came shouting
into the kitchen.

"Blackberry pie!" they yelled.
"When will it be ready?"

"When it is cooked," she said
crossly. "Let me finish then we can
all eat." But the boys just ran about
the hot kitchen, pushing and shoving

each other and leaving great muddy bootmarks all over the clean floor.

"Oh, can't you be quiet! I wish, I wish you were ravens instead of great noisy boys," she cried. But then her eyes widened in horror as the boys shrank, and feathers covered their arms. Their mouths turned into beaks, and with seven deep croaks they flew out of the door. Anne rushed to the window, but the ravens were already out of sight. Together mother and daughter sat weeping, and not even the smell of burning pie could rouse them.

But the next day Anne said to her mother, "I am determined to find my brothers and bring them safely back home."

So she set off with nothing but her needle and thread

and scissors in her pocket. She walked and walked and came across a curious little house in the woods. It was made of silver, and the woman who opened the door was dressed in a long silver robe. But she was not friendly.

"I am all behind today, and my husband will be home soon. There is no supper ready, and I have to mend his cloak," she said all in a rush.

"I could mend the cloak," said Anne taking out her needle, "and then you can cook the supper."

Well, the woman was delighted and opened the door wide. Anne sat quietly in the corner and with the tiniest stitches ever mended the beautiful cloak. When the husband, who was also dressed all in silver, came in he was very impressed with Anne's work, and invited her to join them for supper which was the most delicious roast chicken.

The silver man asked Anne where she was going so she told them the whole story of her brothers.

"Perhaps we can help you," said the silver man. "We are the moon's helpers and she sees most things on earth. I will ask her if she knows where your brothers are."

As the wife cleared the table after supper, she gave Anne the chicken bones.

"Keep these in your pocket, you never know when they might come in useful," and Anne did so.

When the silver man returned the next morning he told Anne that the moon had seen seven ravens flying round the Amber Mountain. When Anne asked him where the Amber Mountain was he told her to follow her nose until she could go no further. Anne thanked the silver couple and set off once again, her nose very firmly in front.

After several days she came to a halt. There in front of her was the Amber Mountain, its sides steep as glass. Anne did not know what to do, but then she remembered the chicken bones. She pushed one into the surface of the mountain and stood on it. Then she put the second bone in a little higher, and stood on that, and so she slowly, slowly climbed to the very top of the mountain. And there she found seven sad-looking ravens. They were her brothers! But there was also an evil old witch sitting there too.

"Well, my dear, your brothers are under my spell, and the only way you can release them is by remaining silent for seven years. Not one single word or you will lose them for ever," and with an evil cackle she flew off.

Anne climbed down the mountain, and when she reached home her mother was delighted to see her. But Anne could tell her nothing. Four years passed in silence until one day Anne was out gathering firewood when a royal hunting party came through the wood. The prince was very struck by Anne's quiet ways, but of course he couldn't get a word out of her. Thereafter he came by every day, and at length asked her to marry him. She smiled her acceptance but never a word did she utter.

Three more years passed, and the prince and Anne had a baby son. Now the queen had never really approved of her son marrying such a poor girl, however pretty she might be, and she never lost an opportunity to make mischief. One day she rushed into the prince and accused Anne of trying to poison the baby. The prince was horrified but, of course, when he asked Anne if she had done such a terrible thing, she was unable to reply. So he sent her to the dungeons, and told her she had three days to explain herself or she would die.

The three days passed with Anne still not uttering a word. On the third day, she was brought out into the courtyard where everyone waited to see what would happen next.

Suddenly there was a great flapping of wings and seven

ravens landed in a circle around Anne. It was her brothers, and in a blink of an eye there they stood, restored to human shape. Well, you can imagine what a lot Anne had to tell! They all talked into the night. The queen had somehow gone missing, but no one seemed to mind too much. The seven brothers went to collect their mother, and when they all came back together the prince promised her that she would never have to do a day's work again!

The Twelve Windows

from 'Told Again' by Walter de la Mare

There was once a princess who lived alone with her father the king, the queen having died many years before. The princess was wise and gentle and loved her father very much, so much so that the king dreaded the day when the princess would marry and leave him alone in the empty palace. But she had promised she would never marry until she met a man who would have three chances to hide himself in the palace so cleverly that she could not see him. Now you might think this was not so difficult but the princess had witch's eyes and she could spy out the smallest thing like an ant or one tiny daisy on the palace lawn. She had a special room at the top of a tower in the palace which had twelve windows that the princess could look out of to practise her great skill.

Many princes and handsome young men came to court the princess but all failed to hide themselves well enough. Now there was a swineherd who would watch the princes and the handsome young men come and go, and after a while he thought he might just as well try himself to see if he could win the hand of the princess. When he arrived at the palace gate, the guards just laughed at him, but the watchman who was passing at the time thought the young swineherd had an honest face. So he lent him a cloak of green velvet, and the swineherd was ushered into the princess's rooms.

Straightaway she saw that he had an honest face, but she also saw his poor clothes under the cloak, and she saw his heart beating against his ribs. She wished him luck, and gave him an hour to hide. The swineherd went down, down deep into the palace dungeons and hid himself under a pile of straw. When the hour was up, the princess climbed up into her special room and looked through the first window. She could see no sign of the swineherd. She looked through the second window. She could see no sign of the swineherd. But then she looked through the third window, and there she could see him, lying under the straw. The princess was sorry as she realised that the young swineherd was the first of the many young men who had come to court her that she actually liked.

The next day, the swineherd went to the palace fish pond and, taking a deep breath, he plunged to the bottom of the pond and hid under the roots of the graceful water lilies. He waited and waited, his lungs bursting. The princess climbed up into her special room and looked through the first window, then the second, the third, the fourth and the fifth. There was no sign of the swineherd, and the princess found she was pleased. She looked through the sixth and the seventh and the eighth. There was no sign of the swineherd and the princess found she was delighted. But then she looked through the ninth, and she saw the swineherd crouched in the pond, under the roots of the water lilies. The princess found she was full of sadness.

The young swineherd realised he was up against some powerful witchcraft, so that night he went to seek out his friend the white fox. He told her all about the princess and her witch's eyes, and he also told the fox that he had fallen in love with the princess. The fox just nodded and told him to get a good night's sleep. She woke him in the morning before it was light. When the swineherd was washed and dressed, the fox touched him with the tip of her tail, and he turned into a beautiful white mountain hare. Then she turned herself into an old woman and, taking the hare in her arms, she walked to the palace and stood by the garden gate.

The princess was walking in the palace gardens, her face sad as she thought of the swineherd who today faced his last chance at becoming her husband. She saw an old woman standing by the garden gate, with a white mountain hare in her arms. The hare looked so beautiful that the princess could not resist going up to stroke its fur. The old woman who, of course, was really the clever fox, gave the hare who, of course, was really the swineherd, to the princess. The princess was amazed by the beauty of the hare and by the softness of its fur, but when she went to give it back, the old woman had disappeared. The princess placed the hare on her shoulder and together they climbed the stairs to the room with the twelve windows.

The hare crept round under the princess's hair as she looked out of the first window. There was no sign of the swincherd. She looked out of all the windows until she came to the twelfth. There was no sign of the swineherd. With a beating heart she went to look out of the last window. She so wanted not to see the swineherd. She looked and looked again. She could not see him! The one thing witch's eyes cannot do is see behind them, and so the swineherd had won the hand of the princess. The hare darted down the stairs while the princess was still crying with delight, and ran out of the palace to where the fox was waiting. She touched the hare with the tip of her tail and there stood the swineherd once again.

He thanked the fox profusely and then ran back to the palace as fast as ever he could. There he found the princess

standing in the garden looking everywhere for him. They
went to see the king, and the whole story came out. The
princess and the swineherd said they loved each other. The
swineherd said he did not want to live anywhere else in the
land. So the king did not lose his daughter. The princess
married a man she really liked. The swineherd gained
everything from just having a try. The white fox was invited
to the wedding, and they all lived happily ever after.

Sleeping Beauty

a retelling from the original tale by Charles Perrault

L ong, long ago, when fairies were still able to grant wishes, there lived a king and queen who wanted, more than anything in the whole world, to have a baby daughter. When their wish was finally granted and a beautiful tiny princess lay in her cradle, the king and queen decided to have a great candlelit party to celebrate. They invited the twelve most important fairies in the land and a great many other people besides.

As well as the thousands of glittering candles, there were golden tables piled high with all kinds of delicious food, and the royal orchestra played their most cheerful tunes. The twelve fairies all lined up to present their christening gifts to the tiny princess. Their gifts were those that only a fairy can give: beauty, kindness, grace, honesty and the like. The princess smiled happily in her cradle as one by one the fairies tiptoed up.

The eleventh fairy had just promised the princess a sweet singing voice, when there was a great roll of thunder and all the candles flickered out. There stood quite the most wicked fairy anyone had ever seen. She was dressed all in black, her long straggly hair was black and her eyes, glittering in rage, were as black as the crow's feathers. Her voice was like a saw as she screeched, "How dare you not invite me to the party! I too have a gift for the little princess," and she smiled a not very nice smile. "Because you have forgotten me, my gift is that when the princess is sixteen she shall prick her finger on a spindle and die!" and with a horrid laugh, the wicked fairy disappeared with another clap of thunder.

As the candles were hastily relit, everyone started talking at once. Then a quiet voice was heard over all the hubbub. It was the twelfth fairy.

"I cannot undo this wicked spell," she whispered, "but I can decree that the princess will not die. She will instead fall into a deep sleep for a hundred years," and all the fairies slipped away leaving the court in despair.

The king, of course, immediately ordered that all the spinning wheels in the land were to be burned. After a while, everyone grew less frightened, and as the princess grew up into the most lovely girl, the wicked fairy's prediction slipped from most people's memories.

On her sixteenth birthday the princess went exploring. At the top of a tower she did not remember seeing before, she found an old woman, sitting at a spinning wheel.

It was, of course, the wicked fairy in disguise. The princess was fascinated and, as she bent forward to look at the cloth, her hand caught the sharp spindle and she immediately fell to the ground as though dead. With a swirl of smoke and a nasty laugh, the wicked fairy disappeared.

Everyone else in the palace fell asleep at the same moment. The king fell asleep with his ministers, the queen and her maids fell asleep in her dressing room. The cook fell asleep in the kitchen in the middle of baking a cake, the groom fell asleep as he fed the horses in the stables and even the little linnet the princess had in a golden cage by her bedside fell asleep on its perch. A great high thorn hedge grew up and soon the palace was completely hidden. Time stood still and all was silent.

Many, many years passed. The tale of the sleeping princess spread far and wide, and many came to try to find her. But no one could get through the thorn hedge. And so after even more years, people forgot what lay behind the hedge.

Then one day a handsome prince came riding through the woods, and as he reached the thorn hedge, thousands of pink roses burst into bloom. The prince walked forward, and a path appeared leading through the hedge towards the palace. It was a hundred years to the day since the princess had pricked her finger. The prince was astonished by the sight that met his eyes. Everywhere people lay asleep, frozen in the midst of whatever they had been doing when the spell caught them.

The prince climbed the tower, and there he found the princess, looking as lovely as ever. He bent over and kissed her, and immediately the spell was broken. The king and his ministers carried on just where they had left off. The queen chose which dress she wanted to wear and the maids brushed her hair. The cook put her cake in the oven and the groom led the horses out into the courtyard. And even the little linnet in her golden cage sang a joyful song.

As for the princess. . . ! Well, she and the prince had fallen in love with each other on the spot, and were married the very next day. They all lived happily ever after, and the wicked fairy was never ever seen again.

Rapunzel

a retelling from the original fairytale by the Brothers Grimm

Once upon a time there lived a man and his wife who for years and years had wanted a child. One day the wife was looking sadly out of the window. Winter was coming but in the next door garden, which was surrounded by a huge great wall, she could just see rows and rows of delicious vegetables. In particular, she could see a huge bunch of rapunzel, a special kind of lettuce. Her mouth watered, it looked so fresh and green.

"Husband, I shall not rest until I have some of that rapunzel growing next door," she whispered.

The husband clambered over the wall and quickly picked a small bunch which he took back to his wife. She made it into a salad, and ate it all up. But the next day, all she could think of was how delicious it had been so she asked him to pick her some more.

He clambered over the wall again, and was picking a small bunch of the rapunzel when a voice behind him hissed, "So you are the one who has been stealing my rapunzel!"

When he spun round, there stood a witch and she looked very angry indeed. The husband was terrified, but he tried to explain that his wife had been desperate for some fresh leaves for her salad.

"You may take all the leaves you require then, but you must give me your first child when she is born," smiled the witch, and it was not a nice smile. The husband was greatly relieved, however, for he knew that there was little chance of his wife ever having a daughter so he fled back over the wall, clutching the bunch of rapunzel. He did not tell his wife of his meeting with the witch for he thought it would only frighten her, and he soon forgot all about his adventure.

But it all came back to him when nine months later his wife gave birth to a beautiful baby girl. No sooner had she laid the baby in her cradle, than the witch appeared to claim the child. The wife wept, the husband pleaded but nothing could persuade the witch to forget the husband's awful promise, and so she took the tiny baby away.

The witch called the baby Rapunzel.
She grew into a beautiful girl with long,
long hair as fine as spun gold. When she
was sixteen, the witch took Rapunzel
and locked her into a tall tower so no
one would see how beautiful she
was. The witch threw away the
key to the tower, and so whenever
she wanted to visit Rapunzel she would
call out, "Rapunzel, Rapunzel, let down your hair,"
and Rapunzel would throw her golden plait of hair
out of the window at the top of the tower so the witch
could slowly scramble up.

Now one day it happened that a handsome young
prince was riding through the woods. He heard the
witch call out to Rapunzel and he watched her climb
up the tower. After the witch had gone, the prince came
to the bottom of the tower and he called up, "Rapunzel,
Rapunzel, let down your hair," and he climbed quickly up
the shining golden plait. You can imagine Rapunzel's
astonishment when she saw the handsome Prince standing
in front of her but she was soon laughing at his stories.
When he left, he promised to come again the next day, and
he did. And the next, and the next, and soon they had fallen
in love with each other.

One day as the witch clambered up Rapunzel

exclaimed, "You are slow! The prince doesn't take nearly as long to climb up the tower," but no sooner were the words out of her mouth than she realised her terrible mistake. The witch seized the long, long golden plait and cut it off. She drove Rapunzel far, far away from the tower, and then sat down to await the prince. When the witch heard him calling, she threw the golden plait out of the window. Imagine the prince's dismay when he sprang into the room only to discover the horrible witch instead of his beautiful Rapunzel! When the witch told him he would never see his Rapunzel again, in his grief he flung himself out of the tower. He fell into some brambles which scratched his eyes so he could no longer see.

And thus he wandered the land, always asking if anyone had seen his Rapunzel. After seven long years, he came to the place where she had hidden herself away. As he stumbled down the road, Rapunzel recognised him and with a great cry of joy she ran up to him and took him gently by the hand to her little cottage in the woods. As she washed his face, two of her tears fell on the prince's eyes and his sight came back. And so they went back to his palace and lived happily ever after. The witch, you will be pleased to hear, had not been able to get down from the tower, so she did NOT live happily ever after!

Teeny-tiny

an English folk tale

Once upon a time there lived a teeny-tiny old woman. She lived in a teeny-tiny house in a teeny-tiny street with a teeny-tiny cat. One day the teeny-tiny woman decided to go out for a teeny-tiny walk. She put on her teeny-tiny boots and her teeny-tiny bonnet, and off she set.

When she had walked a teeny-tiny way down the teeny-tiny street, she went through a teeny-tiny gate into a teeny-tiny graveyard, which was a teeny-tiny shortcut to the teeny-tiny meadow. Well, she had only taken a few teeny-tiny steps when she saw a teeny-tiny bone lying on top of a teeny-tiny grave. She thought that would do very well to make some teeny-tiny soup for supper so she put the teeny-tiny bone in her teeny-tiny pocket and went home at once to her teeny-tiny house.

Now the teeny-tiny woman was tired when she reached her teeny-tiny house so she did not make the teeny-tiny soup immediately but put the teeny-tiny bone into her teeny-tiny cupboard. Then she sat in her teeny-tiny chair and put her teeny-tiny feet up and had a teeny-tiny sleep. But she had only been asleep a teeny-tiny time when she woke up at the sound of a teeny-tiny voice coming from her teeny-tiny cupboard. The teeny-tiny voice said, "Where is my teeny-tiny bone?"

Well, the teeny-tiny woman was a teeny-tiny bit frightened so she wrapped her teeny-tiny shawl round her teeny-tiny head and went to sleep again. She had only been asleep a teeny-tiny time when the teeny-tiny voice came from the teeny-tiny cupboard again, a teeny-tiny bit louder this time. "Where is my teeny-tiny bone?"

The teeny-tiny woman was a teeny-tiny bit more frightened than last time so she hid under the teeny-tiny cushions, but she could not go back to sleep, not even a teeny-tiny bit. Then the teeny-tiny voice came again and this time it was even a teeny-tiny bit louder. "Where is my teeny-tiny bone?"

This time the teeny-tiny woman sat up in her teeny-tiny chair and said in her loudest teeny-tiny voice, "TAKE IT!"

There was a teeny-tiny silence, and then a teeny-tiny ghost ran out of the teeny-tiny house, down the teeny-tiny

street, through the teeny-tiny gate into the teeny-tiny
graveyard – with the teeny-tiny bone clutched very tightly
in its teeny-tiny hand! And the teeny-tiny woman never
took even a teeny-tiny walk there ever again!

CLASSIC STORIES

FOR 7–9 YEAR OLDS

Within the pages of this section children will find tales full of wonder, magic, adventure and laughter. Much-loved classics sit alongside legends from faraway places, making this a collection for children and parents to cherish. The beautifully told stories include *The Pied Piper of Hamelin*, *Ali Baba and the Forty Thieves* and *The Emperor's New Clothes*, all especially chosen for 7–9 year olds. Each tale will excite imaginations and help to foster a lifelong love of books and stories.

245 SPELLS AND ENCHANTMENT

FAVOURITES 296

341 FEATHERS, FUR AND FANGS

GIANTS, WITCHES 375 AND ENCHANTMENTS

ROYAL 418 ADVENTURES

455 MYTHS AND LEGENDS

Spells and Enchantment

The Pot of Gold
an Irish folk tale

iall O'Leary was sitting on a gate in the sunshine, day-dreaming quite happily, when – TIC! TIC! TIC! – he became aware of a sharp sound coming from the field behind him.

"Now what on earth can that be?" Niall wondered to himself. "It's too loud to be a grasshopper . . . and it's too quiet to be a bird."

TIC! TIC! TIC! it went.

Niall O'Leary swung his legs over the gate and turned around. He blinked in astonishment. There in the long grass of the field was the tiniest man Niall had ever seen, no higher than his boot. The tiny man had his back to Niall, but Niall could see that he was dressed all in green, with a long white feather in his cap. A tiny leather shoe lay before him on a rock, and he was banging away at it with a tiny stone hammer.

Niall's eyes lit up. A leprechaun! A real, live leprechaun! Niall licked his lips greedily.

Every tiny leprechaun had a huge pot of gold hidden somewhere. And as everybody knew, if you caught hold of a leprechaun and squeezed him tightly enough, he would have to tell you where his treasure was buried.

Quietly, quietly, Niall O'Leary got down from the gate.

TIC! TIC! TIC! went the leprechaun's hammer.

Quietly, quietly, Niall O'Leary crept through the grass.

TIC! TIC! TIC! went the leprechaun's hammer.

Quietly, quietly, Niall O'Leary reached out with his large, meaty hands . . .

"GOTCHA!" cried Niall O'Leary, and he squeezed and squeezed the wriggling leprechaun with all his might.

"Ooooof!" cried the leprechaun. "Let me go, you big bully!"

"Tell me where your gold is and I will!" boomed Niall.

"I can't tell you anything while you're squeezing the breath out of me," the leprechaun gasped, looking rather purple.

"Oops, sorry!" blustered Niall, and he relaxed his grip a little.

"That's better," wheezed the leprechaun, taking big gulps of air. "Now put me down and I promise I'll show you where my gold is hidden."

A broad grin spread across Niall's face as he lowered the leprechaun back down to the grass. "A leprechaun can't break his promise!" he chuckled.

"No," grumbled the leprechaun rather crossly, "and my gold is buried under here." He leapt a few steps into the middle of the field and pointed at a clump of dandelions. "You'll need a spade, mind," the leprechaun added thoughtfully. "You'll have to dig quite a way down."

Niall's face fell. "But I haven't got a spade with me," he said, glumly. "What shall I do?"

"Why don't you tie your handkerchief around the dandelions so you don't forget where the gold is buried," the leprechaun suggested. "Then hurry back home and fetch a spade. I promise on my word of honour that I won't untie the handkerchief."

Niall's face brightened once again. "What a great idea!" he beamed. He fumbled in his pocket, brought out a rather grubby red silk handkerchief, and tied it around the clump of dandelions. It waved at him in the breeze like a cheerful flag. "Thank you Mr Leprechaun," Niall remembered to say politely. "You've been mighty helpful." Then in a few strides, he was back over the gate and away home, humming merrily.

As soon as Niall had grabbed the biggest spade he could find in the garden shed, he set off back to the field at once. All the way down the lane, he day-dreamed of what he would do with the gold. But when Niall O'Leary reached the gate, he stopped stone-still and his mouth hung open. He dropped the spade and scratched his head. "Well, blow me down," gasped Niall. All over the field, thousands of red silk handkerchiefs were tied onto clumps of dandelions and fluttering in the breeze. And Niall could hear the sound of gleeful leprechaun laughter floating over the grass on the wind.

So Niall O'Leary never got his pot of gold after all. But that is how he came to own the most successful silk handkerchief shop in the whole of Ireland . . .

The Wild Swans

a retelling from the original story by Hans Christian Andersen

A long time ago, in a land far away, there lived a king whose wife died, leaving him with eleven little sons and a baby daughter, Elise. The king married again and the children's new stepmother was cruel and jealous. She seemed to put the king under a wicked spell which made him forget all about his beloved children. So the queen sent little Elise away from the palace to be brought up by a peasant couple who lived in the forest. Then she used witchcraft to turn the princes into swans and she sent them flying off from the palace forever.

Many years passed and Elise thought she would never see her brothers again. Then one evening, as she was sitting by a lake watching the sun set, she saw a line of swans come flying like a white ribbon across the sky. They alighted next to her, and at the exact moment when the sun melted into the lake, the swans disappeared in a flutter of feathers. In their place stood eleven princes. They were Elise's long-lost brothers! They recognised each other at once, and they ran to hug each other, weeping tears of joy.

"We have to live as swans by day," the princes explained, "but at night we return to our true selves. Our wicked stepmother banished us to live in a country which lies across a wide sea and we are only allowed to return here once a year for just eleven days. Tomorrow is the day that we must leave once again. Little sister, it is a dangerous journey, but now we have found you, we will take you with us."

All night long, the princes gathered willow bark and tough reeds and rushes and Elise wove them into a strong net. By sunrise, as the princes fluttered back into swans, Elise was lying in the woven mesh, fast asleep. The swans seized the net strings and, with a few powerful wingbeats, sped off into the sky. And so the brothers carried their sister, right across the land and over the churning sea . . .

High above the waves, Elise dreamed she saw a beautiful fairy who smiled sadly and said, "If you are very brave, you can set your brothers free from their enchantment. You must go to the churchyard and pick the stinging nettles that grow on the graves there. They will burn and blister your skin, but you must pick them with your bare hands and then crush them with your bare feet. Twine the nettles

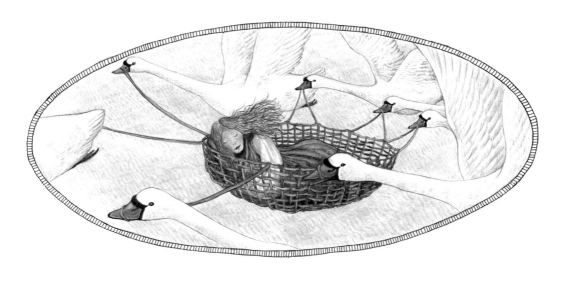

into flax and weave eleven shirts with long sleeves. The second that you throw the shirts over your brothers, they will be swans no longer. But mark this well, from the moment you start your task, you must not speak. If you utter a single word, it will be like a dagger through your brothers' hearts and they will surely die."

Elise awoke with a start to find herself lying on a bed of moss in a great cavern, shaded with vines and creepers. Her brothers were flown, and strangely there was a stinging nettle lying next to her. At once, she slipped away to find the churchyard. The graves were silent and spooky, but Elise clambered all over them collecting the nettles that sprang there in thick clumps. How the nettles burnt and blistered her hands! Elise hurried back to the cave and trampled on the nettles until they were crushed and her feet swollen and sore. Finally, she twisted the stalks into flax and began carefully to weave . . .

Elise's work was clumsy and slow due to her red, painful hands and arms. But by the evening when the swans returned, she had woven nearly half of the first shirt. The princes were upset by Elise's strange task and scared by her silence. But when they saw the spark of hope in Elise's eyes, they realised that she must be suffering for their sake. The youngest brother wept for his sister's pain, and as his tears fell onto her injured arms and hands, the blisters healed themselves and disappeared.

Elise would have worked around the clock, until all eleven shirts were finished and the spell finally broken. However, the next day, her hiding place in the cavern was sniffed out by hunting dogs and a royal hunting party burst in upon her. Elise was terrified, but she knew that if she uttered a single word, her brothers would die. The king thought that Elise was the most beautiful girl he had ever seen. "Don't be afraid," he said gently to her, as she stood trembling and silent. "Whoever you are, you can't live here in this cave. You will come back to my palace and I will make sure you are looked after and taken care of." The king lifted Elise up behind him on his horse and they were off like the wind over the hills.

Elise wept without a word as the ladies of the court dressed her in silks and satins, threaded pearls in her hair, and led her into a splendid banquet which the king had ordered in her honour. "You will be my queen," the king told Elise gently after the feast, "but I do not want you to be sad. I want you to be happy here with me." The king led Elise down a corridor to a small door. He opened it and Elise's mouth widened into a perfect "O" of surprise. The room was adorned with green hangings, to look just like the cave in the forest. And on the floor was the shirt she had finished and all the bundles of nettles from the churchyard. Elise flung her arms around the king and kissed his face and hands as he handed her the key to the little room.

After that, Elise spent every day at the king's side. She could see that he was good and kind and thoughtful, and she longed to tell him how much she had begun to care for him – but she dared not utter a sound. Every night, Elise crept down the corridor in her nightdress to her secret little room and continued with her weaving. Her heart was heavy with the thought that her brothers did not know where she was and must be searching anxiously for her.

Night after night, the pile of flax grew lower and lower, and by the time the tenth shirt was finished, Elise was in desperate need of more nettles. There was nothing for it but to creep out of the palace by moonlight, and hurry down the dark paths all the way to the churchyard. When Elise reached the graves, her blood ran cold with horror. Witches sat on the tombstones, reaching down into the earth with their bony fingers. Elise thought of her brothers and forced herself to walk past the witches and collect huge armfuls of the burning nettles. Then she was away, hurrying back to the palace before dawn . . .

Unbeknown to Elise, the king's chief advisor had spied on her. He had always been jealous of the wild, silent girl from the cave who had won the king's heart and now sat at the king's

side instead of him. His wicked heart leapt for joy as he hurried to the king the very next morning. "Your majesty," the chief advisor whispered, "I am sorry to tell you that I saw your bride-to-be at the churchyard last night, surrounded by witches. She can only have been performing black magic."

252

The king shook his head vigorously. "You must be mistaken," he said. "I do not believe it."

"Go to Elise's room and see the new pile of churchyard nettles she collected for her spells," the chief advisor insisted. "She is a witch and she must be burnt. The people will find out and they will demand it."

The king hung his head in sorrow. He felt as though his heart was breaking.

Next morning, guards broke into Elise's chamber and hauled her away to a dark, damp prison. They left her with only her nettles for a pillow and the shirts she had woven to keep her warm but they were all Elise wanted. Elise didn't know what she had done wrong, but she knew she was going to die and that she didn't have much time left. Her hands trembled as she hurried desperately to finish the final shirt. As she twisted and plaited and wove, a swan came flapping his wings against the window. Elise recognised her youngest brother and she ran to thrust her fingers through the bars and stroke his feathers. She couldn't say a word to tell him what had happened, and tears sparkled in her eyes as she waved him away and hurried back to her work . . .

All day and all night, Elise's sore fingers worked faster than ever. As the sun's rays stretched through the bars, the final shirt was nearly, nearly finished . . . Elise didn't stop frantically working even when the guards thrust her into a smelly cart and they went bumping through the streets. Crowds of people threw mud at her and jeered. "Look at the witch!" they shouted. "See, she's working on some evil spell!"

Then the cart arrived at the bonfire and the executioner stepped forwards to drag Elise to her death. But suddenly, eleven huge white swans swooped down out of the sky. Quick as a flash, Elise grabbed the shirts and threw them over the birds.

The crowd fell back in terror as there was a huge flash of lightning. The swans disappeared and in their places stood eleven handsome princes – although the youngest had a swan's wing instead of one arm, for Elise had run out of time to finish the final sleeve of his shirt.

"Now I can speak!" Elise sobbed. "I am innocent!" She sank into her brothers' arms and the princes explained all that had happened. Then the people began to cheer and the church bells rang out for joy, and the king took his beautiful bride and her brothers back home to his palace.

The Pied Piper of Hamelin
a German legend

Imagine what it would be like to live in a town overrun by rats. Rats in the streets, the shops, the gardens! Rats in the town hall, the hospital and police station! Rats in your school corridors, your classroom, your desk! Rats in your kitchen, your bath, your bed! Well, that's what it was like to live in the town of Hamelin, which lay beside the River Weser.

No one knew where the rats had come from or how they had managed to take over the town in such numbers. The townspeople of Hamelin were desperate to be rid of them. They couldn't eat without rats nibbling off their plates. They couldn't get dressed without uncovering rats nesting in their clothes and boots. They couldn't put their babies down to sleep without finding rats cuddled up in the cradles. They couldn't even chat to each other in comfort, for the noise of all the squeaking and scampering! So you can see why the mayor put up a poster outside the town hall saying:

There will be a reward of
ONE THOUSAND GUILDERS
to anyone who can get rid of the rats!

255

Yes, one thousand guilders! Everyone began to imagine what they would do with such a huge fortune – but of course, they could only dream. No one had the first idea how to begin claiming their town back from the rats.

By the time the stranger came knocking on the door of the town hall, the mayor was panic-stricken. He would have listened to anybody who said they could help. So when the stranger announced confidently, "I can get rid of all the rats for you," the mayor didn't worry too much about the stranger's odd, multicoloured costume. The mayor paid no attention to the stranger's extraordinarily long fingers and the unusual pipe that hung on a cord round his neck. The mayor didn't think too much about the sad smile on the stranger's face or the wistful gleam in his eyes. The mayor just beamed with relief and said, "GREAT! When can you begin?"

"Right now," replied the stranger, and he raised his pipe to his lips. Off he went, out of the town hall and into the street, playing a lilting tune that filled the air. Instantly, all over town, the rats stopped scuffling, pricked up their ears, and listened. For the first time in many, many months, there was silence for a moment. Then the scampering and squeaking began again, as the rats ran to follow the Pied Piper.

The townspeople of Weser couldn't believe their eyes. All through the town strolled the Pied Piper, his fingers continually moving on his pipe and the haunting notes rippling through the air. And out of all the houses swarmed the rats; out of every garden and gutter, out of every nook and cranny they came streaming. Down stairwells and through streets, out of passages and alleyways, over rooftops and along roads the rats came hurrying after the strange musician. And the Pied Piper didn't stop playing all the way to the wide River Weser. He didn't stop playing as he dipped one brightly coloured foot into the rushing waters and the thousands of rats began to plunge off the bank into the river. He didn't stop playing until the very last rat had drowned.

Then the church bells rang out in celebration, the townspeople started hugging each other, the children began dancing and singing – and the Pied Piper strode quietly back to the town hall to fetch his reward.

"My one thousand guilders, if you please," said the Pied Piper, calmly.

The mayor just smiled what he thought was a charming smile. Now the rats were dead and gone he certainly didn't plan on giving away what was nearly the entire contents of the town council bank account! "Come, come now, my dear fellow," the mayor coaxed. "One thousand guilders is somewhat over-the-top for playing a pretty ditty on a tin whistle, surely you'll agree! Why don't we settle on fifty guilders, and I'll throw in a nice bronze medal and even put up a statue of you and me together in the market place, eh?"

The Pied Piper simply turned on his heel and walked out into the street.

As he went, he once more lifted his pipe to his lips. But this time, he played a different tune. Enchanting notes rippled all around and down the roads the children came dancing, running and leaping after the Pied Piper.

The men and women of Hamelin were struck still with horror as the children swept past them and were gone through the town. Playing his strange melody, the Pied Piper led the children past the River Weser and skipping happily along a path that led up to a steep, craggy mountain. He piped a burst of airy notes and a little door appeared in the mountain slope. The Pied Piper led the children inside. The townspeople could hear the echo of his pipe and the children's laughter grow fainter and fainter as they went deeper and deeper into the earth. Then suddenly, the little door slammed shut and disappeared. The children were gone – all except for one little boy who was lame and so hadn't been able to keep up with the others. He stood on the mountainside and sobbed, calling out for his friends. But the little door had vanished.

No one ever saw the Pied Piper or the children again. But on sunny days, some townsfolk swore they could hear ripples of childish laughter floating down from the mountain. And from that day to this, there has never been a single rat in the town of Hamelin.

Belle and the Beast

a retelling from the original tale by Madame Leprince de Beaumont

here was once a businessman who had made a fortune by trading overseas. He lived in a magnificent mansion staffed by servants and with a TV in every room – including the indoor swimming pool. The businessman's wife had died, so he had brought up their three beautiful daughters on his own. Unfortunately, the two eldest girls, Bianca and Bettina, lazed about all day watching chat shows, flicking through magazines and day-dreaming of marrying professional footballers. But Belle, the youngest daughter, was a great help to her father in running his business. She also enjoyed reading books on engineering and space exploration, for she was as intelligent as she was beautiful, and she had an avid interest in rocket science.

The businessman once had to go away on an important trip for work.

"Don't forget to bring us back some jewellery!" yelled Bianca.

"And some perfume!" bellowed Bettina.

"Is there nothing you would like, darling?" the businessman asked Belle.

Belle thought for a while. "Just a beautiful rose, please Daddy," she smiled.

"That's my girl!" the businessman said, and gave a cheery wave as he drove away.

But when the businessman finally returned, he was downcast and empty-handed.

"I'm afraid your dear old Dad has had it," the businessman explained. "I was on my way back last night, but it was dark and raining and somehow I got completely lost in the middle of nowhere. The only house for miles around was a spooky old mansion, and I went to ask for help. The lights were on, the front door was open, but nobody seemed to be at home. I thought it was very strange, but I was so desperate that I crept inside and stayed the night. Early this morning, as I was hurrying off through the grounds, I stopped to pick a rose for Belle. 'STOP THIEF!' someone roared. 'This is my house and those are my roses! Is this how you repay my hospitality? I am going to kill you!' The man who came striding towards me was uglier than a monster in a film. He had a hairy face and bloodshot eyes, a snout for a nose and teeth like fangs. His hands were clawed and his body huge and hulking. I realised that the beast was deadly serious, so I fell on my knees in terror and begged for mercy. 'I will give you three months to say goodbye to everyone,' he growled. 'After that, you must return here to die . . . unless you have a daughter who is willing to come in your place and live here with me forever.'"

Bianca and Bettina stood gawping in horror. "Oh Daddy," they wailed, "who is going to look after us when you're gone?"

"Don't worry, Daddy," Belle comforted her father. "I can't let you die. I will go instead of you."

"Belle, you will do nothing of the kind!" her father protested. "You haven't seen this guy!"

"I don't care!" said Belle, resolutely sticking out her chin. And nothing Belle's father could say would make her change her mind. "If you sneak off without me, I shall just follow you," was her final word on the subject. So three months later, the broken-hearted businessman accompanied his brave daughter to the door of the huge, lonely mansion and kissed her for the last time. He could hardly see through his tears as he turned and walked away . . .

"Right," Belle said to herself firmly, though her bottom lip was trembling. "Let's find the library. Maybe it has a good science section." She set off through the stone corridors and oak-panelled halls, exploring. It was an eerie feeling to be all alone in such an enormous old place. Suddenly, Belle stopped in surprise. There, right in front of her was a door marked 'Belle's room'. She put her hand on the iron handle and gently pushed. It swung open with a creak. Belle gasped with delight. Inside, was everything she could possibly have wished for. There was a soft, white bed. Wardrobes full of beautiful clothes. But best of all, lining the walls was shelf after shelf of books.

"The owner of this place can't be all bad," Belle murmured to herself. She drew down the nearest book. It was bound in ancient leather and had gold-edging. She read the first page:

Belle, you have a heart of gold
Like girls in fairytales of old.
Whatever you wish, it will come true.
There's magic waiting here for you.

"Hmmm," wondered Belle. "Well, the only thing I really wish is that I could see if my Dad is okay."

At that very moment, Belle noticed a mirror on the bedroom wall begin to cloud over. Mists swirled across the glass, and when they cleared, instead of her own reflection, she saw a picture of her father, sitting at home sadly without her. After a few moments the picture vanished, but Belle was very grateful to have been able to see her father at all. *The owner of this place is actually very kind*, Belle thought to herself.

Just then, Belle heard the dinner bell ringing from the great hall. She hurried along and found a delicious meal laid out for one. No sooner had she swallowed three mouthfuls than she heard a shuffling and a snuffling. The food stuck in her throat and her heartbeat quickened. Belle forced herself to turn round and face her host.

Her father had been right. He was truly hideous.

"I'm Belle," she whispered, remembering her manners, like the well-brought up girl she was. "My room is wonderful – thank you."

"Call me Beast," said the monster gruffly, a look of pleasure lighting up his sad eyes. "Did you really like everything?"

"Yes, of course," said Belle. "Particularly the books. I love books, especially those on rocket science."

"They are your books now," said Beast. "Everything here is yours. I give it all to you. You can do with everything just what you wish. That goes for me, too. If I'm bothering you just tell me to go away and I will." The Beast looked down at his huge, flat feet. "I know I'm exceedingly ugly. I might put you off your food." He sighed a deep sigh. "And not only am I ugly, I'm very stupid too."

"Now, now," comforted Belle. "I'm sure that's not the case. Anyone who is ready to say they are stupid can't possibly be stupid. The only people who really are stupid are those who won't admit that they're stupid!"

"Do you really think so?" sighed the Beast.

"Yes, of course!" laughed Belle. "And if you're really worried about being stupid, I can teach you all about rocket science. Let me get my books . . ."

A sheepish smile came over the Beast's ugly face as he listened to Belle read. After a while, he suddenly interrupted her.

"Belle, will you marry me?" he asked.

Belle was extremely taken aback. She looked at the monster as he crouched adoringly in front of her. "I'm sorry," she said. "I wish I could, but I really don't want to."

And so the time passed. Each day, Belle read in her room and walked in the beautiful grounds, admiring the roses. And each evening, the Beast came to visit her. As the weeks went on, Belle began to enjoy his company and looked forward to seeing him. But each night the Beast asked her to marry him, and even though Belle liked him more and more as a friend, she simply couldn't – well, *fancy* him.

Belle's only other worry was her Dad. Each day she saw in the mirror that he was pining more and more without her. Her sisters were selfish, unkind and thoughtless, and her father had grown quiet and pale and thin.

"Dear Beast," Belle begged one night, "allow me to go back to see my dad. I am afraid that he is dying of a broken heart."

Much to Belle's surprise, the Beast nodded his agreement. "Of course, Belle," he said, "if that is what will make you happy. Only I don't know what I'll do without you . . ."

"Darling Beast," whispered Belle, stroking his matted, shaggy hair, "I promise I'll be back in a week."

"Then I promise you that when you wake up tomorrow morning, you'll be at home with your father," sighed the Beast. "Take this ring. When you're ready to leave, just put it by the side of your bed at night. As you sleep, it will bring you back here."

Sure enough, next morning Belle woke up back in her old bed. Her dad couldn't believe his eyes! He and Belle hugged and laughed and spent a wonderful holiday doing all the things they used to enjoy doing together – going through his accounts, visiting the science museum, watching old musicals on TV . . . The week flew by in the twinkling of an eye. "Please, Belle, don't go," begged her dad, and Belle didn't have the heart to leave.

But several nights later, Belle had a terrible dream. She saw the Beast lying in the garden of his mansion, under the rose bushes that he loved so much. Belle knew that he was dying. "Daddy," she sobbed the next morning. "I'm worried that something dreadful has happened to the Beast. He's my best and truest friend – and it's all my fault!"

That night, Belle put the Beast's ring by her bedside. It didn't seem as if she'd been asleep for five minutes when she woke up in her beautiful white room in the mansion. Belle sped off into the moonlit garden and there, lying under the rose bushes just as in her dream, lay the Beast. She flung herself down by his side and heaved his big, heavy head into her lap. Her tears plopped one by one onto his hairy face.

Weakly, the Beast opened his eyes and smiled. "I thought you had forgotten your promise," he whispered. "Now I have seen you once again, I can die happily."

"No!" Belle cried. "You can't die! You mustn't leave me! I love you!" And she kissed him.

At that very moment, the night sky was lit up by a million rainbow-coloured fireworks. Belle gazed upwards in surprise – she thought things like that only happened in films. When she looked back down at the Beast again, the monster was gone. Lying in her lap was a handsome, happy prince. He sprang up and lifted Belle to her feet with joy in his eyes.

"My darling Belle," he told her, "Thank you for setting me free! I have lived under a wicked enchantment for years which forced me to appear as the Beast – not only ugly but stupid, too – until a beautiful girl willingly fell in love with me. You are the only person in the world who saw through my ugly appearance and sensed what I was really like inside. Now we will live together happily forever."

And that's exactly what they did. But this is a real tale, not a fairytale, and real tales don't have entirely happy endings. The prince took Belle to live at his palace – and her dad went to live with them too. But Belle's selfish sisters got what they deserved. They were turned into statues and set at the palace gates until such time as they began to think about other people rather than themselves. As far as I know, they're both there still . . .

Pandora's Box

a Greek myth

hen the world was first created, it was a happy place of light and laughter; there was no such thing as sadness or pain. The sun shone every day and the gods came down from heaven to walk and talk with the humans who lived on earth.

One afternoon, a man called Epimetheus and his wife, Pandora, were outside tending their flower garden when they saw the god Mercury approaching. He was bowed down by a dark wooden chest that he was carrying on his shoulders and he looked hot and tired. Pandora rushed to get the worn-out god a cool drink, while Epimetheus helped him lower the chest onto the ground. It was tied shut with golden cords and was carved with strange markings.

"My friends, would you do me a great favour?" sighed Mercury. "It is so hot today and the box is so heavy! May I leave it here while I go on an errand?"

"Of course you can," smiled Epimetheus.

The man and the god heaved the chest indoors.

"Are you sure that no one will find it?" asked Mercury

anxiously. "NO ONE under ANY circumstances must open the box."

"Don't worry," laughed Epimetheus and Pandora, and they waved the god off through the trees.

All of a sudden, Pandora stopped still and frowned. "Listen, Epimetheus!" she hissed. "I am sure I heard someone whispering our names!"

Epimetheus and Pandora listened hard. At first, they heard nothing but the twittering of the birds in the sunshine and the rustling of the leaves in the breeze. Then, they heard the distant sound of "Epimetheus! Pandora!" being called from outside.

"It's our friends!" cried Epimetheus, happily.

But Pandora looked puzzled and shook her head. "No, Epimetheus, those aren't the voices I heard," she said, firmly.

"They must have been!" Epimetheus laughed. "Come on now, let's go and see everyone."

"You go," Pandora insisted, with a frown. "I'd rather stay here for a while."

Epimetheus shrugged, kissed Pandora on the nose, and strode outside. As soon as he was gone,

Pandora hurried over to the strange box and waited. After only a few seconds, she heard it again – distant voices calling "Pandora! Pandora!" The voices were so low and whispery that Pandora wasn't sure whether she really was hearing them or was just imagining it. She bent down closer and put her ear to the lid. No, this time she was sure. The box was calling to her! "Pandora!" the voices pleaded. "Let us out, Pandora! We are trapped in here in the darkness! Please help us to escape!"

Pandora jumped back with a start. Mercury had expressly forbade them or anyone else to open the box . . . and yet the voices sounded so sad and pitiful.

"Pandora!" they came again. "Help us! Help us, we beg you!"

Pandora could stand it no longer. Hurriedly, she knelt down and worked at the tight golden knots. All the time, the whispering and pleading voices filled her ears. At last the knots were undone and the gleaming cords fell away. She took a deep breath and opened the lid.

At once, Pandora realised she had done a terrible thing. The box had been crammed with all the evils in the world – thousands of tiny, brown, moth-like creatures that stung people with their wings and caused hurt and misery wherever they went. Now, thanks to Pandora, the evils were free! They flew up out of the chest in a great swarm and fluttered all over Pandora's skin. For the very first time, Pandora felt pain and regret. She began to wail with despair, and all too late, she slammed the lid back down onto the box.

Outside, Epimetheus heard his wife's cries and came running as
fast as he could. The little creatures fluttered to sting and bite him,
before speeding off through the window into the world beyond. For
the first time ever, Epimetheus began to shout at his wife in anger.
Pandora yelled back, and the couple realised in horror that they were
arguing.

"Let me out!" interrupted a high voice. Pandora and Epimetheus
grabbed onto each other in a panic. The voice was coming from
inside the box. "Don't be afraid of me! Let me out and I can help
you!" came the voice once more.

"What do you think?" Pandora whispered to Epimetheus, wide-
eyed.

"Surely you can't do any more mischief than you already have
done," he grumbled. So Pandora shut her eyes and opened Mercury's
chest for a second time.

Out of the deep, dark box fluttered a single shining white spirit
like a butterfly. It was Hope. Pandora and Epimetheus sobbed with
relief as she fluttered against their skin and soothed their stinging
wounds. Then she was gone, darting out of the window and into the
world after the evils. And luckily, Hope has stayed with us ever since.

Tomlin

a Scottish folk tale

Carterhaugh Wood was thick and green and dark, and people said it was the home of fairy folk. One bright summer's day, Janet, the earl's daughter, made up her mind to go and explore it for herself. She crept out of the castle and set off down a narrow path deep into the woods. After a while, Janet reached a small stone well in the middle of a clearing. There were roses climbing all over it – far more beautiful than any in the castle gardens – and Janet bent to pick one. No sooner had the stem broken off in her hand than Janet heard a voice that said, "Naughty-naughty, Janet. Who said you could come here into our wood and pick one of our roses?"

Janet straightened up with a start. There before her stood the most handsome young knight she had ever seen. She tossed her hair proudly and replied, "How dare you speak to me like that! These woods belong to my father, the earl. I shall go where I choose and pick whatever flowers I like!"

Delight sparkled in the young man's eyes at her bold answer and he threw back his head and laughed. "I am Tomlin," the knight said, taking Janet's hands and spinning her round, "and today you shall stay here in the forest with me and we shall play."

All day long, Tomlin and Janet wandered through Carterhaugh Wood. They danced and sang and told each other stories. And by the evening, they were both deeply in love.

"I will not return to the castle without you," Janet vowed. "You must come with me and I will beg my father to let you stay."

"I cannot leave the wood," replied Tomlin sadly. "I was once human, but many years ago, when I was riding through the forest, the Fairy Queen caught me and enchanted me. Now I am an elf-knight, and I must ride by the side of the Fairy Queen to protect her for ever more. I only wish that I could be a man again, for then I would surely marry you."

"Is there no way to break the spell?" Janet sighed.

"There is," Tomlin said gently, "but you must be very brave."

"Tell me what I must do," Janet whispered.

"This very night is Halloween," Tomlin explained, "a night when fairies, goblins and witches ride abroad. You must go to Mile Cross and hide there until midnight, for then I will come riding by. First you will see a troop of riders on black horses. Then there will be a troop on brown horses. Next will come riders on horses as white as milk – and in the middle of them will ride the Fairy Queen herself. I will be among the elf-knights at her side, and I will wear only one glove so you can find me quickly among the throng. When you see me, you must run to my horse, seize its bridle and drag me down. You must then hold me fast, no matter what happens – for the fairy folk will cast all sorts of spells on me to try to keep me. If you have the strength and courage not to let go, the enchantment will at last be broken and I will be yours." Tomlin took Janet's hand. "Do you think you can do all this?" he asked quietly.

"Yes," breathed Janet. "Yes, I will."

Later that night, when everyone else was safely inside the castle with the doors and windows barred, Janet hid in the darkness on the moor at Mile Cross. Just before the stroke of midnight, she heard the thunder of hooves and out of the night appeared hundreds of black horses, bridles jangling and manes flying. On their backs were witches with bony fingers and sunken faces with dead, staring eyes.

Next, the brown horses galloped past, whinnying and snorting. The wrinkled goblins who rode them whipped them with willow switches and clutched the reins with wizened fingers.

Then the white horses came like glowing ghosts through the gloom, wild-eyed and foaming at the mouth, and at the centre of the riders Janet saw the beautiful Fairy Queen, sitting tall and fierce and proud. Quickly, Janet searched for a rider with only one glove. She plunged in among the pounding hooves, pulled down the enchanted elf-knight and held Tomlin to herself as tight as she could.

The Fairy Queen sent up an unearthly wail that tore through the darkness and all the hundreds of riders thundered around, shrieking and howling. Suddenly Janet felt Tomlin grow in her arms and she realised she was holding a huge, hairy bear. Still she held him fast, and he writhed into a hissing snake. Still she clutched him in her arms, and he bucked into an angry, snapping wolf. Still she held on tight, and he turned into a blazing branch that burnt into her flesh. Still Janet refused to let go, and in a flash of cold lightning she saw she was at last holding a naked, human man. As she wrapped Tomlin in her cloak, a haunting cry came from the Fairy Queen: "Tomlin, I would rather have changed your eyes to wood and your heart to stone than lost you!" Then suddenly the wild hunt was gone, disappeared into the night, and Janet and Tomlin were left alone on the dark, windy moor to make their way home to the castle together.

Hop-toads and Pearls

a retelling from the original tale by Charles Perrault

"G o and fetch the water!" yelled the widow at her younger daughter. "You can finish that sweeping later! And hurry back with it". You've still got to light the fire and peel the potatoes for dinner."

The poor girl hurried to rest her broom in the corner and wipe her dusty hands on her tattered apron. She never grumbled about being treated like a slave because she was good and kind and couldn't think badly about anybody. But how she wished that her mother and her sister might help her out a little with all the housework now and again . . .

As the exhausted girl stumbled out to the well with the cumbersome bucket, the widow's elder daughter looked up from her comfy chair by the window and smirked. Fanchon was like her mother in every way: how she looked (very ugly), how she spoke (sharp and nasty) and how she acted (selfish and lazy). This was the reason why her mother adored her so: whenever she looked at Fanchon, she saw herself.

The widow's younger daughter reached the well and heaved up

a heavy, full bucket. Suddenly, she noticed that an old beggar-woman had joined her. The toothless crone wheezed, "My dear, I'm hoarse with thirst. Could you spare me a little drink?"

"Of course," the kind girl answered, and hurried to unhook the dripping bucket and help the beggar-woman to a ladleful.

Little did the younger daughter know that the hag who stood in front of her was actually a powerful fairy, who had disguised herself to put the girl to the test. The younger daughter kindly helped the beggar-woman to another ladleful of water and chatted politely to her for a while, before hauling the bucket back home.

How the girl's mother and her sister yelled and screamed and swore at her for taking so long at the well! "I do beg your pardon," the poor girl apologised. "I will be quicker next time." To everyone's surprise, a shining white pearl dropped from her lips with every word.

The stunned widow woman picked up a pearl from the floor, bit it hard between her teeth, and held it up to the light to examine it. "They're real!" she exclaimed, with a greedy twinkle in her eye. "What on earth happened at the well this evening? Tell me everything, or I'll lock you in the coal cellar all weekend."

The younger daughter was just as amazed as her mother and sister, and truthfully told them that she had done nothing but give a drink to a woman she'd met at the well. Pearls continued to drop from her lips as she spoke, and as fast as they fell, the widow scooped them up greedily into her pockets.

"Did you hear that, Fanchon?" she screeched delightedly. "Get yourself down to that well immediately!"

"Get lost!" the rude girl snorted. "I'm not fetching and carrying like a slave for anything!"

"I said GO!" the widow roared, cuffing the horrified Fanchon round the head. "Find that woman and give her a drink, whether she wants one or not! We're going to be rich, rich, rich! . . ."

Fanchon sulked and pouted, grumbled and cursed with every step that she lugged the splintery bucket – and it was only fear of her mother's temper that made her do it at all. She flung the bucket angrily into the well and moaned and groaned to herself with every wind as she pulled it back up. No sooner had she finished, than she noticed she had been joined by an elegant young woman dressed in fine robes. (It was the fairy again, but this time she had disguised herself as a princess.) "Good evening," the princess said politely, "would you be so good as to allow me a drink?"

"Oh, it's you, is it?" Fanchon sneered. "You're the reason why I've got splinters in my hands, splashes all over my dress, and my arms are killing me. You'd better make it worth my while and give me diamonds instead of pearls, that's all I can say." With that, Fanchon angrily flung the wooden ladle at the princess and dumped the bucket at her feet. "Go on then," she snapped.

No sooner had the princess taken one sip than Fanchon snatched the ladle back and humped the bucket back to the house. "There!" she yelled at her mother. "Happy now?" To everyone's horror, three great hop-toads leapt from her lips and sprang across the floor, croaking. Fanchon clapped her hands over her mouth in alarm.

"Whatever's happened?" cried the widow. "Where are the pearls?"

"I don't know!" wailed Fanchon, and three more hop-toads bounced, bulging-eyed, from her mouth. She began to scream and stamp her feet.

"This is all your fault, you ungrateful wretch!" the widow yelled at her younger daughter. She shoved the startled girl outside and slammed the door in her face. The poor younger daughter wandered off into the forest, sobbing . . .

The girl would almost certainly have got lost in the woods forever if the prince hadn't spotted her on his way back from a hunting trip. The prince was fascinated by the pearls that fell from her mouth, but he was even more charmed by the forgiving, kind way in which she spoke of her obviously horrible family. He took the lovely girl back to his palace at once, and after she had got to know and love him, he married her.

As for the nasty elder daughter, well, even her own mother tired of her moaning in the end. Besides, who wants to live with a house full of hop-toads? The widow threw the girl out, and they both lived the rest of their lives with only their miserable selves for company.

The Firebird

a Russian fairytale

Long ago in Russia, in the days when witches lurked in the forests and dragons flew over the plains and demons hid in the mountains, there lived a lord called Tsar Andronovich who owned a magnificent garden. At the centre of the garden lay a beautiful orchard, and in the middle of the orchard lay Tsar Andronovich's favourite tree – a tree which grew precious golden apples. Tsar Andronovich had given strict orders that no one was allowed to touch the golden apple tree except for himself. But one night, an amazing firebird with wings of flame and eyes of crystal came blazing into the orchard and stole some of the precious fruit.

"I must have this amazing firebird alive!" Tsar Andronovich marvelled. "This creature seems even more splendid than the golden apples she has been stealing!"

Half an hour later, the Tsar's three sons were galloping out of the gates in search of the firebird. The eldest and middle son, Dimitri and Vassili, thundered off together. They had teamed up to find the firebird and agreed to split their father's fortune between them. The youngest son, Ivan, was left to go off sadly on his own.

Ivan rode for three days and nights without any idea of where he was going and without seeing any sign of the firebird. His food and water began to run low and his horse was exhausted. Just as Ivan was thinking things couldn't get much worse, he heard a blood-curdling howl behind him and out of a dark forest ran a huge grey wolf. Ivan's horse shot away from under him, throwing him into the dirt. But it didn't escape very far. The grey wolf sprang onto it and gobbled it up.

"Eat me quickly and have done with it!" Ivan cried at the panting beast.

"I am not going to eat you," grinned the wolf. "I have to repay you for eating your very tasty horse! Now, I can't help noticing that you look worn out. Ride on me, the grey wolf. I will take you where you want to go."

Ivan was too tired and lonely to argue. He climbed onto the grey wolf's back and explained all about his quest to find the firebird. He had hardly finished speaking when the grey wolf leapt away like an arrow. It seemed like only a few seconds before they came to a halt before a stone wall.

"Ivan, climb over this wall and you will see the firebird in a golden cage," the wolf explained. "Take the firebird, but whatever you do, do not steal the golden cage."

Trembling, Ivan clambered over the wall and found himself in a courtyard below. Hanging from a tree in the middle was a golden cage with the firebird inside, just as the wolf had said. Ivan crept up to the leafy boughs, opened the jewelled door, and drew out the beautiful firebird. To his great surprise, she didn't flap or cry out or make any fuss at all. *Hmmm*, thought Ivan to himself. *I really need the cage as well, or else where am I going to keep the firebird?* He reached up into the leaves and unhooked the cage. At that very moment, ear-splitting alarm bells began to ring and guards rushed into the courtyard from all sides. They roughly dragged Ivan off to see their master, the Tsar Dolmat.

"You must pay dearly for trying to steal my precious firebird," boomed Tsar Dolmat, his face dark with anger. Then he rubbed his beard and thought for a second. "UNLESS," he added, "you go to the ends of the earth and bring me the horse with the golden mane. If you can do this, I will give you the firebird with pleasure."

Ivan crept back to the grey wolf hanging his head in shame. But his friend simply said, "Ride on me, the grey wolf, and I will take you where you want to go."

The grey wolf sprang away to the ends of the earth faster than the wind. It seemed like only a couple of minutes before they came to a stop outside some stables.

"Ivan, go into these stables and take the horse with the golden mane," the wolf told him. "But whatever you do, do not steal its golden bridle."

Cautiously, Ivan edged into the stables, crept up to the horse with the golden mane, and began to lead it out of its stall. *Hmmm,* thought Ivan, as he looked at its golden bridle hanging on the wall. *I really need the bridle as well, or else how am I going to ride the horse?* The moment he lifted down the bridle a clanging peal of bells broke the silence. Soldiers dashed into the stable and hauled Ivan away to see their master, the Tsar Afron.

"You must pay dearly for trying to steal my wonderful horse with the golden mane," raged Tsar Afron, shaking with fury. "UNLESS," he added, "you go to the other side of the world and bring me Tasha the Beautiful to be my bride. If you can do this, I will gladly give you the horse with the golden mane."

Ivan could hardly bring himself to tell the grey wolf that he had disobeyed him a second time. But when the wolf saw Ivan returning empty-handed he simply said, "Ride on me, the grey wolf, and I will take you where you want to go."

Ivan jumped onto the grey wolf and he sped away to the other side of the world as quick as lightning. It seemed like only an hour or so before they drew up outside a glorious palace.

"Ivan, this time I am going to be the one who goes inside and you are going to be the one who waits," said the wolf and he sprang over the palace wall with one mighty bound. Ivan hardly had time to draw breath before the wolf came springing over again – this time with Tasha the Beautiful tossed onto his back. Ivan leapt onto the wolf's back and they were off through the air like a shooting star.

By the time the
three arrived back at Tsar
Afron's home, the grey
wolf was highly surprised
to find Ivan weeping bitterly.

"Why are you crying?"
the grey wolf asked. "If we
give Tasha the Beautiful to Tsar
Afron, you will get the horse with the
golden mane. If we give the horse with the
golden mane to Tsar Dolmat, you will get the firebird. If we give the
firebird to Tsar Andronovich, your father, you will get all the wealth
he possesses."

"But I have fallen in love with Tasha," Ivan protested, "and she
has fallen in love with me!"

The grey wolf looked at Tasha the Beautiful and she nodded
sadly, biting her lip.

"Oh very well," sighed the grey wolf. "I will turn myself into
the form of Tasha the Beautiful. You can present me to Tsar Afron in
her place and he will give you the horse with the golden mane. When
you are safely two mountains away, think of me, the grey wolf, and I
will be back at your side."

And so it all happened. Tsar Afron was tricked and soon Ivan
was once again mounted on the grey wolf while his sweetheart Tasha
the Beautiful rode prettily on the horse with the golden mane.

As they drew near the villa of Tsar Dolmat, Ivan sighed a deep
sigh. "Oh grey wolf," he began, "I would so like to keep this horse
with a golden mane. Would you turn into the form of the horse, as
you disguised yourself as Tasha before? Then I could take you to

Tsar Dolmat and win the firebird. When I am safely two forests away, I will think of you and you will return back to my side."

The grey wolf looked at Ivan and bowed slightly. "For you, I will do this," said the wolf gruffly. And so it all came to pass. Tsar Dolmat was tricked, and Ivan was once again mounted on the grey wolf while his sweetheart Tasha the Beautiful rode prettily on the horse with the golden mane and carried the firebird.

By and by, the companions came to the very spot where the grey wolf had set upon Ivan's horse and eaten it. Then it was the grey wolf's turn to sigh a deep sigh. "Well, Ivan, here I took a horse from you and here I now return you with another horse – and a beautiful bride and a firebird, too! You no longer need me and I must go!" And the wolf loped off into the woods and was gone.

Ivan and Tasha went on their way in sadness, weeping for their lost friend. When they were very nearly back home at Tsar Andronovich's house, they stopped to rest and sank into an exhausted sleep. Even the firebird was so soundly asleep that she didn't notice two figures come creeping out of the shadows. It was Dimitri and Vassily, who had returned from their travels empty handed and were enraged to find their little brother not only with the firebird but also with Tasha the Beautiful! In their bitterness, the brothers drew their swords and stabbed Ivan where he lay dreaming. Then they swept up Tasha the Beautiful and the firebird and were off to their father's mansion, to pretend that the treasures were theirs. "Breathe a word of this and we'll kill you," they hissed into Tasha's ear, and Tasha shook with sorrow and fear . . .

Ivan's body lay lifeless and cold as snow started to cover him like a thick blanket. A few bold birds and woodland creatures began to creep closer to find out what type of thing would lie so silent and still in the freezing weather – and among them came a grey wolf with yellow eyes and drooling jaws. He stalked right up to Ivan's body and sniffed all round. Then he sat in the snow, threw his head back and howled a spine-chilling howl. Slowly and gently the wolf began to lick the wound in Ivan's chest. And suddenly, Ivan sat up and began to shiver. "What am I doing asleep in this snowstorm?" he asked the grey wolf.

"Ride on me, the grey wolf," came the gruff voice, "and I will take you where you want to go."

"Home," whispered Ivan into his friend's ear, "I want to go home." And no sooner had he finished saying the words than they were there.

Of course, when Tsar Andronovich learnt the truth, he threw the wicked Dimitri and Vassily in a dungeon, where they belonged. Ivan and Tasha the Beautiful were married – Ivan rode his faithful grey wolf to the wedding ceremony and Tasha arrived on the horse with the golden mane. As for Tsar Andronovich, well he got his precious firebird after all – and he loved her so much he even let her eat the golden apples from his favourite tree whenever she wanted.

The Red Shoes

retold from the original tale by Hans Christian Andersen

here was once a woman who was so poor that she couldn't afford to buy her daughter, Karen, any shoes. The woman often wept to see Karen's feet all rough and blistered. She would have been overjoyed to know that the shoemaker's wife felt so sorry for Karen that she was making her a pair of red shoes from some of her husband's left-over leather. But the woman never found out. She died the very day that the red shoes were finished and Karen wore them for the first time as she walked behind her mother's coffin on the way to church.

The shoemaker's wife couldn't sew very well and the shoes had turned out to be rather clumsy and misshapen. But Karen thought that her soft, red shoes were the most wonderful things in all the world. However, the old lady who kindly took Karen in said, "You can't possibly go walking around in those odd things. Whatever will people think?" She threw the red shoes onto the fire and bought Karen a pair of sensible, sturdy black ones.

It was the sensible, sturdy black shoes that Karen was wearing when the old lady took her to the palace to see the parade for the little princess's birthday. The king and queen stood with the little princess on the balcony, waving and smiling. But Karen didn't look at the gracious expressions on their faces, or their fine rich robes. Karen couldn't take her eyes off the red shoes on the little princess's feet. They were magnificent – made out of satin instead of leather, so they actually shone like rubies. *Those really are the most wonderful things in all the world*, thought Karen.

From that moment, whenever Karen buckled on her sensible, black shoes, she thought of the little princess's beautiful red ones. Whenever Karen took off her sensible black shoes, she thought of the princess's beautiful red ones. And she longed for those beautiful red shoes with all her heart.

One day, the old lady who looked after Karen looked at her sensible, black shoes and tutted, "My, my! Those are looking rather old and shabby – and they're too small for you now. We can't have you going along to church in those tomorrow." The old lady handed her a purse full of money. "Buy yourself some new ones," she smiled.

Karen walked all the way to the shoe shop with a thumping heart. First, she tried on some sensible, sturdy black shoes – but there were none to fit her. Then she tried on some smart, lace-up brown shoes – but they still either slopped up and down or cramped her toes. Then Karen peered up at a high shelf and saw a red pair exactly like the ones the little princess had worn. They fitted her perfectly. Karen held her breath as she handed over her money and stepped out of the shop. Her feet gleamed and twinkled in the sunlight. She could hardly believe it. Her dream had come true.

Karen knew full well that the old lady wouldn't approve at all of her choice. But luckily for her, the old lady's eyesight wasn't what it was, and the colour of Karen's new shoes was just a dark blur. Karen kept quiet, saying nothing of the truth.

Next day, Karen's heart nearly burst with excitement as she slipped on her red shoes. She tripped gaily all the way to church, and even though it was a beautiful day and there were many finely dressed people about, she had eyes for no one and nothing except the red shoes. She twisted and turned as she walked, so her toes and heels shone in turn. She hoped that everyone would see them.

Even when Karen was sitting in her church pew, she couldn't take her eyes off her red shoes. Even when the priest was praying, she couldn't take her eyes off her red shoes. Even when the organist began to strike up a joyful hymn of praise, she couldn't take her eyes off the red shoes. The statues of the angels and saints seemed to frown down sternly upon her, but Karen didn't notice. She still couldn't take her eyes off the red shoes.

As the choir started to sing out and their voices filled the air, Karen felt a strange sensation in her feet. Her toes began to twitch inside the red satin. Her heels began to quiver to and fro. Suddenly, Karen's feet began to dance. Right there and then in church, Karen's red shoes forced her to stand up and leap and turn and skip. With the eyes of the whole congregation staring at her, Karen's red shoes danced her down the aisle and out into the sunlight. "Help me!" she cried, but no one knew what to do. The red shoes danced Karen all around the graveyard and out of the church gate. Then they danced her round and round the churchyard wall and off down the street . . .

By day and by night, the enchanted red shoes carried Karen along, twinkling wickedly. They danced her in and out of houses and up and down stairs. They danced her right through the city gates across the fields and into the dark forest. They danced her out of the trees and through meadows, until Karen had quite forgotten how long she had been dancing . . . and

still they made Karen dance. "Forgive me!" the sobbing girl cried out. "Forgive me for thinking of these foolish pretty things above everything else!" At last, the red shoes were still. Utterly exhausted, Karen collapsed into a heap and closed her eyes. And when her soul reached heaven, she never had to dance or think about red shoes ever again.

The Magic Tinderbox

retold from the original tale by Hans Christian Andersen

A soldier came marching down the road – left, right! left, right! left, right!

"Good morning, sir," croaked an ugly witch sitting at the roadside. "If you do as I say, I will make you very rich. You see that huge tree there –" the witch pointed over to an old oak – "it is quite hollow." You must climb to the top, wriggle through a hole and then lower yourself down the inside of the trunk all the way to the bottom. You will see three doors. Open the first one and you will find yourself inside a room where a frightening dog sits on a box full of money. Spread my blue-and-white checked apron on the floor, put the dog onto it, and he won't bother you at all. Then you can open the box and take out as much money as you can carry. In this first room, the money will be copper. If you'd rather have silver, you must face the even scarier dog in the second room. If you'd prefer gold, you must go into the third room – but there the dog is yet more terrifying."

"What do you want for yourself?" the soldier grinned.

"I don't want a single coin of the money," the witch cackled. "Just bring me a rusty old tinderbox that my granny forgot last time she was in there."

"Very well," agreed the soldier, and the witch gave him her apron. Then the soldier shimmied up the outside of the old oak tree, wriggled through the hole, and lowered himself down . . . down . . . down the inside. He found himself in a long corridor lit by one hundred burning lanterns, and sure enough, there were three doors in front of him. The soldier bravely put his hand on the first doorknob and turned it.

"Great Scott!" he cried, springing back in alarm. There in the middle of the room was a dog with eyes the size of teacups. The soldier tore his eyes away from its staring gaze, lay the witch's apron on the floor and lifted the dog on to it. Then he unlocked the box the dog had been sitting on. Amazing! It was filled to the brim with shining copper coins. The soldier gleefully grabbed huge handfuls and stuffed them into his knapsack, his pockets and even his boots.

The second dog couldn't possibly have eyes bigger than that first one, the soldier thought to himself. Boldly, he walked to the second doorknob and turned it . . .

"Good lord!" he yelled. There in the middle of the room was a dog with eyes the size of mill-wheels. Round and round and round they churned – it made you dizzy just to look at them. Once again, the soldier forced himself to look away. He laid the witch's apron down, heaved the dog onto it, and unlocked the box on which it had been sitting. Fantastic! There before him was a treasure trove of silver! The soldier got rid of all the copper coins quick as quick and filled his knapsack, pockets and boots.

"Surely the third dog's eyes can't be any bigger than that!" the soldier said to himself, laughing at his good luck. He went to the third doorknob and turned it . . .

"Heavens above!" he cried. The third dog had eyes the size of the Round Tower of the city of Copenhagen. Not only that, but they whizzed round and round in his head like Catherine Wheels. It was several minutes before the soldier found he could look at something other than the dog's enormous spinning eyeballs. Then he laid down the witch's apron, hauled the dog onto it, and unlocked the box it had been sitting on. Unbelievable! There was enough gold to buy the palace of the King of Denmark himself! Chortling with joy, the soldier emptied his knapsack, pockets and boots of every last silver coin and crammed them with gold instead. He hurried off down the corridor, found the tinderbox, and then climbed up . . . up . . . up and out of the tree.

"Where's my tinderbox then?" the witch cackled.

"Tell me why you want it so badly and I'll give it to you," replied the soldier, firmly.

"Where IS IT?" the witch shrieked in annoyance.

"If you don't tell me why you want it, I'll cut off your head," insisted the soldier.

"GIVE ME MY TINDERBOX!" the witch howled in frustration.

"Very well," said the soldier, and he drew his sword and cut off the witch's head. Then he went on his merry way down the road, with his knapsack, pockets and boots weighed down with gold, and the witch's tinderbox tucked safely inside his jacket.

At the very next town, the soldier booked into the best hotel, ate in the most expensive restaurant, and went to the most exclusive shop to buy himself new clothes. At once the soldier found he had a lot of new friends and they told him of all the wonders to be seen in the town – particularly the beautiful princess, who lived in the castle on top of the hill.

"How can I get to see this princess?" the soldier asked.

"You can't," his new friends explained, "no one can. For it has been prophesied that she will one day marry a common soldier, and the king and queen keep the princess locked up so this can never happen."

Day after day, the soldier spent his gold on the finest things money could buy for himself and his friends. It was a horrible shock when he went one morning to fill his pockets and found that all the gold was gone. Suddenly, the soldier's friends disappeared. The soldier had to move out of the grand hotel and into a dingy attic at the top of fourteen flights of stairs. He didn't even have enough money for a candle to cheer things up with a bit of light. Then the soldier remembered the witch's tinderbox. Surely he could use that to give him a few sparks to start a warming fire? No sooner had the soldier struck the tinderbox once with the flint than there was a flash of lightning and the dog with eyes the size of teacups appeared.

"What is your command, sir?" the dog growled, bowing its head respectfully.

Once the soldier had got over the shock, he stammered, "Well, I suppose I'd really like you to get me some money."

The dog immediately vanished – but reappeared an instant later with a purse of money clamped between its jaws.

The soldier whooped and danced about with delight. Suddenly he understood the secret of the tinderbox. Strike it once, twice or three times, and the dog from the first, second or third room appeared to grant his wishes!

Soon the soldier was richer than ever. He moved back into the grand hotel, ate at the expensive restaurant once again, bought himself new suits of fine clothes, and found himself surrounded by friends once more. He had everything he could wish for – except for a wife to share it all with. *That princess must be very bored locked up there in the castle,* the soldier thought to himself.

The soldier waited till it was dark, then struck the tinderbox once. In a flash, the dog with the eyes like teacups appeared. "I would like to see the beautiful princess," the soldier said. Before he could blink, the dog ran off and then reappeared with the princess lying on its broad back, fast asleep. She was indeed very beautiful and the soldier couldn't resist bending over to give her a kiss. The dog then disappeared and the princess was gone.

Next morning, up in the castle on the hill, the princess remembered what had happened as if it had been a strange dream, and she told her mother and father all about it. The king and queen were deeply worried. The clever queen sewed a pretty silk bag, filled it with flour and tied it around her daughter's neck when she went to bed. Then the queen pierced a tiny hole in the bag, tucked the princess in and kissed her goodnight.

Of course, the soldier had fallen deeply in love with the princess and that night he sent the dog to fetch her again. Neither the dog nor the soldier noticed the thin line of flour that ran down from the silk bag and left a tell-tale trail all the way from the castle to his door. And in the morning, when the princess was safely back in her bed, the soldier was woken by royal officers breaking down his door. They grabbed him and dragged him away to be hanged.

A huge crowd of townspeople had gathered to watch the soldier die, and opposite the gallows sat the smug king and queen and all the members of the town council. Just as the hangman put the noose around the soldier's neck, the desperate man had an idea. "Will you grant me one last wish?" he yelled out to the king. "I would like to smoke a pipe of tobacco before I die."

The king thought for a moment. He didn't want to seem merciless in front of all the people, so, "Very well," he said. To the soldier's great delight, the hangman untied his hands and offered him a pipe and some matches.

"Don't worry," the soldier grinned, "I have my own light," and he pulled out his tinderbox and struck it three times.

At once, the dog with the eyes as big as teacups, the dog with the eyes as big as mill-wheels, and the dog with the eyes as big as the

Round Tower of the city of Copenhagen stood before him. "Save me," the soldier cried, "or I will surely die!" The dogs growled like rumbling thunder and sprang among the crowd, scattering them everywhere in terror. They made straight for the king and queen and the table of town councillors. One by one, the dogs picked them up in their jaws and hurled them far, far away over the most distant hills. "Hooray!" the townspeople cried. "We never liked them anyway. We'd much prefer the brave soldier to be our king and the beautiful princess to be our queen!" And that's exactly what happened. They were married straight away – and the three dogs were guests of honour at the wedding feast.

Seven at One Blow

a traditional folk tale

There was once a little tailor who was a very cheeky chap. Maybe he was a cheeky chap *because* he was little, I don't know. In any case, he was little and he was cheeky and he was a tailor – and that's the truth of it.

The little cheeky tailor was sewing one day and nibbling on a thick slice of bread and jam (it was strawberry – his favourite) when several big fat flies started buzzing round the jam pot. "Get lost!" he spluttered through a mouthful of crumbs. "Buzz off!" He flicked at the flies with his sewing, but the stubborn insects just buzzed round the jam pot more determinedly than ever. "I'll show you!" the little cheeky tailor murmured, and he jumped down from his sewing stool and fetched his broom from the corner. Very slowly (so as not to arouse the flies' suspicion), he lifted his broom high above his head and – THWACK! – brought it down swift and hard right on top of the jam pot. When the little cheeky tailor looked underneath, his chest puffed up with pride. "Well, look at that!" he crowed. "I've killed seven at one blow! What a hero I am!"

The little cheeky tailor put aside his work, found some silver material, and quickly ran himself up a wide belt. He decorated it with sparkly glass beads and embroidered it in gold thread with the words: SEVEN AT ONE BLOW. Then the little cheeky tailor buckled it around his waist and stood in front of the mirror. *"My, my!"* he breathed. "What's a splendid champion like me doing in a dingy little workroom like this? I should be out and about in public, so everyone can admire me!" With that, the little cheeky tailor left his sewing shop for the last time and set off down the road, humming merrily to himself and tipping his hat politely to all he met.

It wasn't long before everyone was gossiping about the hero who had killed seven at one blow. "Just imagine slaying seven men at one blow!" the people exclaimed.

"No, it wasn't seven men," others insisted, "it was seven trolls!" "You are wrong," yet more protested. "It wasn't seven trolls, it was seven dragons!"

Eventually, even the king got to hear of the very small, but very brave, champion and he ordered him to the palace at once.

"You see, my problem is this," the king explained, bending low so that he could see eye to eye with the little cheeky tailor. "There are two giants who keep robbing my villages and killing my subjects. If you get rid of them, I'll give you half of my kingdom."

"And . . ." said the little cheeky tailor (because he was very cheeky like that).

"And what?" said the king, very puzzled.

"And your daughter's hand in marriage," chuckled the little cheeky tailor. "It's only usual in cases like this."

"Oh very well," grumbled the king, "I'll throw in my daughter's hand in marriage, too."

"Very well," chirped the little cheeky tailor. "Two giants mean nothing to me. Don't forget that I have killed seven at one blow." And with a wink he strode off, his belt sparkling in the sunlight.

When the little cheeky tailor found the giants, they were both asleep under a huge, shady oak tree. The little cheeky tailor patted his belt comfortingly, picked up two large, round pebbles, and tucked them into his shirt. Then he tried to creep up to the tree. He had problems getting close, because each time he walked forward, the giants' enormous snores blew him back. Finally, he made a mad run for it and – looking a little windswept – reached the trunk. He climbed nimbly into the branches and chuckled to himself. Then – PLOP! – he threw one of the stones down at the first sleeping giant and hit him smack on the nose.

"OY!" roared the giant, waking up at once and turning on his brother. "What did you do that for, dungbreath?"

"Do what?" mumbled the second dozing giant.

"You know!" bellowed the first giant. "Just don't do it again!" And he settled back to sleep.

High up in the tree, the little cheeky tailor giggled and dropped his other stone. PLOP! Again, it hit the first giant's conk.

"OY!" he boomed, sitting bolt upright and glaring at his brother. "I told you not to do that, thunderpants!" And he socked the second giant right in the mush.

"What on earth did you do that for, mouldybeard?" the wounded giant roared, and he punched his brother in the mouth.

That was the start of a giant fight that raged so hard and long the people in the nearby village thought there was an earthquake. The little cheeky tailor was very nearly shaken out of the oak tree, but at the end of it, the giants both lay dead beneath him and he had nothing worse than a bruised bottom.

And that is how a little tailor came to win half a kingdom and marry a princess all through being a very cheeky chap. Maybe he was a cheeky chap *because* he was little, I don't know. In any case, he was little and he was cheeky and he was a tailor – and that's the truth.

Ali Baba and the Forty Thieves

a tale from The Arabian Nights

Listen, O my beloved, and I will tell you the tale of a man called Ali Baba. Ali Baba worked as a woodcutter and was as poor and generous as his merchant brother, Kasim, was rich and mean. But the time came when Allah (may His name be praised forever!) smiled on Ali Baba and changed his fortunes forever.

Late one afternoon, the woodcutter was leading his pack mules down a rocky valley when he saw a cloud of dust in the distance, approaching fast. Ali Baba hurried to hide himself and his mules among the cliffs, where he could peep out unseen from behind a boulder. It wasn't long before forty horses carrying forty bandits came thundering into the valley, led by an ugly robber chief on a jet-black stallion. Ali Baba's legs turned to jelly as the vicious-looking thugs slid off their wild-eyed horses and walked straight towards the rock face. The robber chief suddenly cried, "Open sesame!" and to the woodcutter's utter amazement, the rock split in two with a groan, leaving an opening in the cliff. The robber chief and his men strode straight inside and the rocks clashed together behind them. Ali Baba was left in the silence of the valley, listening to the whinnying of the horses and the pounding of his own heart.

After what seemed like ages (although Ali Baba knew it must only be a few minutes), the men reappeared, each carrying a heavy saddlebag. "Yalla!" cried the robber chief, and he and his bandits jumped onto their stamping steeds and raced away, leaving a whirlwind of dust behind them.

"May Allah be merciful!" gasped Ali Baba, and he scrambled down the cliff face as fast as his short legs would carry him. "Open sesame!" he cried, as loud as he could manage. The cliff face split asunder and revealed the entrance to a huge cavern filled with treasure from years of bandit raiding. Jewelled swords and golden plates and silver lanterns hung from the walls. Earrings and necklaces and bracelets spilled out from huge chests. Rolls of expensive silks were stacked up next to jars containing precious spices. And gold coins spilled onto the cavern floor from thousands of overflowing sacks.

Ali Baba stood open-mouthed for just a few seconds. Then he sprang into the cave and the rocks smashed shut behind him. Working quickly, Ali Baba filled his pockets and some empty sacks with coins and other treasures. "Open sesame!" he cried again, and to his great relief the entrance reappeared. He hauled his booty outside and loaded up his mules while the rocks slid seamlessly together. Ali

Baba hurried home under cover of darkness, murmuring prayers of gratitude all the way.

Being a good, generous man, the first thing Ali Baba did after telling his wife about his good fortune was to tell his brother and offer to share half of his treasure with him. But being a jealous, greedy man, this wasn't enough for Kasim. He insisted that Ali Baba describe to him exactly where to find the magical cliff and exactly how to open the entrance.

At first light the very next day, Kasim rode out to find the bandits' cavern for himself. He arrived at the rock face, cried "Open sesame!" and ran delightedly into the treasure cave. But when he had filled all his bags to bursting and it was time to go, Kasim began to panic. "Open barley!" he cried – nothing happened. "Open wheat!" – again, nothing. Kasim knew that the magic word was some type of cereal, but he couldn't for the life of him remember which. "Open oats!" he tried, and "Open maize!" –

but not even as much as a fine crack appeared in the rock. As Kasim
sat dejectedly on the cavern floor he felt the ground underneath him
tremble. A few seconds later, the cliff in front of him opened with a
crack of thunder. The robber chief and his bandits had returned . . .

As you can imagine, O my beloved, Kasim did not return home
that night . . . nor the next . . . nor the next. And when Ali Baba went
searching in the valley for his brother, he found Kasim's body
displayed inside the robbers' cave in four bits. Now, as everyone
knows, all good people like to be buried in one piece. So the grieving
Ali Baba took home Kasim's remains and paid a tailor to come
blindfolded to his house and sew the pieces of his brother back
together without asking any awkward questions.

Of course, as soon as the bandits returned to their treasure cave
and found the pieces of their victim missing, they realised that
someone else knew the whereabouts of their lair and the all-
important magic password. "We will search every street in Arabia
until we find this intruding dog!" the robber chief roared, and the
bandits galloped off at once.

It was the robber chief himself who made the all-important
discovery. Lurking in the marketplace just before dawn, he
stopped and admired the nimble work of a tailor

who was already at his stall and sewing in the half-light.

"This is nothing!" laughed the tailor. "Last week I had to sew a man's dead body together with my eyes covered!"

At that, the robber chief grabbed the tailor by the scruff of the neck and lifted him into the air with one hand. "Show me where you did this, or I'll personally turn you into a human pin-cushion," the robber chief growled.

"Whatever you say," gasped the tailor, "but I was blindfolded, so I'll have to try to remember the way with my eyes shut."

The tailor screwed his eyes up tight and groped his way through the streets all the way to Ali Baba's front door.

"Are you sure this is the one?" spat the robber chief.

"May the fleas of a thousand camels infest my armpits if I am wrong," gulped the tailor.

So the robber chief marked Ali Baba's door with a tiny red cross and disappeared into the morning hustle and bustle.

That night, a merchant with a train of mules carrying forty huge jars of oil came knocking at Ali Baba's door, asking for shelter for the night. Little did Ali Baba know that the merchant was really the robber chief in disguise. And never could he have guessed that only one of the jars actually contained oil. Hidden inside the other thirty-nine jars were the remaining thirty-nine bandits, waiting to jump out whenever the robber chief gave the word and slay everyone in Ali Baba's household!

Ever-generous, Ali Baba welcomed the merchant into his house and told his servants to set the oil jars down in his courtyard. Soon the robber chief found himself sitting at his sworn-enemy's table, being served a delicious feast.

While Ali Baba entertained his guest, his slave girl, Maryam, ran back and forth in the kitchen preparing dish after dish of tasty food. Half-way through the cooking she realised with a shock that she had

run out of oil – then heaved a sigh of relief as she remembered all the jars of oil out in the yard. *Surely my master's guest won't mind if I take a little of his oil in return for our hospitality,* Maryam thought to herself.

As soon as Maryam's footsteps padded close to the first jar, she was shocked to hear a voice hissing at her from within: "Is it time yet?" Now Maryam was a clever girl, and she realised at once that the merchant and his oil jars could not possibly be what they seemed. "No, not yet," Maryam replied into the air hole in the lid, in as deep a voice as she could manage, and she passed onto the next jar. Again the same thing happened . . . and again as she approached the third jar – and every time until she reached the fortieth jar. Then she realised who the oil merchant really was and what exactly was inside his thirty-nine jars of oil!

Quickly and quietly, the brave girl dragged the fortieth jar into the kitchen and poured the oil into a huge kettle that hung over the fire. As soon as the oil was smoking and boiling away, Maryam filled a large pitcher and poured the burning liquid into the air holes of all thirty-nine jars. "Ha!" she said, as the last of the boiling oil trickled away. "That's the end of you lot!"

Next Maryam hurried to her chamber and dressed in her dancing costume. How beautiful she looked, wrapped in her coloured scarves and tinkling with golden chains and sequins! And how she delighted Ali Baba and his guest when she made her entrance, elegantly twirling to the music. The so-called oil merchant grinned a toothy smile and beckoned for Maryam to come closer . . . and closer . . . He was still smiling when Maryam floated right up beside him, swiftly pulled a silver dagger out from under her costume and stabbed it down hard through his heart.

Ali Baba jumped to his feet and tore at his hair in shock. "Look what you've done!" he howled. "You've killed our guest! Surely you will bring down the wrath of Allah upon us!" But Maryam whipped off the oil merchant's false beard and eyebrows, and stripped him of his turban and his robes – and there lay the robber chief, cold and still.

"But – how –" spluttered Ali Baba, and Maryam grabbed him by the hand, led him out into the courtyard and uncovered the dead thirty-nine robbers in the oil jars.

Ali Baba was so grateful that he gave Maryam her freedom at once. She married his son and became a proper member of the family. With the forty thieves out of the way, Ali Baba was the only person in the whole world who knew the whereabouts of the bandits' treasure cave and the magic words, "Open sesame". He and his family shared a lot of their riches among the poor, as Allah in heaven wants us all to do. But there was more than enough left over for Ali Baba and his family to live in happiness and wealth for the rest of their lives.

The Little Matchgirl

retold from the original tale by Hans Christian Andersen

It was New Year's Eve and bitterly cold. Snow and ice lined the streets like an untrodden white carpet, for all the people were indoors, happily preparing to bring in the New Year. All alone in the windy square by the fountain, the poor girl who sold matches shivered. She pulled her ragged shawl a little closer around her thin cotton dress. She rubbed her hands together and blew on her fingers and stamped her feet, but freezing wet snow came swamping through the holes in her boots.

The little matchgirl hadn't sold one box of matches all day and she was too frightened to go home, for her father would be extremely angry. "Someone will surely pass this way and buy in a minute," she told herself. But how cold she was, how cold! "If only I could light one of my matches," she murmured, "that would warm me a little." With fingers stiff with cold, the little matchgirl falteringly took out one of her matches and struck it.

The tiny wooden splinter blazed into a bright little flame and the little matchgirl cupped her hands over it, craving its spark of warmth and light. As she stared into the orange centre of the flame, she saw herself standing in front of a roaring stove, giving out heat that warmed her from the tips of her toes to the top of her head. Suddenly, the match's flame went out and the vision died with it. The little matchgirl somehow felt even colder than before.

The little matchgirl didn't dare light another match for a long time. Then "Just one more," she whispered, through her chattering teeth. Shaking, the little matchgirl drew out another of her precious wares and struck it on the wall. The glimmer from the little matchstick seemed to light up the stone until it was clear and glassy, like a crystal window. Through the window, the little matchgirl could see a room with a welcoming fire and bright candles and a table laden with delicious things to eat, and she held out her hands towards it. It seemed as if she was going to be able to reach right through the glass and into the wonderful room – then the match died out. The magical room vanished, and huge tears filled the little matchgirl's eyes.

Her poor numb hands fumbled to light another, and her pale face lit up with wonder in the glow of the third flame. Suddenly a magnificent Christmas tree sparkled before the little matchgirl in the light. It shimmered with glassy balls of many colours and glittered with tinsel, and tiny dots of candlelight danced all over its thick green needles. "How beautiful!" breathed the little matchgirl, her eyes big and round. Then the match scorched her fingers and she dropped it, black and twisted, into the snow. The Christmas tree was gone, but the glimmering lights from its candles were still there, rising up and up into the night sky until they mingled with the twinkling stars. Suddenly, one of the lights fell through the darkness, leaving a blazing trail of silver behind it. "That means someone is dying," the little matchgirl murmured, remembering what her Granny used to say whenever they saw shooting stars.

As the little matchgirl stood dreaming of her beloved, dead grandmother, she unthinkingly lit up another match – and there was her granny before her in the light of the flame. "Granny, don't go!" sobbed the little matchgirl, as she lit one match after another, so the vision wouldn't fade like all the others. "Let me stay with you!" she begged, and the old lady smiled and held out her arms for the little matchgirl to run into, just as she always had done.

It was midnight, and all over the city the church bells pealed out to welcome in the New Year. Revellers poured out of the inns and houses to dance and sing and shake hands with strangers and wish each other well. There, lying in the snow by the fountain, was a little girl's thin, lifeless body, surrounded by spent matches. For the little matchgirl had left it there when she had gone away with her grandmother. She had no need of it in the place where they were going: a place without cold, nor hunger, nor pain – just happiness.

St Christopher

a European legend

Once there was a man called Christopher, who saw God all around him in the world and loved the Lord very much. As Christopher pulled endless weeds out of his vegetable patch he would pray, "Thank you, God, for sending the sunshine to make crops grow." As Christopher hammered away at his leaky roof on stormy nights he would pray, "Thank you, God, for sending the rain to water the land and fill the rivers and seas."

Christopher felt that because God did so much for him, he wanted to spend his life doing things for God in return. He knew that holy men like monks worked for God by spending their lives shut away in monasteries, praying. But Christopher didn't think that would suit him at all. He was very tall and very strong, and was much better at *doing* things than keeping still and silent.

Christopher's little wooden house lay by a wide, churning river, and it was while he was watching the raging waters one day that he had an idea. There was no bridge across the river and no ferryman either. But Christopher was sure that he could wade through the river carrying the travellers on his shoulders. Christopher knew that each

trip would be ice-cold, exhausting and dangerous, but he was
determined to work for God by helping other people.

   And that's exactly what he did. No
matter what time of day or night
travellers arrived at his hut,
Christopher stopped whatever
he was doing, stripped off his
shirt, and plunged into the
freezing river. Time and time
again Christopher carried
men, women and children
across to the other side – and
often back again, too – and never
took a single penny from anyone for
his efforts.

   One day, a little boy knocked on Christopher's door, all on his
own. "Will you carry me across, mister?" he asked.

   "No trouble at all," smiled Christopher. He caught the child up
in his big, safe hands and tossed him high into the air a few times
until he was chuckling with delight. Then Christopher swung the
little boy onto his shoulders and strode out into the water, bellowing
a rousing song to drown out the scary rushing of the river.

   Christopher was only waist-deep when he realised he was in
trouble. Somehow, the little boy had suddenly become heavier than
three fully grown men put together. And with every step deeper into
the swirling water, the child weighed more and more – heavier than
an ox . . . heavier than a load of bricks . . . heavier than his entire
house! Christopher sank into the riverbed under the immense burden,
and the waters came rushing around his chin. Still Christopher strode

on, but the waters came crashing over his face, filling his nose and mouth with liquid instead of air. Still he pressed forwards – even when the river rose above his eyes. His one desperate thought was to keep the child above water and get him safely to the far bank. Just when Christopher thought his lungs were about to explode and he would surely drown them both, he felt the steep uphill slope underfoot that led to the opposite bank. Christopher ploughed out of the river with his last drop of energy, lowered the little boy to the ground, and collapsed on all-fours in the sunshine.

"Thank you," came the child's soft voice, "for carrying God's son for a while and taking the weight of all the sins of the world onto your own shoulders."

Christopher's heart leapt for joy as he realised at last that the mysterious little boy was Jesus Christ himself. Gasping, he looked up – but the child had already vanished . . .

Many people today pray to St Christopher to look after them and help them when they are going on a journey. And now you know why he is always pictured wading through a river with a little boy on his shoulders.

Thumbelina

retold from the original tale by Hans Christian Andersen

 nce upon a time there was a woman who wanted more than anything in the world to have a child – but she didn't know where to get one. She went to see a witch about it and the witch gave her a special seed. The woman planted the seed in a flowerpot and it grew . . . and grew . . . and grew . . . into a bud that looked very much like the bud of a tulip. "What a beautiful flower!" the woman murmured one day, and she leant over and kissed the closed petals. POP! The bud exploded into an open flower, and there sitting in the middle of it was a tiny little girl, no bigger than the woman's thumb. The woman was overjoyed with her beautiful daughter and named her Thumbelina. The woman

 thought that her tiny daughter was utterly delightful and looked after her tenderly. But one night, a big, fat toad came hopping through a broken pane of glass in the woman's window. *Hmmm*, thought the toad, as her bulging eyes caught sight of Thumbelina sleeping in half a walnut shell. *She would make a perfect wife for my son*. The toad picked up the dreaming little girl, bed and all, and hopped away to the marshy river where she lived. The toad swam out to where the water ran fast and deep and placed Thumbelina in her walnut shell on a broad, flat lilypad. *Now you can't run away*, the toad thought, and she swam off to break the good news to her son . . .

When Thumbelina woke up and saw that she was not only lost, but trapped too, she began to cry bitterly. The fish wiggled up to see what was causing all the tiny splashes and ripples, and they took pity on the sad, tiny girl. Quickly and silently, they nibbled through the lilypad's green stem and Thumbelina went floating off down the river.

Soon, she was far out of the toads' reach . . . and still the lilypad raft floated on. Thumbelina sailed past towns and was swept out into the countryside. Thumbelina liked it among the fields. It was sunny and peaceful, and a pretty white butterfly fluttered down to keep her company. Suddenly a large flying beetle dive-bombed the lilypad and wrapped his legs around Thumbelina's tiny waist. In a flash, Thumbelina found herself sitting on a twig with the beetle high up in a tree, watching her lilypad drift away without her.

Hundreds of the beetle's curious friends came crawling out of the bark to peer at what he had brought home. "Urgh! Look, it's only got two legs," the beetle children squealed.

"Where are its feelers?" some of the lady beetles murmured.

"Hasn't it got a slim bottom?" other lady beetles gasped in horror, admiring their own round shiny ones.

"It is rather ugly," the male beetles had to admit. "Let's get rid of it." And they flew down from the tree with Thumbelina and sat her on a daisy.

Poor Thumbelina felt very much like crying. But just then she noticed a little hole in the earth below her that looked very like it was a type of doorway. She jumped down from the daisy and peered into the gloom. "Hello!" she cried. "Is anyone at home?"

After a few seconds, out popped a fieldmouse's head. She looked Thumbelina up and down, and tutted loudly. "Dear, dear!" the fieldmouse scolded. "You look exhausted and hungry. If you're as lost as you look, you're very welcome to stay here with me – in return for keeping my rooms nice and clean and tidy."

So all winter Thumbelina lived with the fieldmouse. Every day, she washed and swept and scoured and polished, and the fieldmouse was very kind to her. Although, truth to tell, Thumbelina found life rather boring. The fieldmouse wasn't at all skilled at making entertaining conversation and neither was her regular visitor, Mr Mole. Mr Mole came once every week in his fine black velvet overcoat. He didn't like to talk. He just enjoyed sitting and peering at Thumbelina through his little, short-sighted eyes, and listening to her sing.

The fieldmouse was delighted that her friend so liked Thumbelina. "I think he's falling in love with you," she whispered to Thumbelina excitedly. The fieldmouse was even more sure that she was right when Mr Mole invited them both to visit him in his splendid underground mansion.

"I have dug a tunnel from your house to mine," Mr Mole informed them, "so you may come and see me in comfort. Only please close your eyes when you are halfway down the passage, for I am afraid that a dead swallow is lying there."

Thumbelina wasn't at all revolted when she came across the dead bird on her first trip to Mr Mole's house. Instead, she felt pity for the poor thing, lying all stiff and still on the cold earth. While the fieldmouse ran on eagerly ahead, Thumbelina bent down and stroked the bird's feathers. "Goodbye, sweet swallow," she murmured, and she laid her head on the bird's soft breast. DUP! DUP! DUP! Thumbelina heard the swallow's heart beating – only very faintly, but Thumbelina knew that the bird was still just alive!

From then on, Thumbelina found as many excuses as possible to creep away from the fieldmouse and into the tunnel to care for the swallow. Over the weeks that followed, she placed leaves under the bird's head and plaited a coverlet of hay to keep it warm. She dripped drops of water into its weak throat and fed it tiny morsels of food – and gradually the swallow began to recover. By the time the weather had begun to grow warmer, the swallow was well enough to stand and hop about. On the first day of spring, the swallow was totally better – and extremely grateful for all Thumbelina's kindness. "One day, I will repay you," he twittered as he hopped up the passageway and soared off into the blue sky.

It was then that the fieldmouse announced to Thumbelina that she had arranged for her to be married to Mr Mole. "He is very wealthy and will take good care of you," the fieldmouse beamed.

But Thumbelina was horrified. "I cannot live my life underground!" she cried, and ran sobbing out into the fields. She held her hands up to the sunshine and looked all around at the flowers, and she felt as if her heart would break.

Just then, Thumbelina heard a familiar twittering above her head. She looked up and saw her friend the swallow swooping down towards her. "Come away with me," cried the swallow, "I know a place where you will be happy. I have seen it on my travels." Joyfully, Thumbelina jumped onto his soft, feathery back.

The swallow flew off with Thumbelina over villages and roads, lakes and forests, snow-capped mountains, to a land where the weather was always sunny, where the breeze was always warm, and where in every flower there lived a tiny person just like Thumbelina. Thumbelina was very happy in her new home. She even married a handsome prince who lived in a rosebud and who was extremely glad that she had never become Mrs Mole! Best of all, the swallow came to visit every year in September, and stayed with Thumbelina and her prince each winter long.

Babushka

a Russian folk tale

There was great excitement in the village where Babushka lived. All the old lady's neighbours were out of doors, peering up at the wintry night sky, where the biggest star anyone had ever seen was shining down at them. "Where has it come from?" everyone gasped in astonishment. "What does it mean?"

Only Babushka stayed indoors, getting on with her housework as usual. "What a lot of fuss about a star!" she muttered to herself as she swept and dusted, scrubbed and mopped, polished and tidied. "I haven't got time to waste, I've got standards to keep up." Babushka's house was always spotless and in perfect order.

RAT-TAT-TAT! came a loud knocking at the door.

"Now who's that interrupting my work?" Babushka frowned. She hurried to the door, plumping up the cushions and tidying a vase of flowers on the way. To her astonishment, three foreign-looking men were standing on the doormat, wrapped in long, embroidered robes and swathed in turbans. Even more surprisingly, the camels they had been riding were tied to the gatepost and were snorting puffs of steam into the crisp, cold air.

"Good evening, Babushka," the first man greeted her. He held out his hand and it jingled with bangles of gold, while jewelled rings sparkled on his fingers. "We are travelling from a far distant country, and we need a place to rest for the night. Would you be kind enough to welcome us in?"

Babushka could clearly see that the men were rich and important. "Of course . . . I would be honoured," she spluttered red-faced, and she welcomed her guests into her little sitting room while she quickly untied her apron and smoothed down her hair.

"What brings you to these parts?" Babushka asked politely, as she bustled about lighting a fire.

"We are following the strange star that shines so brilliantly," the second man explained.

"Really?" smiled Babushka, as she went to bring three plates of bread and cheese and pickles from the kitchen.

"We believe that it will lead us to a new king – the king of all heaven and earth," continued the third man.

"Well, fancy that!" remarked Babushka, scurrying to fetch three steaming mugs of hot chocolate.

"Why don't you come with us, Babushka?" the first man urged. "We will be leaving tomorrow with our gifts of gold, frankincense and myrrh."

"Thank you, but I can't possibly come with you," said Babushka. "If I were to go away, who would air the beds and sweep the stairs and dust the shelves and scour the sink? Besides, I don't have anything that would be suitable as a gift for a king!"

"This king is newborn," the second man said kindly. "He is still only a tiny baby."

Babushka paused with a tray full of washing-up. "I had a baby boy once," she said in a whisper, "but he died."

The third man rose to his feet and put his hand gently on Babushka's arm. "Come with us," he said, softly. "Come with us to see the baby saviour of the world."

Babushka stood and thought for a while. Her eyes had a faraway look in them and there was a sad smile on her lips. "Maybe just this once . . ." she murmured to herself. Suddenly – CUCKOO! CUCKOO! CUCKOO! – the clock in the hall noisily broke the silence. "Oh dear, is that the time?" cried Babushka, springing back into action. "I must go and make up the guest beds!" and she sprang off up the stairs.

Next evening, the star shone brighter and higher in the sky than ever. "Are you sure you won't come with us, Babushka?" the three men pleaded as they mounted their camels ready to go.

"I'd love to, but I've got too much to do," the old lady blustered.

The three men waved sadly as they lurched away.

Babushka's heart was strangely heavy as she shut the door and went back inside her little cottage. She left her broom standing in the corner, the washing-up in the sink and the crumbs under the table, and she went and unlocked a cupboard in the corner of the sitting-room instead. Babushka sighed a deep sigh as she gazed at the shelves in front of her. They were stacked with toys of every size and colour. Babushka ran her fingers lovingly over them, wiping off a layer of dust. "My little son's toys would make a perfect present for the new baby king," she murmured.

It took Babushka all night to wash and dry and polish all the toys, until every single one was as good as new. As the sun came creeping through her window, she packed the toys in her shopping bag, put on her overcoat and headscarf, opened her cottage door and locked it behind her. Then she was off down the path.

Babushka walked and walked and walked – through villages and towns and cities. She lost all track of time, but she noticed one night that the star faded from the sky. A few days later, she came to the little town of Bethlehem. "Have you seen three men on camels, looking for a baby?" Babushka asked a local innkeeper.

"Why, yes," replied the innkeeper. "The three men were here all right. In fact, the baby was born in that very stable over there." He pointed to a dingy hut at the back of his inn. "The three men didn't stay long – just as well, really, because just after they'd gone, a group of shepherds came to see the baby too." The innkeeper laughed. "It would have been a bit crowded with everyone there at once! But I'm afraid you're a bit too late. After all the visitors had gone, the parents left with their baby last week."

Babushka looked from the empty stable to her full bag of toys. "I will go on searching until I find the baby," she decided. "I will give him my presents and ask him if he will be my king too." Then she turned on her heel and strode away determinedly . . .

Babushka is still wandering over the world today, looking for the baby king. No one notices her as she goes quietly from house to house, but whenever she sees a good girl or boy, she dips into her shopping bag and places a toy by their bed. It is only on one day every year that the children find Babushka's gifts – and that is Christmas Day, the birthday of Jesus, the baby in the stable.

Rip Van Winkle

an American legend

n a village in the foothills of the Catskill Mountains of America lived a man called Rip Van Winkle.

Everybody liked Rip. He was a generous, easy-going man who was always glad to lend a hand to his neighbours. In fact, Rip Van Winkle was always to be found doing anybody else's work except his own. And didn't his wife remind him about it all the time! Nag, nag, nag it was, all day long. "Rip, if you're not too busy varnishing Mrs Green's fence today, you can mend the holes in the shed. Instead of helping to burn the farmer's rubbish, you can feed the chickens and milk the cows. Then if you can stop yourself from building Arne Jacob's wall for him, there's our potatoes to dig up and the wagon to be washed down and the gutters to be cleared out and the yard to be swept and . . ." And so it was every day, on and on and on and on.

Every now and again, Rip Van Winkle whistled for his faithful dog Wolf, shouldered his gun, and strode away from his wife without a word. Off he would stroll up the mountainside, along the river and through the pine forests until his wife's screeching voice had

grown so faint that he could no longer hear it, and he was
surrounded only by the twittering of the birds, the rustling of the
trees in the breeze and the panting of his companion by his side. Rip
always knew there would be heck to pay when he got home. But a
day off in the peaceful sunshine was well worth it!

One day when Rip had disappeared on one of these rambles,
he was taking a rest under a shady tree, when he heard a voice calling
his name. "Rip Van Winkle! Rip Van Winkle! Rip Van Winkle!" came
the high, shrill cry.

Wolf's ears flattened against his skull and he gave a long, low
growl. Rip looked in the direction Wolf was snarling and there among
the long grass was a nodding green feather. The nodding green
feather was tucked into a bright red cap. The cap was on the head of
a bearded man no higher than his own boot, struggling under the
weight of a big beer barrel.

"Rip Van Winkle! Rip Van Winkle! Rip Van Winkle!" shouted
the dwarf, crossly. "Will you get yourself over here and give me a
hand with this barrel before it squashes me!"

Rip was so used to doing what he was told that he jumped up to help at once.

"That's better," wheezed the dwarf, as Rip took one end of the heavy barrel. "Now up we go!" Rip nearly tripped over as the dwarf stomped away up the mountain, pulling the barrel and Rip Van Winkle with him.

After at least an hour's tramping and much huffing and puffing, the dwarf led Rip Van Winkle straight behind a thundering waterfall, through a hidden door and into an enormous cavern.

Dwarfs were swarming everywhere. Some were dressed in aprons, pouring endless tankards of beer out of big kegs just like the one Rip was helping to carry. Others were playing nine pins, rolling smooth round black rocks at copper skittles and cheering loudly. Yet more dwarfs were drinking and clinking their tankards together, singing noisy songs.

"Pull up a chair," Rip's new friend invited him, lowering the barrel to the floor and passing him a tankard. "Help yourself to a drink. You must be gasping thirsty after that climb – I know I am!"

The stunned Rip Van Winkle did just that. "My, that's mighty powerful stuff!" he spluttered, as he swallowed down a huge gulp of the dwarf beer. "But whatever it is, it's very good!" He licked his lips and poured himself another tankardful. None of the dwarfs was taking a blind bit of notice of him, so Rip Van Winkle sat back and began to watch the nine pins competition. "Well, this is a most pleasant way to spend the afternoon," he thought, helping himself to another beer . . . and another . . . and another . . . and another. And before Rip Van Winkle even realised he was drunk, he had slumped forwards onto a huge flat rock and was snoring loudly.

When Rip woke up, the dwarfs were gone and the cavern was empty. "Come on, Wolf," he yawned, and they both stood up and stretched. "We'd better hurry back or we'll never hear the last of it." Through the little door they strode and out from behind the waterfall and off down the mountain. "Wait for it," he murmured to his dog as he climbed the porch steps to his house. "Any minute now, that wife of mine will start screeching fit to wake the dead." Rip put his hand on the doorknob and turned. He nearly walked smack-bang into the door as it failed to open. "Well, this needs a bit of oil," he murmured to himself. He rattled the knob and twisted it about. "Funny," Rip remarked, "I think it's locked. She never locks the door, never."

At that very moment, the front door opened and there stood a woman with an angry face. "Who are you?" the woman snapped.

"What are you up to, trying to get in my front door?" She was not his wife. In fact, Rip Van Winkle had never seen her before.

"Who are you?" gasped Rip. "What are you doing in my house?"

"*Your* house!" the woman scoffed. "I've lived here for over nineteen years!"

Rip Van Winkle backed off the porch and looked around him. He scratched his head and stared. The woman was right – it *wasn't* his house. Well, it looked similar to his house, but the curtains at the window were different. There were strange chairs on the verandah. The wagon in the yard was not his wagon.

"But – I – How –" stuttered Rip. "Where's Mrs Van Winkle?"

"Mrs Van Winkle?" the puzzled woman gawped. "She left here nearly twenty years ago, just after her husband wandered off and disappeared. Now, be off with you or I'll call the police!"

"*Twenty years!*" marvelled Rip Van Winkle, as he wandered away stroking his beard. His beard! Suddenly Rip realised that his beard hung down to his knees. The woman's words had to be true! He had been asleep for twenty years!

Rip Van Winkle's hands trembled with the shock as he reached down and patted the bemused Wolf comfortingly. Then his mouth began to curve upwards in a small smile. "Just imagine, Wolf," he murmured. "No more nagging – ever!" Rip Van Winkle turned and strode across the street, whistling a merry tune. Happily, the inn was in the same place it always had been – and when the townspeople heard his story, he never had to buy himself another pint of beer again.

A Tall Story
an Indian folk tale

F ive blind men were once sitting under a shady palm tree
by the bank of the River Ganges in India, when they
sensed that someone or something had silently crept up
and joined them. "Who's there?" asked the first blind man. There was
no reply, so he got to his feet and walked forwards with his
arms outstretched. After a few steps, his hands hit
something flat and rough and solid in front of him.
"It's a wall!" he cried, triumphantly.

"Don't be stupid!" cried the second blind man,
standing up. "How could someone have built a wall right
under our noses without us hearing?" He, too, felt about in front of
him. "Aha!" he said, delightedly, as he ran his
hands down a hard, smooth, stick-like thing.
"It's a spear, definitely a spear!"

At that, the third blind man got up to
join them. "A wall and a spear!" he sneered.
"Obviously, neither of you have any idea
what this thing is." His fingers closed around

something tatty and wiggly. "It's nothing more than a piece of old rope!" he laughed.

"How can you say that?" argued the fourth blind man, who had jumped up and joined in without anyone noticing. "I'm standing here with my arms wrapped around something so big that my fingers are barely touching together. It's a tree trunk, I'm telling you. A tree trunk!"

"I suppose I'll have to settle this," sniffed the fifth blind man, as he rose. He stuck out his hand confidently and grabbed hold of something long and swaying. "HELP!" he shouted. "It's a snake! It's a snake!"

Suddenly, whoops of laughter filled the air and the five blind men heard a little boy giggle, "You're ALL wrong! You're actually holding parts of an elephant – and you all look REALLY SILLY!"

At that, the first blind man stopped patting the elephant's side. The second blind man stopped stroking the elephant's tusk. The third blind man stopped holding the elephant's tail. The fourth blind man stopped hugging the elephant's leg. And the fifth blind man let go of the elephant's trunk. And from that moment on, the five blind men never argued again.

The Adventures of Sinbad the Sailor
a tale from The Arabian Nights

Many moons ago, Sinbad the Sailor weighed anchor and sailed his merchant ship away from the ancient and magical city of Baghdad. The brave men voyaged into unknown waters for weeks, and by the time they spied land, they longed for the feel of solid ground underneath their feet. It was only a very small island that they saw – covered in sand, the grey of sea mists and with just two or three lone palm trees. Yet Sinbad and four others jumped into a little rowing boat and went ashore in case there might be coconuts or a pool of fresh water to top up their supplies.

Sinbad and his men were only halfway across the sandy island when a huge fountain of water suddenly jetted into the sky and the ground began to rock beneath their feet. As the sailors struggled to stay upright, they saw horror on the faces of their fellow crew members who had stayed on-board the ship. Their panic-stricken voices floated to them across the waves: "Whale!. . . It's a whale!" Then Sinbad realised they were not on an island at all, but on the back of a huge sea-creature who had been asleep for centuries. Sand had been blown there by the wind and a handful of palm tree seeds had put down shallow roots and sprouted. But at last the footsteps of Sinbad and his men had awakened the monster whale and now it was diving!

As the "island" began to sink into the sea, Sinbad watched his terrified crew hoist the sails of his ship and speed away. The ship disappeared from view just as the last patch of the whale's back vanished beneath the water, leaving the merchant and his men splashing and choking among the huge salt waves. One by one, Sinbad's men sank down after the whale into the depths, but Allah the merciful took pity on Sinbad and sent a barrel floating towards him on the waves. Sinbad collapsed exhausted over it as it bobbed like a cork on the swell.

The next thing Sinbad knew, he was waking up on a sandy beach, with the barrel beside him and gentle breakers lapping at his feet. He had no idea where he was. Jungle and mangrove swamps were on all sides. The only sign of habitation was a white dome a little way off and Sinbad set off at once towards it.

Sinbad found that the white dome wasn't a temple or a house. It was as smooth and curved underneath as it was on top, and there was no sign of a door. Sinbad sank down next to it, very frustrated. All at once, a huge shadow blotted out the sun and there was an ear-splitting "SQUAWK" as a giant eagle came wheeling down out of the sky. In a rush of wind, it settled its feathery bottom on top of the dome, smothering Sinbad underneath as if a soft mattress had been thrown on top of him. *"An egg!"* breathed Sinbad to himself, and after recovering from the shock, he thought up a brilliant plan to

escape from the island. With much
huffing and puffing, Sinbad wriggled
himself into a position alongside the
mammoth talons of the enormous
bird. He unwound his long silk turban
and tied himself as tightly as he could to
the gigantic claw. Then Sinbad waited until
in a rush of air, the eagle took off from her nest and soared into the
sky, carrying the gasping merchant with it.

Sinbad shut his eyes tight against the glare of the sun as the
eagle hovered higher and higher on the wind. On and on they flew
before finally Sinbad's stomach gave a sickening lurch as the eagle
swooped down to land in the middle of a rocky valley. Hurriedly,
Sinbad untied himself and dashed away from the bird and its vicious
beak. He hid behind a boulder for a while, trying to get his breath
back, and as he took in his surroundings, his eyes opened wide with
astonishment. Everywhere Sinbad looked, the earth was glittering
with jewels! Diamonds and rubies and sapphires and emeralds
carelessly covered the ground like pebbles on a beach. Sinbad stuffed
his pockets and filled his boots until he couldn't carry even one jewel
more. Then suddenly his face fell. How was he to get out of the
rocky valley? Steep cliffs rose around him on all sides, impossible to
climb. "What's the good of having pockets full of treasure," Sinbad
pondered, "if all I can do with it is sit here and count it till I die?"

THWACK! A massive slice of raw meat fell from the sky and
hit Sinbad on the head. "What in heaven – ?" began Sinbad. Then he
realised what was happening. Back in the inns of Baghdad he had
heard travellers' tales about a wonderful valley of jewels. Its cliffs
were so sheer that no one was able to descend into the valley to

reach the gleaming treasure. Instead, merchants threw down hunks of meat, in the hope that some of the jewels would stick to it. They then waited for the giant eagles who lived on the island to pick up the meat and carry it out of the valley. The merchants knew the eagles' favourite eyries, and they simply hid and waited and took the treasure.

Sinbad couldn't believe his good fortune. It was this very valley in which he found himself now!

Once again, Sinbad unwound his long, silk turban. This time he tied himself to the great big slice of meat that had fallen on his head. He was just in time. Almost immediately, an enormous eagle swooped down and snatched the meat – with Sinbad attached – and soared off into the air. Up flew the eagle, right out of the valley and away from the cliffs, alighting with a flutter on a rocky mountain ledge. While Sinbad untied his turban, a merchant popped up from behind a boulder to collect his booty. Of course, he was expecting to see jewels, not Sinbad, but when Sinbad offered to share his pockets of treasure, the merchant grinned a broad grin and promised to help him all he could . . .

By nightfall, Sinbad found himself in a crowded, prosperous port. After trading only a handful of his diamonds and rubies and sapphires and emeralds, he had enough money to buy not just one new ship, but an entire fleet – and to load them with cargoes of satins and silks and spices, too. And Sinbad sailed away across the even seas, hungry for more adventure . . .

The Old Woman and her Pig

a traditional folk tale

Long ago, an old woman found a bright, shining sixpence and went to market to buy a pig. She set off home with the pig trotting quite happily at her side. But when they were nearly there, they came to a stile and the pig wouldn't jump over it.

So the old woman went on a little further. She met a dog and said, "Dog! Dog! Bite pig. Pig won't jump over the stile, so I won't get home tonight." But the dog wouldn't.

So the old woman went on a little further. She met a stick and said, "Stick! Stick! Beat dog. Dog won't bite pig, and pig won't jump over the stile, so I won't get home tonight." But the stick wouldn't.

So the old woman went on a little further. She met a fire and said, "Fire! Fire! Burn stick. Stick won't beat dog, dog won't bite pig, and pig won't jump over the stile, so I won't get home tonight." But the fire wouldn't.

So the old woman went on a little further. She met some water and said, "Water! Water! Put out fire. Fire won't burn stick, stick won't beat dog, dog won't bite pig, and pig won't jump over the stile, so I won't get home tonight." But the water wouldn't.

So the old woman went on a little further. She met a horse and said, "Horse! Horse! Drink water. Water won't put out fire, fire won't burn stick, stick won't beat dog, dog won't bite pig, and pig won't jump over the stile, so I won't get home tonight." But the horse wouldn't.

So the old woman went on a little further. She met a rope and said, "Rope! Rope! Lasso horse. Horse won't drink water, water won't put out fire, fire won't burn stick, stick won't beat dog, dog won't bite pig, and pig won't jump over the stile, so I won't get home tonight." But the rope wouldn't.

So the old woman went on a little further. She met a rat and said, "Rat! Rat! Gnaw rope. Rope won't lasso horse, horse won't drink water, water won't put out fire, fire won't burn stick, stick won't beat dog, dog won't bite pig, and pig won't jump over the stile, so I won't get home tonight." But the rat wouldn't.

So the old woman went on a little further. She met

a cat and said, "Cat! Cat! Scare rat. Rat won't gnaw rope, rope won't lasso horse, horse won't drink water, water won't put out fire, fire won't burn stick, stick won't beat dog, dog won't bite pig, and pig won't jump over the stile, so I won't get home tonight."

"All right," said the cat, " – if you get me some milk."

The old woman was highly surprised and fetched a saucer of milk at once.

The cat scared the rat, so the rat gnawed the rope, so the rope lassoed the horse, so the horse drank the water, so the water put out the fire, so the fire burnt the stick, so the stick beat the dog, so the dog bit the pig, so the pig jumped over the stile – and that's how the old woman got home that night!

The Brave Tin Soldier

retold from the original tale by Hans Christian Andersen

little boy was once given a box of twenty-five tin soldiers as a gift. They wore smart uniforms and proudly shouldered their guns, and the little boy was very pleased with them. Only one of the tin soldiers wasn't quite perfect, for he had just one leg. He and his brothers had all been made from the same tin spoon, and there hadn't been quite enough metal to finish him off. Still, it was because he stood out as being special that the little boy put him to stand guard at the gates of the toy castle, instead of keeping him in the box with the others.

The tin soldier was very honoured to have been given an important duty, and he stood to attention, staring straight ahead. His gaze landed on a beautiful tiny doll whom the boy had placed in the open castle doorway. She was made of the very best plastic and wore a ballet dress of thin muslin, tied at the waist with a shiny blue ribbon. She held both her arms gracefully over her head and she balanced beautifully on one leg, for just like the tin soldier, she had one leg missing. (Well, in actual fact that wasn't the truth. The girl's other leg was extended out behind her because she was a dancer. But the tin soldier wasn't in a position to see it.) *That would be just the wife for me*, the tin soldier thought at least ten times every day. But the tin soldier dared not go and tell the girl of his love for her, for he was on duty.

One morning, the tin soldier was unexpectedly relieved of his post. A sudden breeze blew through the open window causing the curtains to flutter and knocking the soldier right off his feet and over the windowsill. Down he tumbled through the air, until he landed headfirst on the pavement.

The tin soldier didn't cry out for he was brave-hearted in the face of danger – not even when big drops of rain began to bombard him from above. *So this is what it feels like to be out on the battlefield,* the brave tin soldier thought.

Eventually the rain stopped falling and two keen-eyed boys came along and spotted the tin soldier among the puddles. The boys quickly folded some newspaper into a boat, popped the tin soldier in the middle, and set him afloat in the rainwater that rushed down the gutter at the side of the street.

They ran alongside the boat as it swirled along, cheering it on its way delightedly. The tin soldier was shaking with fear inside, but he didn't flinch or move a muscle – even when the rushing water carried his newspaper boat down a drain and into the darkness under the pavement.

Suddenly a huge water-rat appeared.

"Who goes there?" it demanded, twitching its whiskers and baring its long teeth.

At last, I face the enemy! thought the brave tin soldier. But before he could lower his gun and aim it, his newspaper boat was carried past the rat on the tide.

A glimmer of light appeared in the distance and the rushing of the water grew louder and louder. The tin soldier realised with horror that he was being swept towards a sudden drop where the drain water casaded in a waterfall into a canal below. Even worse, the churning waters were splashing over the sides of the newspaper boat and the bottom was growing soggy beneath the tin soldier's feet. "Steady! Steady! Hold the line!" the brave tin soldier told himself. Suddenly the bottom of the boat ripped and gave way. The tin soldier plunged into the deeps and the icy waters closed over his head.

Surely now I am done for! thought the tin soldier, as he sank downwards through the murky wetness. Then all at once, everything went black as a fish swallowed him. The tin soldier choked and spluttered as he was gulped down into the fish's gullet, then the waters drained away and he was left lying on his back, holding tightly onto his gun. Even though the tin soldier couldn't see in the darkness, he could just about breathe in the stinking, rotten air. *So this is what it's like to be a prisoner of war in a dungeon,* the brave tin soldier thought to himself. And to keep up his spirits, he concentrated hard on the beautiful dancing girl he had left behind him at the castle.

The tin soldier lost track of time inside the fish, but eventually he was flung to and fro as the creature was caught on a hook and struggled to escape. Then everything went quiet and still for quite a while, until suddenly the fish was cut open. "I don't believe it!" came a voice "Here's the missing tin soldier," and a woman with a kind face reached in and pulled him out. She gave the brave tin soldier a shower under a running tap, carried him into the drawing room and set him back in his old position outside his very own castle.

The tin soldier puffed out his chest with pride. *The war is over. I am back where I belong*, he thought to himself. He stared straight ahead, and there was his love, his sweetheart, the beautiful little dancing girl. *Tomorrow, as soon as I am off duty, I will definitely ask her to marry me*, the tin soldier decided. But then he felt an icy wind around his ankles, and a breeze coming through the window once more swept him off his feet and into the air. This time he landed in the blazing flames of the open fire – but the brave tin soldier didn't mind, for the dancing girl was blown in too and landed at his side. "Be brave, my love!" cried the tin soldier, holding his gun on his shoulder, and the dancing girl burst into flames and was gone. Then the tin soldier himself began to melt . . . and the next day, when the woman with the kind face was raking over the ashes, she found a tiny tin heart that the fire had been unable to burn away.

Feathers, Fur and Fangs

Puss in Boots

retold from the original tale by Charles Perrault

certain miller was so poor that when he died, all he left his three sons were his mill, his mule and a cat.

"Bagsy me the mill," said the eldest son.

"Bagsy me the mule," said the middle son.

"Oh, great!" said the youngest son. "I suppose I'm left with the cat then." (As you can tell, he wasn't very happy about it. But youngest children often start off with a bad deal in fairytales, so he should really have seen it coming.)

"Stop your moaning!" scolded the cat. "If you stick with me, I can guarantee that you'll be thanking your dear old dad later. Now fetch me a large bag and leave me to get on with things. Oh – and get me a smart pair of boots made from the finest red leather, just like I've always wanted . . ."

The youngest son didn't argue. Firstly, the cat had never talked before, so he was speechless with shock. And secondly, he didn't have a better plan to suggest anyway. So he took what little money he had saved under the mattress and did exactly what the cat had told him . . .

As soon as Puss had finished purring with delight at how fine he looked in his smart boots of the finest red leather, he hurried along to a field and lay down quite still with his bag wide open beside him. After a while – hop! hop! hop! – along came a plump bunny. Pop! the silly rabbit jumped straight into the bag. Zip! Puss shut the bag. Whistling merrily, he took his catch to the palace and presented it to the king. "My master, the Marquis of Carabas, sends you this gift," Puss announced, bowing low.

"Give him my warmest thanks," the king announced, smiling graciously.

As soon as Puss was gone, the king turned to his chamberlain and whispered: "Whoever this Marquis is, he must be very rich and important to send his messengers in such smart boots!"

The next day the cat was back again – with a present of two partridges. And the day after that – with three pheasants. Every day for three months, Puss arrived at court with a gift for the king from his master, the Marquis of Carabas. "What a thoughtful, kind-hearted man this Marquis of Carabas is!" the king exclaimed as his royal pantry filled up with delicious game.

One day, Puss learned that the king was going to take a drive along the river with his beautiful daughter. "Right, you're going for a swim!" the cat commanded the miller's youngest son.

"But – but – I don't have any swimming trunks!" the Marquis of Carabas protested, but Puss was already dragging him along to a certain spot on the riverbank. Before he knew it, the cat had taken away all his clothes and he was swimming around obediently among the waterweed.

Just then, the royal carriage came trundling by. "Help! Help!"' shouted Puss, running out onto the road and flagging it down. "The Marquis of Carabas is drowning!"

The princess squealed with fright as she peered out of the carriage and saw a man splashing about in the water. At once, the king ordered his guards into the river to pull him out.

"Your majesty," purred the cat, as the soldiers began trying to give the startled miller's son the kiss of life. "As if it wasn't bad enough that the Marquis of Carabas has nearly drowned, while he was in the water, robbers have stolen all his clothes!"

The king tut-tutted and sent his chamberlain galloping back to the palace to bring a selection of his very own robes for the Marquis to wear. Soon the miller's son was looking exceedingly handsome in the king's best suit, and the princess was blushing a deep pink. "It's the very least I can do in return for all the kind gifts you have been sending me!" the king said earnestly.

The miller's son had no idea what the king was talking about, but he thought it best just to nod and smile all the same. "You will come and ride with us a while, won't you?" insisted the king, and the miller's son was ushered up into the royal carriage to sit next to the princess.

Puss was highly excited that his

scheme was working, and he ran ahead down the road. By and by, he came to a hayfield of mowers, and he said, "Good people, if you don't tell the king that this field belongs to the Marquis of Carabas, I'll make you all into cat food."

It wasn't long before the royal carriage passed by and, sure enough, the king leaned out of the window and asked, "Who does this land belong to?"

"It b-b-b-belongs to the M-m-m-arquis of C-c-c-arabas," the terrified mowers stuttered.

"You have a fine estate," the king beamed at the miller's youngest son, and the so-called Marquis nodded and smiled.

Soon the royal carriage came to a cornfield of harvesters. The miller's youngest son was just as surprised as the king to learn from the harvesters that the cornfield belonged to him, too! A little further down the road, and a group of dairymaids insisted that their cows belonged to the Marquis of Carabas.

"My!" the king grinned. "What splendid lands you have!" And the princess's cheeks turned quite rosy with pleasure.

While the royal carriage rolled along, Puss was a long way down the road at a fearful ogre's castle. It was the ogre who owned all the land that Puss had been giving to the Marquis of Carabas (though luckily, the ogre didn't know about that!). "Mr Ogre," began Puss politely. "I have come to pay my respects to you because I have heard that you have remarkable powers. Is it true that you can turn yourself from a big, hulking ogre into a tiny, sneaky mouse?"

"Easy-peasy!" growled the ogre. He disappeared before Puss's very eyes and suddenly there was a mouse scurrying about on the floor. It took Puss only a few seconds to pounce and gobble him up, and that was the end of the ogre.

By the time the royal carriage pulled up outside the castle, Puss was waiting outside to greet it. "Welcome to the home of the Marquis of Carabas," Puss announced proudly. The cat ushered the highly surprised miller's youngest son and his stunned royal guests inside, where they found a delicious banquet the servants had prepared for them at Puss's instructions.

"My dear Marquis," beamed the king. "I am most impressed with your riches – er, I mean generosity. If there's anything I can do for you, just say the word."

The miller's son glanced at the princess, who hissed under her breath, "Go on! Ask him!"

So the Marquis of Carabas cleared his throat and said, "Actually, I'd quite like to marry your daughter!" and the king roared with happy laughter.

The couple were married that very day, and the miller's youngest son lived as the rich and prosperous Marquis of Carabas for the rest of his life. So his story has a happy ending after all. (And that's what happens in fairytales, so he should really have seen it coming.) As for Puss – well, he lived happily at the castle too. There were plenty of mice to catch, and that's all he needed to be content – as well as his smart boots of the finest red leather, of course!

The Wonderful Tar Baby

retold from the original tale by Uncle Remus

rer Fox was doing what he usually did – trying to catch Brer Rabbit. But he'd be danged if this time he didn't catch that pesky varmint once and for all! Brer Fox mixed up a big pot of sticky tar and pulled and patted it into the shape of a baby. Then he lolloped up the road, set the tar baby sitting in the dust, and went to lay low in the ditch.

By and by, Brer Rabbit came bouncing down the road. "Good morning," he greeted the tar baby, "nice day, ain't it?"

But the tar baby didn't utter a word.

"I SAYS," shouted Brer Rabbit, just in case the tar baby hadn't cleaned his ears recently, "GOOD MORNING! NICE DAY, AIN'T IT?"

The tar baby just stared straight ahead.

"Ain't you got no manners?" Brer Rabbit asked, crossly.

Still the tar baby stayed silent.

By this time, Brer Rabbit was hopping from foot to foot, madder than a snake in a wasps' nest. "You'd better speak to me civil-like or else!" he hollered.

But the tar baby simply ignored Brer Rabbit.

"Well I guess you've done gone and asked for this!" Brer Rabbit shrieked. BLIP! he thumped the tar baby straight in the mouth – and his fist was stuck fast to the tar baby's face. "You let me go!" Brer Rabbit yelled. "Let me go – or I'll let you have another!" BLAM! Brer Rabbit socked the tar baby again and his other fist was glued tight to the tar baby's head. "I've warned you!" bellowed Brer Rabbit. SMACK! He kicked the tar baby and was left hopping around on one leg. "Don't make me do this!" Brer Rabbit shouted. WALLOP! Another kick and the tar baby was holding him off the ground. "Right, you've really had it now!" Brer Rabbit screamed. THUNK! He head-butted the tar baby and found himself stuck eye-to-eye with the cheeky critter.

All this time, Brer Fox had been holding on to so much laughter he thought he was going to burst. Now he leapt out of his hiding place and howled, "My, oh my, Brer Rabbit! What type of mess have you got yourself into this time?"

"I suppose you're gonna have yourself a tasty barbecued bunny for supper this evening," Brer Rabbit admitted.

"Yep! You said it," grinned Brer Fox, licking his lips.

"Well I'm glad you're going to dress me up with some sauce and warm me over your fire," Brer Rabbit smiled. "I'd much rather you did that than throw me in that briar patch over there."

Hang on a minute, thought Brer Fox, and his face fell. *That no-good rabbit seems quite pleased about being roasted!* "I've changed my mind," Brer Fox said out loud. "I'm gonna hang you instead."

"Ain't I glad it's good ol' hangin' and not being thrown in the briar patch!" sighed Brer Rabbit.

Brer Fox frowned. "I mean, I'm going to drown you!" he snarled.

"Fine, fine . . ." smiled Brer Rabbit gaily. "Dip me in the water and at least I'll die clean. Just don't throw me in that there briar patch, that's all!"

At that, Brer Fox was sure that the very worst thing he could do to Brer Rabbit was to hurl him into the briar patch. He grabbed him round the waist and pulled him hard and – SHLUP! – Brer Rabbit came unstuck from the tar baby. Brer Fox spun round and round and round and – WHEEEEEEEE! – Brer Rabbit went sailing high into the air and came down – DONK! – into the briar patch.

Brer Fox began to smile contentedly. "I've bested that bunny once and for all!" he chuckled, as he wiped his hands.

A high-pitched giggle came from the far side of the briar patch, and when Brer Fox squinted into the sunshine, he could just see Brer Rabbit hopping away into the distance. "I was born and bred in a briar patch, Brer Fox!" he was singing. "Hee hee! Born and bred in a briar patch!"

Brer Fox boiled with rage and thumped the very first thing that came to hand. And you know what that was, don't you?

The Dragons of Peking
a Chinese folk tale

Once there was a prince so poor that he only ruled over a handful of peasants who lived in a cluster of wooden huts among some dry, dusty fields. The sad little place was called Peking. However, the prince was good-hearted and determined and had grand dreams of building Peking into a splendid city. The first thing he did was to work hard with all the men, women and children in the village to build a high, solid wall with broad gates to keep out bandits.

The people were delighted. But little did they know that with all their digging and clearing and carrying and building they'd disturbed two dragons who'd been asleep in an underground cave for thousands of years. And you can imagine how grumpy the dragons felt when they were woken from their lovely long nap! "Who does this prince think he is," the first dragon growled, "getting his people to come banging around our cave like that!"

"Let's teach them all a lesson," the second dragon snorted.

That night, the two dragons wove a spell that turned themselves into an old man and an old woman. Using magic, they crept past the royal guards and through several locked gates and doors, and stole into the very room where the prince lay, snoring soundly. The wrinkled couple asked, "O wise and gracious lord, we have come to ask your permission to leave your city of Peking and to take two baskets of water with us."

The prince stirred slightly in his sleep and murmured, "Why, of course you may!"

The old man and woman hurried off to the river excitedly. It was a narrow, muddy sort of river, but it was Peking's main source of water. They dipped their baskets into the stream, and in only a matter of minutes, the river dwindled to a trickle, then dried up completely. For the disguised dragons' water baskets weren't normal water baskets. They were enchanted water baskets that could never be filled, even if an entire ocean was to be poured into them. Next, the old man and woman took their water baskets (which were no heavier than before) off to the village spring. Soon, where there had once been a bubbling gush of water, there was just a muddy puddle. Then the old man and woman visited every house in the village, draining all the people's water baskets of every last drop. Finally, the bent-over pair hobbled off with their water baskets down the road that led out of Peking.

By the time the sun rose, the wicked old couple were far, far away. Shouts of horror rose up from all over Peking as the people woke up and discovered there was no water. Before long, there was a clamouring crowd outside the prince's house. "What shall we do?" they shouted. "Our lips are parched. We can't boil any rice for breakfast. Our crops are drying and withering in the sun before our very eyes!"

The prince wrinkled up his nose as a stinky smell wafted underneath his nostrils. "Oh dear," he sighed, "and none of you has been able to have a bath this morning, have you?"

The people shuffled about and looked down, red-faced.

Then suddenly the prince remembered his dream about the two old people and their water baskets. Being a wise person who believed in magic, he was very suspicious and dashed off to see his faithful old advisor straight away. The faithful old advisor said, "Aha!" and smiled a knowing smile, and waggled his finger a lot, and took the prince straight off to the dragons' cave outside the city. When the faithful old advisor saw the cave was empty, he said "Well, there you are then."

"Well, there I am – what?" said the prince, rather frustrated.

"My father was told about this cave by his father, who was told by his father, who was told by his father, who was –"

"Yes, yes!" cried the prince impatiently. "Get on with it!"

"The two dragons who were asleep here obviously weren't very impressed with your plans to improve the city. They've taken your water and gone!"

At once the prince called for his spear and his horse, and was gone down the road in a cloud of dust. There were many travellers on the road that morning, but the prince glanced at them all briefly and thundered past without stopping. At last, after hours of hard riding, he recognised the old couple from his dream and reined in his panting horse. "I gave my permission for an old man and woman to take my water," the prince yelled, "not the two dragons that you two really are!" He plunged his spear into each of their baskets and water immediately began to gush out in a cascading torrent. With a spine-chilling roar, the old couple began to change back into dragons before the prince's horrified eyes. But before the fire-breathing creatures could pounce on him, they were swept off in one direction by the swirling waters, while the prince on his horse was carried off in the other. All the surrounding countryside was submerged into a vast sea, and the prince's horse scrambled onto a jutting crag that poked up out of the water. It had once been the tip-top of a gigantic mountain.

"Now what am I to do?" frowned the soaking prince.

"I shall pray to Heaven for help," came a voice. The prince looked round in surprise and saw that it came from a Buddhist monk, who had been sitting there so silent and still that he hadn't even noticed him. The monk shut his eyes and bowed his head . . . and as he prayed – to the prince's enormous relief – the waters vanished. The prince thanked the Buddhist monk earnestly and began galloping back to Peking.

As soon as the prince neared the high, solid wall he had built around his city, his people came pouring out of the gates with happy faces. "You'll never believe it!" they cried. "All our water has come back. But best of all, a brand new fountain has sprung up! It has swelled the river with water more sweet and crystal clear than any we have ever seen!"

Thanks to the magical fountain, the land around Peking stopped being dry and dusty and became green and beautiful. The prince fulfilled his plans of making the city one of the most splendid in the world, and – as far as the people know – the dragons have never come back.

The Hare and the Tortoise

retold from the original fable by Aesop

T he day that Tortoise challenged Hare to a race, all the animals laughed so hard that their tummies ached. But Tortoise was fed-up with Hare whizzing round him all the time, teasing him about how slow he was. *I'll show that Hare, if it's the last thing I do!* Tortoise promised himself.

Hare thought that Tortoise's little joke was extremely funny. For that's all Hare thought it was – a joke. Hare never expected that Tortoise would actually go through with his mad idea. So his eyes nearly popped out of his head when he arrived at the starting line to see Tortoise already there, limbering up in a very slow, stiff, creaky sort of way.

"Be careful there, old chap!" Hare worried, as he realised his friend was serious. "You don't want to do yourself an injury."

"Don't worry about me," replied Tortoise. "You should be working out how you're going to beat me. Ha! You won't see me for dust!"

A huge crowd of animals had gathered to watch the race and they all cheered and clapped and jumped up and down at Tortoise's bold remark.

Suddenly, Hare started to feel rather annoyed. "All right then. If that's the way you want it!" he snapped. "I was going to give you a headstart, but obviously you won't be wanting one."

"No need," breezed Tortoise, although his little heart was pumping inside his shell. "First one to the windmill's the winner."

Hare peered into the distance. The windmill was three fields away. He could get there in under a minute without even losing his breath. But surely it would take Tortoise all day to reach it!

"Three! Twit-Two! One!" cried Barn-Owl, and Tortoise lifted one leg over the starting line amid thunderous applause.

The stunned Hare watched in amazement as Tortoise began to crawl slowly away. *Well, you have to hand it to Tortoise!* Hare thought, seeing the funny side of things again. *He's certainly got a good sense of humour and a lot of guts!*

Hare sat down next to the starting line under a shady tree. It was a beautiful sunny day and it was very pleasant to sit there in the dappled light, watching Tortoise amble peacefully into the field. Hare's eyes shut and his head drooped before he even realised he was sleepy . . .

Meanwhile, Tortoise was remembering what his dear old mum had told him as a child: *Slow and steady does it, son. Slow and steady does it.* And Tortoise kept on going and didn't give up . . .

Hare didn't wake up until the night air was so cold that it was freezing his whiskers. *Where am I?* he thought. And then suddenly he remembered the race. Hare leapt to his feet and squinted into the moonlight, but there was no sign of Tortoise. All at once, he heard a faint sound of cheering coming from a long way off, and he saw tiny dark figures jumping up and down around the windmill. "Surely not!" Hare gasped, and shot off over the fields like an arrow. He arrived at

the windmill just in time to see all the animals hoisting Tortoise – the champion! – on their shoulders. And of course, after that, Hare never ever teased his friend about being slow again.

The Elephant's Child

retold from the original tale by Rudyard Kipling

There was once a time when the elephant had no trunk. All the elephant had for a nose was a blackish bulgy snout, which could sniffle and snuffle but couldn't pick anything up. And at this time there lived a very, very young elephant's child – so young that the world was still strange to him and he was finding out all about it by asking his family and friends a lot of questions. The elephant's child found out about things such as: where the sun slept (deep inside the lake); why his friend zebra had stripes (because he would have looked very silly with spots); and why ant-eaters ate ants (because they weren't called pigeon-eaters or turtle-eaters, were they?). But there were still a couple of things that the elephant's child didn't know: What did Mr Crocodile look like? And what did Mr Crocodile have for his dinner? And because the elephant's child had no more family or friends left to ask, he wandered away on his own to find out.

By and by the elephant's child reached the great grey-green, greasy Limpopo River, set all about with fever-trees. There he came across a lumpy log of wood lying in the water, blinking its yellow eyes and smiling a toothy grin.

"Excuse me," said the elephant's child, "can you tell me what Mr Crocodile looks like?"

"Well yes I can," said the lumpy log of wood. "I am Mr Crocodile and I look like this."

"Thank you very much," said the elephant's child. "I don't mean to be a bother and a nuisance, but can you also please tell me what Mr Crocodile has for his dinner?"

"Now that's a big secret," beamed Mr Crocodile. "Kneel down and bend close to me and I'll whisper it into your ear."

All excited, the elephant's child knelt down and bent close to Mr Crocodile.

SNAP! Mr Crocodile opened his long, razor-sharp jaws and clamped them firmly around the elephant's child's nose.

"Ow!" yelled the elephant's child. "Led go! You are hurtig be!"

But Mr Crocodile didn't let go. He held on tighter than ever and pulled and pulled and pulled.

Now the elephant's child liked swimming, but he didn't want to go into the water today, thank you very much. So he sat back on his wrinkled trousers and pulled and pulled and pulled.

Mr Crocodile thrashed with his wide, flat tail, sending water splashing everywhere. And he pulled and pulled and pulled.

And the elephant's child dug deep with his broad, round feet into the mud. And he pulled and pulled and pulled.

Just when the elephant's child thought that he was going to have to take a dip anyway, a friendly bi-coloured-python-rock-snake wriggled past and saw that he was having a bit of trouble. The friendly bi-coloured-python-rock-snake helpfully tied his head end around the elephant child's waist and looped his tail end around a handy nearby boulder, and pulled and pulled and pulled.

Suddenly the elephant's child's nose came free with a PLOP! that echoed all around the fever-trees up and down the great grey-green, greasy Limpopo River. "Thank you very much," the elephant's child said to the friendly bi-coloured-python-rock-snake, and he began to wrap his very sore nose in cool banana leaves. But the elephant's child didn't like the feel of what had happened to it. His nose felt longer and thinner and definitely – well, *stretched*. He sat in the mud looking dejected and touching it tenderly.

"That's a fine long trunk you've got there," said the friendly bi-coloured-python-rock-snake. "I'll bet you can pick things up with that and use it to shower yourself with water, and all sorts!"

"Really?" said the elephant's child, brightening up.

"I'd say that trunk is very useful and very handsome too," said the friendly bi-coloured-python-rock-snake. "I'll bet that when you go back home, all the other elephants will want one just like it." And so he wasn't surprised at all when, some weeks later, he saw a long line of elephants all queueing up on the banks of the great grey-green, greasy Limpopo River, set all about with fever-trees, to see Mr Crocodile and ask him what he had for dinner.

The Moon in the Pond

retold from the original tale by Uncle Remus

Every now and again Brer Fox and Brer Rabbit would shake hands and make peace for a while and, following their example, all the critters would forget their arguments and get along together just dandy. It had been like this for some weeks when Brer Rabbit ran into Brer Turtle and they got talking.

"It sure is peaceful around here now," sighed Brer Rabbit.

"Yep," nodded Brer Turtle, who was a man of few words.

"It sure is quiet," sighed Brer Rabbit.

"Yep," nodded Brer Turtle.

"Peaceful and quiet is good, but it ain't fun like in the old days, is it Brer Turtle?" asked Brer Rabbit.

"Nope," agreed Brer Turtle.

"I think that the folks round here could do with a dose of fun again," sighed Brer Rabbit.

"Yep," nodded Brer Turtle.

Brer Rabbit bounced to his feet with a chuckle. "Then I'm going to invite everyone to a little fishing frolic at the pond tomorrow night," he said. "I'll do all the talking as long as you back me up with your 'yep' and 'nope' now and then." And Brer Rabbit and Brer Turtle shook hands. Brer Rabbit loped off to do the inviting and Brer Turtle set out for the pond, so as he'd be sure to get there on time . . .

Sure enough, the following night, everyone was there at the pond. Brer Bear and Brer Wolf had brought their hooks and lines. Brer Turtle carried a pot of wriggling bait. Brer Fox brought his fishing net.

Miss Meadows and Miss Motts brought themselves, dressed up to the nines.

While Brer Turtle shook his pot at Miss Meadows and Miss Motts and made them squeal with delight, Brer Bear announced he was going to fish for mud-cats. Brer Wolf said he was going to fish for horneyheads. Brer Fox declared he was going to fish for perch for the ladies. And Brer Rabbit winked at Brer Turtle and said he was going to fish for suckers.

So everyone got busy with their hooks and their lines and their bait, and Brer Rabbit went to cast his line first. "I don't believe it!" he gasped, peering into the water and scratching his head. "The moon has done gone and fell in the water!"

Everyone looked serious and gathered round and tut-tutted and well-welled and my-myed as they looked into the pond and saw the moon floating there like a big pale coin. "There ain't no fish gonna come swimmin' through this water unless we get the moon out of the way," said Brer Rabbit. "Isn't that so, Brer Turtle?"

"Yep," nodded Brer Turtle, with a twinkle in his eye.

"So how we gonna get the moon out, Brer Rabbit?" worried Miss Meadows.

"Hmm," pondered Brer Rabbit, thoughtfully. "I've got it! We borrow Brer Turtle's drag net, and we drag it across the pond, and we drag the moon right out!"

"That's it!" breathed everyone, excitedly.

"That's surely it!"

"It don't bother you none if we borrow your drag net, does it Brer Turtle?"asked Brer Rabbit.

"Nope," replied Brer Turtle, trying hard not to collapse into laughter.

Then Brer Rabbit leapt off to fetch Brer Turtle's drag net and was back again before anyone could say 'lickety-spit'. "I think I'd better be the one to do the dragging," Brer Rabbit sighed. "It needs someone mighty clever and mighty musclcy."

At that, Brer Fox and Brer Bear and Brer Wolf sprang forward and insisted on taking the drag net from Brer Rabbit. After all, they didn't want to look like saps in front of the ladies, now, did they?

Brer Fox and Brer Bear and Brer Wolf walked gingerly down to the edge of the pond with the net. They cast it into the water, dragged it along, and heaved it out, dripping. When the ripples had settled on the pond, there was the moon, shining just as bright in the water as before.

"Nope!" cried Brer Rabbit. "You need to go deeper."

Brer Fox and Brer Bear and Brer Wolf waded knee-deep into the cold pond. Once again they cast out the drag net, and once again they pulled it in without having caught the moon.

"Try again a little deeper," yelled Brer Rabbit from the nice, dry bank. "You'll surely get it next time." And Miss Meadows and Miss Motts eagerly waved them further out.

Brer Fox and Brer Bear and Brer Wolf took one more step and

suddenly the bottom of the pond fell away steeply and there was no more mud under their feet and they were ducked right under the water! Up they popped, choking and splashing and spluttering.

Miss Meadows and Miss Motts giggled and snickered as Brer Fox and Brer Bear and Brer Wolf hauled themselves out of the pond. They were a sight for sore eyes, dripping water from every hair and covered all-over in waterweed.

I've heard that the moon will always bite if you use fools for bait, Brer Rabbit giggled, looking them up and down. Now if you're asking me, "you gentlemen ought to get yourselves home and into some dry clothes." And as Brer Fox and Brer Bear and Brer Wolf slopped and slapped away into the moonlight, Brer Turtle and Brer Rabbit went home with the girls.

The Last of the Dragons
by E Nesbit

f course you know that dragons were once as common
as motor-omnibuses are now, and almost as dangerous.
But as every well brought-up prince was expected to kill
a dragon, and rescue a princess, the dragons grew fewer and fewer till
it was often quite hard for a princess to find a dragon to be rescued
from. And at last there were no more dragons in France and no more
dragons in Germany, or Spain, or Italy, or Russia. There were some
left in China, and are still, but they are cold and bronzy, and there
were never any, of course, in America. But the last real live dragon
left was in England, and of course that was a very long time ago,
before what you call English history began. This dragon lived in
Cornwall in the big caves amidst the rocks, and a very fine dragon it
was, quite seventy feet long from the tip of its fearful snout to the
end of its terrible tail. It breathed fire and smoke, and rattled when it
walked, because its scales were made of iron. Its wings were like half-
umbrellas – or like bat's wings, only several thousand times bigger.
Everyone was very frightened of it, and well they might be.

Now the King of Cornwall had one daughter, and when she

was sixteen, of course she would have to go and face the dragon: such tales are always told in royal nurseries at twilight, so the Princess knew what she had to expect. The dragon would not eat her, of course – because the prince would come and rescue her. But the Princess could not help thinking it would be much pleasanter to have nothing to do with the dragon at all – not even to be rescued from him. "All the princes I know are such very silly little boys," she told her father. "Why must I be rescued by a prince?"

"It's always done, my dear," said the King, taking his crown off and putting it on the grass, for they were alone in the garden, and even kings must unwind sometimes.

"Father, darling," said the Princess presently, when she had made a daisy chain and put it on the King's head, where the crown ought to have been. "Father, darling, couldn't we tie up one of the silly little princes for the dragon to look at – and then I could go and kill the dragon and rescue the prince? I fence much better than any of the princes we know."

"What an unladylike idea!" said the King, and put his crown on again, for he saw the Prime Minister coming with a basket of new-laid Bills for him to sign. "Dismiss the thought, my child. I rescued your mother from a dragon, and you don't want to set yourself up above her, I should hope?"

"But this is the last dragon. It is different from all other dragons."

"How?" asked the King.

"Because he is the last," said the Princess, and went off to her fencing lessons, with which she took great pains. She took great pains with all her lessons – for she could not give up the idea of fighting for the dragon. She took such pains that she became the strongest and boldest and most skilful and most sensible princess in Europe. She had always been the prettiest and nicest.

And the days and years went on, till at last the day came which was the day before the Princess was to be rescued from the dragon. The prince who was to do this deed of valour was a pale prince, with large eyes and a head full of mathematics and philosophy, but he had unfortunately neglected his fencing lessons. He was to stay the night at the palace, and there was a banquet.

After supper the Princess sent her pet parrot to the prince with a note. It said:

Please, Prince, come on to the terrace. I want to talk to you without anybody else hearing. – The Princess.

So, of course, he went – and he saw her gown of silver a long way off shining among the shadows of the trees like water in starlight. And when he came quite close to her he said: "Princess, at your service," and bent his cloth-of-gold-covered knee and put his hand on his cloth-of-gold-covered heart.

"Do you think," said the Princess earnestly, "that you will be able to kill the dragon?"

"I will kill the dragon," said the Prince firmly, "or perish in the attempt."

"It's no use your perishing," said the Princess.

"It's the least I can do," said the Prince.

"What I'm afraid of is that it'll be the most you can do," said the Princess.

"It's the only thing I can do," said he, "unless I kill the dragon."

"Why should you do anything for me is what I can't see," said she.

"But I want to," he said. "You must know that I love you better than anything in the world."

When he said that he looked so kind that the Princess began to like him a little.

"Look, here," she said, "no one else will go out tomorrow. You know they tie me to a rock and leave me – and then everybody scurries home and puts up the shutters and keeps them shut till you ride through the town in triumph shouting that you've killed the dragon, and I ride on the horse behind you weeping for joy."

"I've heard that this is how it is done," said he.

"Well, do you love me well enough to come very quickly and set me free – and we'll fight the dragon together?"

"It wouldn't be safe for you."

"Much safer for both of us for me to be free, with a sword in my hand, than tied up and helpless. Do agree."

He could refuse her nothing. So he agreed. And next day everything happened as she had said.

When he had cut the cords that tied her to the rock they stood on the lonely mountain-side looking at each other.

"It seems to me," said the Prince, "that this ceremony could have been arranged without the dragon."

"Yes," said the Princess, "but since it has been arranged with the dragon –"

"It seems such a pity to kill the dragon – the last in the world," said the Prince.

"Well then, don't let's," said the Princess, "let's tame it not to eat princesses but to eat out of their hands. They say everything can be tamed by kindness."

"Taming by kindness means giving them things to eat," said the Prince. "Have you got anything to eat?"

She hadn't, but the Prince owned that he had a few biscuits. "Breakfast was so very early," said he, "and I thought you might have felt faint after the fight."

"How clever," said the Princess, and they took a biscuit in each hand. And they looked here, and they looked there, but never a dragon could they see.

"But here's its trail," said the Prince, and pointed to where the rock was scarred and scratched so as to make a track leading to a dark cave. It was like cart-ruts in a Sussex road, mixed with the marks of sea-gulls' feet on the sea-sand. "Look, that's where it's dragged its brass tail and planted its steel claws."

"Don't let's think how hard its tail and its claws are," said the Princess, "or I shall begin to be frightened – and I know you can't tame anything, even by kindness, if you're frightened of it. Come on. Now or never."

She caught the Prince's hand in hers and they ran along the path towards the dark mouth of the cave. But they did not run into it. It really was so very dark.

So they stood aside, and the Prince shouted: "What ho! Dragon there! What ho within!" And from the cave they heard an answering voice and great clattering and creaking. It sounded as though a rather large cotton-mill was stretching itself and waking up out of its sleep.

The Prince and the Princess trembled, but they stood firm.

"Dragon – I say, dragon!" said the Princess, "do come out and talk to us. We've brought you a present."

"Oh yes – I know your presents," growled the dragon in a huge rumbling voice. "One of those precious princesses, I suppose? And I've got to come out and fight for her. Well, I tell you straight, I'm not going to do it. A fair fight I wouldn't say no to – a fair fight and no favour – but one of these put-up fights where you've got to lose – no! So I tell you. If I wanted a princess I'd come and take her, in my own time – but I don't. What do you suppose I'd do with her, if I'd got her?"

"Eat her, wouldn't you?" said the Princess, in a voice that trembled a little.

"Eat a fiddle-stick end," said the dragon very rudely. "I wouldn't touch the horrid thing."

The Princess's voice grew firmer.

"Do you like biscuits?" she said.

"No," growled the dragon.

"Not the nice little expensive ones with sugar on the top?"

"No," growled the dragon.

"Then what do you like?" asked the Prince.

"You go away and don't bother me," growled the dragon, and they could hear it turn over, and the clang and clatter of its turning echoed in the cave like the sound of the steam-hammers in the Arsenal at Woolwich.

The Prince and Princess looked at each other. What were they to do? Of course it was no use going home and telling the King that the dragon didn't want princesses – because His Majesty was very old-fashioned and would never have believed that a new-fashioned dragon could ever be at all different from an old-fashioned dragon. They could not go into the cave and kill the dragon. Indeed, unless he attacked the Princess it did not seem fair to kill him at all.

"He must like something," whispered the Princess, and she called out in a voice as sweet as honey and sugar-cane:

"Dragon! Dragon dear!"

"WHAT?" shouted the dragon. "Say that again!" And they could hear the dragon coming towards them through the darkness of the cave. The Princess shivered, and said in a very small voice:

"Dragon – Dragon dear!"

And then the dragon came out. The Prince drew his sword, and the Princess drew hers – the beautiful silver-handled one that the Prince had brought in his motor-car. But they did not attack; they moved back as the dragon came out, all the vast scaly length of him, and lay along the rock – his great wings halfspread and his silvery sheen gleaming like diamonds in the sun. At last they could retreat no further – the dark rock behind them stopped their way – and with their backs to the rock they stood swords in hand and waited.

The dragon drew nearer and nearer – and now they could see that he was breathing fire and smoke as they had expected. He came crawling slowly towards them wriggling a little as a puppy does when it wants to play and isn't quite sure whether you're not cross with it.

And then they saw that great tears were coursing down its brazen cheek.

"Whatever's the matter?" said the Prince.

"Nobody" sobbed the dragon, "ever called me 'dear' before!"

"Don't cry, dragon dear," said the Princess. "We'll call you 'dear' as often as you like. We want to tame you."

"I am tame," said the dragon – "that's just it. That's what nobody but you has ever found out. I'm so tame that I'd eat out of your hands."

"Eat what, dragon dear?" said the Princess. "Not biscuits?" The dragon slowly shook his heavy head.

"Your kindness quite undragons me," it said. "No one has ever asked any of us what we like to eat – always offering us princesses, and then rescuing them – and never once, 'What'll you take to drink the King's health in?' Cruel hard I call it," and it wept again.

"But what would you like to drink our health in?" said the Prince. "We're going to be married today, aren't we, Princess?"

She said that she supposed so.

"What'll I take to drink your health in?" asked the dragon. "Ah, you're something like a gentleman, you are sir. I don't mind if I do sir. I'll be proud to drink your and your good lady's health in a tiny drop of" – its voice faltered – "to think of you asking me so friendly like," it said. "Yes, sir, just a tiny drop of puppuppuppuppupetrol – tha-that's what does a dragon good, sir –"

"I've lots in the car," said the Prince and was off down the mountain like a flash. He was a good judge of character and knew that with this dragon the Princess would be safe. "If I might make so bold," said the dragon, "while the gentleman's away – p'raps just to pass the time you'd be so kind as to call me Dear again, and if you'd shake claws with a poor old dragon that's never been anybody's enemy but his own – well, the last of the dragons'll be the proudest dragon that's ever been since the first of them."

It held out an enormous paw, and the great steel hooks that were its claws closed over the Princess's hand as softly as the claws of the Himalayan bear will close over the bit of bun you hand it through the bars at the zoo.

And so the Prince and Princess went back to the palace in triumph, the dragon following them like a pet dog. And all through the wedding festivities no one drank more earnestly to the happiness of the bride and bridegroom than the Princess's pet dragon – whom she had at once named Fido.

And when the happy pair were settled in their own kingdom, Fido came to them and begged to be allowed to make himself useful.

"There must be something I can do," he said, rattling his wings and stretching his claws. "My wings and claws and so on ought to be turned to some account – to say nothing of my grateful heart."

So the Prince had a special saddle or howdah made for him – very long it was – like the tops of many tramcars fitted together. One hundred and fifty seats were fitted to this, and the dragon, whose greatest pleasure was now to give pleasure to others, delighted in taking parties of children to the sea-side. It flew through the air quite easily with its hundred and fifty little passengers – and would lie on the sand patiently waiting till they were ready to return. The children were very fond of it, and used to call it Dear, a word which never failed to bring tears of affection and gratitude to its eyes. So it lived, useful and respected, till quite the other day – when someone happened to say, in his hearing, that dragons were out-of-date, now so much new machinery had come in. This so distressed him that he asked the King to change him into something less old-fashioned, and the kindly monarch at once changed him in to a mechanical contrivance. The dragon, indeed, became the first aeroplane.

Giants, Witches and Enchantments

Baba Yaga, the Bony-legged Witch
a Russian folk tale

There was once a wicked woman who hated her stepdaughter so much that she pushed the little girl out of doors and told her to go and borrow a needle and thread from Baba Yaga, the bony-legged witch. The girl's stepmother did it when her husband was out at work, so the little girl had no one to turn to and she was terrified. Baba Yaga had iron teeth, and lived in the middle of the deep, dark forest, in a hut which moved about on hens' legs. Neverthless, the girl dared not disobey her cruel stepmother. So off she went into the deep, dark forest.

The little girl was soon among tall, prickly trees that whispered all around her, and she quite forgot which way was which. Big tears began to glisten in her eyes.

"Do not weep, little girl," came a cheerful voice. The little girl looked up to see that a little nightingale was talking to her. "You are a kind-hearted girl and I will tell you what I can to help you. Pick up any things that you come across along the path and make sure you use them wisely."

So the little girl set off again, further into the deep, dark forest.

As she walked
along, she saw a
neatly folded handkerchief
lying among the pine-needles, and she
put it in her pocket. A little further on, she took
some ribbons that were dangling from the branches. A
few steps on, she picked up a little can of oil that lay amongst some
rocks. Next, she came across a big, juicy bone and then a large
maple-leaf sprinkled with some tasty-looking morsels of meat – and
then her pocket was full.

It wasn't long before some big iron gates came into view up
ahead, and beyond them was Baba Yaga's hut, running about on its
hens' legs. The little girl shivered with fear. Suddenly a howling wind
rose up which sent the branches of the trees whipping fiercely around
her head. *I'll never get near that horrible hut at this rate*, the little girl
realised, ducking the boughs coming at her thick and fast. She
thought quickly. She pulled out the ribbons and tied them onto the
trees, and as soon as she did so, the wind dropped to a gentle breeze
and the branches became still.

Then the little girl tried to push open the gates, but a dreadful
creaking and groaning tore the air. The girl took the oil can from her

pocket and gave the hinges a good oiling. After that, the gate opened without a squeak, and the girl passed through.

All of a sudden, a drooling, snarling dog came running at her out of nowhere, barking fit to wake the dead. Quick as a flash, the girl grabbed the big, juicy bone and threw it to the dog. He forgot his attack immediately and lay down and began to gnaw.

Now the girl faced the hut itself, scuttling about on its awful scaly legs. And there on the steps stood BABA YAGA THE BONY-LEGGED! "Come in, my dear!" grinned the witch, showing her iron teeth. "While I'm searching for that needle and thread you want, you can have a nice bath and do my spinning for me."

Baba Yaga gripped the girl's arm with her claw-like fingers and pulled her up the steps into the house. "Run her a bath and be quick about it!" she screamed at her pale-faced maid, before whispering "Make sure you scrub her well, all ready for eating." Then Baba Yaga the bony-legged bustled away.

The pale-faced maid began to hurry about filling the bath with water, and the little girl saw that she was trembling with fear of Baba Yaga the bony-legged. "I am sorry for you having to live and work here," the little girl said. "Here, have this handkerchief as a little present to cheer you up."

"Oh thank you," the pale-faced maid sighed, gazing in delight at the lovely embroidery. "I will use a teacup instead of a jug to fill the bath, so you have more time to escape."

Then the little girl noticed a skinny black cat in the corner. "You don't look as if you've eaten properly for ages," she said, stroking his tatty fur. "Here, have these scraps of meat."

"Oh thank you," the skinny black cat purred, neatly washing his paws. "I will do the spinning for you, so you have more time to escape. Now take this magic towel and comb and run for your life. When you hear Baba Yaga coming, throw each of them behind you, one by one."

So the little girl took the magic towel and comb and began to run for her life through the deep, dark forest, while the cat sat down at the spinning wheel, tangled the wool into a big mess and hid behind it, and began to spin.

Several times, the witch passed the open door of the room and peered in. But when she heard the whirr of the spinning wheel and saw the pile of tangled wool, she went away content that the little girl was working hard. But by and by, the witch began to get suspicious that the pile of wool wasn't getting any smaller. "Are you sure you know how to spin properly, little girl?" she screeched.

"Yes, thank you," yowled the cat, trying to sound like the little girl but failing terribly. Then Baba Yaga the bony-legged screamed with fury. She rushed into the room and grabbed the cat by the scruff of the neck. "Why did you let the girl escape?" she howled.

"You've never given me anything to eat but left-overs," the cat hissed. "That kind-hearted girl gave me tasty morsels of meat."

Then Baba Yaga stalked over to the pale-faced maid and slapped her. "Why did you let the girl escape?" she howled.

"You've never given me a single present," the pale-faced maid shouted. "That kind-hearted girl gave me a lovely hanky."

Then Baba Yaga stormed outside and threw a stick at the dog. "Why did you let the girl escape?" she howled.

"You've never given me a bone," the dog barked. "That kind-hearted girl gave me a big, juicy one to chew on."

Then Baba Yaga kicked the iron gates. "Why did you let the girl escape?" she howled.

"You've let us get all stiff and rusty," they creaked. "That kind-hearted girl soothed our aching joints with lots of lovely oil."

Finally, Baba Yaga punched the birch trees. "Why did you let the girl escape?" she howled.

"You've never once decorated our branches," they roared, "but that kind-hearted girl tied beautiful ribbons all over us."

Then Baba Yaga gnashed her iron teeth and jumped on her broomstick and raced off through the deep, dark forest after the little girl. The little girl heard the swish of the air and knew she was coming and threw down the magic towel. Suddenly a wide rushing river appeared before Baba Yaga, splashing all over her broomstick and soaking it so badly that it could no longer fly. Spitting and cursing, Baba Yaga had to get off and slowly wade across. Then Baba Yaga was off and running . . .

The little girl heard the pounding of Baba Yaga's footsteps and knew she was coming, and she threw down the magic comb. All at once, a jungle sprang up in front of Baba Yaga, so thick and dense and tangled that Baba Yaga the bony-legged could do nothing to find her way through it. She squawked and screamed and gnashed her iron teeth, and stormed back to her horrible hut, shouting all the way.

The little girl saw her father standing at the door of their house, and she rushed to tell him all about her stepmother's evil plot. Her father pushed the wicked woman out of doors and drove her into the magic jungle – after which, she was never seen again. Then the little girl and her father lived happily on their own, and the nightingale came to visit every day.

The Selfish Giant

retold from the original tale by Oscar Wilde

Once there was a beautiful garden in which the children used to play every day on their way home from school. The children didn't think that the beautiful garden belonged to anyone in particular. But one day a huge giant strode in and boomed, "What are you all doing here? This is MY garden. Get lost!" Seven years ago, the giant had gone to visit his friend the Cornish ogre. Now he was back and he wanted his garden all to himself.

Of course, the children ran away at once. But the giant wasn't satisfied. Straight away, he put up a high fence all the way around his garden with a noticeboard outside which read: TRESPASSERS WILL BE PROSECUTED. He really was a very selfish giant.

Now the poor children had nowhere to play. But the giant didn't give any thought to that. He was too busy wondering why the blossom had fallen from the trees, why the flowers had withered, and why all the birds seemed to have flown away. *Surely it is meant to be the springtime,* the giant thought to himself as he looked out of the window and saw huge flakes of snow beginning to tumble from the sky. Frost painted the trees silver. A blanket of ice chilled the ground and hardened the plants into stiff, lifeless spikes. Day after day, the north wind roared around the giant's garden, zooming around his roof and howling down his chimney pots. And the hail came to visit too, battering on the giant's windows until the giant bellowed with annoyance and clapped his hands over his ears against the noisy rattling.

Then one Saturday, the giant woke up to hear a sound he had almost forgotten – it was a bird, chirruping and cheeping in his garden. A beautiful perfume tickled the giant's nose . . . It was the scent of flowers! "Spring has come at last!" the giant beamed, and he pulled on his clothes and ran outside into his garden.

The giant couldn't believe what he saw. The snow had melted, the frost and ice were gone, the sky was blue and the breeze was gentle and warm. And there were children everywhere. They had crept back into his garden through a hole that had worn away in the fence. Now children were sitting in trees heavy with ripe fruit. Playing among flowerbeds filled with nodding blossoms.

Running over emerald green grass scattered with daisies and buttercups. And the sound of their happy laughter filled the air.

Only in one corner of the garden was it still winter. A little boy was standing in a patch of snow, looking up at the bare branches of a chestnut tree and crying because he couldn't reach it. The giant's heart ached as he watched. "Now I know what makes my garden beautiful," the giant murmured. "It is the children. How selfish I have been!"

The giant strode through the garden towards the sobbing little boy. The giant scooped him up gently and set him among the icy boughs of the chestnut tree. At once, broad green leaves appeared all over the branches and down below, the snow vanished and it was spring. The little boy's face brightened into a huge smile and he reached his arms up around the giant's neck and hugged him.

"It is your garden now, little children," laughed the giant, and the children skipped about delightedly. The giant took his axe and knocked down the fence and had more fun than he had ever had in his life by playing with them all day. Only one thing spoiled the giant's new happiness. He looked all over his garden for the little boy whom he had helped into the tree, but he was nowhere to be found. The giant loved the little boy the best, because he had kissed him, and he longed more than anything to see his friend again.

Many years passed by and the children came every day to play in the beautiful garden. The giant became old and creaky and eventually he could no longer run about and let the children climb over him as he had done. The giant sat in a special armchair so he could watch the children enjoying themselves. "My garden is very beautiful," he would say to himself, 'but the children are the most beautiful things of all." Sometimes the giant's huge grey head would nod forwards and he would begin to snore, and the children would creep away quietly so they didn't disturb him. And one afternoon, the giant woke from such a little doze to see an astonishing sight.

In the farthest corner of his garden was a golden tree he had never seen before. The giant's heart leaped for joy, for standing underneath it was the little boy he had loved.

The giant heaved himself up from his armchair and shuffled across the grass as fast as his old legs would take him. But when he drew near the little boy, his face grew black as thunder. There were wounds on the little boy's palms and on his feet. "Who has dared to hurt you?" boomed the giant. "Tell me, and I will go after them with my big axe!"

"These are the marks of love," the little boy smiled, and he took the giant's hand. "Once, you let me play in your garden," the little boy said. "And today, you shall come with me to mine, which is in Paradise."

And when the children came running to play that afternoon, they found the giant lying dead under the beautiful tree, covered with a blanket of snowy-white blossoms.

Aladdin and the Lamp

a tale from The Arabian Nights

Aladdin's father had died years ago, abandoning Aladdin with no education, no job and no money. And so Aladdin lived life as a street urchin until there was a knock at his mother's door one evening and in strode a tall, turbaned man with a flowing cloak and the longest moustache Aladdin had ever seen.

"May Allah be praised! At last I have found you both!" the man cried, smiling broadly at Aladdin's mother. "I am Aladdin's long-lost uncle, a wealthy merchant, and I offer my nephew Aladdin the chance to come and work for me and make his fortune."

At this, Aladdin's mother's eyes opened wide and round. "I'm sure your father never mentioned a brother," she hissed under her breath to her son. "But don't be so foolish as to point it out!" And she set about making the merchant truly welcome.

Next morning, Aladdin was horrified to find that he was woken up at sunrise, forced to wash and tidy his hair, and pushed out of doors to begin his new career. Still half-asleep, he ran to keep up with his so-called uncle as he strode at a cracking pace through the bazaar, past the harbour, and right into the burning hot desert. "Find some wood and build a fire," his uncle ordered, and from the tone of his voice, Aladdin thought it was best not to argue. His uncle scattered some strange-smelling powders into the flames and chanted words in a weird language. There was a blaze of green fire and the ground trembled under their feet. When the smoke cleared, a trapdoor had appeared in the earth before them.

Aladdin's uncle heaved it open and bellowed at Aladdin, "Go down and find me a lamp!"

Aladdin was frozen with fear. His teeth chattered and his knees knocked with terror at all that had happened.

"You useless boy!" Aladdin's uncle roared, sounding highly like Aladdin's mother. He took a ring from his hand and shoved it roughly onto Aladdin's finger. "This magic ring will keep you safe. Now go!" And he pushed Aladdin through the trapdoor and onto the staircase.

Down, down, down into the darkness went Aladdin. He hurried through several gloomy caves and finally reached a beautiful garden. Many trees were growing there, covered in brightly coloured fruits. Aladdin couldn't resist picking handfuls of the glassy fruits and filling his pockets and shirt. He gasped with relief as he saw a rusty lamp resting on the grass, and he stuffed that into his shirt too. Then he was off back through the caves . . .

Now Aladdin hadn't spent all that time on the streets without becoming very streetwise. He was highly suspicious about his so-called uncle and, of course, Aladdin's suspicions were right. The merchant was in fact an evil sorcerer who knew powerful black magic. The sorcerer's wicked arts had shown him the whereabouts of the cave and the powers of the secret lamp that lay within, and he had worked hard for years to try to find a way in. Eventually, the sorcerer discovered that no one was allowed to enter the cave and take the lamp for themselves. Someone else had to do it for them – someone like a street-urchin, who wouldn't be missed. Because that someone had to remain locked in the cave forever!

Now Aladdin could see the sorcerer's eyes glinting greedily down through the square hole that led to the upper world. "Give me the lamp!" the sorcerer barked.

All Aladdin wanted to do was to get out of there as quickly as possible. "Help me out first and then I'll give it to you," he shouted back.

"I said, give me the lamp!" the sorcerer insisted.

Aladdin wasn't stupid. "Sure," he yelled, "just as soon as you get me out of here!"

"GIVE ME THE LAMP, YOU STUPID BOY!" roared the sorcerer.

Well, that did it. Aladdin hated people telling him he was worthless. "NO!" he shouted. "I found it and now I'm going to keep it!"

The sorcerer hopped about with rage, cursing and spluttering. "Then have it," he screamed, "and enjoy it in the darkness forever!" He thundered out the magic words and the trapdoor slammed shut with a massive crash. When Aladdin put his hands up and felt about, the opening was gone.

"What have I done!" Aladdin moaned, wringing his hands. As he did so, he happened to rub the sorcerer's ring. There was a blinding flash and a huge genie stood before him.

"I am the genie of the ring!" the massive apparition thundered. "Speak your wish, O master, and I will obey."

"I wish to heaven I was out of this cave!" Aladdin howled.

At once, Aladdin found himself back on the sands of the desert, blinking in the hot sunlight. He raced home and blurted out his whole sorry adventure to his mother. At first she thought he was telling one of his usual stories, but then Aladdin showed her the multi-coloured glass fruits and rusty old lamp.

"If we sell these glittery baubles and this old lamp," his mother sighed, "we'll at least have some pennies to buy some bread and cheese to go with our soup tonight."

"But we won't get the best price for the lamp unless I try to clean it up a bit," said Aladdin. He picked it up and began to rub at it with his sleeve.

Once more, there was a blinding flash and a genie even bigger than the genie of the ring stood before him. "I am the genie of the lamp!" roared the enormous spirit. "Speak your wish, O master, and I will obey."

"Bring us some food!" was the starving Aladdin's command.

Suddenly there was a table before them, covered with huge golden platters laden with delicious food. Aladdin and his mother could hardly believe their eyes. In a few minutes, their stomachs were more full than they had been in years. And after they'd sold one of the gold platters in the market, their purses were too.

After that, the lives of Aladdin and his mother changed for the better. They were clever not to arouse suspicion by selling the gold platters only one at a time, when their purses were becoming empty. No one would have called them rich, although they lived much more comfortably than they had before. And so life would probably have gone on, if Aladdin hadn't been caught up in town one day in a great procession. Hundreds of slaves with swords at their sides came marching through the bazaar, and in the middle of them, high on their shoulders, was a magnificent litter of gold and silver. As the litter was carried past Aladdin, the swishing silk curtains swung just a little to one side, and inside Aladdin glimpsed the beautiful Princess Balroubadour.

From that moment on, Aladdin was head over heels in love. He couldn't speak, he couldn't eat, he couldn't sleep, for thinking of the beautiful Princess Balroubadour. Aladdin's mother watched her son grow thinner and paler by the day, and finally decided she had to do something about it – even if it was the most foolish thing she had ever done in her life. She loaded up one of the golden platters with the coloured, glassy fruits that Aladdin had brought back from the sorcerer's cave, and she went to see the princess's father – the Sultan of Baghdad himself!

Of course, the sultan realised what the jewels were at once – and he had never seen such huge, fine diamonds, emeralds, rubies and sapphires in his life. Being a greedy man, and hoping that there were more where those came from, he agreed at once that Aladdin should marry his daughter and become his son-in-law.

Aladdin was overjoyed, and that night he dared to use the lamp once more and conjure up the genie. By morning, a splendid palace with golden domes and pearl spires and nine hundred and ninety-nine stained glass windows had been built exactly opposite the sultan's own palace. The sultan clapped his hands with delight, the wedding festivities were held that very afternoon, and Aladdin took his beautiful bride to live in his splendid new home.

It was fortunate that Princess Balroubadour felt the same way about Aladdin as he felt about her, and together they were completely happy – until one day, when Aladdin was out hunting, a ragged old pedlar came through the streets of the bazaar shouting, "New lamps for old! New lamps for old!" The princess and her maid rushed to the eighty-eighth window of the palace to look out on the funny little man who was offering to swap good wares for bad.

"How silly!" the maid giggled, and rushed to exchange the rusty old lamp in Aladdin's room. As soon as Aladdin's lamp was in the pedlar's hands, he gave a little cry of excitement and disappeared through the streets. A few seconds later, the princess, her maid and the entire palace had vanished, too! As you have probably guessed, the pedlar was none other than the wicked sorcerer.

Aladdin returned from his hunting trip to find his wife missing, his palace gone and his father-in-law furious! "Bring me my daughter within forty days," the Sultan roared, "or I'll stuff your precious jewels into your mouth and make you eat them!"

Worst of all, Aladdin no longer had his wonderful lamp. "What am I going to do?" he moaned, standing all alone in the spot where his palace had once been. He wrung his hands in despair, and as he did so, he rubbed the sorcerer's magic ring. In a flash, the genie of the ring stood before him once more. "Speak your wish, O master, and I will obey," boomed the mighty spirit.

"Bring back my palace, with everyone and everything in it!" yelped the delighted Aladdin.

But the genie shook his head firmly and said, "I cannot, master. The palace is under the power of the genie of the lamp."

Aladdin thought hard for a couple of seconds and then his face brightened. "Then take me to my wife!" he yelled.

Suddenly, Aladdin was standing in his palace in front of his startled – but overjoyed – wife. "Hurry," Princess Balroubadour urged. "The sorcerer is out at the moment, but he keeps the lamp with him at all times. We have to think of a way to get it from him."

The quickwitted Aladdin mixed a sleeping powder into a goblet of wine, gave it to the princess, and then hid behind a screen. Only a few moments later, the sorcerer came striding in, his cloak billowing out behind him. The smiling Princess Balroubadour rushed to offer him a refreshing drink – and as soon as the sorcerer had thirstily drained the sleeping potion, he collapsed on the floor in a crumpled heap.

Aladdin sprang out from behind the screen and fumbled in the sorcerer's clothes. At last, he held his wonderful lamp in his hands! He rubbed it . . . gave the order . . . and in the twinkling of an eye, he, his wife, his palace – and the sorcerer – were back in Baghdad.

Aladdin and Princess Balroubadour breathed a sigh of relief. "I don't know about you," Aladdin said to his beautiful bride, "but I've had quite enough magic for one lifetime – and besides, now I've got you, I've got everything in the world I could possibly want."

The princess nodded her agreement, and Aladdin once more rubbed his wonderful lamp. "I give you your freedom!" he told the genie, and in a blinding flash the overjoyed spirit was gone from the lamp forever.

Aladdin and the Princess Balroubadour (and of course, Aladdin's mum) lived happily ever after. And when the sorcerer eventually woke up, he got what he had always wanted – the rusty old lamp, no more and no less.

In the Castle of Giant Cruelty

retold from an original tale in John Bunyan's
The Pilgrim's Progress

There was once a dark, ugly city where no one seemed to be happy. But none of the grumpy, scowling citizens ever thought of leaving because they knew nothing of life outside the city walls. Huge, flat plains of mud surrounded the city as far as the eye could see. No one had ever braved the danger of trying to wade through them, so no one even knew if there was anything beyond the swamps. There were rumours of a far distant city where the sun always shone and where the people lived happily together – but no one really believed it existed . . . that is, except for a man called Christian.

For a long time, Christian had been growing more and more miserable with his life in the grim, depressing city. But it was the strange, glowing light that finally made him decide to leave. It was some weeks ago that Christian had first glimpsed the light, far away in the distance, beyond the mud flats. No one else seemed to be able to see it. They just shuffled around with their hands in their pockets, looking at the pavements as usual. But Christian thought the light was beautiful. "I shall leave this dreadful city and somehow reach the place the light is coming from," he decided. "Or I shall die in the attempt," he added.

Christian didn't take anything with him. He just got up the next morning and instead of making his usual way to work, he walked towards the gates that led out of the city. As people realised that Christian meant to leave town, they began to laugh and jeer at him. "You must be mad!" they mocked. "You'll be floundering in that mud by nightfall and no one will come to rescue you!" But Christian didn't listen to them. He just heaved open the rusty, creaky city gates and strode out into the swamps.

As soon as Christian was outside the city, he felt as if he had left his cares and troubles behind him. Determinedly, he began walking towards the light in the distance. He walked . . . and walked . . . and walked . . . until he had left the city so far behind that he

couldn't see its dark, smoky outline anymore. He walked and walked until he dropped with thirst and hunger and exhaustion. Christian didn't have the strength to lift himself back up. He closed his eyes and everything went black.

It was having a huge bucket of water sloshed over his face that finally brought Christian back to his senses. He sat bolt upright, gasping and choking and spluttering out the iciness that filled his nose and mouth.

"I am the Giant Cruelty!" boomed the loudest voice that Christian had ever heard. He looked up and began to tremble. He was in a stone room the size of a cave, and standing over him was a man as tall as his house back in the city. The giant had blood-shot eyes and blackened teeth and long, claw-like nails. "What were you doing, trespassing on my land?" Giant Cruelty thundered.

"I'm v-v-very s-s-s-orry," Christian stuttered. "I d-d-didn't realise I was trespassing."

"That is a pitiful excuse!" the giant bellowed. "Now you are no longer a trespasser. You are a prisoner.." The giant's eyes lit up with amusement and he cackled evilly. "I shall enjoy watching you rot in my dungeons!" he boomed, and scooped Christian up in his mighty fist.

Christian's heart thumped as he felt himself being carried down a long flight of steps. He shivered at the echoing of the giant's footsteps all around and at the damp chill in the air. He wrinkled his nose in disgust as a vile stench filled his nostrils.

Suddenly, the giant's fist opened and Christian was thrown onto the stone floor of a dungeon. A rat scampered up and squeaked in his face, and Christian sprang to his feet with shock.

"Have this bread and water," Giant Cruelty ordered, hurling a mouldy loaf at Christian and slamming down a bucket of foul-smelling water. "You have to stay alive so I can come back tomorrow and watch you scream and cry and beg for mercy."

Giant Cruelty chuckled. He slammed the door of the dungeon, locked it with a massive iron key, and stomped back up the stairs.

Christian swallowed hard and turned away from the locked door. He wasn't the only prisoner after all. Six faces peered out at him from the shadows – faces that looked even more hungry and thirsty and despairing than his own.

"How long have you been here?" Christian gulped.

"So long that we have forgotten our own names," one man sighed.

"The giant only feeds us once a week," a woman whimpered, eyeing Christian's bread and water.

"Here," Christian decided at once. "Come and join in my share with me. If we all stay strong and help each other, maybe we can find a way out of here together."

The desperate men and women didn't need inviting twice. They crept out of the shadows and fell on the loaf ravenously.

At that very moment, a spine-tingling CREAK! filled the air and the dungeon door swung wide open. To Christian's astonishment, a golden key had appeared in the lock. There were words down the shaft which read: the Key of Kindness.

Christian didn't stop to wonder at the strange key. He just grabbed it and urged, "Come on everybody!", and hurried everyone out of the dungeon and up the stairs. The Key of Kindness somehow fitted every locked door they came to and the giant seemed to have disappeared altogether.

Christian and his new friends didn't stop running until they had left the castle far behind them. Then they hugged each other, panting, and turned towards the glowing light. Christian smiled. Now he could see the faint outline of a golden city – and it was much, much closer than before. As he set off on his journey once more, he felt a new feeling in his heart. It was hope.

Freya and the Brising Necklace

a Norse myth

The beautiful goddess Freya wandered through the halls of her palace, counting her blessings. She had a wonderful husband, the god Odur, and two lovely daughters, as fair as flowers. They had an elegant home and splendid garden in the heavenly realm of Asgard, surrounded by their friends. Still, Freya's heart was restless, yearning for excitement.

Preparing her carriage pulled by cats, she decided to go on a journey. First, she travelled through Midgard to see the world of humans. Then she journeyed through the land of the light elves, Alfheim, home of her dear brother, Frey. Finally, she found herself at the borders of Svartalfheim, the rocky realm of the black dwarves.

A wicked dwarf called Dvalin and his three equally wicked brothers learned that the beautiful goddess was coming and set a trap for her. Deep inside a dark cave, they built a workshop and busied themselves with an anvil, hammer and a fiery furnace. As Freya wandered along, the noise of the dwarves sparked her curiosity and she drew closer.

Lit only by a raging furnace, Freya found four dwarves hard at work. They pretended not to notice her arrival. Looking around, she suddenly caught sight of their anvil and gasped in astonishment. There, glittering and gleaming in the golden flames, was the most beautiful necklace she had ever seen. Unbeknown to the unfortunate Freya, the necklace was enchanted. From the moment the goddess laid her eyes on it, the charms began to take effect and she felt an uncontrollable need to possess it.

"You have surely crafted the most exquisite necklace in the universe," Freya breathed, her heart pounding. "How much silver do you ask for it?"

"The Brising Necklace is indeed the most desirable adornment in all creation," Dvalin replied, "but we could not sell it for all the silver in the world."

Freya's pulse raced. She could not take her eyes off it. "Then how much gold do you ask for it?" she said.

"The Brising Necklace is not for sale for any treasure of gold," Dvalin countered.

Freya began to feel desperate. She could not walk away without it. "There must be some treasure you will take for the necklace," she implored. "Please tell me, what is your price? I am willing to pay whatever you want!"

The dwarf brothers exchanged evil glances. "The only treasure we will exchange for the necklace is you," Dvalin stated firmly. "You must be married to each of us for one day and one night, and in return, the necklace will be yours."

Freya was so enchanted that she did not hesitate. "So be it," she agreed, and the deal was done.

As soon as Freya held the Brising Necklace as her prize, she came to her senses and felt ashamed and guilty. How she regretted betraying her beloved Odur. The only solution was to keep the necklace hidden away, so no one would ever see it and find out what she had done.

Hurrying home to Asgard, she stowed the necklace safely in her chamber, setting strong magic onto the door and window locks so that only she was allowed to enter. Freya breathed a heavy sigh of relief. She never dreamed that anyone would find out about the four dwarf weddings, held deep underground in Svartalfheim. Her secret was safe forever…

However, the mischievous god Loki made it his unofficial business to find out about everything that went on in the universe. He soon discovered all about Freya's misdemeanour and, being the troublemaker he was, he delighted in telling all to Odur.

Odur was furious, not at Freya, but at Loki. "How dare you
enter my home and accuse my wife of such unfaithfulness, without a
shred of evidence!" Odur roared. "I utterly refuse to believe it. Unless
you can bring me this Brising Necklace as proof, I shall tear you limb
from limb if you cross my path again. Now get out of my sight!"

Fuming, Loki slunk away. He was determined to make Odur
eat his words by somehow stealing the necklace and showing it to
him. Loki knew that Freya had sealed the chamber with magic, so
trying to break in was out of the question. Instead, he turned himself
into a fly and zipped around the door and windows, searching for a
tiny hole to squeeze through. At last he found one right at the top of
a window seal – it was no bigger than the eye of a needle, but it was
enough.

Holding his breath, Loki wriggled through, and found himself
inside Freya's chamber. There she was, curled up asleep on her bed,
wearing the cursed Brising Necklace. Even Loki had to admit that it
truly was a priceless work. Silently, he turned himself back into
human form, and gently slid the necklace from around her throat.
Quietly unlocking the door, he stole away into the night.
When Freya awoke the next morning, finding the necklace gone and
her door unlocked, she knew at once that her guilty secret had been
discovered. Beside herself with anguish, she hurried to find her
husband to confess everything. However, Odur was nowhere to be
seen. Freya searched high and low in a panic, but her cherished
husband was gone.

Distraught, Freya dashed to the mighty Odin and threw herself
at his feet. Weeping bitterly, she told all. "I shall never rest until I find
my husband and beg his forgiveness," she sobbed.

Odin looked grave. The all-seeing father of the gods knew all about Freya's sin, and how her estranged husband had stridden away, heartbroken. He also knew where Odur was … but he decided the goddess had to learn a bitter lesson. "Wander the universe until you find Odur and win his pardon," Odin announced. "But you must wear the necklace forever more, as a permanent reminder of your mistake."

Odin sent the messenger, Heimdall, to retrieve the necklace from Loki, and soon it was clasped around Freya's neck once more. With a heavy heart, Freya wandered away from Asgard, searching for her husband. Wise Odin watched her go with fondness, knowing that all would soon be well again between them.

David and the Giant

a tale from the Old Testament of the Bible

ow David wished he could be just like his three older brothers! They were away fighting in the war with the fierce Philistines. But David was too young to join the great army of King Saul, like them. He was too young to strap on his armour and gird on his sword and face the pagan warriors, like they had. He was too young to fight to defend his country and his religion, to fight for his God, like they were.

Well, that's what David's father, the white-haired Jesse, kept telling him, anyway. So David found himself stuck at home looking after his father's sheep and listening to his father worry day and night about his other sons away at the battlefront.

One evening, David returned home from his peaceful day out on the pastures to find that his father was packing some grain, bread and cheeses. "I'm sending you to take these supplies to your brothers, David," said old Jesse, with an anxious look on his face. "It will be a dangerous trip, and I'm in half a mind not to send you at all. But they can't have very much to keep them going – and besides, I'm desperate to hear news of how they are."

David's heart leapt within his chest. At last, he was going on an adventure! He tried not to look too excited to be leaving his old father all alone at home, but he couldn't help the bright glint in his eye as he waved goodbye and set off on his horse.

After several days of hard riding, David had gained a bruised bottom and an aching back, and had lost a little of his reckless enthusiasm. In fact, when David finally reached King Saul's army camp, he no longer felt very excited at all. He found the soldiers exhausted and running away from the battlefield as fast as their wobbly legs would carry them. The retreating troops threatened to trample David underfoot as they swarmed back into the camp, and David was very glad when he finally recognised the familiar faces of his brothers among the retreating troops. "Whatever is going on?" David gasped.

"It's a giant – a real, live giant!" one of his brothers panted. "Whenever we go out to face the Philistine army in a battle, their troops don't come out to meet us. Instead, they send the giant Goliath, who challenges us to settle things by a duel – just him against one of us. It sounds fair enough – but you ought to see the size of him! There's no way any one in their right mind would face him alone! So we run away and Goliath and the Philistines stand there hurling insults at us."

At that, little David felt his blood begin to boil. You mean to say that no one has tried to beat this giant? he marvelled. Our whole army is a laughing stock? And he marched off to find King Saul. At first, King Saul was highly amused when his guards showed a little shepherd boy into his tent, who demanded, "I want you to let me fight Goliath! God has given me the strength to fight lions and bears when I'm looking after my sheep, and now he'll give me the strength to fight the giant, too!" There was a strange light of faith gleaming in the boy's eyes, so, much against his better judgement, King Saul decided to let the little shepherd boy have a go after all.

The king brought his own, very best, armour for David and helped dress him up in it. But the armour totally swamped him and he could hardly move in it. So David took the whole caboodle off again. There he stood in his simple shepherd's robe with his crook, his catapult and a bag of five round stones. And that's how he strode out to face the giant . . .

Goliath was far and away the biggest man that David had ever seen. He had legs like tree trunks and carried a spear the size of a battering ram. When the giant saw the tiny figure of the little shepherd boy coming out to meet him, he threw back his head and roared with laughter. Then he stomped forwards over the earth, ready to rip David apart like a rag doll.

David gulped as the mighty man came storming towards him. He could feel the ground shaking as the giant thundered nearer, and he set a stone onto his catapult. Now he could see the big scar on the giant's chin and the way his bristly eyebrows joined in the middle. David took aim and fired – WHAM! The little stone sank right into the centre of the giant's forehead.

"What happened?" Goliath gasped, as he collapsed.

He never found out, because David rushed up, drew the giant's own sword and hacked off the wicked giant's head. And King Saul's army chased the stunned Philistine soldiers all the way back to their own cities.

The Fisherman and the Bottle

a tale from The Arabian Nights

he fisherman was having a very bad day. The first time he had cast his nets in to the Arabian Sea, all he had pulled out was an old boot. The second time, all he had pulled out was a broken pot full of mud. The third time he had cast his nets, and all he had pulled in was an old copper bottle. But there was something about the bottle that stopped the fisherman from hurling it back into the deeps. Perhaps it was the way the stopper glinted in the light. Or maybe it was the strange wax seal around the neck, highly decorated with strange markings. It might even have been the fact that the fisherman could have sworn he heard a faint noise coming from inside. In any case, something made the fisherman plunge his hand into his pocket for his penknife, slash the wax seal around the neck, and draw out the heavy stopper.

The fisherman turned the copper bottle upside down and shook it. All that came out was a trickle of dust as fine as sand . . . a trickle of dust that seemed to blow upwards with the wind, instead of falling down . . . a trickle of dust that became a wisp of smoke . . . a wisp of smoke that became a puff of mist . . . a puff of mist that

became a cloud
billowing overhead . . . a cloud
that formed huge feet and legs, and an
enormous body, and strong arms and hands –
and a massive, fierce, bald head with golden earrings
and a long moustache and cruel eyes. In other words, there
was a gigantic genie towering over him.

"Kneel before me, you spawn of a quivering jellyfish!" the
genie roared. "And prepare to meet your death!"

"What have I done?" the terrified fisherman begged, falling to
the sand. "I know the story of Aladdin and the genie of the lamp.
Haven't I set you free? Aren't you meant to grant me wishes?"

"You have indeed set me free," the gigantic genie bellowed,
"but it is FAR TOO LATE for wishes! For the first hundred years
that I was trapped inside that copper prison, I did indeed swear
that I would grant three wishes to anyone who set me free – no
matter how greedy they were. But no one helped me, and I grew
impatient. For the next two hundred years, I swore that I would
give never-ending riches to anyone who set me free. But no one
helped me, and I grew angry. For the next five hundred years, I

swore that I would give an entire kingdom to anyone who set me free. But no one helped me – and I grew furious. It was then that I swore that the very next person I saw would taste my revenge. Now I have been trapped inside that copper prison for TWO THOUSAND YEARS. And it is you who will have the honour of receiving my punishment!"

The fisherman shuddered as the genie drew an enormous, shining, curved sword from his belt. He began to think fast if there were some way he could save himself . . .

To the genie's astonishment, the fisherman gave a friendly wink. "Come on now," the fisherman smirked, "enough of this fooling around. The way you appeared from nowhere like that was really very impressive, but I should tell you that I simply don't believe in magic."

"What do you mean, you don't believe in magic?" the genie roared, his face as black as soot.

"Well, sorcerers and genies and spells – no one believes in all that old rubbish nowadays," sniggered the fisherman, scornfully.

"Old rubbish!" blustered the genie, quite lost for words.

"So we've both had a bit of a laugh and a joke, haven't we?" continued the fisherman, quite calmly. "Now, you just tell me where you hid to make it look like you came out of the bottle, and I'll congratulate you on your fantastic trick. Then you can tell me where you're going to perform your conjuring show next time and I'll promise to bring lots of gullible friends who'll pay good money to watch you. And then we'll both shake hands on it and go home to our wives. What do you say?"

"How dare you call me a fake!" boomed the raging genie, as green smoke hissed out of his ears. "I'll show you that I'm real! I'll show you that I'm the most terrifying genie that ever came out of a bottle – I'll prove it to you, by getting back into it right now!"

Suddenly the genie's massive face began to melt, his arms and legs began to blur, his huge body began to shimmer in the air. His features became formless and shifting like a great cloud of mist. Then the cloud narrowed into a spiral of smoke that funnelled round and down and round and down . . . and right into the neck of the bottle. As the very last wisp disappeared inside, the fisherman grabbed the heavy stopper and rammed it into the neck of the bottle as hard as he could.

"I shall never cast another net as long as I live," gasped the sweating fisherman, and he hurled the bottle as far as he could out into the ocean.

So if you're ever at the beach and you see a copper bottle bobbing about in the water or washed up on the shore, be very careful before you open it, won't you . . .

The Giant's Wife

an Irish legend

I n the days when giants lived in the north of Ireland, Finn McCoull was the biggest, strongest, most handsome of them all – or so he thought. Finn could rip a pine tree out of the ground with his bare hands. He could leap across a river in one bound. He could split a boulder in half with one swish of his axe.

Now Finn had heard that there were clans of giants living in Scotland who had tree trunk-throwing competitions and boulder-carrying contests for fun. That sounded to him like great crack. So Finn decided to build a road right across the sea, so he could walk across to see these Scottish giants without getting his feet wet. Finn pulled on his big black workboots, kissed his wife Oonagh goodbye, and promised, "I'll be back in a week – ten days, tops." Then he strode off over hills and forests to the coast.

Finn began to work hard, ripping rocks from the mountains and throwing them into the sea until they piled up above the water and began to form a road. However, he was only three days into the job when a friend of his arrived at the seashore. "Finn, I don't mean to worry you, to be sure," his friend said, "but there's gossip about a strange giant who's on his way to your house to flatten you. Some say that he's leapt across the sea from Scotland without needing a boat or a bridge. People say he keeps a thunderbolt in his pocket. I've heard, too, that he has a magic little finger with as much strength in it as ten men put together!"

"Pah!" cried Finn, "I don't believe a word of it!" But secretly, he had begun to feel a little uneasy.

"One thing's for sure," his friend continued, "the stranger knows that everyone thinks you're the biggest, strongest, most handsome giant in all Ireland and he doesn't like it one little bit. He's made up his mind to find you and mince you into pieces!"

"We'll see about that!" bellowed Finn. "I'm going home right now to sit and wait for this pipsqueak of a giant, and if he dares to show his face at my front door, I'll stamp on him and squash him like an ant!" But even though Finn sounded brave, underneath it all he was really rather worried.

The minute that Finn arrived home, he sat down glumly at the kitchen table and told Oonagh all about the stories of the strange giant. "If it's true, he'll beat me into mashed potatoes!" Finn moaned.

"You men are always boasting about your muscles, but sometimes you should use your brains instead!" Oonagh laughed. "Now do as I say and leave everything else to me . . ."

Oonagh quickly found nine round flat stones and put them on a plate with a round flat oatcake, which she cleverly marked with a thumbprint so she could see which one it was. Meanwhile, Finn built an enormous baby's cradle and put it by the fireside, just as Oonagh had told him. Just then, Finn and Oonagh felt the ground begin to shake underneath them and a dark shadow fell across the house. "It's him! He's here!" panicked Finn, running to and fro in a tizzy.

"Whatever shall I do?" "Calm down!" urged Oonagh, handing her husband a bonnet and a nightdress. "Put these on and climb into the cradle!"

Finn was far too scared to argue, and soon he was dressed up like a baby and lying cuddled up in the crib. Oonagh shoved a huge bottle of milk into his mouth and went to answer the door.

"WHERE IS FINN McCOULL?" roared the massive giant who stood on the doorstep. He was certainly the biggest giant Oonagh had ever seen – and the ugliest! "WHEN I FIND HIM, I'M GOING TO RIP HIM TO SHREDS!" the giant bellowed.

"I'm afraid you've missed my husband," Oonagh smiled sweetly. "He's away at the coast, building a road across the sea to Scotland. He started this morning and he'll be finished by teatime. You can come in and wait for him if you like."

The massive giant growled something under his breath that may or may not have been "thank you".

Oonagh just laughed and gaily beckoned. "Well, you'd better

come in and have something to eat," she sang. "You'll need to get your strength up if you're going to fight my Finn. I have to say you look like a dwarf next to my fine husband!"

In the cradle, Finn's teeth began to chatter. What on earth was his wife annoying the monster giant like that for?

"Have an oatcake," Oonagh offered the stranger politely, putting one of the round, flat rocks on his plate.

The greedy giant crammed it into his mouth and took a huge bite. "OW!" he roared, spitting bits of broken teeth all over the table.

"Oh dear, didn't you like it?" Oonagh fussed. "To be sure, they're the baby's favourite!" She strode over to the cradle and gave Finn the oatcake with the thumbprint. He munched on it happily.

The strange giant peered into the cradle and his eyes opened wide. "That's Finn McCoull's baby?" he remarked, highly surprised. "My, he's a whopper of a lad, isn't he?"

"Yes," sighed Oonagh, tickling her husband under the chin while Finn cooed and gurgled as best he could. "He's got teeth all ready, you know. Here, put your finger into his mouth and feel . . . Go on."

Slowly, nervously, the giant put his magic little finger inside Finn's mouth.

CRUNCH! Finn bit down as hard as he could – right through the bone!

"AAAAAAARRRRRRRGGGGGHHHHHHH!" roared the giant. "If Finn McCoull's baby is that powerful strong, I'm not hanging around to find out what Finn McCoull is like!" And he was out of the door and away over the hills before Finn McCoull could leap out of the cradle.

Finn McCoull never did finish his road across the sea. If you go to Ireland today, you can still see it poking out into the water, half-finished. He wanted nothing more than to stay at home and enjoy the rest of his days with his beautiful, clever wife. So that's exactly what he did.

The Thunder God Gets Married
a Norse legend

U p in heaven, Thor the thunder god was furious. Someone had stolen his magic hammer. Thor's magic hammer was the terror of the gods. Whenever he threw it, it killed anything that it touched and it always returned to his hand. It was perhaps the most deadly weapon that the gods possessed to protect them against their enemies, the giants.

Now the raging Thor's roaring sounded like the clouds were clashing together. His face was so black with anger that it sent a dark shadow over the whole sky. As Thor grabbed blazing lightning bolts and hurled them through the clouds, the mischief-maker god, Loki, came nervously to see him. "I have good news, my angry friend," Loki explained. "I have used my cunning to find out that it is the giant Thrym who has stolen your hammer. He has agreed to give it back on one condition – that he has the most beautiful of all the goddesses, Freya, as his bride."

The thunder god's sulky face brightened a little and he charged off to find Freya straight away. "Put on your best dress, Freya!" Thor boomed, throwing open her wardrobe doors. "You have to marry the giant Thrym so I can get my magic hammer back."

Freya's eyes flickered with cold fire. "Excuse me, Thor," she said, calmly. "Would you care to repeat that?"

"You-have-to-marry-the-giant-Thrym-so-I-can-get-my-magic-hammer-back!" the impatient thunder god cried at top speed.

Freya stood glaring, her hands on her hips. "Firstly Thor, as the goddess of beauty I don't *have* to do anything."

Thor's face reddened.

"Secondly," Freya continued, "I wouldn't marry that ugly monster Thrym if he were the only creature left in the world."

The ashamed thunder god hung his head.

"Thirdly," Freya finished, "it's your problem, *you* sort it out."

"Sorry, Freya," Thor mumbled, shuffling about a bit. Then he turned and stormed back to Loki. The two gods sat down glumly and wracked their brains to come up with another way to get back the hammer.

"How about . . ." Thor started to suggest. Then he shook his head. "No, no good."

"What if . . ." Loki began. Then his face fell. "No, it would never work."

It looked as if Thor's magic hammer would have to stay in the land of the giants forever – until the god Heimdall had an idea.

"That's absolutely out of the question!" Thor thundered.

"Outrageous!" Loki squealed. "I'll never do it!"

"Well, you come up with another plan then," Heimdall laughed, knowing that there wasn't one.

That night, the giant Thrym was delighted to see a chariot with a bride and bridesmaid in it rumbling up to his castle steps. "It's Freya!" the gormless giant gasped with delight. "I shall gladly give back Thor's magic hammer in return for the most beautiful wife in the world!" The overjoyed giant commanded a magnificent wedding banquet to be prepared and his guests to be sent for at once.

But Thrym wouldn't have been so overjoyed if he could have seen what was underneath the veils of his bride and bridesmaid – the angry, highly-embarrassed faces of Thor and Loki! As it was, the giant was far too excited to notice how big and clumsy the bride and bridesmaid looked in their frilly dresses. Thrym didn't take in that the women had low, gruff voices and huge, hairy hands. And he hardly thought twice about the way that Freya swigged down two whole barrels of beer and devoured an entire roast ox.

When all the guests had eaten and drunk their fill, the beaming Thrym got to his feet to make a speech. "My wife and I," he began, blushing bright red, "would like to thank you all for coming here today to celebrate this happy occasion with us. Freya has made me the luckiest being in the whole universe. And now, I will keep my word and give back the magic hammer I stole from that ugly thug of a thunder god."

There was a roll of drums as one of Thrym's servants brought in the magic hammer on a cushion. Thrym held it high in the air for his marvelling guests to admire, then with a grand flourish, he presented it to his bride.

"The ugly thug of a thunder god thanks you!" roared Thor, ripping off his veil and springing to his feet. And before Thrym and his guests could really take in the trick, they were lying dead on the floor and the wedding feast was unexpectedly over.

All the gods were truly relieved to have the magic hammer back in Thor's hands in heaven, where it belonged. But it was a long time before Thor and Loki could laugh with the other gods about how charming they both looked in a dress!

Royal Adventures

The Emperor's New Clothes
retold from the original tale by Hans Christian Andersen

There was once an emperor who loved new clothes above everything else. Designers, tailors, clothmakers, dyers, and specialists in all sorts of needlework travelled to his city from all over the world. Anyone who could suggest flashy, fancy new outfits for the emperor was always very welcome at the palace.

One day, it was the turn of two weavers to be ushered into the emperor's dressing room. The emperor, his butler and all his Officers of the Royal Wardrobe, gasped with amazement as they listened to them describe their work. "We have created a special type of fabric that is so light and airy the wearer cannot feel it is there," the first weaver announced.

"Our samples are top secret, which is why we have not been able to bring any to show you," the second weaver explained.

"However we can assure you that not only are our designs and patterns exquisitely beautiful," said the first weaver, "but the fabric has the unique advantage that it is completely invisible to anyone who is not worthy of his job –"

"– or who is just plain stupid!" laughed the second weaver, and the emperor and all his courtiers gasped and chuckled along.

"We would be honoured if you would like to order the very first suit of clothes made out of this extraordinary fabric, your imperial majesty," said the first weaver, bowing low.

The emperor clapped his hands with delight. "I'd like to place an order right away!" he commanded, and he gave the two weavers a large sum of money so that they could buy the rare, expensive materials they needed and begin their work without delay.

The weavers set up their looms in the palace studio and got going right away. News of the strange cloth spread round the city like wildfire and soon everyone was talking about it. But the weavers worked behind closed doors and no one got even a glimpse of what they were doing. Still, day and night everyone heard the looms clicking and the shuttles flying, and work on the magical cloth seemed to be progressing well.

As the days went on, the emperor began to feel rather uneasy about seeing the cloth for the first time. *Imagine if I can't see the fabric myself!* he thought to himself. *How dreadfully embarrassing that would be!* The worried emperor decided to send his trusted old butler to see how the weavers were getting on. He was sure that his butler was both fit for his job and very wise, and would be sure to see the wonderful material.

The weavers bowed low and ushered the butler into the studio. But the butler couldn't see anything at all. *Heavens above!* the butler thought to himself. *Those looms look totally bare to me! I must either be a very bad butler, or else I'm an idiot. No one must ever find out . . .* So he praised the material that he could not see, told the king that the weavers' work was indeed magnificent, and everyone in the city heard that the cloth was truly unbelieveable!

Soon afterwards, the weavers sent word to the emperor that they needed more money to buy essential items for the work. The emperor had been so delighted with the butler's report that he sent them twice as much money as before.

The emperor was more excited than ever. "I'm going to have the most amazing suit of clothes in the world!" he giggled to himself ten times a day.

Eventually, just as the impatient emperor thought he was going to explode with waiting, the weavers announced their work was finished. They went to the dressing room to present the material to the emperor amid fanfares of trumpets. "Is the cloth not beautiful beyond all imagining?" the weavers sighed.

The emperor smiled a wide smile, trying to hide his horror. All that the weavers appeared to be holding up before him was thin air. The emperor's worst fear had come true – to him the cloth was invisible! *I cannot be thought to be a fool or not worthy to be ruler,* the despairing emperor thought. So he beamed and leant forwards and inspected the air. "Wonderful! Splendid! Magnificent!" he cried, and his butler and all the Officers of the Royal Wardrobe nodded and cried out compliments. None of them could see anything either, but they weren't about to risk losing their jobs by admitting it.

So the weavers got out their tape measures and their scissors and they set about cutting the thin air (or so it seemed) into a pattern. All night long they sewed with needles which appeared to have no thread, and in the morning they announced that the emperor's new clothes were ready. "Now if your imperial majesty would care to disrobe, we will dress you in the amazing garments."

The emperor swallowed hard and took off all his clothes. The weavers helped him on with the underpants and trousers and shirt and jacket that he couldn't see. "Aren't they lighter than cobwebs?" they sighed. The emperor spluttered his agreement. He couldn't feel that he had any clothes on at all.

The emperor stood back and looked at himself in the mirror. According to what he saw, he didn't have a stitch on! But he turned this way and that, pretending to admire himself. And the butler and all the Officers of the Royal Wardrobe cried out, "How wonderfully the new clothes fit you, sire!" and "We have never seen the like of the amazing colours!" and "The design is a work of genius!" – even though it looked to them as if the emperor was as naked as the day he was born.

Everyone else can see my new suit except me, the emperor thought to himself glumly. And he walked out of the palace to parade before the people in his marvellous new clothes.

The streets were lined with hundreds of men and women who *ooohed!* and *aaaahed!* over the emperor's invisible new clothes – for none of them wanted to admit that they couldn't see them.

Suddenly, a little boy's shrill voice rose over the applause of the crowd. "But the emperor has nothing on!" the child shouted. "Nothing on at all!" Suddenly there was a stunned silence and the little boy found that hundreds of pairs of eyes were staring at him. Then someone sniggered . . . someone else tried to stifle a giggle . . .

another person guffawed and snorted . . . and the whole crowd burst out into uncontrollable peals of laughter.

The emperor's face turned as red as a ripe tomato. "I am indeed a fool!" he murmured. "I have been swindled by two tricksters!" He ran back to the palace as fast as his short, naked legs could carry him – but the clever (and now very rich) weavers were long gone!

The Little Mermaid

retold from the original tale by Hans Christian Andersen

F ar, far out in the ocean, the water is as blue as cornflowers and deeper than the tallest mountain. It is there that the sea-people live, and in the very deepest waters lies the Sea King's palace of coral and mother-of-pearl. The Sea King's beloved wife had died, so his mother, the old queen, took care of his six beautiful mermaid daughters. All day long, the princesses sang and danced, swimming in and out of the pillars and halls of the palace. Sometimes shy, brightly coloured fish swam up to eat out of their hands. And at other times, each would tend the little garden that she cared for in the royal grounds. Each mermaid princess gave her garden its own particular style and design: one was shaped like a whale; another had a rockery of shells; yet another had flowerbeds where the sea-horses came to graze. But the youngest mermaid's garden was shaped like the sun that shone on the world above the sea, and the flowers that grew there blazed red and orange and yellow like the sunlight.

The little mermaid had never been up to the ocean's surface and seen the upper world, for the princesses were only allowed to do

so when they reached fifteen years
old. But the little mermaid longed
for that day to come. She loved to
hear the stories her grandmother told
of people and ships and cities and
animals and meadows and forests and
the like. And many a night the little
mermaid stood at her open chamber
window, peering up at the watery reflections of
the moon and the stars and the dark shapes of
ships as they passed like clouds above her.

When each of her sisters came of age, the little
mermaid begged them eagerly to tell her everything they
had seen. Then at last, she turned fifteen and it was her turn to see
the upper world for herself.

The little mermaid thought it was more beautiful than she had
ever imagined. Her head broke through the foam when the sun had
just gone down and the clouds looked as if they were on fire with red
and gold. The sound of music and singing was coming from a tall-
masted ship bedecked all about with coloured flags and banners.
Suddenly rockets zoomed up from it into the sky which exploded
into stars that fell glittering all around her – the little mermaid had
never seen fireworks before. When she was lifted up on the swell of
the sea, she saw onto the ship's magnificent deck and understood the
reason for the wonderful celebrations: it was the birthday party of a
prince, more handsome than any merman she had ever seen.

As the little mermaid gazed with delight at the prince and his
ship, she heard a familiar rumbling stirring deep within the sea. A
storm was coming! All at once the sky darkened. Sheets of rain lashed

the ship. The waves towered into mountains that hurled the ship upwards and sent it crashing down towards the depths. The little mermaid saw with alarm that the ship wouldn't be able to hold out against the might of the weather and the ocean, and she ducked under the waves as wooden planks and other pieces of the ship came flying out of the darkness at her head. Through the murky waters, the little mermaid was horrified to see human bodies come floating down around her – and among them was her beautiful prince, choking and gasping for air.

The little mermaid shot through the water and clutched him close to her, and began swimming up to the light until his head was above water. The little mermaid hauled the exhausted prince to the shore and let the waves wash him onto the sand, and she stayed in the foam and watched him until the storm had died away and the morning sunlight came streaming warmly through the clouds. Then she saw the green hills for the first time and heard the peal of bells, and she saw a group of young girls come skipping out of a white building with a cross on the top. One of the girls noticed the prince where he lay. She ran to him and laid his head in her lap, and slowly the prince opened his eyes. He looked up at the girl and smiled, and the little mermaid turned away sadly, for she knew the prince thought it was that girl who had rescued him. Down, down, down, the little mermaid dived into the deeps – and her heart ached all the way back to her father's palace.

From that moment on, the little mermaid was thoughtful and sad. She longed to see her handsome prince again, to tell him that she loved him and wanted to be with him forever. She wanted to be human more than anything else in the whole world. There was only one thing she could do: make the dangerous journey to the cold, dark depths of the ocean to see the Water-Witch.

The Water-Witch's lair was set about with the skeletons of humans she had drowned and the remains of ships she had wrecked. The little mermaid trembled with fear as she explained why she had come.

"What you long for is extremely difficult to give," the Water-Witch cackled. "I can make your tail disappear and give you legs so that you can walk about with the humans in the world above. But every step you take will be as painful as if you are treading on knives. And I cannot make your prince fall in love with you. It is up to you, and you alone, to do that. If your prince marries another, the morning afterwards your heart will break and you will turn to foam on the water."

The little mermaid shuddered, but she bade the Water-Witch continue.

"The price for such strong magic is very high," spat the witch. "Once I have given you legs, there is no changing your mind. You will never be able to return to the sea as a mermaid to see your family . . . And there is one more thing. I cannot mix the potion you need unless you give me your voice."

The little mermaid longed so badly for her prince and for a human soul that she whispered, "So be it." The words were the last sounds she ever uttered. For then the Water-Witch took the little mermaid's voice and brewed up an evil-smelling potion for her in exchange.

The little mermaid felt as if her heart would break with grief as she swam back past her father's palace, leaving her sleeping family for the world above. She splashed onto the sand, half-choking through her tears and half-gasping for air, and looked at her beautiful silvery fishtail for the last time. Then the little mermaid raised the witch's brew to her lips and drank deeply. At once pain wracked her body and she fell into a dead faint . . .

The little mermaid awoke to find her handsome prince standing over her, looking worried. "Are you all right?" he asked, but the little mermaid couldn't reply. Instead, she smiled as she looked down at her body and saw that she had the prettiest pair of legs she could have wished for. Falteringly, she stood up for the very first time. The little mermaid put out her foot – and it was true, each step was like treading on knives. But soon she was dancing and running and skipping along the beach for joy, and the prince was utterly enchanted.

The prince took his new little friend back to the palace and dressed her in fine robes of silk and satin. He didn't seem to mind that she was dumb, and kept her by his side at all times, calling her "my beautiful little foundling".

Yet although the little mermaid was happier than she had ever dreamed was possible, there was a sadness in her eyes and a heaviness in her heart. Each night, she would creep out of the palace and go down to the seashore. Sometimes she saw her sisters way out among the surf, and they would sing to her sadly as they floated on the waves. Once, she even thought she glimpsed the golden crowns of her father and grandmother – but perhaps it was just the moonlight glinting on the water.

Eventually a day came when the prince led the little mermaid onto a fine ship just like the one from which she had rescued him. They sailed for a night and a day, and all the time the little mermaid longed to leap into the waves and dive down to see her family far below. The ship finally arrived in the harbour of a neighbouring kingdom, and all the people lined the streets to meet them, waving flags and cheering. "See how they welcome me," the prince whispered to the little mermaid. "For today I am going to marry their princess."

The little mermaid felt as if someone had grabbed her heart with icy fingers. Surely it couldn't be true? But when the prince's bride came running down the palace steps to meet him, the little mermaid understood. It was the girl who had found him on the beach; the girl whom the prince thought had saved him from the sea; the girl whom the prince thought was the little mermaid.

That afternoon, the little mermaid stood in church dressed in silk and gold, holding the bride's train. And all the way back to the ship, she cried silent, dry tears.

That night, as the splendid ship floated on the waves, there were flags and fireworks and music and dancing – and the little mermaid felt no more a part of the celebrations than she had when she had watched the prince's birthday party from afar.

The little mermaid stood on the deck all night and listened to the sighing of the sea. She felt the warm night wind on her face and her hair floated in the damp sea mists. When the first rays of the dawn lit up the horizon, the little mermaid prepared herself to dissolve into foam on the waves. But instead, she saw transparent beings of light flying to her through the air. They lifted her up on their wings and soared off into the sky, and the little mermaid found that she was one of them. "We are the daughters of the air," the beautiful beings explained. "We do not have an immortal soul, but if we perform enough acts of goodness and kindness, we will one day win one for ourselves. And this is your reward for the suffering you have endured."

The little mermaid raised her hands towards the sun and the tears in her eyes were tears of joy. She looked down upon the prince and his bride on their ship. They were searching for her sadly in the water, thinking she had fallen overboard. But the little mermaid didn't stay to watch them for long. She blew them a kiss and flew onwards with the daughters of the air.

The Golden Touch
a myth from Ancient Greece

There was once a king called Midas who loved gold more than anything in the world. Each day, he spent hour after hour in his treasure house, running his hands through his sacks of gold coins, admiring his golden jars and statues, and holding up his golden jewellery to the light to watch it gleam and shine. Midas thought that the precious metal was a much more delightful colour than the emerald green of the grass or the sapphire blue of the sea. He thought it was far more beautiful than the gold of waving fields of wheat, the gold of his wife's hair – even the gold of sunshine.

The king once helped the god Dionysus by taking care of one of his friends who was lost. Dionysus was very grateful and insisted, "Let me repay you for your kindness by granting you a wish! Now think hard . . . Make it something good! . . . Whatever you like . . ."

Midas knew exactly what he wanted. "I wish for everything I touch to turn to gold!" he declared.

"Are you sure about that?" Dionysus asked. "Are you quite, quite sure?"

"What could be better?" cried Midas, delightedly.

"Very well then," sighed the god. "It is done."

Midas couldn't wait to try out his new powers. He hurried over to a tree and snapped off a twig. Unbelievable! It immediately grew heavy and bright. It had turned to solid gold. Joyfully, Midas rushed around touching everything in his royal garden. Soon the apples hung on the trees like golden baubles. The flowers hardened into gold sculptures. The fountain froze into a spray of golden glitter and the grass solidified into a gold pavement.

"How wonderful!" laughed Midas, clapping his hands. "Now for my palace!" and he picked up his robes and ran inside. By the time Midas reached the cool of his great chamber, his clothes had stiffened into a fabric woven from pure gold thread. "Ooof!" puffed Midas. "That's a little heavy!" The weight of his golden clothes were dragging him down, slowing him up and making his shoulders ache. *Still,* thought Midas, *that's a minor botheration compared to how beautiful my robes now look!* He set off through the halls and corridors, touching pillars, pictures, doors, furniture, floors . . . until everything glowed gold.

Phew! It was hungry, thirsty work! Midas sank into one of his new golden chairs at his new golden dining table and called for his servants to bring him his lunch. He wriggled about a bit on his rock hard seat, but couldn't get comfy. "Never mind!" said Midas to himself, as the servants brought in platter after platter of delicious food. "I don't know any other king who is rich enough to eat off gold plates!" And he touched each serving dish and bowl and saw them gleam.

"Amazing!" Midas whooped, and licking his lips, he reached for a juicy chicken leg. "OWWW!" he yelled, biting down on hard metal and breaking a tooth. He reached for a goblet of wine and took a gulp. "AAARRGH!" Midas roared, as the mouthful of gold got stuck in his throat. The king pushed his chair back, spitting out the hunk of treasure.

"Oh, no!" the king moaned. Suddenly he realised what the god Dionysus had been trying to warn him about. "I'm going to have a whole kingdom full of gold, but I'm not going to be able to eat or drink anything!"

At that very moment, Midas's golden doors swung open and his little daughter came running towards him. Midas backed away in horror – but it was too late. "Daddy!" the little girl cried, flinging her arms happily around him. Suddenly the king's beloved daughter was no more than a lifeless statue. Midas howled with misery and huge tears began to stream from his eyes. "I would gladly give away every piece of gold that I own to have my little girl back again," he wailed. "How foolish I have been! There must be some way to take back my wish!"

Desperately trying not to touch anything else, Midas hurried to Dionysus and begged him to undo his magic. "Go and wash in the River Pactolus," the god instructed him. As soon as the king had done so, he was hugely relieved to find that his golden touch was gone. All the things Midas had turned into gold were back to normal – including his beautiful little daughter. After that, if the king had had his way, he would never have looked at another nugget of gold as long as he lived. But the god Dionysus turned the sandy bed of the River Pactolus gold for ever more, so that every time Midas walked along its banks, he would remember his greedy mistake.

The Nutcracker Prince

retold from the original tale by Ernst Hoffmann

r Drosselmeier was an old man with a secret. In his youth, he had been the most nimble-fingered, highly skilled craftsman in the entire royal court. Dr Drosselmeier had made clocks that were mechanical wonders. Some chimed with a hundred tinkling bells. Others were decorated with tiny musicians that danced and played their instruments as they struck the hour. Some even had secret doors, out of which little birds fluttered and flew around the room, chirruping the passing minutes. Yes, Dr Drosselmeier's clocks had been the talk of the palace. But the most amazing thing he had ever made was a mouse-trap.

Dr Drosselmeier had invented a brilliant clockwork trap that caught mice in their hundreds, twenty-four hours a day. Everyone in the palace had been delighted – except for the Mouse King. He too had lived in the palace with his subjects. Now, he was forced to leave and find another home, and he was furious about it. The Mouse King knew powerful magic and he took his revenge on Dr Drosselmeier by turning his nephew into an ugly, wooden doll.

The doll wore a painted soldier's uniform and it had a prince's

crown painted mockingly
onto its head, and its jaws moved so it could
crack nuts between its teeth. The Mouse King's spell
was so strong that there was only one way to undo it. Firstly,
the nutcracker prince had somehow to kill the evil Mouse King. And
secondly, a little girl had to love him, in spite of his ugliness. Well,
Dr Drosselmeier had no idea where the Mouse King had gone, and
he certainly didn't know a little girl kind enough to take pity on the
poor, ugly wooden doll. And so his nephew had stayed a nutcracker.

From that moment on, Dr Drosselmeier had never made
another clock. He lost all heart for mechanical things and so he lost
his job at the palace, too. Dr Drosselmeier blamed himself entirely for
his nephew's dreadful disappearance and he had never breathed a
word of what had happened to anyone. But ever since, he had been
trying to find a way to break the Mouse King's spell . . . and at last,
he thought he had.

Dr Drosselmeier's goddaughter, Clara, had grown into the
kindest little girl anyone could wish to meet. If any little girl was
going to take pity on the stiff, glaring nutcracker prince, it would
be Clara.

Now it was Christmas Eve, and Dr Drosselmeier had arrived at Clara's house trembling with excitement. He wasn't excited because there was a party going on with games and music and dancing. No, Dr Drosselmeier was excited because tonight was the night he hoped the evil magic would be undone and his nephew would return to life. While the party guests talked and joked and laughed together, Dr Drosselmeier set about emptying the huge bag he had brought with him. It was filled with gingerbread and shortcake, candy walking sticks and sugar pigs, nuts and bon bons, nougat and humbugs . . . High and low, in every corner of the room, Dr Drosselmeier heaped piles of all the Mouse King's favourite things to eat. *That should tempt him out from wherever he's hiding*, thought Dr Drosselmeier, determinedly.

Then it was time to give Clara her Christmas present. The little girl's eyes opened wide with excitement as she stripped off the sparkly paper. But her face suddenly fell as she saw the ugly nutcracker prince. Then, gently, Clara stroked the doll's face. He wasn't cute, he wasn't cuddly – he wasn't even new! But that was exactly why Clara decided she loved him. She couldn't bear to think of leaving him all alone, laughed at and unloved – especially at Christmas time. Clara clutched the nutcracker prince close to her and hugged him tight. And Dr Drosselmeier slipped away from the party, his heart light with hope . . .

When the party was over and it was bedtime at last, Clara tucked the wooden doll up next to her. "I love you," she whispered, just before she fell asleep. "I'll look after you always." And that night, Clara had a very strange dream. She dreamt that the nutcracker prince woke up beside her. He smiled at Clara and held her hand, and led her downstairs. There was scuffling and squeaking coming from the drawing room, and when Clara peeped around the door she saw a terrible sight. There were mice everywhere! They were climbing all over Dr Drosselmeier's goodies, fighting and biting each other to get at the sweets. And worst of all, a horrible seven-headed mouse was standing in the middle of the carpet, cackling with glee at all the arguing and the mess. The seven-headed mouse wore seven golden crowns and Clara could tell at once that he must be the king of the evil creatures.

Very bravely, the nutcracker prince charged at the gruesome Mouse King with a sword glinting in his hand and began to fight furiously. But he was completely outnumbered. The mice swarmed to their king's defence. They dragged the nutcracker prince to the ground and he disappeared under a thousand biting, clawing bodies. Just as the Mouse King threw back his head and began to laugh, Clara tore her slipper off her foot and threw it at him with all her might. WHAM! It hit the Mouse King on four of his seven horrible heads. He staggered to and fro for a second, and then collapsed dead to the floor.

As soon as the mice saw that their leader was no more, their courage deserted them. They hurried to scoop up his body and then they were gone, streaming off through cracks in the wall, holes in the skirting and gaps in the floorboards.

The nutcracker prince ran to Clara and kissed her. "Thank you for all you have done for me," he whispered, and there were tears sparkling in his painted eyes. "Let me repay you by taking you on a wonderful journey to my kingdom, the realm of sweets . . ."

It was the most wonderful dream Clara had ever had. She travelled through forests made of barley sugar, crossed rivers that ran with lemonade, picked flowers of sherbert, walked on paths of chocolate, and visited the nutcracker prince's gingerbread castle. In fact, Clara was very sorry to be woken up – even though it was Christmas Day itself! She hugged the wooden doll and told him, "You're the best present I've ever had," and she could have sworn that his smile was even broader than usual.

Meanwhile, across the city, Dr Drosselmeier had also woken up to find the best present he'd ever had. There sprawled underneath his Christmas tree, sleeping an exhausted but peaceful sleep, was his brave, handsome nephew . . .

The Sword in the Stone
a Celtic legend

he blacksmith's anvil had suddenly appeared in the courtyard of the cathedral on Christmas morning. No one knew how it had got there. The anvil had a sword stuck into it and stood on a huge stone. Words were carved right round it which read: *Whoever pulls out this sword is the rightful king of the Britons.*

Many a proud lord had stepped up and tried to pull the sword out of the mysterious anvil. But even though they had heaved and sweated and grunted and pulled and pulled and pulled, all of them had walked away disappointed. Now almost a week had passed. It was time for the New Year's Eve jousting festival, and still the anvil stood on the stone in the courtyard with the sword sticking out of it.

Every year, bold knights came to the capital city from all over the kingdom to ride against each other in the New Year's Eve jousting festival and show off how brave they were. This year, Sir Ector's son, Sir Kay, would joust for the very first time. Sir Ector's younger son, Arthur, was going along too, as Sir Kay's squire. Sir Ector and his sons lived in the very furthest corner of the kingdom – so far away from the capital city that news of the strange anvil hadn't even reached them. It took them three days of hard riding until they saw the towering cathedral spire and the bright fluttering flags of the jousting field in the distance. Then a dreadful thing happened. Sir Kay put his hand down by his side to pat his trusty sword – and there was nothing there. "My sword!" Sir Kay gasped. "It's gone!"

Arthur turned quite pale with horror. It was a squire's job to make sure that a knight was properly equipped. "We must have left it at the lodging house we stayed at last night," he groaned. "Don't worry, Kay. I'll dash back and fetch it." Before anyone could argue, Arthur had wheeled his horse around and was galloping at full tilt back down the road. There wasn't a second to lose.

But when Arthur arrived back at the lodging house, there wasn't a sign of Sir Kay's sword anywhere. Arthur raced his horse back to the city wondering how on earth he was going to break the bad news to his brother. He was very nearly at the jousting field when he galloped past the cathedral courtyard and saw the sword

sticking out of the magical anvil on the stone. Arthur reined in his panting horse at once and looked all around him. There was no one about; everyone was at the jousting competition. It certainly didn't look as if the sword would be missed if he borrowed it for a while. "I promise I'll bring it back later," Arthur muttered out loud to no one in particular. He dashed over the snow, jumped up onto the stone and grasped the sword. It slid out of the anvil as easily as a needle pulls through cloth. "Gadzooks!" Arthur breathed, as he gazed at the mighty, jewelled blade in

his hands. "This is the most magnificent weapon I have ever seen!"
Then he remembered that the competition was about to begin. He
sprinted back to his horse, leapt into the saddle, and arrived at the
jousting field just as the first fanfares were being trumpeted.

Sir Kay was astonished at the superb weapon that his younger
brother handed him. He and his father had just heard all about the
mysterious anvil from the other knights at the jousting competition,
and he realised at once where the strange sword must have
come from. "See, father!" he cried over the crowds,
brandishing the sword over his head. "I must be
the new king of the Britons!"

Sir Ector came running at once and gasped
at the magnificent weapon in Kay's hands.
"How have you got this?" he demanded.

Kay's face fell. "Arthur brought it to
me," he mumbled.

Sir Ector's face was grave. "Who pulled
this out of the stone and gave it to you?" he
quizzed Arthur.

"N-n-o one," stammered Arthur. Quite a
few people had gathered around by now,
pointing and shouting and staring, and
suddenly he felt very nervous. "I pulled it out
of the stone myself. I was going to put it back
when Kay had finished with it, honest!"

Sir Ector led Arthur back to the
cathedral and into the courtyard, with a huge
and excited crowd following hot on their heels.
"Put the sword back where you found it, son," he told Arthur.

"All right," shrugged Arthur. He climbed onto the stone and thrust the sword back into the anvil.

First, Sir Ector himself tried to pull it out. Then Sir Kay heaved at it with all his might. The sword didn't budge an inch.

"Now show us how you did it, son," said Sir Ector, his voice trembling slightly.

Everyone held their breath as Arthur stepped up to the anvil. As he pulled the sword out effortlessly, the cheer that went up could be heard all over the capital city and beyond.

And that is how a young boy called Arthur, who wasn't even a knight, was crowned king of the Britons and eventually became the greatest of all the heroes who ever lived in the Celtic lands.

Ricky with the Tuft

retold from the original story by Charles Perrault

aaarrggh!" cried the queen, as she saw her newborn son for the first time. "Surely this baby can't be mine! He's hideously ugly!"

The fairy midwife sighed. It was true. The tiny face of the queen's new baby boy was swamped by a huge red nose. He was cross-eyed and his shoulders were humped. One of his legs was much shorter than the other. And to top it all, the baby was totally bald except for a single tuft of hair sticking up in the middle of his head. "Never mind your little boy's looks, your majesty," the fairy midwife comforted the queen. "I promise that your son will grow up to be far more intelligent, witty and charming than other people, and everyone will love him for it. What's more, I'm going to give him a gift. I'm going to give him the power to make the girl he falls in love with as intelligent as he is, so he won't ever get bored with her company . . . Now, what are you going to call your special little son?"

"Ricky . . ." the queen decided, making up her mind that she loved her son after all. "He's my little Ricky with the Tuft."

Not long afterwards, the queen of a neighbouring kingdom

gave birth to twin daughters. The first tiny girl to be born was so perfect that the queen at first thought she was looking at a little angel from heaven. But the second baby was as ugly as her elder sister was beautiful.

"Oh dear," said the fairy midwife – the same one who had helped at the birth of Ricky with the Tuft. "I have to tell you that your elder daughter will grow up to be incredibly stupid . . . However, there is some comfort. Your younger daughter will stay ugly, but she will be so clever that no one will even notice."

The queen was relieved that her younger daughter's fate seemed to be taken care of, but she was very worried about her elder daughter. "Can't we somehow give the elder one some of the younger one's intelligence?" the queen suggested.

"I'm afraid that's beyond my powers," the fairy midwife replied. "However, what I can do for her is to make her more beautiful than any girl in the world. What's more, I'll also give her a gift. The boy she falls in love with will become as beautiful as she is, so she'll never tire of looking at him."

Sixteen or so years passed, and the two princesses grew up exactly as the fairy midwife had said they would. Strangers were at first entranced by the beauty of the elder princess. However, they would soon creep away because trying to make conversation with her was as difficult as digging a field with a spoon. The strangers would then turn to the younger princess and be captivated by her intelligent and entertaining chat. Everyone totally forgot how plain and ungainly the princess was after only five minutes in her enchanting company.

Unfortunately, the beautiful elder sister knew very well that she was exceedingly stupid and embarrassing. She often stole away into the woods to be on her own – and it was on one of these lonely walks that she first encountered Ricky with the Tuft.

It wasn't an accident that the princess and the prince came to meet each other. Ricky with the Tuft had fallen desperately in love with the pictures of the princess that were for sale in all the shops. After collecting every single one, sticking them all over his bedroom walls, and gazing at them adoringly for hours on end, Ricky with the Tuft had decided that he wanted to marry the real thing. He had set off determined to find her.

"My lady, I feel as if I have been looking for you all my life," sighed Ricky with the Tuft, bowing low to the princess.

The princess just shrugged, as she couldn't think of anything to

445

say to the remarkably ugly prince who stood before her.

"I have never seen a girl as beautiful as you," admitted Ricky with the Tuft. "And as I should know more than most, beauty is an important blessing that shouldn't be taken for granted."

The sad princess blurted out, "I would much rather be as ugly as you are, if only I could be a little less stupid!"

Luckily, Ricky with the Tuft wasn't offended. "I have the perfect solution," he smiled. "I love you with all my heart, and if you will only consent to be my wife, you will become as wise and witty as you could ever wish to be."

The princess wasn't sure if she understood or not what the ugly prince was saying. She stood gaping open-mouthed.

"I can see you are a little taken aback by the suddenness of my proposal," said Ricky with the Tuft, kindly. "So I will give you a whole year to get used to the idea."

The princess said nothing to disagree, and so Ricky with the Tuft trotted off home, his heart full to bursting with happiness.

From that moment on, the princess discovered that she was as intelligent and entertaining as she was beautiful. The news spread rapidly, and princes and lords and earls came from kingdoms far and wide to seek her hand in marriage. Of course, in all the excitement, the princess quite forgot about Ricky with the Tuft. Her mind was completely taken up with one big worry. The princess thought each suitor very handsome in his own way, but now that she herself was so clever, she found them all extremely boring! "How can I marry a man whose conversation sends me to sleep within five minutes?" she sighed wistfully.

One day, the princess decided to wander alone into the woods to think the problem over. She hadn't been gone long when she came across a hundred servants preparing a banquet among the trees. They were hanging flags and balloons and coloured lanterns in the branches; they were scurrying to and fro in a vast outdoor kitchen, cooking a delicious feast; they were setting up a dance floor and a bandstand, and laying thousands of tables and chairs – all beautifully decked with flowers. "Whatever is going on?" the astounded princess asked one of the servants. She had attended many wonderful balls, but had never been to one on such a grand, gorgeous scale. "The person giving this banquet must have a very important reason to throw such a wonderful party."

"Tomorrow our master, Ricky with the Tuft, is getting married," the breathless servant replied. "He loves his bride with all his heart and is throwing the best wedding feast ever!"

The princess gasped as she suddenly remembered the squinting, limping, hunchbacked prince with the huge nose and the strange tuft of hair, whom she had met exactly a year before. *I gave him the impression I would marry him!* she thought in horror.

The princess suddenly saw Ricky with the Tuft himself heading through the trees towards her. "Good afternoon, my darling," he cried. "I have kept my word and have come to see how you feel about marrying me now."

The princess hung her head in shame. "There is no doubt in my mind that you are the kindest, most honourable, most intelligent person in the world," she sobbed. "I would love to be with you forever – but I can't! I am deeply sorry that I can never marry you, for I can't get over your terrible ugliness!"

To the princess's amazement, Ricky with the Tuft laughed out loud. "Well, I do believe that you've fallen in love with me after all," he cried. And when the princess looked up, she saw that Ricky with the Tuft had become as handsome as she herself was beautiful. "Didn't you know you had the power to do that?" the prince beamed.

The princess fell into his arms, and the very next day, she and her prince had the best wedding feast ever – just as Ricky with the Tuft had wanted.

The Happy Prince

retold from the original tale by Oscar Wilde

The statue of the Happy Prince stood high up above the city on a tall column. He glittered in the sunlight, for he was painted all over in gold leaf and had a glowing ruby set into his sword hilt and two sparkling sapphires for eyes. The people of the city often looked up at the Happy Prince and sighed, for they admired his beauty and envied his contented smile.

One evening, a little swallow came fluttering through the skies and landed between the prince's golden feet. It was well past the end of the summer and the wind had grown chilly. The swallow's friends had set off several weeks ago for a warmer land. The swallow had stayed behind because he had fallen in love with a slender reed by the river, and he could not bear to leave her. But the wind had grown chilly and the bite of frost had crept into the air. The shivering swallow had realised that to stay any longer would mean certain death from the cold. He had begged the reed to travel with him, but the reed had simply shaken her head. So the swallow had been forced to fly sadly off without her. Tomorrow he would fly away and catch up with his friends. Now the little bird tucked his head under his wing and prepared to get some rest for the long journey. But just as the swallow began to drift off into dreams, large raindrops started to fall on his head. The swallow looked up in puzzlement at the clear night sky and saw that the statue above him was crying.

"Who are you and why are you weeping?" the little swallow asked, as the statue's tears shone in the moonlight like diamonds.

"People call me the Happy Prince," replied the statue, "but in truth, I am full of sadness. They have set me up here so high that I can look out over the whole city and see all its ugliness and misery. Tonight, I can see a poor woman sitting in a house near the edge of town. The woman is thin from hunger and pale from tiredness, but she is still at work, sewing passion-flowers onto a gown for one of the queen's maids-of-honour. In the corner of the room, her little boy lies very ill in bed, asking for oranges. But the woman has no money to buy him anything, so all she can give him is water." The Happy Prince sighed. "Little swallow, will you pluck out the ruby from my sword and take it to the woman, so that she might sell it to the jeweller for money? My feet are fastened to this pedestal and I cannot move."

The Happy Prince looked so sad that the swallow agreed to be his messenger. The little bird pecked the ruby out of the prince's sword and flew away with it in his beak over the rooftops. He flew in at the window of the woman's house and found her slumped over her work in a worn-out sleep. The swallow laid the jewel down next to her thimble, then he flew gently round the bed, fanning the feverish, sick boy with his wings until he looked much cooler and more comfortable. Then the swallow flew back to the Happy Prince and told him what he had done. "It's strange," the bird remarked. "I feel a warm glow inside me, even though the weather is so cold."

"That is because you have done a good deed," explained the Happy Prince, as the tired little swallow closed his eyes.

Next day, the swallow flew all over the city bidding goodbye to everyone and everything. "I am leaving tonight for Egypt!" he cried. But when in the evening he came to say farewell to the Happy Prince, he found that the statue was crying once again.

"Far across the city I can see into an attic where a young man leans over a desk. He is struggling to finish a play for the Director of the Theatre, but he is too cold to write anymore. His fire has died away and he has no money to buy either wood or any food for his supper." A glistening tear rolled off the end of the Happy Prince's nose and sploshed onto the swallow's head. "Little swallow, will you stay with me one more night and be my messenger? Will you pluck out one of my sapphire eyes and take it to him?"

"Dear prince," said the swallow, "I will not pluck out your eye." and tears gleamed in his own.

"Little swallow, please do as I ask," begged the Happy Prince, and he looked so sad that the swallow fluttered up and plucked out one of his sapphire eyes and flew away with it to the young man in the attic. The little swallow was very relieved when he returned to nestle at the Happy Prince's feet, for the air underneath his wings had really become very cold indeed.

The next day, the swallow flew down to the harbour and watched all the big ships sailing away to lands where the breezes were warm and the days were long. "I am leaving too, tonight!" he sang out to everyone he saw. At sunset, the swallow flew off to the Happy Prince to say goodbye. "In the square below," said the Happy Prince, "I can see a little matchgirl whose matches have all spilled into the gutter. She is crying because she can make no money and if she goes home empty-handed, her father will beat her." The Happy Prince smiled sadly. "Little swallow, pluck out my other eye and take it to the little matchgirl so she can be happy."

"But then you will be blind!" cried the swallow.

"Little swallow, please do as I ask," whispered the Happy Prince, and he looked so sad that the bird did as he wanted.

"Now you can no longer see," the little swallow said, as he fluttered back to the statue. "I will stay with you always."

"But little swallow," protested the Happy Prince, "your friends will be waiting for you on the hazy banks of the River Nile."

"I will stay with you always and be your eyes," the swallow promised, and he slept between the prince's feet.

Next day, the swallow flew all over the city and told the Happy Prince what he had seen there. "I have seen the rich making merry in their beautiful houses while beggars lie outside their gates," the swallow murmured. "I have seen old people who sit all day on their own, cold and lonely. I have seen small children tremble in front of bullies. I have seen much suffering and misery."

"Little swallow," said the prince, "with your beak, peel off the fine gold that covers me. Fly with leaves of it to all the poor people of my city."

The little swallow sighed heavily, but he did what he was told. Then the statue of the Happy Prince was quite dull and grey.

As the faithful bird finally settled down between his friend's feet, the snow began to fall in thick white flakes. The streets glistened silver with a lining of frost. Icicles hung like shards of glass from the rooftops. And the little swallow shivered at the foot of the Happy Prince. He tried beating his wings to keep warm, but eventually he knew that he was going to die. The little swallow used his last drop of strength to flutter up to the prince's shoulder. "Goodbye, Happy Prince," he cried. "I will not see you again."

"I am glad you are finally going to where the sun will warm your wings," the Happy Prince said.

"I am not going to Egypt," murmured the swallow, "I am going to sleep forever." And he kissed the Happy Prince on the lips and fell down dead at his feet.

That very moment, a strange cracking noise came from within the Happy Prince. It was so loud that the Mayor heard it way down below. He peered up at the statue for the first time in months. "Good lord!" he remarked. "However did the Happy Prince get that shabby? We'll have to replace him with something else."

The very next day, workmen pulled down the Happy Prince from his column and threw him into a furnace. They cleared away the dead swallow and then put a statue of the Mayor on the column instead. But the Happy Prince knew nothing about all this, because his heart had broken. In fact, when the workmen opened the door of the furnace, they saw his cracked lead heart for themselves, because it would not melt away. They threw it onto the same rubbish dump on which the dead swallow was lying. And when God asked his angels to bring him the two most precious things in all the city, they took the Happy Prince's heart and the little swallow with them up to heaven.

Myths and Legends

The Beginning of Life
an Aboriginal myth

 ong, long ago was the Dreamtime. Everywhere was bare, flat and empty. There was only stillness and quietness all over the surface of the world.

However, underneath the surface, deep in the earth's crust, all sorts of creatures were sleeping. Animals, birds and reptiles lay cocooned in the land, dreaming peacefully.

One day the Rainbow Serpent opened her eyes and found herself in complete darkness. Flexing and stretching her coils, she began to push her way through the earth. Finally, she broke through the surface, bursting out into the sunlight. The featureless land stretched in all directions. She set off to explore.

Slithering all over the land, the Rainbow Serpent's strong winding body carved out valleys and heaped up land into ridges. She journeyed for many moons, travelling over the whole earth until she arrived back where she had started. Exhausted, she coiled herself up and rested.

After a long nap, it occurred to her that all the other creatures were still asleep deep inside the earth. With as much energy as she

could summon, the Rainbow
Serpent called and called, and
gradually, her voice penetrated
the layers of the earth and began
to stir the creatures from their
deep slumbers.

The frogs awoke first. Slowly,
they began to move up through the earth,
with their bodies full of water. Delighted, the
Rainbow Serpent tickled the frogs, making them
laugh so hard that they coughed up their stores of
water, which flowed out over the earth. Some of the water
gushed into channels and pits formed by the Rainbow Serpent's

wanderings, creating streams, rivers, waterfalls and lakes. Other trickles of water ran away over the soil and were absorbed by the land. In these places, tiny green shoots appeared. Soon, in all directions there were patches of soft grass, clumps of leafy bushes and bright flowers, and clusters of tall, spreading trees.

As the land sprang to life, all the other reptiles, birds and animals burst out from under the ground. The Rainbow Serpent led them across the earth and they all found suitable homes. The birds were delighted to swoop through the skies and nest in the treetops. The reptiles were comfortable sheltering among cool stones and damp, shady nooks and crannies. The Rainbow Serpent was acknowledged by all as the mother of life. She set laws, so that all the creatures could thrive together and the earth remain healthy forever.

As time passed, the Rainbow Serpent noticed that some creatures were particularly excellent at keeping her laws. She gave these creatures human form and told them that they were in charge of looking after the land and everything that lived in it. Each human had a totem pole of the tribe they came from, whether from an animal, reptile or bird. The Rainbow Serpent instructed all the tribes that they were allowed to eat creatures from any totem pole except their own – that way, there would be enough food for everyone.

The Rainbow Serpent chose other creatures that she was very pleased with and turned them into rock. They were sent to stand forever as hills and mountains, acting as the guardians of the tribes living on the land.

And so the tribes and the land lived and prospered together. A man called Biami grew to be an exceptionally wise human. Knowledgeable, honest and kind, he took great care of the earth. When he became old, the Rainbow Serpent did not let him die, but gave him a spirit form, so he could live forever among the tribes as a protector.

It wasn't long before Biami was faced with evil. Calmly, Biami cast the man and his selfish, devious ways out from his tribe. Abandoned and angry, the wicked man used all his cunning to discover how to take on spirit form. He became an evil spirit called the Bunyip.

Alarmed, Biami warned the tribes to keep away from the Bunyip and have nothing to do with him. Even more furious, the Bunyip determined to have revenge. He decided to use his evil to wreak chaos among the tribes and bring as much trouble and sorrow to everyone as he could. The Bunyip raged and swore hatred, and threatened to steal any tribe member he could lay his hands on – and devour them.

From that day to this, everyone has lived in fear of the Bunyip. He lurks in gloomy, remote places such as waterholes and rainforests, luring travellers to their deaths. He delights in snatching and eating children, and ensnaring people to become his evil slaves for eternity.

The Creation of the Navajo People
a Native American myth

T he First World was black. The only light came from burning flames around it. It was a small, stifling place. Its inhabitants, the insects, didn't like living in such a dark, cramped place. One day, they flew up to the roof of the world and fluttered about, searching for a way out. Eventually, Locust saw a glimmer of blue light filtering through a tiny crack. He squeezed through the space, and the other insects followed.

The insects found themselves in the Second World. This was a blue world, much larger and lighter than the world they had left behind. Although flat and rather bare, there was much more space to fly about – and grasses and bushes. The insects flew off to explore. However, before they had gone far, huge birds flew in from all directions. "This is our land!" the birds cried. "And there is not enough food here for all of us. You must leave at once!" As they spoke, mighty flocks from far and wide swooped towards the unwelcome insects. Terrified, the insects swarmed up towards the roof of the world where they found a small hole and escaped through it.

The insects found themselves in the Third World. This was a yellow world, even bigger and lighter than the blue world. As well as grasses and bushes, there were trees, forests, mountains and rivers. The world was inhabited by all kinds of creatures. Some had fur, some had feathers, and some had scales. Some crawled on the ground, some swam in the sea, and some soared through the air.

Time passed, and four holy spirits appeared before the creatures – White Spirit, Blue Spirit, Yellow Spirit and Black Spirit. They silently made signs, instructing the creatures to wash themselves clean, before vanishing completely. The creatures did as they were told, and waited.

Some days later, the holy spirits returned, bringing several sacred objects. Firstly, they spread a buckskin on the ground, then laid two ears of corn on top, and placed two eagle feathers under the corn. Then they covered everything with a second buckskin. Finally, the spirits called the white east wind and the yellow west wind to blow life into the ears of corn. The ears of corn became the first man and woman. Welcomed eagerly by the creatures, the humans lived happily in one society, all speaking the same language. Together, they were all known as the First People.

Many years passed and the First People lived happily and peacefully, multiplying in number. However, there came a time when there were so many of them that food began to run short. Chaos broke out as those who were swift and strong took what food was left, and those who had none tried to steal it from them. The First People realized they needed a ruler to judge wisely and fairly, and keep order among them. They called a great assembly, and creatures from all four directions put forward their candidates.

The eastern creatures suggested Wolf. He offered gifts of a white springtime cloud, the white light of the morning, and a stalk of young corn. The southern creatures suggested Bluebird. She offered gifts of a blue summertime cloud, a piece of blue sky, and a stalk of growing corn. The western creatures suggested Lion. He offered gifts of a yellow autumn cloud, the yellow light of the evening, and a stalk of ripe corn. The northern creatures suggested Hummingbird. He offered gifts of the multi-coloured northern lights of winter, multi-coloured dried grains and beans, and a multi-coloured storage bowl. The First People could not choose among the candidates – their gifts were all equally as important. So they eventually decided that they should be ruled by all four wise creatures, working together as a council to make important decisions, and create new laws.

The council decided that the First People would have to leave the Third World or they would starve. They flew up to the roof and looked for a way out. Suddenly, voices called them from above and the First People realized that they could fly around the edges of the roof.

One group flew around the eastern edge. In the Fourth World, they became the Navajo people. A second group flew around the southern edge. In the Fourth World, they became the bird people. A third group flew around the western edge. In the Fourth World, they became the animal people. A fourth group flew around the northern edge. In the Fourth World, they became the insect people.

In the Fourth World, the days were white and the nights were black. The voices that had called them to the new world belonged to tribes of people, including the Hopi, the Comanche and the Apache. Among them also lived spirits – the hard-working Badger, the evil Water Monster, and the trickster, Coyote.

There came a time when the wicked Water Monster decided to flood the Fourth World, killing everything in it. The First People gathered their most precious treasures, including seeds of every living plant. In terror, they fled to the top of the tallest mountain. There, Navajo medicine men planted bamboo, and prayed for the shoots to spring up.

After five days, the bamboo towered above them. The stems had tangled into a mass rather like an ancient, gnarled tree, which was hollow at the centre. The First People carved a door in the side, squeezed in, and began to climb up the middle. Up they went, until they emerged one by one, blinking into the sunlight of the Fifth World. Here, all the creatures of the First People settled and here they have stayed ever since.

Ra's Secret Name

an ancient Egyptian myth

Before time began, nothing existed except an endless dark ocean of chaos. Forming himself out of this nothing, the creator then made a world in the middle of the ocean. He lit the world with his own brilliance – the light of the sun, and then made other gods and goddesses to keep him company. Next came the humans, to be his children.

Every day, the creator sailed across the sky in a boat of blazing light, surveying the world. Each evening, his sun boat sank, into the underworld. Using his powers to protect himself from the clutches of the dead, he journeyed through their kingdom to fight the evils. Every morning, he sailed safely back up into the sky.

Out of all the other gods and goddesses, Isis was the strongest. Clever and cunning, she made it her business to become the wisest of them all. Patiently, she travelled all over the world, discovering the hidden properties of everything the creator had made. Eventually, she knew millions of spells and secrets – except for one. She did not know the secret name of the creator himself – the root to all his power.

Isis was well aware that Ra would never give up his secret name, unless he was forced. However, Isis also knew that nothing could harm Ra – his spirit of creation was far too strong for that.

Isis thought long and hard. She realized that Ra could only be affected by something from his own body. But even if she could get hold of a strand of hair or a flake of his skin, how could she make a dangerous weapon?

Biding her time, one day, Isis saw her opportunity. Sometimes, Ra would leave his sun-boat in the heavens and descend down to earth on foot. On such a walk, Ra paused to talk to a group of gods. Suddenly, Isis saw a drop of spittle fall from

his mouth. As swift as the wind, she caught the spittle and whisked herself away.

Hidden in her palace, Isis mixed the spittle of the mighty Ra with some earth, making clay. Muttering words of strong magic, she shaped the clay into the form of a snake. Then, closing her eyes, Isis carefully spoke the secret words of creation.

The great goddess stood back and watched. It was only a moment before bright colours wrapped themselves all around the clay creature from the tip of its nose to the point of its tail. With a wriggle, the snake reared its head and opened its eyes, hissing and flickering its forked tongue. It was alive.

Isis clapped her hands with delight, her eyes shining. Cautiously, she picked up the creature and carried it to a spot on one of Ra's favourite walks. Staring deep into its eyes, she whispered its instructions, then let it ripple away across the earth. As the snake found a shady hiding place and disappeared from view, Isis hurried away into the shadows.

That very day, Ra happened to stroll along that way, admiring the beauty of his creation. Suddenly, without warning, he received a terrible shock. He felt something he had never felt before – pain. Screaming in agony, he collapsed to the ground, clutching his foot. In his pain, he did not notice a strange snake slithering away from him – Isis' snake.

Ra howled as burning poison began to spread through his flesh. Hearing the cries of the great creator, the other gods and goddesses came running to him in alarm.

"Something has hurt me! I didn't see it and I cannot guess what it might have been, for nothing I have made can hurt me!" the creator gasped. "Help me!" Ra begged, growing pale and sweating. "I fear that I am dying."

Panicking, the gods and goddesses tried all the magic they knew, making every desperate effort they could think of to heal the creator. Nothing made any difference. Ra shook as the poison began to stiffen his muscles

Then, Isis stepped forward. "Great father," she said, her voice filled with fake concern, "I think I know a spell that could save you – but it will only work if I use your secret name."

Ra groaned – not only in pain, but also in horror. He had no choice. Summoning all his remaining energy, he feebly beckoned Isis to bend down close to him. The goddess struggled to contain her excitement, and put her ear to the creator's lips.

"I will tell you my secret name," Ra murmured, his breathing becoming shallow. "But only if you never reveal it to anyone."

"I promise!" Isis agreed, eagerly.

At last, Isis had the power she wanted. She healed Ra as the other gods and goddesses stood back in awe of her incredible magic. Fully restored, Ra rose through the heavens into his sun-boat, and light shone down on the world once more.

The Murder of Osiris

an ancient Egyptian myth

The creator, the sun god Ra, ruled the heavens and gave the god, Osiris, the task of looking after the world. Osiris made his home in Ra's favourite country, Egypt. There, he ruled as king with his wife, the mighty goddess Isis, as his queen.

Wise and fair, Osiris cared deeply for his people and, in return, his people loved him. Under his guidance, the Egyptians learnt how to farm the land and tend the animals. The great god brought law and order to the country. Most importantly, he taught everyone how to worship the other gods properly. Before long, Egypt became a prosperous place where all the people lived happily.

Everyone loved Osiris – except, that is, for his youngest brother, the god Seth. Seth was jealous of Osiris and exceedingly bitter that Ra had chosen Osiris to be king of Egypt instead of him.

The more Seth brooded on this, the more hatred burned in his heart. The day came when Seth decided that he could bear it no longer. He would have to take the throne from his brother. Seth knew that he couldn't fight Osiris. Raising an army would be impossible because the Egyptians loved and supported their king. Besides, Isis knew very strong magic – it was rumoured to be as strong as the magic of Ra himself – and she was always with her husband, protecting him. No, thought Seth, force was not the answer. He would have to be much more cunning than that.

Seth waited until Osiris went away, then he seized the opportunity to bribe the royal craftsmen and courtiers into helping him. He paid them handsomely, and they listened carefully to his plan…

Months later, when Osiris returned from his travels, there were great celebrations throughout Egypt. The people feasted in their homes, and sang and danced in the streets. A mighty banquet was held at the palace – and of course, Seth was one of the guests.

Usually at royal parties, Seth sat in a corner and glowered. But today was different. Today his heart was filled with a gleeful secret, and Seth couldn't stop himself from smiling and laughing along with all the other guests. Admiring the beautiful decorations of garlands, banners and scented candles, he helped himself to platefuls of the tasty food and drank goblet after goblet of wine. When the musicians began playing, he clapped along, and roared with delight at the acrobats and jugglers. Finally, when everyone had eaten, Seth stood up and bellowed for silence.

"Welcome home, brother Osiris!" he announced, with a grand flourish. "In honour of your return, I have arranged some very special fun for us all."

Seth clapped his hands, and beckoned his group of courtiers to enter the banqueting hall. Everyone turned and watched as the men came in, carrying in a long, narrow chest, made of gold and decorated with precious gems in intricate designs. The banquet guests all gasped in admiration of the beautiful object.

"Brother, this wonderful chest, shining like the rays of Ra himself, has been made by your own royal craftsmen," Seth explained – not mentioning that he had bribed them to make it in a very special

way. "It is the prize in a new game – one that is very
easy to play. Each of us will take turns to lie inside it,
and whoever fits exactly – head touching one end and
feet the other, with the sides snug around them – wins
the chest!"

The banquet guests were thrilled and hurried to queue
up to take their turn in the game. One by one, they all lay down in

the chest, and one by one, they were all disappointed. They were either too tall or too short, too big or too small. At last, only Osiris himself was left.

"Come, brother!" Seth encouraged. "Let us see if fortune is smiling upon you this evening."

Gathering his robes around him, Osiris stepped carefully into the chest. Then the courtiers helped him to lie down. It was a tight squeeze, but if he held his breath, he fitted exactly inside!

The watching guests all went wild with delight.

"We have a winner!" Seth cheered. "Congratulations brother!"

Motioning for the musicians to strike up and play, he seized Isis and swept her off in a joyous dance. Everyone joined in, laughing with pleasure – leaving Osiris lying in the chest, trapped.

Soon only the courtiers remained around the chest – everyone else was whirling around the dance floor, enjoying themselves, the game quite forgotten. Quick as a flash, without anyone noticing, the courtiers slammed the lid shut. Then they picked the chest up and hurried out of the banqueting hall.

Leaving the revellers dancing and singing, the courtiers took the chest to the river Nile and threw it into the deeps – just as Seth had paid them to. The golden coffin sank down deeper and deeper into the dark waters … where Osiris eventually suffocated to death. Meanwhile, Isis searched high and low for Osiris, but he did not reappear that night, nor the night after, nor any of the nights after that. As time passed, Egypt mourned, but it eventually became clear that there was no option but to declare Seth the new king. However, while Seth was triumphant, Isis was heartbroken. She swore never to rest until she found out what had happened to her beloved husband.

The Trojan Horse

from the epic poem Iliad

When Prince Paris of Troy stole away the beautiful
Helen, wife of King Menelaus of Greece, the outraged
Greeks were determined to win her back. The finest
warriors in the swiftest ships sailed in a mighty fleet to the shores of
their enemy. Eventually hundreds of warriors swarmed up the
beaches, laying siege to the immense, high-walled city of Troy.
The Trojan princes often descended from their lofty towers to pit
their strength against the Greeks on the broad plain outside the
steadfast gates. Among the armies of both sides were the greatest
heroes the world has ever seen. At their hands, the battlefield ran red
with rivers of blood by day, and burned with smoking funeral pyres
by night.

After ten long years, even the Trojan princes Paris and Hector,
and the Greek warrior of warriors Achilles, were ranked among the
slain. Yet the Greeks were still no closer to breaching the towering
stone stronghold. Battle-weary, disheartened and homesick, the great
army was out of ideas – until the great king Odysseus hit upon a
daring new plan. If they could not win the city of Troy by force, they

might instead win it by cunning.

Odysseus ordered soldiers to a nearby forest on Mount Ida to cut down trees and chop them into planks. Then the famous carpenter, Epeius, set to work with the wood. After three days, he had crafted an enormous wooden horse that was stunning to behold. It was so magnificent that no one guessed it was in fact hollow. A hidden trapdoor led up into the empty body of the beast.

At dawn the following day, the sentries positioned high on the battlements of Troy could not believe their eyes. Every morning for the past ten years, they had been greeted by the sight of the Greek camp spreading along the shore, their banners fluttering in the breeze, their armour glinting in the sunlight, their ships filling the water as far as the eye could see. But this morning, the beach was empty! Or nearly – among the smoking heaps of burning huts was the incredible sight of the giant wooden horse, standing still and silent on the golden sands. The sentries sounded the alarm at once.

When old King Priam of Troy surveyed the scene for himself, he was nervous that the Greeks might have set an ambush. A group of scouts marched down to the seashore to investigate – but they found only one Greek soldier hiding among the rocks. Terrified, he begged the Trojans to spare his life, telling them that the Greeks had sailed for home, leaving the horse as a gift and himself as a sacrifice to the gods, to ask for a safe voyage.

Joy rushed into the hearts of the Trojans and after endless battles, they had cause to celebrate. Throwing open the gates of the city, the men, women and children ran down to the sea for the first time in ten years. Singing and dancing, they attached ropes to the wooden horse and laid rollers in front of it. By nightfall, they had heaved it into the heart of Troy. Then the elated citizens ate, drank and danced until the early hours, when everyone fell asleep – even the sentries.

Alas for Troy! Fortune was not smiling on the city after all. The Greek warrior had courageously volunteered to weave a web of lies. As soon as the Trojans had started feasting, the entire Greek fleet had sailed back to their beaches from a nearby cove. Now, in the city, with the Trojans soundly snoring, the trapdoor in the wooden horse slid open. Odysseus and a band of the finest Greek warriors descended from inside. Some of the warriors headed straight for Helen's chamber, while the others opened the gates of Troy, unleashing hell on the great city.

The Trojans had no chance and were slaughtered in their beds. In triumph, the victorious Greeks led Helen down to their ships and set their torches to the great city. Finally, as the sun rose, the Greeks set off on their long journey home, leaving Troy to burn.

Kotan Utunnai

a Japanese myth

I was raised by a young woman I called my older sister –
although she was not my sister by blood. My sister's
people were the people of the sea, enemies of my people
– the people of the land. My sister told me that my father and mother
were great warriors, who died bravely together in battle when I was
only a baby. The woman I now call my sister took pity on me and
from then on, took care of me and gave me all the love I could ever
need – even though she was of the enemy. So, I was brought up here
in this lonely place, far away from humans and their dangers.

When I was little, I sometimes heard a rumbling sound far off.
My sister said this was the sound of her people's gods fighting. When
I grew older, I sometimes heard a rumbling sound overhead, upon
the roof of our grass hut. Somehow I knew that this was made by the
spirits of my own people. When I told my sister, she revealed that
I had an older brother who had also survived, and who had declared
war on the people of the sea, to avenge the death of my parents.
I knew I had to find him.

I asked my older sister for my father's clothes, which she had saved carefully. Soon I stood proudly in my father's war robes, with his helmet on my head, and his sword thrust into his belt at my waist. Feeling my father's spirit rush into my body, I was suddenly whisked with my sister up through the smoke hole of our hut and we were carried away on the wind.

Up through the skies we were blown in a blur, and finally dropped gently on the shores of a sandy beach, not far from a range of towering mountains. With great leaps and bounds, my sister and I set off over several forests, which we realized were made of strange

metal trees. Finally, we came to a great bonfire, surrounded by six men wearing stone armour, six men wearing metal armour, twelve women, and a monstrous, revoltingly ugly demon.

To my horror, tied to the top of one of the metal trees was a terribly wounded man. Although I had never laid eyes on him before, I knew at once that he was my older brother, Kamui-otopush.

"Do you admire our prisoner?" growled the demon. "We are taking him as a sacrifice to our leader and ruler, Shipish-un-kur!"

Outraged, I instantly drew my sword to do battle for his life. With one stroke, I killed three of the stone warriors and their wives, and with a second stroke, I killed three of the metal warriors and their wives. Meanwhile, my sister sprang to the top of the tree and freed Kamui-otopush. Within minutes, she had spirited him away to safety, and returned to my side.

Together, my sister and I took on the hideous demon and the remaining men and women. Our sword blades flashed as we slashed and sliced through the air in the direction of the mountains. I prayed to the gods for help, and felt my father's fighting spirit flood through me afresh. One by one, I killed them all – even the terrible demon. One by one, their spirits left their bodies and flew rumbling away into the west.

Perplexed, my sister and I felt the need to face Shipish-un-kur and punish him for wanting Kamui-otopush killed.

Following our instincts, we journeyed for half a day before we finally came to Shipish-un-kur's house. Peering in cautiously at the window, we saw that Shipish-un-kur was only a young man, with scarcely any hairs on his chin. Sitting next to him was the most beautiful young woman I had ever seen – his younger sister, Shipish-un-mat. Without further hesitation, I left my sister and flew up onto the roof of their house, stomping about to make as much noise as possible. With one swift movement, I dropped down the chimney and seized Shipish-un-kur. "You would have taken my older brother as a trophy!" I roared. "Instead, you will face my sword. Now fight me – or die like a coward!"

Letting go of Shipish-un-kur, I grabbed his sister, thinking to use her as a shield. But Shipish-un-kur was not deterred, and simply stabbed her repeatedly. This filled Shipish-un-mat with such fury that she turned against her brother and began to fight on my side. Up, down and around we flew inside the house, springing off the rafters, smashing into the walls and bouncing off the floor, entangled and entwined in combat. Hearing all the noise we were creating, an army of Shipish-un-kur's finest warriors hurtled

in to defend him. Fortunately, I was not alone and in a rush of air, Kamui-otopush was suddenly fighting at my side.

Even though I fought with my father's sword, I could not match my brother's skill. Kamui-otopush had the strength of one hundred men, and as he swiped his sword gracefully through the air, the evil warriors fell without a chance.

All at once, Shipish-un-mat screamed out a prophecy, "Your older sister has travelled to a far-distant land. She is fighting demons and is sorely wounded. She is in dire need of your help!"

"Go!" cried Kamui-otopush. "I will finish off these vermin and then I will join you."

Shipish-un-mat and I flew up into the heavens. My sister's spirit led me to her, and to my dismay I saw that Shipish-un-mat's words were true. Lifting my sister's crumpled body to the heavens, I begged the gods to restore her to health. To my eternal joy, they answered my prayer and she was well again.

And so my sister married the hero Kamui-otopush. I married the beautiful Shipish-un-mat. And from then on, the people of the sea and the people of the land have lived together in peace and harmony.

The Hound of Culan

an Irish legend

Midway through chieftain Sualtim's wedding day, his beautiful young bride, Dechtire, mysteriously disappeared. Sualtim's advisors sought her high and low, but to no avail. It was as if she had vanished into thin air. At first, Sualtim was furious. It had not been an easy job persuading King Conor of Ulster to let him marry his sister. But finally he had won the hand of the fairest woman in the land and secured an alliance with the most powerful ruler in all of Erin. Now, it seemed that Dechtire had run away, ruining not just his romance but also his political plans. However, Amergin the wise Druid advised Sualtim not to be too hasty. Amergin could sense ancient magic in the air … and what could humans do against the will of the almighty gods?

So Sualtim waited patiently and a whole year passed by, until one day Dechtire came walking out of the forest, carrying a baby in her arms. She told Sualtim an amazing story … the heroic god Lugh swooped down on the day of her marriage to Sualtim and whisked her off to the Land of Fairy. Lugh was also the father of the child that she held so tenderly in her arms.

Sualtim was in a quandary. If Dechtire had borne a child by another mortal, he would have hunted the man down, slashed off his head and paraded it for all to see. However, as Amergin pointed out, Sualtim had been paid a great honour by the gods. So, from the moment Sualtim laid eyes on the child, he thought of him as his own and brought him up as his rightful heir.

Many thought that Sualtim was foolish for believing Dechtire's wild tale. But as time went on, even the most hardened sceptics began to think that perhaps her story was true.

The child, who Dechtire named Setanta, was markedly different from other children. He began to walk before most children his age could even crawl. He learned to read before other children could speak. When he started lessons, he showed an attentiveness and intelligence that surprised all his teachers. By the age of only eight, Setanta spoke with the thoughtfulness of Amergin himself, and could hold his own in combat with the fastest, strongest, most experienced of Sualtim's warriors.

Sualtim often thought that his chest would burst with love and pride when he watched his adopted son. But he also realized that he had already taught Setanta all he had to offer. "You will always be my son," he told the boy tenderly, "but you were borne of the god Lugh and you are clearly destined for greatness. If you wish to learn more, you must go to the very best in the land – to the court of your uncle, King Conor. Be wary of him as he is cunning and slippery, and will wish to avoid his duty to you. But, my golden son, I have no doubt that you will find a way to win him over."

On the day Setanta arrived at the king's fortress in Emain Macha, the men and women of the court were out watching their sons compete in an annual hurley match. As Setanta joined the cheering crowd of spectators, he immediately saw a way to get the attention of the king.

Grabbing a spare hurley stick, he ran out to join the game, tackling the player with the ball and siezing it from him with great skill. Then he set off down the pitch, swiftly sprinting past the players, dodging between them or shouldering them out of the way as they came out to tackle him – all the while with the ball dancing at the end of his stick. By the time Setanta reached the goal, the players were left motionless, totally dumbfounded, while the crowd were roaring and leaping about with delight. Setanta smashed the ball through the goalkeeper's legs and the crowd went wild!

"Tell that boy to come here at once, whoever he is!" roared the stunned King Conor. "I will not have people just waltzing in here, without my permission." However, when he found out that the extraordinarily talented hurley player was in fact his nephew, he was pleased to claim him as his own kin.

From then on, Setanta was instructed in the arts and skills of a noble warrior by the finest teachers of the court. And it became one of King Conor's greatest pleasures to show Setanta to all the chieftains who owed him allegiance.

Once, when Setanta was a teenager, the king asked the lad to accompany him to the home of Culan, the master blacksmith. However, as Setanta was playing hurling, he told his uncle not to wait for him, and he would follow on later.

By the time Setanta had finished his game and arrived at the home of Culan, the warriors were inside feasting, and the gates were closed.

Pacing the grounds was Culan's enormous, drooling guard dog, renowned for being a bloodthirsty, vicious maneater. Spotting Setanta, the brute bounded towards him, growling and barking ferociously. Without a moment's hesitation, Setanta drew out his hurley stick and ball. Taking perfect aim, he struck the hound directly between the eyes. The creature keeled over dead before it had even sniffed a hair on Setanta's head.

Culan heard the commotion and came rushing out, his
sword at the ready. He was truly astonished at the sight of
Setanta standing unharmed over the body of the beast – and
somewhat annoyed that he was now without a guard dog!

"Until you find and raise another hound, I will be your guard
dog and keep watch at your fortress," promised Setanta.

And that is how Setanta became known as Cuchulain, meaning 'the
hound of Culan'. The blacksmith's guard dog was only the first of
many monsters Cuchulain vanquished. Witches, magicians and
creatures of evil that faced him met certain death.

Whenever Cuchulain went into battle, a strange frenzy came
over him, which was terrifying to behold. And in all the time from
those ancient days to the present, there has never been a greater hero
in the land of Erin.

Yama-Kumar and the Healing Gift

an Indian legend

Take heed! Live a good life. Be kind and honest. Be respectful to the gods and to each other. For then, when you pass from the bright land of the living into the dark underground kingdom of the dead, you will have no fear of facing the lord of death, Yama.

When Yama examines your soul, he will smile upon you, whisper words of comfort, and send you on your way to one of the blessed, joyful heavens. But if you spend your time on this earth doing evil, spreading misery and causing people pain, then prepare to grovel before Yama and quake with terror. He will banish you to the deepest dungeons of his realm for punishment, and he will harden his heart against your screams and begging, for it will be too late for repentance or forgiveness.

Sometimes the just, fair Lord Yama wanders among the living and observes how his future subjects are paving their way to his kingdom, with either good or bad deeds. Concealing his true nature behind a human disguise, no one would suspect that he is anything other than an ordinary man.

Once, on one of Yama's journeys through the land of the living, he met a beautiful mortal woman and fell in love. The woman had no idea that she was being wooed by the ruler of the underworld. Overcome by his charms, the unsuspecting woman became the wife of the lord of death. Yama was delighted, although his happiness proved to be short-lived. His new bride soon became difficult and quarrelsome. Yama was horrified to find himself nagged all day long. His wife made his life a misery.

The couple were thrilled when a baby son came along, and they named him Yama-Kumar. However, to the proud father's dismay, his wife became even more bad-tempered and demanding. There came a day when the lord of death could stand his wife's scolding, screeching, shrieking voice no longer. He vanished, fleeing back to his underground realm. His wife was mystified – and determined to track her absconded husband down and make his life a hundred times more miserable.

Yama could not forget his little son, who he loved very much. From the safety of his underground kingdom, he kept a careful eye on the boy and watched him as he grew up. He was dismayed to see that his wife was not looking after the boy as she should. She either ignored him, or burdened him with boring, tedious chores. Yama-Kumar grew up without learning anything. By the time he was a young man, his father was very concerned that he had no way of making a living for himself. The ruler of the underworld decided he had to help his son, and one night, he appeared to Yama-Kumar in a dream.

"Do not be afraid," he whispered into Yama-Kumar's sleeping mind. "I am the lord of death, but I am also your father. I want to give you a very special gift. Work hard to become a doctor, learning all about medicinal herbs and plants, and I will bestow on you the power of healing. You will be able to cure anyone who is ill – unless you see me sitting at your patient's head, waiting to catch their soul, for this means that they will surely die."

When Yama-Kumar woke up, he was full of excitement. Sure enough, he did as his father had instructed and threw himself into studying medicine. He was so keen that he became a doctor in half the usual time. Yama-Kumar quickly discovered that the lord of death kept his promise. He seemed to be able to cure anyone, no matter how ill they were, no matter how unusual the problem was. Even if other doctors declared the patient a hopeless case, Yama-Kumar could cure them – unless, of course, he saw his father sitting grimly at the patient's head. Yama-Kumar became famous far and wide, and was soon known as the greatest doctor in all the land.

After some years, Yama-Kumar was called to the royal palace itself. The king and queen's beloved daughter had fallen ill, and now

they feared she was dying. As
Yama-Kumar entered the
patient's bedroom, his heart
sank. There was the shadowy
figure of his father, sitting at
her head. Yama-Kumar looked
at the beautiful young princess
lying in front of him and
listened to the sobbing of the
king and queen, and all the
courtiers, who loved her very
much. He bowed his head and
prayed, pleading with his
father not to take her. The lord
of death sighed. "She can have
three days more, my son," he
murmured, and faded silently
away.

The king and queen had,
of course, seen and heard
nothing. "Take heart," Yama-
Kumar told them, "I cannot
promise, but I am going to do
my very best to heal your
daughter." For two days and
nights, he sat at the pale girl's
bedside, wracking his brains to
come up with a plan to save
her. On the third day, Yama-

Kumar finally saw the shape of his father looming into view before him.

"Beware, father!" he cried, before the lord of death could take the princess. "Allow this young woman to live to a ripe old age or I shall tell my mother who you really are and where she can find you."

Yama stopped and thought about the terrible threat. A cold shiver ran down his spine. "So be it, my son," he nodded, and disappeared hastily into the shadows.

Yama-Kumar immediately set about curing the princess with his herbs and medicines. By the time she was well again, they had fallen deeply in love. The king and queen were delighted to marry their daughter to the talented young doctor who had saved her life. And Yama-Kumar and the princess lived happily together forever.

Daedalus and Icarus

a Greek myth

Daedalus was renowned all over Greece for being a famous craftsman and architect. People from far and wide travelled to Daedalus' workshop in Athens to beg for his help in designing stunning landmarks and amazing inventions. No one could come up with such brilliant new ideas as Daedalus … until one of his apprentices, his nephew Talos, started to amaze everyone with his own talents. Daedalus should have been proud of his young protégé, but he wasn't. He was unbearably jealous. In cold blood, Daedalus lured his rival to the roof of the great temple, then pushed him over the edge to his death.

The Athenian court banished the great inventor from the city forever. Daedalus fled to the island of Crete, which was ruled by the mighty King Minos. Daedalus knew that Minos would be delighted to have the world's most famous inventor at his court, and would pay him handsomely for his expertise.

One of the first tasks King Minos set Daedalus was to devise a lair for a monstrous creature called the Minotaur, which was half-man, half-bull. Daedalus created an underground labyrinth of

criss-crossing corridors and alleys that twisted their way to dead-
ends. The Minotaur was let loose to roam about in its depths.
Every year, King Minos fed the monster by forcing a group of young
Athenian men and women into the labyrinth and leaving them to be
hunted down and devoured.

From then on Daedalus' life became better and better. He fell in
love with a royal lady-in-waiting and was thrilled when one year
later, she bore him a son who they named Icarus. At last, Daedalus
was happy and content.

One fateful day an Athenian hero, Theseus, managed to kill the
Minotaur and emerge alive from the maze. King Minos was outraged,
and Daedalus and Icarus hid themselves away, afraid of his wrath.
Daedalus decided that they had to escape from the island – but it was
not going to be easy. Minos' soldiers stood guard at all the sea ports,
harbours and coves, and would catch them wherever they tried to
board a boat. Daedalus wracked his brains to come up with an
escape plan. In the end, he could only think of one way – they would
have to flee by air.

Daedalus set about fashioning huge wings for himself and his
son. He collected sackfuls of feathers, and glued them into shape
with wax. It was a long, painstaking job, but finally Daedalus gave
the wings a careful inspection and pronounced them ready. He
strapped one pair onto his son and the other onto himself. Then the
intrepid pair prepared to jump off a high cliff.

"Listen carefully, my son," ordered Daedalus. "Do not soar too
high, or the sun will scorch your wings. And do not dip too low, or
the spray of the sea will soak them. Just follow me and do as I do."

Daedalus shut his eyes and prayed a silent prayer to the gods.
Then he and Icarus launched themselves off the cliff. It worked!
Wings outstretched, they were lifted aloft on the breeze, gliding over
the ocean, floating away from Crete and cruel King Minos.

Icarus whooped, wide-eyed with excitement. He felt such a
thrill that he totally forgot his father's warning. He soared upwards
and hovered in the heat of the sun. Then his joy turned to pain as

burning wax began to drip down his arms. "Help me, father!" he screamed, as he realized what was happening. "My wings are melting!"

Daedalus was horrified, but there was nothing he could do. He watched, helpless, as his son dropped out of the sky and splashed into the sea, struggling, spluttering and sinking.

The gods had chosen to punish the great inventor for murdering his young nephew. And even though the master craftsman made it to safety, he lived for the rest of his days with a broken heart that not even he could mend.

The Death of Baldur

a Norse myth

Baldur and his twin brother, Hodur, were the sons of the chief god, Odin and the beautiful Queen Frigg. Although they loved their sons dearly, Baldur was their clear favourite. Hodur had been born blind, and so could not share the joys of life in the same way as his brother. Yet, the twins loved one another very much. Baldur was often found with his arm linked through Hodur's, making sure he wasn't left out and lonely.

Baldur not only lifted the heart of Hodur, but of everyone in Asgard. Every god and goddess always cheered up at the sight of Baldur's shining face. Baldur was also loved by all the humans of Midgard.

Over time, Baldur became deeply troubled by nightmares of death. He could no longer smile. Instead, the light went from his eyes and his forehead became creased with a permanent furrow.

For the humans of Midgard, there was no greater joy than to die a courageous death on the battlefield. The daughters of the great god Odin himself, Valkyries, would then swoop down and take them away to live in Valhalla, the hall of the slain. There they would feast and fight to their heart's content for ever more. However, humans dreaded wasting away of old age or sickness, for then their spirits would drift down into the silent underground kingdom of Niflheim, ruled by the ghoulish queen, Hel. Baldur became consumed by a feeling of impending doom. His nightmares vividly showed his descent into the underworld for eternity, though he knew not how or why.

When Odin saw how tormented his beloved son had become, he disguised himself as a messenger, mounted his eight-legged horse Sleipnir, and raced out of Asgard faster than lightning. Without stopping, he rode furiously until finally he crossed the bridge over the black stream that bordered Hel's kingdom. Odin searched the land of the dead until he found the grey barrow of the prophetess, Volva the Wise. Chanting the strongest words of ancient magic, Odin watched as the dead woman rose, pale and ghastly, from the earth. "Tell me, who shall cause the death of my son, Baldur the Bright?" the father of the gods demanded.

"Hodur shall take his life," Volva the Wise whispered, sinking back into her grave with a great sigh.

Odin felt as though his heart was breaking as he rode the long pathways back to Asgard. Desperately, he tried to devise a way to cheat destiny, to save each of his sons from their terrible fates.

As Odin entered the halls of his palace, Queen Frigg threw her arms around him. "Put aside your fears!" she laughed. "I have saved our son! I have journeyed around the universe and spoken with every bird, every insect and every animal; every leaf, every twig, and every blossom; every dwarf, every troll, and every giant;

every illness, every disease, and every poison; every man, every woman, and every child. All things under the heavens have sworn an oath not to hurt our beloved Baldur!"

"Can this really be true?" breathed Odin, a spark of hope flickering inside him.

"Come and see for yourself," Queen Frigg laughed. She led her husband away to the lush garden of Gladsheim, where a crowd of gods and goddesses had gathered, cheering and clapping with glee. Making his way to the front of the throng, he saw for himself what was entertaining them so delightfully. A chill ran down Odin's spine. The gods and goddesses were taking turns to throw objects at Baldur. They were lobbing rocks, firing arrows and hurling knives. However, to Odin's astonishment, the missiles were turning themselves and veering aside from his son, who was beaming and laughing once more. Odin could hardly believe his eyes, but at the same time he was deeply comforted. Heaving a sigh of relief, he allowed himself to smile.

Amid all the laughter, Loki, the troublemaker god, stepped forward. "Shame on you all!" he cried, bringing the sport to a halt. "You are all forgetting poor Hodur! Is no one going to help him join in the fun? Come on, Hodur. Your old friend Loki will take care of you. You want to have a go, don't you?"

Everyone began cheering once more. "Yes, Hodur – have a go!" they cried. "Come and take your turn. No matter what you do, your brother will come to no harm."

Hodur was embarrassed and protested, but Loki insisted, giving him a dart of mistletoe. Then Loki guided Hodur's hand in the right direction, and urged, "One … two … three … fire!" The mistletoe dart sped from his fingers.

Hodur realized at once that something was terribly wrong. The crowd around him suddenly fell silent – then terrible screams and wailing tore through the air. The mistletoe dart had fired straight into Baldur's chest and pierced his heart! The stunned god had fallen to the ground and now lay dying.

"NO!" bellowed Odin. "How can this be!" With a roar, he drew his sword to smite Loki – but the sly god had vanished silently. "It is my fault. Mine!" howled Queen Frigg, on her knees in the dirt, cradling her son's lifeless body. "I never dreamed that a tiny shoot of mistletoe might somehow be of harm. The plant was the one thing in the universe I forgot to make take an oath."

Although the tragedy was no accident, it was certainly not the fault of Queen Frigg. The jealous, cunning Loki had somehow found out her mistake and engineered Baldur's murder. With his pale body in his mother's arms, Baldur's spirit rose up and drifted away towards the murky gloom of the underworld. In his grief, Odin swore that he would track the trickster down to the ends of the earth, and make Loki regret his evil deed for all eternity.

Index of Stories

Adventures of Sinbad the Sailor, The 330

Aladdin and the Lamp 384

Ali Baba and the Forty Thieves 300

Amal and the Genie 189

Androcles and the Lion 88

Baba Yaga, The Bony-legged Witch 375

Babushka 318

Beginning of Life, The 455

Belle and the Beast 259

Brave Tin Soldier, The 337

Cat and the Mouse, The 103

Chicken Licken 76

Cinderella 36

Creation of the Navajo People, The 461

Daedalus and Icarus 501

David and the Giant 401

Detah of Baldur, The 505

Dick Whittington and his Cat 154

Dragons of Peking, The 349

East of the Sun and West
  of the Moon 135

Elephant's Child, The 357

Elves and the Shoemaker, The 55

Emperor's New Clothes, The 418

Firebird, The 278

Fisherman and the Bottle, The 405

Freya and the Brising Necklace 396

Frog Prince, The 31

Giant Who Counted Carrots, The 202

Giant's Wife, The 409

Gingerbread Boy, The 169

Golden Touch, The 431

Goldilocks and the Three Bears 146

Greedy Dog, The 100

Hansel and Gretel 183

Happy Prince, The 449

Hare and the Tortoise, The 354

Hop-toads and Pearls 274

Hound of Culan, The 489

How Jumbo Went to the Moon 113

In the Castle of Giant Cruelty 392

Jack and the Beanstalk 172

Kaatje's Treasure 121

Kotan Utannai 483

Lad Who Went to the
North Wind, The 117

Last of the Dragons, The 365

Liam and the Fairy Cattle 178

Lion and the Mouse, The 69

Little Matchgirl, The 307

Little Mermaid, The 424

Little Red Riding Hood 165

Magic Porridge Pot, The 19

Magic Tinderbox, The 289

Mermaid of Zennor, The 207

Moon Caught in the Marsh, The 129

Moon in the Pond, The 360

Murder of Osiris, The 473

North Wind and the Sun, The 133

Nutcracker Prince, The 434

Old Woman and her Pig, The 334

Pandora's Box 266

Peter and the Wolf 150

Pied Piper of Hamelin, The 255

Pot of Gold, The 245

Precious Stove, The 159

Princess and the Pea, The 61

Puss in Boots 341

Ra's Secret Name 467

Rapunzel 231

Red Shoes, The   285

Ricky with the Tuft   443

Rip Van Winkle   323

Rumpelstiltskin   48

Selfish Giant, The   380

Seven At One Blow, The   296

Seven Ravens, The   211

Sleeping Beauty   225

Snow Daughter and Fire Son   125

Snow White and Rose Red   42

Snow White and the Seven Dwarfs   194

Sorcerer's Apprentice, The   142

St Christopher   310

Star Maiden and the
   Flax Flowers, The   108

Sword in the Stone, The   439

Tall Story, A   328

Teeny-tiny   237

Three Billy Goats Gruff, The   96

Three Little Pigs, The   78

Three Wishes, The   65

Thumbelina   313

Thunder God Gets Married, The   414

Tomlin   270

Trojan Horse, The   479

Twelve Dancing Princesses, The   26

Twelve Windows, The   218

Ugly Duckling, The   91

Why the Manx Cat has no Tail   72

Why the Robin has a Red Breast   84

Wild Swans, The   248

Wonderful Tar Baby, The   346

Yama-Kumar and the Healing Gift   495